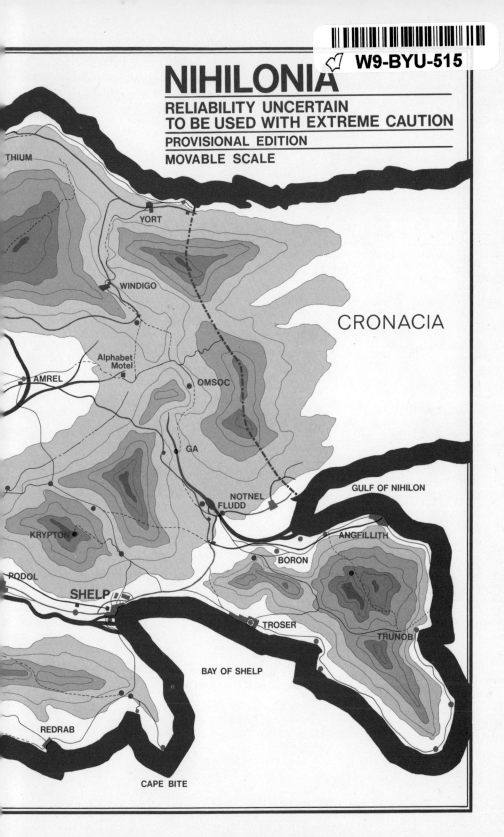

NIHILONIA

RELIABILITY UNCERTAIN
TO BE USED WITH EXTREME CAUTION
PROVISIONAL EDITION
MOVABLE SCALE

THIUM

YORT

WINDIGO

Alphabet Motel

AMREL

OMSOC

CRONACIA

GA

NOTNEL
FLUDD

GULF OF NIHILON

KRYPTON

ANGFILLITH

BORON

PODOL

SHELP

TROSER

TRUNOB

BAY OF SHELP

REDRAB

CAPE BITE

Travels in Nihilon

ALAN SILLITOE

New York

CHARLES SCRIBNER'S SONS

Travels in Nihilon

Prologue

More than twenty-five years have gone by since a guidebook to Nihilon was published. A committee of editors has therefore decided to collect information for a new and more up-to-date volume. This is a difficult undertaking because Nihilon is, by and large, that undiscovered country from which few travellers can be expected to return. Nevertheless your Chief Editor hopes to complete the writing of this handbook when his five more active collaborators—soon to be introduced—have come back from Nihilon itself.

The reason for publishing a handbook to Nihilon is that tourists seeking strange meetings and unexpected thrills, travellers with unusual desires, and people wanting merely to live in that country, need the experience of others on which to plan their hopes and expectations. Although it is true that out of many who have gone to Nihilon, few have returned with enough lucidity to give information or tell of their adventures, it must be said that guidebooks are not written for those who come back, but to prime those with the impetus to go, and to help those ardent spirits who have the good fortune to arrive.

In any case, that little-known country of Nihilon can claim certain achievements worth showing to the world. Its nihilism, they say, is second to none. Its nihilistic principles are applied to modern life in such a way that, as one lands at Nihilon City Airport, being only permitted to approach at dusk, a string of immense and lit-up letters nearly two kilometres long spells out the coruscating message:

NIHILISM WORKS!

Such a country ought to be explored and, if possible, described.

At the same time we also believe that whatever dangers are to be met with in Nihilon will be effectively dispelled if sufficiently written about. Indeed it is our fond hope that a thorough guidebook to a country

7

whose life and economy is based on nihilistic principles could certainly be not a little responsible for undermining the very foundations of the country itself, and bringing about a new and more lawful era in its history. Man, by nature, is not nihilistic, and in order to make him behave and live in such a fashion, one can assume that certain 'principles of nihilism' have been formulated by the one man who runs the country, and whom we hope to meet in the course of this narrative. Though Nihilon, through him, has devised the perfect system of regimented chaos as the best way of safeguarding the eternal spirits of its citizens, this is no proof that a better method could not safeguard them even more.

Since most of the capitalistic freedom-loving nations are going in the same direction, we feel it our duty to show the truth of what Nihilon claims to have achieved by way of constructive nihilism. We will also fill in the pot-holes of its recent history, and instruct in geography, as well as voice a few opinions on the arts and other matters —about which recent travel and encyclopaedic works are all too vague.

Certain documents have already arrived from my five collaborators in the field, and I will incorporate other material in this book as it comes to hand. It will be necessary to adjust the prose here and there, since the styles of the reports too often betray touches of panic and hysteria, a tone that may not commend itself to the general reader.

Some might say that the original reports, being more in tune with events related, should have been left as they were written, and that the style I have adopted may be less vivid. To which I reply that since the documents came into my hands and not those of my forewarned critics, then I am the one who will have the final word on it. A guidebook to such a country as Nihilon puts me into an unbending frame of mind, which I feel is necessary if I am to maintain strict control over such disordered nihilistic material.

I spoke to all five members of this perilous expedition before they set out, and from everyone received permission to arrange their notes as I thought fit. Whether this compliance was because they were visiting Nihilon, and not another more civilised country, I have as yet no way of knowing, though I decided that this may well be the truth on reading the preliminary despatches.

If it is eventually plain that Nihilon will not after all submit itself to having a guidebook written about it, then this work will have to be presented in the form of a novel. I hope novelists will forgive me for this, because it seems that after sifting through the basic material to hand, I may well find it necessary to move into their territory.

But this Guide to Nihilon comes from underground, and may have been tainted by the nihilistic quality of the material in question. However that may be, let us begin the story of five people who travelled to Nihilon. They were foolhardy, but who is not?

Chapter One

The frontier area was shrouded in mist, a factor that Adam had not reckoned on as he cycled away from his Cronacian hotel after breakfast. It simply meant that he would not need to use his poetic talent on a long description of the area, which he had been told to do as one of his contributions to the guidebook. When the hotel manager said that the Nihilon authorities often put up artificial mist to obscure the mind and eyes of both friends and enemies alike, Adam had taken it as a subtle hint that much would be deliberately hidden from him in the country he was about to visit. This was what he expected, anyway. But though it was a real mist, there was no distance behind it so early in Spring. It was a veil of promise that, at this early hour, gave off a smell of suave Nihilonian warmth.

Following the Editor's instructions Adam had come by train along the southern coast to the last town in Cronacia, travelling a day and a night sitting in an empty carriage because, for quite unfounded reasons, he worried for the safety of his bicycle in the neighbouring luggage van. Stowed in the lightweight pipes of the aluminium frame were two thousand travellers units—the currency for his daily expenses through Nihilon. He had never possessed such wealth before, and balancing this concern was a feeling of security at the thought of it, causing him to marvel again at the ample but mysterious financial help that the projected guidebook must have received, and glad that after so many indigent years he had been called on to work for it. Frugal living had kept him thin for his age of forty, and his muscles had hardened since the trip began, though he had not yet done much cycling.

The road went straight up the steep hill, to the customs post at the top. As he approached, pushing his bicycle, which was burdened by panniers on either side of the back wheel, he perceived through the dispersing mist a large sign saying:

WELCOME TO ALL TRAVELLERS WHO COME WITH
FRIENDSHIP. SIGNED: PRESIDENT NIL.

On the olive-tree side of the route, groves of twisted grey trunks descended by an undulating landscape to the sea a few kilometres away. Soldiers standing behind concrete blocks bore sensitive but uneducated faces, and submachine guns. On the oak and coniferous flank of the road, the land climbed gently at first, then more sharply to the stony plateaux and snowy heads of the Nihilon Mountains. Trenches were dug behind thick entanglements of wire, because relations between Nihilon and Cronacia had never been good, and flared occasionally into open warfare. It distressed Adam that no trouble was ever taken to disguise this tender situation, or to remedy it. The socialist regime of Cronacia was mild and orderly, in no way quarrelsome regarding its black-hearted neighbour of Nihilon. But Nihilon bristled with wild dreams, was inwardly polluted with nightmare (so the manager of the hotel in Cronacia had said), and therefore not to be trusted along the one frontier it possessed, which Cronacia's fair land had the misfortune to share.

He was the only tourist crossing at that time of day, and the mist finally cleared as he approached the sentry at the wicket gate. On the handlebars of his bicycle an unobtrusive Tonguemaster had been clipped, an ingenious instrument that enabled him to understand and be understood in the many languages and dialects of Nihilon. He felt confident and fit, full of sensibility and wellbeing, and free of responsibility, as if he had been put back to a younger age when faith or lack of it had not yet risen to the peak of spiritual turmoil that had tormented him before taking this job. The sentry thrust an ugly-looking bayonet towards his stomach: 'Passport.'

Adam handed it to him with a pleasant smile. Glassy splinters of sunlight spread over them both. The sentry gave it back without looking at it, and said: 'Can I have a ride on your bicycle? I can control a tank, but I've never used a bicycle, though ever since I can remember I've longed to join a circus.' His face was earnest and sad and good-natured, and even had it not been, Adam would have let him borrow the bicycle, because he invariably became friendly and pliant whenever he held out his passport at a frontier. He took the sentry's gun, while the sentry clumsily mounted the frame and pedalled along the road, and was soon lost to sight around a bend.

To pass the time till he returned Adam inspected the rifle, a compact well-made bullet-gun that, because he had never been near a factory, seemed a miracle of human ingenuity. He had always been awed by machines. Even a bus or a bicycle might send him into realms of dreamy respect when he stood by the side of the road in a certain mood of physical uncertainty or disorientation. He lifted the gun up, as he had seen it done, and squinted along the line of the barrel. The fine steel of the curving trigger drew his finger, and when he stroked the shining polish there was a thump at his shoulder, and noise hammered forth and reverberated like whipcracks in all the mountains around, breaking the misty stillness of the dawn.

Another note sounded, similar though more distant, and a faint burn passed along his elbow like an angered wasp, followed by the thud and splintering of bullets into the nearest tree. When it was obvious that they came from the opposite direction, he fell to the ground for shelter, cheek against stones and soil, tears on his skin as machine guns tore the air open from Cronacia. Retaliatory bursts from Nihilon sent out rhythmical loud strings of similar noise from the concrete stumps picketing the forward slope of the frontier post, and in the occasional peace used by both sides to draw breath he heard shouting from nearby soldiers and laughter as, without orders, they gladly took up emergency positions to break what must have been several days of tedious inaction.

Adam slithered backwards, still gripping the guilty gun, filled with vain and bitter regret that he had mindlessly taken the rifle when the soldier had pedalled away on his bicycle. But such thoughts were drowned in the clatter of small-arms fire which at first hindered his progress to a position of safety. Chips of wood fell against his back, and stony earth spat around him. As minutes passed and the furore increased he felt less in danger of death, and moved with more skill.

A mortar began thumping up bombs to his left. He had both expected and dreaded this. Down and across the valley in Cronacia smoke puffs lifted along the hillside like large birds taking off in alarm. His belly detected a violent upheaval of the earth not far away, as the veteran Cronacian defenders of their soil commenced an artillery fireplan against this barefaced provocation of territorial integrity, unwittingly set in motion by Adam. Heavier guns from Nihilon phlegmed out smoke and fire from the heights behind, and during the momentary peace of his own mind he counted the explosions and noted their patterns of white and dark-green gradually spreading in a single pall over the whole hillside.

Retaliation couldn't be long in coming. Adam, with an exceptionally refined sense of self-preservation which, though it acted for him at moments of extreme physical danger, rarely warned him of the more devastating psychic upsets, ran on hands and feet between tree boles pitted with bullet marks. He reached the lea-side of a concrete lean-to, choking with fear and excitement, wondering how he could get free of the battle and find his bicycle, still clutching the rifle that might lead him to it.

Petrol fumes reeked in the air. The frontier post was burning, and all he had to show for his entry into Nihilon was an unstamped passport, and a rifle. The fact that he had so far escaped injury did not weigh much with him, for he was beginning to feel, as he sat on a fallen tree trunk some way back from the worst of the shelling, that without his bicycle he would soon cease to exist. In it was all his money, as well as pens, ink-bottle, maps, paper, and change of shirt. The best plan, he decided, was to follow the main road away from the frontier, and look for his bicycle as he went along. At least he had got into the country. Having been told to expect a savage and rigorous customs check, it now seemed as if no such establishment existed at this entry point. Or if it did it had probably been concussed into a smoking ruin. That was one thing to be thankful for, at least.

Chapter Two

Benjamin Smith, who had stayed late in his hotel bed, and did not approach the frontier till almost midday, specialised in politics and military history. Being fat and bald, and confident with his senior age of fifty, he had been nominated chief field-worker on the collection of data for the guidebook to Nihilon. He did not know why this was so, yet realised that it was just, and therefore saw no reason why he should hurry on what promised to be nothing more than a month's exploring holiday in Nihilon. He drove a black Thundercloud Estate car along a well-made road that curved up to the highest pass, and in spite of the gradients, and the great weight of his equipment, he did over eighty kilometres an hour. The sun's heat beamed on him, but he wore a dark-green eye-shield fixed across his forehead, happy and free in such heat, though not especially grateful in case it should put him off a lunch of local delicacies once he had broached the border.

He had been warned of difficulties that might tax his skill getting into Nihilon, but no border had ever fazed such a master of extensive travels around the world as Benjamin Smith. He stopped by the road-side and lit a cigar, then continued the winding ascent. At the next sharp bend a pair of sentry huts signalled the last outpost of Cronacia, and the guards there did not stop him to look in his passport, but indicated that he should go on. As if in acknowledgement of his comradely wave, they pointed at his car and laughed so hilariously that, catching a last view in his rear mirror, he saw them actually rolling on the asphalt surface at some joke that he was now too far off to share. A brief question as to what could be so amusing at that par-ticular time of day flashed through his mind, but was soon pushed out by a bout of speculation on what different fundamentals of life he would find once he had passed into Nihilon.

There was little time to think, for the glittering white-and-olive line of one-storied police posts stretched before him like a clean new town, a sight which reminded him to switch on his Tonguemaster for the inevitable parleying to come. On a high pole waved the flag of the People's Capitalist Republic of Nihilon. Its emblem was a large nihilistic black ink-blot, splayed on an immense white sheet of cloth. When he paused to make sure his papers were ready, an old white-overalled road-cleaner with a square grey moustache leaned on his window:

'It's a beautiful pattern, sir,' he said, 'and a lucky man who had the genius to think it up. It's copyright, sir, you know.'

'Spectacular,' said Benjamin nonchalantly, though it looked almost truly so against the pale blue of the Nihilon sky. The road-duster went on to say that the author of this design had made a fortune in royalties, since every postcard or lapel button, car window or steamer funnel that displayed it contributed to his unparalleled riches.

'Some people are born lucky,' the old man muttered as he went away, shaking his head at the cruelty of such injustice.

When Benjamin drove forward and stopped at the kiosk, a policeman strolled over to him, smiling pleasantly. Across the road, painted along one of the white buildings, and intended mainly for tourists leaving the country, was the cryptic but worrying legend:

SELF-EXPRESSION PLUS SELF-INDULGENCE EQUALS
NIHILISM.
SIGNED: PRESIDENT NIL.

'No one is allowed into our wonderful country today,' said the policeman.

'On whose authority?' Benjamin demanded, turning his window lower.

'Mine, and the rest of us,' the policeman grinned. 'We just feel like being awkward. It's part of our self-expression. Sometimes we let them in, sometimes we don't. Today we don't.'

Four loudspeakers attached to the flagpole emitted a shattering roar of what Benjamin could hardly call music, as if it were played by a collection of brass bands, a few hundred fire engines, a thousand blacksmiths' hammers, and the amplified reproduction of a force-twelve wind. The policeman looked towards the flagpole with rapture, hands pressed together. Seeing the alarmed and puzzled look on Benjamin's face, he took out a tiny square notebook, for it was impossible to be heard, and passed a scribbled message through the car window, which said: 'It's our National Hymn to Nihilism. Don't you think it's beautiful?'

Benjamin tried to smile, while gritting his false teeth to stop them rattling. 'What's it called?' he wrote facetiously on his own square of paper, imagining that such monstrous noise could not possibly have a title.

The policeman grimaced, as if maliciously imitating him: 'I'm glad you asked that. It's called "The Hammer and Chisel Forever!"'

Benjamin sweated for almost half an hour, and though both hands were clamped on his ears, the vibration of the symphony for loud-speakers shattered every vein. The policeman stayed close, and occasionally broke out of his rapture to scribble further little notes: 'It's our Geriatrics Symphony Orchestra playing,' 'That's my favourite part,' 'I hope they play it again tomorrow,' or 'I could listen to it forever, couldn't you, dear traveller?', at which Benjamin Smith could only nod and grin, and observe other Nihilonians gently gazing at the loudspeakers, as if by looking they'd be able to hear better.

He opened his briefcase and found the official letter from the Nihilonian Ambassador which said that Mr. Benjamin Smith, as a bona fide traveller to Nihilon, was to be admitted to the country and allowed to wander at will without let or hindrance. It was covered with stamps, seals, photographs, fingerprints, dates, and obscene marks of every colour and description. In tiny smudged print at the bottom was a statement saying that anyone disobeying these commands or rendering them null in any way would be shot by order of President Nil. This was a document that Benjamin had thought to use only in absolute necessity, but now that the music had stopped he pushed it towards the frontier guard, disturbing him in the act of filing his nails, for he considered it of vital importance that he should cross the frontier on the same date as Adam the poet, who had no doubt already done so near the coast, a hundred and sixty kilometres to the south.

The policeman looked at the paper closely, to show this supercilious traveller that he could read, and Benjamin got out of his car in case he should need help in its interpretation. Several minutes passed while the reading took place. Then the policemen's face became blotched with rage, as he ripped the paper into small pieces, and threw them in the air so that they were scattered by the wind back towards Cronacia. 'Why did you do that?' Benjamin demanded.

The policeman drew himself to his full height, and stuck out his chest proudly. 'Because I'm a Nihilist, you Red Fascist Pirate, that's why.'

'Oh, are you?' Benjamin cried, and gave him a great blow in the stomach, then punched him so violently in the jaw that the policeman went sprawling across the pavement. Panting with rage, he stood ready to hit him again should he try to get up, or to fight anyone else who might attempt to arrest him. But the few onlookers smiled, fellow policemen and local cleaners, who obviously thought he had acted properly. The policeman, with a look of tearful despair as he lay on the ground, wearily waved him on.

This is obviously the thing to do, thought Benjamin, as he hurriedly started his car and moved forward. I'm learning once again how to behave in this cesspool of President Nil.

Chapter Three

Adam remembered that ice-maps of the Alpine regions had been prepared by the cartographic staff of the guidebook, but he had not been allowed by the General Editor to bring them with him. This was just as well, for they were no doubt totally inaccurate, and in any case he had no intention of cycling through mountain country if he could help it, much less on ice and snow. His only desire at the moment was to get clear of the too sensitive frontier and find the soldier who had unwittingly taken his one means of sustenance and locomotion.

A short distance from the border, when the sun was drawing sweat through his vest and into his jacket, and his feet were beginning to ache, and also his arms from the effort of carrying the rifle, he entered an area where the road and its confines were an overlapping spread of craters. Between the trees he saw a solitary soldier lying on the lip of one, a stream of ochred blood colouring the soil by his left boot. The face was turned sideways, and going close, Adam recognised it as that of the soldier who had taken his bicycle—which he now saw lying under a tree, unharmed, both panniers intact.

The soldier was still alive, and looked at him: 'Help me,' he said, trying to smile from behind his shield of pain. Adam opened the panniers to make doubly sure that everything was still there. Then he went back to the soldier, who by this time had crawled from the shell hole and lay on the flat earth under a tree. He was tying to speak, so Adam gave him a drink of water, hoping he might say something that would be useful for his guidebook. When he put his ear close, the soldier whispered into it: 'Long live nihilism,' then fell back dead.

On examining the rifle more closely Adam noticed that the butt was hollow, and, pressing part of it, the steel cap fell on to his hand. He took out a tightly folded map, and put it into his pocket without opening it, then threw the rifle into one of the shell holes.

Trudging along the road with his bicycle, he did not consider what had so far happened to be the best introduction to Nihilon. Of course, frontier skirmishes took place every day, for what border could be more nervous than that of a nihilistic country? And also, no doubt, soldiers died in them, but he felt it would have been better if he could have made his entrance without this onus on his soul. It's all part of life, he mused, and there's not much anybody can do about it, above all in a Nihilon.

Birds sang from the trees, which was an improvement, especially when he reached level ground and was able to ride his bicycle. The road went down into a wooded valley, and a fine cantilever bridge at the bottom crossed the spinning roar of the river. He leaned over the parapet to get some of the cool air sprayed from below, then took the fieldbook from his jacket pocket and noted that the road so far had been well paved, though he made no reference to the unfortunate incident at the frontier, sounds of which rolled like thunder behind him. It was once more necessary to push the laden bicycle, for the road went uphill.

He had not eaten since breakfast, and thought that any wayside shack selling bread and drink would be useful to him at this moment, in spite of the clear and beautiful landscape that was beginning to inspire his soul. An old woman blocked his way and asked for money, but when he said that he hadn't any Nihilon cash, she retorted that a cigarette would do, since he was so destitute. He was happy to meet someone as human as a beggar, and in spite of her insults he gave her two. But when he wanted to go on she stood stolidly blowing smoke from her toothless mouth, and would not let him pass.

'What do you want?' he asked.

'Nothing,' she said.

'Who are you, then?'

'I'm a scout,' she answered, 'from a battalion of old-age pensioners being sent to fight in the war. We're glad to die for our country, you know.' She gripped the lapel of his jacket, as if wanting to take that too, but he pushed his bicycle around her, thinking she was far gone in senility, and pedalled away.

After another three kilometres he saw a building by the roadside displaying the notice PARADISE BAR above the doors. A further advertisement regarding its functions was painted on a nearby billboard: 'Last chance to eat before the front.' The final word had at one time been 'frontier' but the ultimate three letters had recently been erased, probably in the last hour. It was a clean-looking, respectable, two-storied dwelling, with a lower floor made of over-lapping planks of wood, and an upper portion of solid concrete.

Adam would not have entered this criminally top-heavy structure on a stormy day, but since the air was still enough he decided to go in and get something to eat. A score of tables on the terrace outside were occupied by crowds of old men, some sitting on the steps, others on the ground or stools, or leaning against the actual walls of the unsafe building. A few stayed at the edge of the throng in wheelchairs, and looked as if they had a very uncertain hold on life. But all had rifles, and ammunition belts around their jackets. Bugles and small flags were distributed among them, and many had folded overcoats by their feet, and shopping baskets with packets of food spilling out. Those dressed in city suits, with smart moustaches and clipped hair, watch-chains curving from their waistcoats, sipped small cups of black coffee and smoked cigarettes or thin cigars. Other men wore smocks and cloaks, had beards and cropped hair, took pipes from between their teeth so that they could drink out of huge glasses of beer. Some were merry and loud in their jokes, while others were reflective and dignified, making casual quiet remarks to each other. A few glanced at the sky as if it might rain, but others had no thought except to eat and drink their fill while they could. All seemed to have some set purpose in their eyes.

He stepped respectfully between them and went into the building itself. Part of the main room was cordoned off as a dining saloon, and that, too, was full of old men with their rifles and equipment. Waiters ran among them taking orders, and Adam noticed that they asked for money when they put the beer or food down, as if their customers might be dead before they could collect it in the normal course of time.

He leaned on the counter and asked the barman for a glass of milk and a sandwich. He thought this would be sufficient for his lunch, but went on to consume twice that amount before his hunger was satisfied. It was harder work cycling in Nihilon than on his practice runs before departure.

'Going far?' the red-faced, harassed, hysterical, youngish barman demanded curtly, snatching his plate away, though there was still a piece of his final sandwich left on it.

'Nihilon City.'

'By Zap?'

'What's Zap?'

'A Zap sports car. You're a foreigner by the sound of it.'

'I am,' he admitted, half sad and half proud.

'Do you like nihilism?'

'I don't know, yet.'

'Don't let any of these Geriatrics hear you say that. They *love* nihilism. Ready to die for it. They're going to, what's more. Tear you limb from limb if they hear you so cool on it. I wouldn't blame them either.' He held out his hand: 'You'd better pay for your lunch, and be off. Forty-two klipps, and I want it now.'

Adam took a travellers unit from his wallet, worth a hundred klipps at the present rate of exchange. 'I'll be glad to go.'

'I can't accept that,' the barman said. 'You should have changed it at the frontier. Or you can wait till you get to the next town, which should be the day after tomorrow if you haven't got a Zap. Do you want to buy a Zap?'

'I'd like to pay for my lunch and leave.'

'Go on,' he wheedled, 'buy a Zap. Be a Nihilist.'

'Who do I buy it from?'

'One of the old folk. The Gerries. They're off to the frontier—front, I mean. Most of 'em have Zaps, and I suppose they wouldn't be averse to letting one go to a foreigner like yourself. Won't cost much. I get a commission, you see, on all secondhand Zaps sold at the Paradise Bar. I've got a wife and four kids, so I need every klipp I can get.'

Adam pushed his travellers unit across the counter. 'I'd like to pay and go now.'

'I've told you, I can't take it,' snapped the barman.

'I'll leave without paying, then.'

The bartender laughed, hysterically. 'Try it! Go on, try it!'

An old man, frail and thin, wearing a suit, a red cravat, and a white flower at his lapel, strolled from a nearby table, a rifle hanging at his shoulder by a sling.

'Are you in trouble, young man?' He appeared to be the most civilised person Adam had met since crossing the frontier, and possibly for a long time before that, with pale-blue eyes, ironic and sensitive lips, and fine hands that had perhaps written books or painted pictures. His brow seemed marked with sound ideas, and crowned a face that must have made women happy to be near him and listen to any word he said. He looked about eighty years of age, and the softening effect of

21

so much wisdom and experience seemed even to lurk in the faint waves of his thick grey hair.

'No trouble,' said Adam, taking him for a friendly spirit, though he was somewhat puzzled by the rifle. The old man relinquished it, the butt rattling as it hit the floor close to Adam's feet, and leaned it against the counter. 'I simply want to pay for my lunch with this travellers unit, and go.'

The old man ceased to smile. 'To want something is not good nihilism. What you want, you never get. To do—that is the way to nihilism. I can tell you're a stranger to our country. When you do something, you get something, but not until.'

'I'm only a tourist.'

'No man is a tourist,' he said, his features taking on a harshness that Adam hadn't read into them at first. The bartender leaned on the counter, entranced at every word from the old man, a fascination expressed mostly by an inane grin. 'Life is the same wherever you are. It is hard in Nihilon, so why shouldn't tourists have to fight in order to exist, the same as we do? Much of my life I've worked as a poet in order to contribute to Nihilon's unique civilisation. I'm an old poet now, but rhymes still rattle their way into my head.'

'I'm a poet as well,' Adam interrupted him, glad that he should have something in common with this fine old man. But the man stared at him coldly: 'You may *think* you're a poet,' he said. 'I wouldn't say you were, you liar!'

'I've had several books published,' Adam said, still trying to smile, though sorry he hadn't one of the volumes with him so that he could present it to his friend.

'You aren't a poet,' the old man cried. 'If you say you are, you're a fraud, an imposter, a saboteur, a renegade, a Cronacian spy!'

Adam stepped away, appalled at this unjust attack. The barman picked up a beer mug to smash his head in for offending the old man, but the old man told him sharply to put it down, then apologised to Adam: 'He's a fool, you see. Always attacking people, and I can't stand it, being a poet. However, just listen to my latest composition.

> *Freedom's fight is my last bride*
> *And Nihilon is by my side.*
> *My last sight shall be the sky*
> *For geriatrics never die.*

I composed it for this march, and we old Gerries (as the young affectionately call us) will sing it as an anthem when we charge into the Cronacian scum.'

'You see,' he went on, 'in this country we don't send our young and able-bodied men to fight. Why should they waste their time? They're too busy working for Nihilon, building it up and breeding children. The principles of rational nihilism never let you down. Since the old have to die anyway, they are sent into battle. Of course, there are disadvantages. Though there is a certain amount of dash, and a great deal of ferocious guts in us Gerries, there can't be much question of a decisive breakthrough into Cronacia, because we're never able to keep up the push for long. Nevertheless, when we storm down the hill towards the Cronacian outposts in brigade column, we put the fear of the devil into them, with flags fluttering, trumpets sounding, and the shrill scream of our throats. I haven't been in a charge yet, but I know what it's like because the fighting we Gerries do is shown all over the country on television and in the cinemas. I've often sat up most of the night at the rest home, cheering them on. The glory won't go unrecorded, and that makes a difference, because our actions are shown to the young fellows and others who stay at home praising our courage and tactics, and who only wait for the day when they'll be old enough to have a go. So I shall be there tomorrow morning, because we're going to deal such a blow against the Cronacians that they won't forget it in a hurry. We'll teach them a lesson for the shooting they started this morning. We were called from our rest homes further up the valley as soon as the news came through. Oh yes, we'll show those pirates. You'll hear what we do to them. Do you want to see President Nil's Atrocity Recommendations?'

He fumbled in his pocket to try and find this revealing document, but then began to cough, bent over till the skin of his skull went red, right to the roots of his grey hair. The bartender had listened with tears streaming down his cheeks, and on seeing Adam again, he stopped weeping and grabbed his collar, saying with a ferocious cry:

'Pay up!'

The old man righted himself, forgetting his search for the piece of paper. 'How much does he owe?' he gasped.

'Sixty-two klipps, sir.'

Adam pulled his travellers unit back across the counter: 'You said forty-two a few minutes ago.'

'He means well,' the old man said to Adam, leaning over and straightening the bartender's tie. He picked up the travellers unit, put on a monocle, and held it to the light. 'Change it for him,' he snapped.

'Certainly, sir,' said the bartender. He took the note, put it into the till, and stood by the mirror with arms folded.

'My change,' said Adam, after waiting for him to give it back.

'Sixty-two klipps to the unit,' said the bartender.

'It's a hundred,' Adam shouted. The old man looked on in disapproval.

'Certainly,' conceded the bartender, 'that's what you get at the bank. But here it's sixty-two. Sixty really, but I'm not going to argue about the other two. Economy is frowned upon in Nihilon, especially among tourists.'

'You'd better accept it,' the old man said to Adam.

'But it's ridiculous,' he complained.

'Life is,' sighed the old man, picking up his rifle and sliding a bullet into the magazine.

Adam walked away from the bar, sensing danger. On reaching the door he turned for a moment to see the old man and the bartender bent over the counter, dividing a heap of coin between them, which no doubt should have been his change. He hurried outside, anxious once more for the safety of his bicycle.

Chapter Four

Jaquiline Sulfer, the only female member of our guidebook staff, knew that the first-class luxury express trains of Nihilon travelled at twenty kilometres per hour. Popular trains, on the other hand, went at eighty kilometres an hour, since if one wanted speed, one was expected to pay for it by discomfort, because popular trains had hard seats and no sides, and the railway line after the passage of such a train was littered with people and their belongings that had fallen off. Popular trains were frequently ambushed and de-railed either by political dissidents, or by railway employees who did not like their work. Only the poor, or the jaded rich in search of thrills, travelled by popular trains because they were cheaper and got them there sooner. Popular trains (known as 'fast trains') went on a narrower gauge of rail than slow express trains, and were sent on more circuitous routes through topographically difficult country—though those passengers who survived made the journey from the northern frontier to Nihilon City in less than half the time of those who travelled by the Grand Nihilon First Class Slow Luxury Wide-Gauge Bed-and-Board Express.

Jaquiline had gathered this elaborate matter on the division of trains from someone who had taken a holiday to Nihilon a few years ago. She worked at that time for an eminent psychiatrist, and had transcribed tape-recordings which he had made at the bedside of a so-called psychotic patient, whose pathetic condition was ascribed to his Nihilon vacation. She now remembered his information word for word, without knowing why, and so was determined to make sure, after crossing the frontier, to get a ticket for the correct train.

Station platforms, even at home, made her feel that she could not altogether rely on knowing who she was if anything unusual happened to her. They were such long, impersonal, dirty, ugly things, with too many goodbyes, lost hearts, and tears stamped into the concrete paving.

The sight of a long empty unfeeling railway platform made her want to throw up her hands and wail. But on this occasion she overcame her urge so successfully, due to her strong character, that she appeared extremely brisk and self-possessed. She was a tall, slim young woman whose chestnut-coloured hair had managed to retain its grooming on the boats and trains she had so far travelled on.

She looked for the way to the Nihilon customs and passport control, making sure that the indispensable Tonguemaster was clipped unobtrusively on to her handbag. Having carried her three suitcases out of the compartment, she now hoped they would be taken by a porter through to the Grand Express on which she wanted to get a sleeping compartment to Nihilon city.

A few people made their way along the platform to the passport control office, though none used a porter. She wrote in her notebook: 'To obtain a porter at the frontier is a near impossibility, and travellers are advised to bring as little luggage as possible.' She crossed out 'a near impossibility' and wrote 'extremely difficult', for she saw a tall well-built man wearing a dark uniform coming towards her. 'Excuse me, madame,' he said, touching his gold-braided cap, 'I'm the station-master. May I help you?'

'I *would* like a porter,' she smiled.

'There are no porters today,' he said. 'They're all across at the hotel waiting to see the Geriatrics charge into action on television. It's a great day for Nihilon. The old folks are rearing to go at Cronacia, because of the treacherous attack. Unfortunately I have to stay here and keep essential services going.'

'I've just come from Cronacia,' Jaquiline told him, 'and it's peaceful there. People are very happy and amiable.'

The stationmaster looked at her sardonically: 'You should try telling that to President Nil. It's difficult for you to understand our situation. Anyway, the incident was in the south, not up here. That's why it's peaceful. Otherwise there'd be war here as well, believe me.' He took a suitcase under his arm, and one in each hand.

'It's very kind of you,' she said, following him.

'You'd better get some of our money,' he told her, a piece of advice he obviously believed in, for he set her cases down before a money-changer's window. 'This is a branch of the Nihilon Bank. They don't change money on the train, except at two hundred to the unit.'

'That's double the rate,' she said, opening her handbag. 'I'll wait till I get on, then.'

He shook his head. 'Don't. It's illegal. The currency they give you on the train is forged. You get real ones here.'

'Oh, I see,' she said and, not to be hurried, wrote in her notebook: 'Travellers are strongly advised to change money on arrival at the Nihilon frontier post, and should on no account attempt to do so on the trains, as such currency as is then given, though twice that of the official rate, is frequently forged.' She then changed twenty units, for which she unknowingly received two thousand forged klipps, and followed him to the passport and visa control office.

No one had ever settled the question as to whether a visa was necessary for a visit to Nihilon. At home, Jaquiline had applied for information to the nearest Nihilonian consulate which, by a happy coincidence, was situated in the same building as the offices of the proposed Guide to Nihilon. The following advice-note was returned to her:

'To enter Nihilon a passport provided with a permanent or transitory visa obtainable from any Nihilon consulate is essential. The former is valid for a stay of one year, while the latter does not permit a sojourn at all.'

In the same envelope was a printed form entitled: 'Visa Application for Sojourn in Nihilon.' The first questions were harmless enough, but they later became more personal, posing such queries as to how many children her four grandparents had had, whether they drank or not, and if so, what diseases and divorces there had been for as far back as she could remember. Then the questions ceased to be merely personal. They became shockingly intimate. Jaquiline, almost thirty, but looking younger, had had a good share of experience, but her upbringing had been strict and proper, so that she had controlled her life with such skilful discretion that hardly anyone suspected her of so many adventures. These questions, therefore, prying into the most intimate secrets of her sex life, made her indignant. Forgetting that she had already filled in the harmless part of the form, she tore it into four pieces, put it into an envelope, and posted it back to the Nihilonian consulate. Two days later, an impressive, gold-lettered, fully signed, and exquisitely stamped visa, reeking of perfume, was sent to her free of charge. This she now took from her handbag, and passed, together with her passport, through the small window of the control post, while the stationmaster waited nearby with her luggage. A loudspeaker, halfway down the wall by which she stood, and level with her knees, demanded:

'Why are you coming into Nihilon?'

'To write a guidebook.'

'Do you have any money?'

'Two thousand travellers units.'

'How long do you expect to stay?'

'A month.'

'What about your accommodation?'

'I shall be staying at hotels.'

'Do you have any letters from your prospective employer?'

'I'm not going to work in Nihilon,' she said, lighting a cigarette. 'I'm only visiting the country.'

'Oh,' the loudspeaker sneered. 'Don't you like our country? Does nihilism frighten you?'

'Not at all,' she answered. 'Perhaps I would even like to live here, but I can't tell yet.'

'Well, you can't anyway,' the man's voice said superciliously. 'You'd never get permission. Only Nihilon citizens can live in this country. Unless you have a bank account in Nihilon.'

'I don't,' she snapped, tired of this interrogation.

'Then how much money do you have with you?'

'I've told you. Two thousand travellers units.'

'You're lying!' he cried. 'Show them to me.' She took the notes from her wallet, and a hand snatched them away. The stationmaster's eyes grew large at the sight of such money. She could hear a rustle beyond the window as it was avidly counted. 'We don't have to let you in,' the voice said smugly, pushing her money back with two notes short, which she was unaware of because she didn't think to check it.

His words alarmed her, for she had work to do on the guidebook. 'I have a proper visa. And please hurry or I shall miss my train to Nihilon City.'

The stationmaster shuffled his feet. 'I have to go now, miss.' But she knew that as long as the stationmaster stayed with her the train wouldn't be able to leave.

'Your visa is no concern of ours,' said the passport official. 'None whatsoever.'

'Your consulate abroad gave it to me.'

He gave a small dry laugh: 'I'm afraid you were the victim of a hoax. However, if you do want to get into Nihilon I can sell you another visa here.'

'How much?'

'Three hundred klipps might help.'

She stamped her foot: 'That's robbery.'

'Robbery does not exist in Nihilon,' a louder voice said from the speaker. 'We are all well paid, happy, prosperous, patriotic, sober, and hardworking British—I mean Nihilonian—officials, while you are a foreign whore who has come to disturb the equanimity of our perfect lives. Four hundred klipps, or get back to those Cronacian bastards and see how *they* rob you.'

She pushed two hundred across the counter, and her correctly stamped passport was returned to her, though with some grumbling. 'Come on,' she said to the stationmaster 'or I'll have to bribe them some more.'

Just as they were entering the customs hall a strangled croak came from the passport booth behind, and a scarcely human voice was shouting and whining about her money being forged, which it was, though Jaquiline had no idea they were referring to her, being pre-occupied at taking her place in a short queue at the customs desks.

It looked like a fairly busy market, with travellers and uniformed officials handling goods they had shaken on to the tables, and shouting prices at each other. Now and again someone would hand over money, scoop his things into a case, clip it shut, and walk away sweating and muttering towards the door leading to the train.

A blue-uniformed customs officer, holding a clipboard which stated in bold black words, as far as Jaquiline could see, that you were forbidden to bring anything at all into the country, leaned across the table and pulled the half-smoked cigarette from her mouth. 'You'll have to pay duty on that,' he said, stubbing it out, and throwing it on to a pair of scales. 'How do you expect our nation of honest shopkeepers to live if we let you bring cigarettes into our Nihilon?'

'They're very strict here,' said the stationmaster. 'This is one of the worst frontier posts as far as the customs people are concerned. Others are quite easy.'

She took up her pad and wrote: 'At the frontier, scenes of great confusion prevail, especially during the so-called customs-house examination. Every case and packet is opened, so that it is inadvisable for ladies to travel alone. She who has no option but to do so will see the most intimate articles of her wardrobe pawed by brutish fingers, and held up to the gaze of other travellers in order that they may leer at them. This they are too ready to do, in the hope that, having fallen in with the customs officer's perverted sense of humour, they may be spared having to pay duty on their own goods. But one is indeed made to pay, for one is literally robbed of one's luggage and then made to buy it back again.' 'It is a most degrading experience,' she wrote later, 'and the female tourist is advised to maintain dignity and patience through her ordeal. This, it must be said, is something of a feat, under the circumstances, for the victim is taken to a room in which her actual person is searched by two poker-faced dragons of Nihilon officialdom. At this stage one may well begin to wonder whether the country is worth visiting at all, but your correspondent had no option except to persevere in her intention to obtain information for the benefit of future travellers. The least that can be said about this infamous procedure is that a cup of coffee was provided after the experience was over, though at a very inflated price.'

Having parted with another five hundred klipps, whereupon everything was put back into her cases, she followed the broad back of the stationmaster to the waiting train. There was a booth open on the platform at which one could buy tickets to Nihilon City, but she got into a long and acrimonious argument with the woman behind the glass, who tried to insist that she pay for a return instead of a single journey. Jaquiline refused to give in on this point, and after snatching the correct ticket, and throwing down the money, she watched her cases taken towards a suitable compartment. The hooter of the train blew a prolonged and urgent note, unpleasant, she thought, if heard in the distance from some comfortable bed at night, but now giving a feeling of actual relief, because in a short time she would be taken out of these bleak and extortionate frontier sheds.

The stationmaster climbed over her cases to reach the door of the high carriage, before pulling each one in after him. He told her to wait on the platform while he took them to her compartment. Through the window, a few yards along the train, she saw his rather long limbs placing her cases respectfully on the racks. It would be difficult to climb those steel steps unaided, so she waited for him to come back and assist her. He had shown such magnificent kindness in this barbaric country that she wondered how to reward him. It would be embarrassing and wrong to tip such an impressive stationmaster, who looked so sincere and dignified in his immaculate uniform, almost like some elderly general about to review his equally smart and elderly soldiers. If she were a man she could offer him a cigar, but then, he wouldn't help a man in this way, so the situation would not arise. It was a quandary that stayed with her till the train began to move during the blast of the final whistle blown by the stationmaster as he leaned far out of the window.

She ran along the platform, unable to mount the steps and get on the train. Drawing level with her compartment, she saw the stationmaster smile ecstatically as he threw his gold-braided cap over her head and as far as he could across the platform. He then unbuttoned his tunic, all set to relax on the long and easy ride to Nihilon City.

Chapter Five

Benjamin Smith laughed at having knocked the policeman down at the frontier, reflecting that it served the bastard right for tearing up his visa certificate—which he'd worked on for three days, a pure sweat of the forger's art. The car droned softly and efficiently on, and at a level stretch across a mountain plateau a red Zap sports car came towards him on the same side, a crimson swift oval flattened on the blue-grey tarmac road. The Zap was far off at first, so that Benjamin thought it was going away from him, that it had appeared from some slip-road while his eyes had wandered, but the car grew and came close, the dare-devil inside dead-set on some vicious suicide game. Benjamin's calculations speeded up rapidly, weighing his own heavy car as three times that of the Zap, but even so, the thought of entering a brick-wall competition didn't appeal to him, since the smoke would be mutual if it came to a smash.

He turned to the other side of the road, choosing safety, but the Zap thought otherwise, and Benjamin sweated at the sight of death coming up so quick. He almost stood on the brakes, and angled the car to the edge of the road he had originally been on, but it seemed as if the Zap was latched at him by some demonically tuned radio beam.

At the last point of evasion he felt that something subtle yet deadly had been done to the camber of the road. It was as if the man in the Zap, having set on him from far away, had planned his tactics knowing that Benjamin would turn off for final safety at this section of the innocent-looking highway, because the heavy Thundercloud Estate car rumbled off it, descended a slope, turned completely over, then righted itself, shaking from side to side, and bouncing on its indestructible springs before settling down to silence.

Benjamin opened his eyes, and reached into the glove-box for his revolver. He didn't know whether he was hurt or not. For all he knew, and he felt it might be so, he could have broken a few limbs and been bleeding at a couple of internal places. But he sprang out of the car as if to murder the first animal or human being he came across, and crawled up the sandy embankment to the road. A smell of heat and pinecones came from sparse forest on the opposite side. He lay in the ditch and listened. The road was empty. A gentle wind turned the sweat cold on his face. He screamed out at the road, and fired a shot in the direction the Zap had taken, then smiled like a baby that was conscious of hearing for the first time, as he listened to the explosion, and its echoes breaking through each barrier of silence.

Chapter Six

A fortnight on the steamship *Nihilon* brought many mundane reflections to Edgar Salt's mind as he paced the decks, or walked between rows of cabin doors listening to the victims of sea-sickness. A disturbing fact about this ship was that there were no lifeboats. At first he had been afraid, because the sea was rough, and the clean uncluttered flanks of the ship often brought to mind the possibility of being drowned. He asked a seaman about this deficiency, and the seaman exclaimed scornfully: 'What do we want with lifeboats? Don't you have any faith in the strength and seaworthiness of Nihilon's ships? Our aim is to defeat the nature of the sea, and how can we be seen to do that if we cravenly steam across it festooned with old-fashioned lifeboats? None of our fine vessels have sunk yet, and don't you dare insinuate that this is going to be the first, because it's not.'

As a geographer Edgar took sightings with his sextant and, aided by a chronometer and tables, plotted the ship's position every few hours of the day. He pencilled its track on a chart in his cabin, and noted that the same line, drawn in broad red pencil on the wallchart of the main saloon by the chief navigating officer for the benefit of the passengers, did not coincide with his own. He supposed they must have their reasons for this, though he thought that those passengers who believed the red pencil to be accurate were unfortunate, and even in many ways inferior to himself and those officers who knew that it was not so.

He stopped an officer, to ask why the saloon chart was so much out of true. They talked urbanely, to the noise of people playing ball games in a nearby space, while sturdy green waves created a swell on which the new white ship laboured heavily. 'It's dishonest to deceive the passengers like this,' Edgar said, his precise geographer's mind hurt by such blatant deviation from the truth.

The officer's uniform was clean, his buttons polished, his shirt white and ironed. But he needed a shave: 'You're only honest when you can't be anything else,' he said, with a mechanical smile. 'Honesty is the lowest form of self-expression. Since you're going to Nihilon I'm telling you this for your own good, because you'll need to keep it in mind, believe me. Honesty is a weapon. If you want to kill someone, never be anything but honest to them.'

A huge wave beat up as far as where the lifeboats should have been. 'We're very philosophical on this ship,' the officer went on, 'and I hope we never meet a real storm, or go too close to a rocky coast! Honesty is an international conspiracy. It's everywhere. It's a haven for dogs who think only of their own safety. We in Nihilon have to stay united and fight it. We must never cease to be vigilant. Cronacia, our vile and diabolical neighbour, is forever preaching law, order, honesty, progress, but above all honesty, which shows how dead set she is to wipe us off the face of the earth. You see, if I want to insult you, I need only be honest. But to be honest in that way is a terrible and inhuman form of cowardice. Apart from that, it would be insulting to your intelligence, and to *my* self-esteem.'

The ship sailed along the inhospitable wall of coast, three-quarters around the country of Nihilon to get to the principal seaport in clear weather. Edgar was busy with plane-table and telemeter, compass and camera, sketching in the white spaces on maps he had bought before setting out. He worked in secret, plotting caves and tidemarks, capes, headlands and lighthouses, filling notebooks with data so as to compile his own maps down in the dimly lit cabin. The floor was covered with heavy and conspicuous equipment, and he used two trunks pushed to-gether as a table on which to spread out his papers.

A few days later the same officer greeted him. He was now smoothly shaved, but his clothes were crumpled and dirty, as if he had slept in them since the last meeting. Edgar asked why there were no good maps of Nihilon.

'No authoritative, authentic maps, you mean,' he said with the same sly smile. 'Well, isn't that as it should be? Why does anybody need maps? If an individual wants them he's a spy. If a country needs maps it's moribund. A well-mapped country is a dead country. A complete survey is a burial shroud. A life with maps is a tyranny!'

He lit a pipe, well satisfied with his rabid lunatic speech, then raised his voice even more as he blew out smoke. 'However, don't think we have no great geographers in Nihilon. There are at least six really inspired ones, and each has his own department in which he endeavours to produce beautiful maps from the imagination. Each seeks to outdo the inaccurate productions of the others. I even believe they're for sale in the shops, though they won't do you much good, because, being works of art, they're too expensive.'

'Which shops?'

The naval officer gave a gentle push. 'Look for them. We're all Nihilists in Nihilon! I have to mark up yesterday's false progress on the saloon chart. Goodbye!'

Such fruitless interviews saddened Edgar, and he tried to keep out of this naval officer's way, an intention in which he was not always successful, so that he was glad when the ship turned the headland into the Bay of Shelp and steamed towards the port at five o'clock in the afternoon.

The city extended nearly five kilometres along the coastal plain, a zone of white buildings behind the docks, with villa suburbs rising on the green hills behind. Ash-grey mountains with jagged summits spread across the sky, and almost surrounded the deep wide bay. Edgar noted forests on the lower slopes, and with binoculars memorised the width and direction of certain roads so as to decide whether or not they were fit for motor lorries, or even a heavier type of vehicle.

The main highway out of town went into a broad valley on its way to Nihilon City, the capital of the country which, as far as he knew from the various maps, appeared to be about two hundred kilometres away. These new views were a feast for his surveyor's eyes, and he was too busy scribbling in his notebook to think of getting luggage-boxes on deck.

Only two other ships were in harbour, one bearing the distinctive blot-emblem of Nihilon on its funnel, the other flying the Cronacian flag of an olive branch from its stern. Women were busy along the wharves, working cranes and driving trolleys, and when the same young officer tapped him on the shoulder, Edgar put his book away, and asked why so many women were toiling on the shore instead of men.

'Well, you see, the women of Shelp were very revolutionary. They demanded equality with men, so we gave it to them—building, digging, driving, carrying, rowing, hauling. Now they are happy, because they are equal.'

'What about the men?'

'They are happy too. They sit in cafés, and work in offices all day. They are not equal with the women, but they are generous and don't mind. Everybody works hard in Nihilon, otherwise we wouldn't have such a good standard of living.'

A dozen small rowing boats came towards the ship, and stout, smiling women at the oars called in throaty melodious voices for the privilege of taking luggage to the shore. 'I thought we tied up at the quay,' Edgar said, a chill vision of his bulky and precious luggage balancing on such frail craft. 'At least that's what it said in the brochure.'

'I know, but the quay is under repair, so you must make your own arrangements to get off.'

'That's scandalous,' he cried. 'I thought the Nihilon Line was a reputable shipping company!'

'If you aren't careful,' said the officer, 'all the boats will be taken, and then you won't get off at all. In an hour our ship sets out on another cruise, and you'll come with it if you're not ashore by then. Nihilon waits for no man.'

Going down to the cabin Edgar had to fight his way past an elderly traveller struggling up the companionway with two formidable suitcases. A sharp corner of one bruised him in the chest, and while he pressed it back the old man used considerable force by leaning on his upturned suitcases as if he would stay there and push forever. Neither of them spoke, but breathed hard, and glared, and sweated, till Edgar managed to hold the suitcases to the wall, almost crushing the old man who, nevertheless, bit him savagely in the arm as he went by.

Edgar cried out, and turned to retaliate, but the old man faced him with such a goodnatured smile that he was disarmed, and realised that to begin a fight just now would delay getting his own luggage on deck.

He had read in his preliminary notes, issued by the Chief Editor of the guidebook before setting out, that it was inadvisable to put one's luggage into large trunks because Nihilon porters were afraid of being ruptured, and so might refuse to handle them. But such was Edgar's fragile equipment, and his lack of apposite travel gear that he had been forced to use bulky pieces after all. But since no porters were available, he need not worry for them, though being thrown on to his own strength was something he hadn't bargained for either, as he pulled and struggled with one of the lighter trunks up the stairs. When a job had to be done, no matter how arduous and unpleasant, Edgar set

37

about it methodically as the best and indeed only way of doing it. Nothing could stand in his path, and he began in the finest of spirits to tackle his daunting work.

The first trunk was placed by the gangplank, where it would stay till a stout boater could assist him with it and others into her craft. Such was his system. He then went below for another box, considering it safe to leave the first where it was because no one, in view of its weight, would be able to walk off with it.

Through the open cabin door he saw a middle-aged man wearing a mackintosh looking into one of his trunks (which he had left locked) and casually sifting through a notebook, examining its cyphers with the aid of a torch. His brown lustreless eyes gazed up: 'Don't reproach me. I'm only doing my duty.'

'Get out,' Edgar said, filled with rage.

'You're a spy. You'd better give me thirty thousand kricks to keep quiet. We put spies up against a wall in this country.'

'I'm not a spy. I'm an ordinary traveller.'

'You're lying. Look at those pretty little maps.'

Edgar rushed forward, and shut the lid of the trunk with such force that if the man hadn't withdrawn his fingers in a practised fashion, they would have been smashed to splinters. 'You're not playing fair,' the man cried out, stunned by this belligerent action from such a fair frail person as Edgar. 'You're supposed to plead with me, or at least haggle about the price.'

'If you don't get out,' said Edgar, 'I'll call the captain.'

The man laughed. 'I *am* the captain. I was getting ready to go ashore. My brother will take the ship on its next stage. When I passed your cabin I wanted to see what you had inside it. We've been watching you because you seemed so openly secretive compared to a good dishonest Nihilonian. But now that I know you're a spy, and that you won't be browbeaten about it, I congratulate you on your profession. I'll help you on deck with the rest of your luggage.'

'That's very kind of you,' said Edgar, inwardly happy at such a turn of luck.

They staggered up with the second trunk to find that the first one had gone. 'Don't worry,' said the captain, 'it'll probably be waiting in the customs shed. There are no thieves in Nihilon. By simply taking everything we need, none of us become thieves. Dishonesty forever means fair shares for all. However, I must get off the ship now.' He held out his hand. 'I expect a good tip for helping you on to the deck with that very heavy trunk.'

This Nihilonian humour did not appeal to Edgar at such a critical time, yet the rapacious glint of the captain's eyes told him that the demand was serious, the threat real.

'Quickly,' he said, 'I have to meet my wife.'

'How much do you want?'

'As much as you can afford,' he replied in a softer tone. 'But don't forget that I'm the captain of a large passenger ship. It took me years to reach such a responsible position. After the last voyage I helped a traveller with his luggage and he offered me five kricks! Can you imagine such a pittance! Fortunately he was rather elderly, so I told him he was a mean and insulting swine for offering so little.'

It had been Edgar's intention also to give him five kricks but now, wanting to be relieved of the captain's offensive presence, he took a ten krick note from his wallet.

'You'd better make it twenty,' the captain said. 'I have to share it with my brother officers.'

'Damn you!' Edgar exclaimed. 'You'll get nothing.'

He pulled out a small whistle and put it between his teeth: 'If I blow on this they'll tumble from their bunks and throw you into the water. Your luggage won't float very well.'

'No,' said Edgar.

'Don't be a fool,' the captain growled. 'You're in Nihilon now. Or will be if you pay up, and are then lucky enough to get a boat. If not, you're with us for three more weeks.'

Edgar handed him another ten krick note.

'A service charge of ten per cent goes on that,' the captain said, 'making twenty-two, all told.' Edgar paid this, also, and last saw the extortionate and piratical captain being rowed ashore by a buxom lady in a red blouse, with whom he soon began flirting and joking.

Chapter Seven

As Adam went down the steps of the Paradise Bar an irascible Geriatric in short trousers put out a spindly leg and tried to send him headfirst. With his younger agility he dodged it, but cried indignantly: 'What did you do that for?'

'That's the fate of all Cronacian spies, and so on,' snapped the patriotic oldster, turning back to his beer.

'We'll give 'em hell,' laughed his toothless companion.

A wavering buglenote sounded from the road, and the warriors began knocking out pipes, finishing dregs of beer or coffee. Certain men were designated as markers, bearing lightweight banners of the proud Nihilon blot, now standing ready so that others could form up on them. They were one company of two hundred all told, and soon arranged themselves in four stalwart platoons.

Adam watched the parade. They sprang to attention at the raucous command of a spruce middle-aged officer. A man in front of the leading platoon pushed a low trolley along the road, on which was a powerful portable radio tuned to Nihilon Channel Three, which played a nondescript composition called 'The Land of Hopeless Gore', so that with rifles at the slope and baskets in the other hand, the old men stepped out to as quick a march as their valetudinary legs would allow. Judging by the occasional heavily-made up face Adam suspected there was a sprinkling of young men in their ranks disguised as oldsters who would, no doubt, lead them in the attack and cure any hanging back when enemy machine guns started spitting.

Waiters and barmen who stood on the steps to see them go, and who were sobbing heavily, began jeering at Adam when he mounted his bicycle and rode towards Nihilon City. But the sun shone, and the sky was blue, and he felt full of momentary energy after his snack. A few miles later he passed a house, one of many on the outskirts of a large village.

A ten-year-old boy dressed in a long-trousered suit, wearing a bow tie, and with his hair slicked flat by grease, lounged under a sign saying WELCOME TO NIHILON, but as Adam rode by a stone caught him painfully on the shoulder. He stopped and shouted: 'You vicious little bastard!'

The child burst into tears, and hearing the disturbance, a man in a customs officer's cap ran from the house, calling:

'Anything to declare?'

Adam got back on his seat and rode straight at him, speeding over the rivulet that ran across the road, so that he splashed the man's overalls and sandals as he began to repeat: 'Anything to declare?'

He went swiftly along the village street towards the main square, his lungs almost bursting in getting clear of this bogus customs man who seemed nothing more than another Nihilon peasant out on the make. If, however, he was genuine, then he could only congratulate himself on having passed through the second and final obstacle into Nihilon so painlessly.

Along one side of the large square was a line of six sky-blue tourist buses. The rest of the space was tightly occupied by a vast crowd of people. Though it was the hottest part of the day, they seemed by and large happy, as if everyone had just eaten an ample and satisfying meal. In the middle of the square, on a raised platform, a young man with long blond hair was about to make a speech. An older man, wearing a dark suit, dark spectacles, and carrying a black briefcase, mounted the platform and began talking to him, as if prompting him on what to say, for the young man listened respectfully.

Adam pushed towards the middle, but couldn't get far among so many people. A young man with a child on his shoulder stood next to him, and Adam asked what was happening.

'You won't travel far on that bicycle,' the man said. 'Why don't you get on one of those buses?'

'I don't want to.'

'They're going to the front.'

'He's a foreigner,' said the child from on high.

'Shut up,' his father snapped. He gave Adam a friendly smile. 'They belong to War Tours, a very popular holiday organisation here that does great business whenever there's an outbreak at the frontier. Of course, they can be expensive, though they cater for all purses. War Tours are cheapest. You just camp on a hill or spur, and are given a bit of a map and binoculars so that you can see what goes on. That's the seven-day tour, and costs a thousand kricks, inclusive. If you take a fourteen-day holiday they drive you close enough to be bombed and shelled, and that's more exciting, but also more expensive. Better still, you can stand in a muddy trench with a rifle and bayonet to beat off an attack. That's an even higher price. But a three-week five-star holiday is best, at ten thousand kricks. You get all the other things plus, at the end of it, the glory of a mass attack over the wire, with the optional extra of an artificial limb after your spell in a tent hospital. Mind you, there's a long waiting-list for all categories, but I'm in the know with the organisers, and I happen to have a few application forms.' He drew a bundle of papers from his back pocket and waved them under Adam's nose. 'So tell me which tour you want, then I'll fill in one of these and get you on a bus tomorrow morning. You'll have the time of your life, believe me.'

'It's very kind of you,' said Adam, 'but no thank you.'

The man's face turned ugly. 'What do you mean?'

'I told you he was a foreigner,' said his son.

'Curse it,' the man said, 'I haven't sold any this week.' He threw the papers in the air, and they blew in all directions, so that people began scrabbling for them, though on learning what they were they dropped them quickly.

The crowd became silent, sensing that the speech was about to begin. 'Gentlemen and Ladies,' shouted the young man, bent and twisted, swaying like a crippled sapling. 'Nihilists! Listen to me. Listen to the greatest news of all time.' For several minutes he mumbled and spluttered, nodding his head and waving his arms, making a few vague references to the goodness of President Nil, and the value of living pure upright nihilistic lives; but finally, ringing clear above all heads, was made a most astonishing claim, directly affecting everyone present:

'We have abolished . . .' Even before the last word, cheering and shouts of glee broke from many parts of the square, as if some of the people's secret hopes had been unwittingly leaked out during sweaty and endless days of discussion:

'We have abolished . . . death!' he shouted.

Wild cheering caught up those thousands in the sunlight as the speech went on, though it was impossible that everyone heard the final words of his dramatic and historical pronouncement. No one had ever said it before, it seemed, and now, for the first time, such a promise had been made! The whole population was caught up in hysterical and genuine happiness, and even Adam was affected by it, as the marvellous words screamed out clear and plain once more: 'We have abolished death!'—a message stroking his fundamental nerves as if heaven, or at least a form of it, were really here at last.

A man nearby, with tears of joy in his eyes, took Adam's lapels and held him fast: 'Oh, my dear friend, it's not the first time. Oh no. It has happened before. We were happy once for three days. A voice of intellect, authority, and youth said that death has been abolished! The whole town went wild with happiness, so that people heard of it in neighbouring villages and came to join in. So much happiness! It went on and on, and the three days seemed an eternity.'

His voice became sad, though his eyes couldn't relinquish their glazed hilarious expectation: 'But then troops were called to restore order, and drive us back to our jobs. It was all right to abolish death, but we still had to work. In the fighting several people had no way of proving whether that young man up there was right or wrong in saying that death had been abolished because we never saw them again. But the temporary joy of the town at his news was certainly genuine, as it is now.' He walked away, weeping and tearing at his shirt.

The whole mass surged against the platform, though Adam made his way to the edge of the crowd, then to quieter streets on the other side of the square, so that he could continue his journey. The monumental insanity of the young man's pronouncement had for a few moments lifted him into the same wild unseeing happiness as the crowd, his eyes brimming with tears, his head spinning, hands at his temples as if ready for some final ecstatic take-off. But, pedalling through emptier streets, the normal bleak expectant sadness of a poet's life returned.

Chapter Eight

It was difficult not to despair when the train pulled out of the station with all her luggage on it. But she bravely fought away the tears, and asked the woman at the ticket booth to direct her to the local police office.

'You wouldn't buy a return ticket,' said the woman spitefully, 'so I'm not going to tell you where the police chief lives.'

Jaquiline opened her purse and passed her a two-klipp coin. 'Three,' the woman said. When Jaquiline gave in wearily, the woman held her hand and commiserated as if they were old friends: 'What a shock for you. I saw it all. He's done that twice this week already. But don't you worry. He's always brought back. Now, if you go right to the end of this platform you'll see a hut, by the siding. Outside it there'll be a man watering his flowers. That's the chief of police. He's the one to tell your troubles to.'

Jaquiline hurried off without thanking her. Like other frontier stations, it was only busy at certain times, and because the main train for Nihilon City had left, it was almost deserted, though she was annoyed to see several porters standing idly around now that they were no longer needed.

The platform was long, and it took some time to get to the end of it and down to the level of the line. She then walked on the small broken stones, a difficult and painful process in high-heeled shoes, and she was more than pleased when she saw the chief of police's hut a few hundred metres away.

His humble dwelling was surrounded by a flower garden, a square of lavish and brilliant colours, through which a neat path led to the door. A porcine yet kindly-looking man wearing riding boots walked slowly up and down with a watering can. A short way beyond this delightful

44

oasis was the dividing line between Nihilon and Cronacia, bristling with enormous coils of rusty barbed wire.

When Jaquiline waved, the chief of police looked up, put down his watering can, and came towards her. 'Hello, my dear! I hope you've had a pleasant trip, so far?'

He took his tunic from the fence, threw himself clumsily into it, and buttoned it tight like a corset. 'Yes,' he nodded hearing her story while they stood on the path, 'that's an extremely serious complaint. You'd better come inside so that I can make my notes. It's too hot out here.'

It was an amiable and pleasant reception, and so she followed him in without hesitation. Nihilon was at last showing humane tendencies, she thought, if it set the chief of police's office among a grove of such beautiful flowers. The hut was sparsely furnished, with a desk down one side, and a bench opposite on which new books were displayed. She went over to look at their covers and titles: 'I'm glad to see you're so interested in the printed word,' she said with a smile.

'The printed word,' he said, looking closely into her eyes, 'is the basis of Nihilon's civilization. I don't know where any of us nihilists would be without the printed word. The printed word is all-powerful if you are striving for absolute nihilism. It was our first ally, the printed word. As soon as we original Nihilists realised the force of the printed word, we knew that sooner or later we must triumph. The printed word is wonderful in that you can do anything with it. Not only can it be read in secret but it can be shouted into a microphone, or splashed on to every wall. They say that President Nil has a printed word illuminated in a niche in the wall of his bedroom, but nobody knows what it is, and no one dares try to guess. But we all adore him even more for this worship of the printed word.'

During what she considered this pernicious drivel she took out her notebook and examined the display of volumes more closely. They were mostly novels with nonsensical titles, though one book, which she picked up to examine, had blank pages inside. Another was no more than a box with an artificial flower in it. One contained printed pages that resembled a railway timetable, while the most interesting novelty had a gun attached to the stiff cover when she lifted it up, as if showing the author's absolute contempt for the printed word, of which there was not a sign.

'I have a shop, you see,' said the chief of police. 'And I sell mainly books and flowers.'

'Your writers are ingenious,' she smiled.

'These books are all collector's pieces,' he sighed. 'I only retail the best. Our writers of Nihilon have no problems. How can they, being Nihilists? There are no rules. They write, and so they are understood. It is automatic, no matter what they write, whether it's history, geography, psychology, pornography, botany, monotony, devilism, syphilism, bigamy, polygamy, or sodomy. You name it, they write it. Half our authors are thin and phthisical, and languish for death; the other half are monstrously fat and slothful, and so are prone to heart attack, high blood pressure, gout and palsy, but with a fantastic built-in drive for life. So if you'd be generous enough, dear lady, to buy one of their books I'd be extremely grateful. And so would they, as you can imagine. Not many cultured foreigners come this way to purchase my wares.'

A large transfer of money would be waiting for her in Nihilon City, so she could afford to be extravagant in face of such extortion which, at this point of her adventures, seemed quite skilful and amusing. 'I'll buy this one,' she said, appearing to choose at random the volume with the gun inside, and paying his price of two hundred klipps.

The back of the hut had an embrasure built into it, out of which pointed a heavy machine gun, mounted on a tripod and pre-aimed at the frontier wire. 'In Nihilon everyone has several jobs,' he told her, putting the money under a blotter on his desk. 'Besides being chief of police of this town, I am a bookseller and a gardener. I'm also em-ployed as a frontier guard, so that for every Cronacian spy I kill as he tries to cross into Nihilon, I'm paid three hundred klipps. It's not much, but if I shoot two a week it helps to keep my wife and nine children, as well as my mistress and twelve children.'

'Twelve?' she exclaimed.

'Soon to be fourteen, alas,' he said. 'But never mind. We don't despair in Nihilon. There can't be too many of us, menaced as we are by the barbarian predators of Cronacia.' He went close and looked into her eyes: 'I love you.'

'I'm sorry,' she said, stepping back, and realising that he was short-sighted, 'I only came here to make a complaint.'

'I know,' he said, 'I arranged it. I have all these different occupations, but in my spare time I play God. Perhaps I'll get that job as well, one day, though President Nil has it at the moment.' He put his arms around her and pulled her close to his large chest.

She struggled. 'Let me go. You must be mad.'

'Do you think so?' he sighed, kissing her lips. 'All my life I've wanted to go mad, and I keep trying very hard, as I suppose everyone does in good old glorious Nihilon, but I can't do it. Not yet. I keep trying though, because I hope to. What bliss it would be to go mad. I can't tell you how much I long for it.' He kissed her again, and she slapped his fat unshaven cheek, momentarily checking him.

'Come away with me,' he pleaded. 'I'll give up everything for you. Let's go to Perver City. Or if you don't like that idea, I'll even go into Cronacia with you. We can step through the wire.' He ran to the desk and held up a gigantic pair of wire-cutters. 'The fellow on the other side, who also has a machine gun, won't shoot me, because we have a secret arrangement to let each other cross if things get too difficult. So if you won't come to Perver City, let's run off to Cronacia. I've heard there are wonderful beaches over there. We can sprawl on the sand all day, drinking and making love.'

For a moment the idea appealed to her as a means of getting to know more about the inside workings of Nihilon than by the tortuous expedient of travelling around the country itself, but she remembered that a meeting had been arranged with her four colleagues in Nihilon City, and so opened her notebook to write: 'Passions run high in Nihilon. It is a country with few moral standards, and ladies travelling alone would do well to remember this.'

'No,' she said to the chief of police. 'In any case, wouldn't you rather go on playing God, in the hope that one day you'll go mad?'

'Don't mock me,' he said, making another half-hearted attempt to embrace her. 'I only played God to lure you here. I saw you get off the train, so I persuaded the stationmaster to help you, which was the first part of my uncannily successful plan. He didn't want to, but I said I'd kill his wife and have him arrested for murder if he didn't. So he helped you through the customs, got you to the Nihilon train, and went off with your luggage. I knew that you would then have to complain to me, and I simply waited for you here. You see, it's not playing God. It's only thinking for oneself in a high and mighty manner!'

'Your plan has failed,' she said sternly. 'If you don't recover my luggage I'll make a strong complaint when I reach Nihilon City. And then we shall see what will happen.'

'You're most uncooperative,' he said, sulking, 'I only wanted to make love to you among the flowers.'

'No,' she said.

'Will you sign a confession, then?'

'Certainly not.'

'That's the least you can do after all the trouble I've taken.'

'Never.'

'You don't even ask what for,' he said bitterly. 'A confession would bring me five hundred klipps, which would fill my Zap sports car with top-star petrol for a week. If only I could rely on the goodness of people to give me a little spiritual assistance from time to time. Life can be very hard for someone like me.'

She smiled at his childishness, but which she didn't like because she detected the ruthlessness lying undernearth it. 'How can you hope for people to be good in Nihilon?' she asked.

'You can hope for anything in this country. The reason it is great is that we're not afraid of hope. What's more, our hopes often come true. When I saw you getting off the train, and fell in love with you, I hoped we'd be able to meet, and here you are.'

She lit a cigarette. 'But you arranged all that. You just said so.'

'You can't hope without giving it some help,' he said, laughing for the first time. He attacked her so suddenly that she dropped her cigarette. A trick of his foot shut the door hard, while the other foot clipped itself between her ankles and forced her into his arms, so that, with great strength he lowered her quickly to the floor. Such was the shock of it that she didn't struggle at first. Then she bit, scratched, and spat. She ripped the red tab from the lapel of his tunic, and this sound of tearing cloth saved her. The price seemed too high for him, water over his passion, and he jumped away before she could do any more damage to his uniform.

Jaquiline thought he had only leapt clear so as to spring down again from a better vantage point. She reached the table and opened the book for which she had already paid two hundred klipps. He put up his hands. 'I love you,' he said with trembling lips, eyes fixed on the revolver and cursing the versatility of Nihilon's writers.

She held it steadily and was ready to fire: 'I want my luggage. I have to be in Nihilon City tomorrow.'

'We'll go and get it,' he smiled, taking a paperclip from his desk and fastening the red tab back in place on his tunic.

'I'll go alone,' she told him, putting the gun in its box.

He opened the door, and gallantly pointed the way into sunlight.

'My Zap sports car is at your disposal, madame. Twenty kilometres beyond this station the Nihilon City Express waits for two hours to take on food, fuel, arms, and spare wheels; if I drive fast we can get there in time to apprehend our criminal stationmaster. I'll have him tried and sent to a special school where he'll be taught a lower-grade job.'

'That's unjust,' she protested, 'since it was all your plan.'

He took her hand. 'He was unjust in agreeing to it. It's brought ashes and ruin on my head. He deserves to be punished. However, since it's your wish, I won't have him arrested, on condition that you come back here with me afterwards so that we can be together tonight.'

'No,' she said firmly. 'And while we stand talking we're wasting time.'

They walked along the platform, the police chief swaggering as became his rank, and went out through the booking hall, to where his Zap sports car was waiting by the roadside.

Chapter Nine

Benjamin sat in his silent car, wondering whether or not it had broken its back in tumbling down the bank. He was also curious as to why the powers of Nihilon were on to him so soon, for the driver in that red Zap was certainly no playboy out for a casual accident before breakfast. He'd tried to kill him, and that was a plain Nihilonian fact. Benjamin brooded that he'd probably betrayed himself by hitting the policeman at the frontier, an act he'd taken gluttonous pride in at the time, but which in the glare of midday he saw as his first and perhaps fatal mistake.

He'd always assumed that people over forty didn't make such blunders, but in Nihilon he was learning certain things all over again. This fractured start threatened the fibres of his normally cool nerve, and as he turned the ignition key, he wondered whether his colleagues were faring any better in their allotted zones.

The ground was firmer under the trees, and he hoped to get back on the road, despite the many boulders scattered around. The engine sounded good, so he let off the brake, slipped into first gear, and went forward. Most of Benjamin's life had been devoted to the study of history, and he had been chosen by the Editor of the proposed guide-book to concentrate, as far as possible, on recent events in Nihilon. This was easier said than done, for Benjamin knew that the history books of Nihilon's more recent past were nothing more than gossip columns. In the country's schools history was scandal. Nothing else was allowed. Dates and facts were hard to come by. Political reality was out. There were only false accounts of drunkenness, greed, bribe-taking, murder, orgy, perversion, incompetence, blackmail and corruption. The children and students loved it.

History, as it is ordinarily known, stopped at the beginning of the present regime which, during its twenty-five years of power, had closed the country off from the world, at least as regards any serious study of it. Tourists had been allowed to sample the nefarious delights of its nihilistic principles, but they had for the most part returned in a state of dumb shock.

Inwardly terrified of being disillusioned, they had praised the country out of all proportion to its negative achievements. In this way they kept faith in themselves, and by encouraging others to go in their tracks, enabled them to do the same. Some tourists had come back with no impressions at all, being none the wiser for their visits.

He cruised through the grove of trees, over ploughed earth and between stones, until an incline towards the road was gentle enough to ascend. Even so, it was steep, and called for the full power of the Thundercloud's robust engine to get him to the top. Just in time, he noticed that a deep drainage ditch bordered the road, blocking him off from it. He cursed, stopped, pulled hard on the handbrake, and wondered how he could get over.

Some months ago a letter had reached him from an aged and venerable philosopher of Nihilon who had written a true and complete history of the last Nihilonian civil war, and of all that had happened since, which he was about to offer to a publisher in the capital. He said he would hide a carbon copy of the book in case the first one not only failed to be published, but was also not sent back to him. Another correspondent later informed Benjamin that the philosopher-historian had been arrested by his publisher and never seen again, adding that the spare copy of the manuscript was hidden somewhere in Nihilon. Benjamin, in his travels, hoped to find this document, but his return to Nihilon put him in great danger, because he had been there as a young man, and certain crimes were lyingly attributed to him. His life wouldn't be worth a bent Nihilonian klipp if he were caught, which was why his encounter with the Zap was so worrying.

He got out of the car, hoping to stop a passing motorist and ask for help. But the road was empty, the sky was clear, the sun just past its zenith. At this rate it would take a week instead of a day to reach Nihilon City, so he decided to collect enough large stones to fill the ditch and then cross over it. Unfortunately, the most suitable stones lay at the bottom of the slope, which would mean great labour in bringing them up, but since it seemed the only solution he took off his shirt and walked down for the first consignment.

Twenty-five years ago there had been a civil war in Nihilon, between the ruling Rationalists, and the usurping Nihilists. Benjamin Smith, as an idealistic young man whose girlfriend had recently agreed to marry someone else, went off to fight, with other outsiders, for the cause of the Rationalists. His disappointment in love made him both cunning and reckless—cunning in military logic, and reckless for his personal safety—so that within a year he had reached the rank of company commander.

A drop of sweat from his forehead glistened momentarily on a large stone, that plunged to the bottom of the trench and gave back a sound of splintering fragments. During this lengthy transporting of boulders, perspiring freely, he recalled those days of battle for the Republic of Damascony—now Nihilon—when he had received the Damson Leaf Award for high and useful services from President Took, the last great Liberal president of the country, who was said to have died after the final collapse of the battlefronts. Benjamin wanted to find out what had really happened to him, and what had become of Took's infant daughter, who would by now be a grown woman—if she had survived. It seemed to him, as he lugged a particularly heavy burden up the hill, that history was a dustbin to root around in occasionally for something spiritually satisfying to ponder on, especially when at the ripe age of fifty he was suffering the desolation of a broken marriage, and had accepted a job as historical adviser to an unnecessary guidebook merely to get away from it.

He recalled how he and his company of Rational Guards, reduced to twenty-five men out of two hundred, had been ordered to defend the town of Amrel, which was of great importance for the safety of Nihilon City a hundred and sixty kilometres to the southwest. But there was little chance of holding back the ever-pressing forces of nihilism, for with terror on their side, the sinuous and pot-holed roads opened before them, and led inexorably towards the centre of government.

Amrel was one of the last remaining blocks to their progress. It stood on a sheer hill, a packed little town of tall and ancient buildings from whose ramparts one could see the long bridge over the River Aznal—an impregnable position, and tactically the right place for a last stand since it overlooked the eastern plateau for a great distance, and would have commanded it in every way if the Rationalists had possessed a dozen heavy machine guns, a battery of artillery, and several hundred fresh, well-trained men, instead of twenty-five worn-out idealistic fugitives who had little food and ammunition left.

Even so, the forward patrols of the Nihilists had suffered at the bridge, as the score of bodies rotting in the sun has proved. Benjamin had gone down the hill himself and laid explosive charges under its supports, wired them skilfully, and trailed the lead up the cliff face to his headquarters in the old palace. He would wait for days if necessary for that armoured group he'd dreamed of all his life, a trio of prime and perfect tanks on a long bridge suddenly convulsed in an earthquake of explosions that dropped them into icy water below.

Such a picture was with him still as he heaved another stone up to the culvert, part of the same hot territory he'd tried to defend so long ago. That classically perfect bridge had never been blown, for a man of the town had approached him one evening, and beckoned him on to the arcaded walk with a wide view over the empty and lustreless plain. He talked for a long time of how the bridge was of great commercial and cultural value to the town, part of its actual life-spirit, a bridge which not only connected it to the rich wheatlands and the pastures of the Alpine regions, but also to the Chimney Zone north of Nihilon City from which came all manufactured goods. The bridge was a vital lifeline of the country that, once destroyed, would take years to rebuild, and in any case it was no longer a question, the man went on, of holding up the Nihilist army. All the Nihilists had to do was cross the river by boat to the north and south, out of range of Rationalist patrols, and the town would fall within a matter of hours.

Benjamin knew he ought to have shot the man dead, and had his body thrown towards the river, as the townspeople slung their dogs when they wanted to kill them, but he hesitated, and went on listening in the dusk. The man offered him a bus, with enough petrol to get his company to Nihilon City, in exchange for leaving the bridge alone. Amrel would fall anyway, even if they died defending it. Benjamin knew that the Rationalist armies were being defeated on all fronts because they lacked supplies and popular support. Walking up and down in the cool moonlight, smoking a cigar and listening to the smooth persuasions of this man, offering him safety in the form of a bus and petrol, he felt for the first time since leaving his own country that he wanted to live. Perhaps if he survived he would even fall in love again, and his nod of acceptance was barely visible in the half darkness.

The following morning he and his soldiers had got into the bus. The man who had provided it, and who had shaken his hand warmly, who had embraced him and called him his own brother as they said goodbye, was an agent of the Nihilists. Halfway to the capital, it was by the merest chance that a bomb was found under one of the bus seats, which was to have destroyed them all. Also, five of the petrol cans were full of water, though this was remedied by taking more fuel from filling-stations at gunpoint.

His company deserted him to a man on the outskirts of Nihilon City, where he was arrested, charged with treason for deserting the bridge, and sentenced to be shot. He had no defence, though he said he was innocent, and that his retreat from Amrel was a tactical move to draw the Nihilists into an ambush, but that his own men had abandoned him before he could carry it out.

A Nihilist column had marched over the bridge into Amrel on the following day, and so all the surrounding region was lost by the Rationalists. Other areas were thus outflanked, and the defenders of each front began to fall back in panic. It was the end of the end. In the general collapse, he escaped from his gaolers, and it was only by raw cunning and infinite privation that he was able to get out of the country some months later. As for President Took, no news of his fate had ever been published by the Nihilists.

The ditch was at last filled, and he drove his car on to the road, reflecting that his first day back in Nihilon had so far been as arduous as when he was fighting to save it from the black threat which had now overtaken it.

After a few kilometres along the empty highway in his fast, comfortable car he came to a barrier with the words: CUSTOMS POST. WE IMPLORE YOU TO HALT in painted white letters across the top. There was a maroon Bivouac salon car in front, and when the gate opened, they advanced between two concrete buildings with armed guards standing outside.

An arrogant young customs officer came out of the first door holding a large steel hammer with which he smashed the windscreen of the Bivouac to pieces. 'You are forbidden to import windscreens into Nihilon,' he sneered.

The blond, fair-haired, tall, blue-eyed man at the wheel jumped out and protested: 'This is ridiculous.'

'And that's treasonable talk,' shouted the customs officer. 'Nothing is ridiculous in Nihilon. Drive on, or I'll pulverise your headlamps. It's also forbidden to import headlamps. It's forbidden to bring anything in at all. I'll tax your toenails if you insult me personally like that.'

The man quickly handed over a bundle of money, and after a big red paint mark had been splashed down the side of his car by a second customs officer, he was allowed to enter the country.

'Good afternoon, sir,' said the customs officer obsequiously when Benjamin drove forward, putting his hammer away into a briefcase. Benjamin was resigned to losing his windscreen, because he had a spare plastic one in his repair kit, but the customs officer asked: 'How much blood do you have in your body, sir?'

Puzzled, he made a wild guess: 'Sixteen litres.'

The customs officer opened the door: 'You're only allowed fifteen. Will you step this way, sir?'

He swore, but inaudibly, deciding to be more patient than he'd been at the first obstacle, and followed the customs man inside.

'May I see your passport?'

Benjamin gave it to him: 'Certainly.'

'It's forged,' the man said with a smile, and Benjamin marvelled at how uncannily quick they were in detecting this fact, which was indeed true, though the falsification was so perfect that he didn't see how they could tell. 'However,' the passport general said from behind the desk, 'we don't worry about such details in Nihilon. Kindly sit in that chair so that we can confiscate your litre of surplus blood, then we'll let you go.'

Benjamin put his passport away, and began to roll up his shirt sleeve. 'What would happen if I had a litre of blood *less* than the normal amount?'

'You'd have a transfusion of the difference. That would be inconvenient, because you'd have to wait a few days until they could do it at the local clinic. And you'd have a big medical bill to pay. But there'd be no trouble. No trouble at all. As a Nihilist I have an answer to every question. There are advantages to this system, as you'll no doubt find before you leave.'

Benjamin flinched and grunted as the needle went in, and turned pale when he saw such a huge flow of his life's blood going out. However, the nurse who extracted it was pretty, so he didn't object, but stood up as soon as it was finished and walked unsteadily back to his car.

'The fact is,' said the young customs official with the hammer in his briefcase, 'no matter how much blood a person says he has we always take a litre out, on this route. We sell it to the Nihilon Blood Bank for use in our war against Cronacia. It not only makes us money, but it's patriotic as well.'

'A charming idea,' said Benjamin, glad to be back in his car, though feeling that he'd need a week to recover from this day's blows.

'Another thing,' said the customs officer, 'do you have a repair kit in your car?'

'Of course.'

'Kindly get it out for me.'

Like a man under interrogation, he had admitted something he thought to be totally innocent, if not irrelevant, only to find it of vital consequence to his exhausted body and irascible mind. 'What the hell for?'

'All repair kits have to be inspected.'

'Is there duty to pay on them?'

The customs man shook his head. With a sigh, Benjamin went to the back of the car, lifted the tailgate, and pulled boxes about till he came to the repair kit.

'Open it,' said the customs officer.

He regarded it as the pride of his travelling equipment, a collection of spare parts and tools which he had chosen with care so as to make sure he could deal with any minor breakdown, having heard of Nihilon's bad and brutal service stations. The customs officer picked over the tools disdainfully: 'Do you think our garages are badly equipped? Or do you suspect that our mechanics are incompetent?'

'I carry such tools in my own country,' Benjamin lied.

'Do they do things better there?'

'I didn't say that,' he said, staggering from weakness.

'Confiscated,' said the customs officer, pulling them to the ground with a clatter. A humble little man in a white overall came with a barrow and carried them away. Benjamin, in no position to fight, walked to the front of his car, intending to drive on. 'One moment,' called the customs officer, drawing the hammer from his briefcase and making purposefully for the windscreen.

Benjamin ran with his remaining strength and, gasping for breath as he opened the door, took the heavy revolver from the glove-box. He pointed it at the customs officer, who also turned pale, and let his hammer drop. 'Put that paint mark on the side of my car and let me go,' Benjamin rasped, 'or I'll blow you to pieces.'

'Yes sir,' said the customs officer. Another man splashed a blue streak down the Thundercloud's door, so that, highly satisfied at his forcefulness, Benjamin drove towards the gate.

A squat-faced soldier with rifle and bayonet turned a mangle-handle to open it. As Benjamin was driving through, obeying the roadsign speed of five kilometres per hour, the soldier took a hammer from his pocket and ran in front of the car, smashing its windscreen to pieces. Benjamin, with wild rage, pressed on the accelerator in the hope of crushing him to death, but the adept soldier dodged clear and waved him on with a smile.

Chapter Ten

Nihilon Airways ran three distinct services into Nihilon from the outside world: first-class, second-class, and a flight that could not be described as of any class at all. The fifth member of the guidebook research team, Richard Lope—a tall, dark, slim and handsome young man who, up to now, had been of a highly nervous disposition, had chosen second-class, or middle-class, and was finding it quite comfortable, though there were still three hours to go before landing. Lope had recently graduated with honours from the university, after three years studying the language of his own country which he had learned to speak at two and read at five. He was destined to become a diplomat, but looked upon the Nihilon trip as a pre-paid adventure before getting down to it.

What fascinated him at the moment was the naked air-hostess walking up and down with a tray of drinks and food. All she wore was a thin belt at the waist from which swung a notepad to take down the passengers' orders. Naked air-hostesses were a speciality of Nihilon Airways, though few people were said to take advantage of the service for that fact alone. Nevertheless, Richard considered it a very pleasant aspect of Nihilonian travel, an encouraging introduction to the country as he gazed at the breasts of a beautiful young woman walking along the gangway with his lunch. Her red made-up lips smiled as she bent down to set the tray before him, one of her nipples only a few inches from his left eye.

What puzzled him, on the other hand, were the several protuberances along both sides of the plane which came awkwardly out towards the seats, and which the passengers unfortunate enough to have such a place—of which he was one—found difficult to sit by. They were a sort of oblong box, from which a long pipe or barrel went through the perspex windows. He imagined them to be the multiple aerials of some new and complicated beam-approach landing system, though he wasn't entirely satisfied by this explanation.

During the meal, which included half a bottle of pink, fizzy and potent wine, he read the instruction booklet attached to the seat in front: 'In case of emergency, passengers are kindly requested to carry on talking, reading, eating or sleeping, because though your lives are in our hands, and we will do our best to preserve them, there will be nothing anybody can do about it. Like all other airlines of the world we carry highly inflammable petrol, fly at a great height, and do not provide parachutes, so in the event of an emergency it is highly unlikely that either passengers or crew would survive. When the aircraft is about to land you may notice, if you are fortunate enough to be near an appropriate window, that the inner-port engine will burst into flames. This is part of our special Thrill Service, so you need not be alarmed. Your captain is quite experienced at this form of landing, because he has already done it many times with this particular type of aircraft. All that remains is for Nihilon Airways to wish you a pleasant trip. You are flying at ten thousand metres. Speed unknown because the pitot tube has snapped off the main chimney, ha-ha! Your aircraft is a Cyclon B Private Enterprise 4-Jet Special, a miracle of modern technology built in the factories of Nihilon.'

Richard Lope copied this into his notebook, then went on to inform future would-be air travellers of the attractive stewardesses circulating on this class of plane. An elderly man sitting next to him said: 'She is good-looking, isn't she?'

'Very,' Richard agreed, as she poured his coffee.

'If you stare too much it embarrasses them,' the man whispered. 'They're liable to slap your face, or spill a lunch tray over you.'

'It's hardly possible not to stare.'

'You are young,' the man laughed, 'I suppose that's why. I'm fifty-five, and I've done this trip many times. I'm a professor of economics at Nihilon University, and I frequently visit other countries to attend seminars and conferences. I'm going back to form a committee for investigating ways of reorganising Nihilon's economy. All is not well in our country, Mr. . . . ?'

'My name is Richard.'

'Richard. There is a great deal of wastage.'

'Too much nihilism?' he laughed.

The professor nodded. 'We may have to alter all that. There is talk that nihilism is not a viable economic proposition, though only a little talk, as yet. Nihilism is so highly regarded by the common people that we intellectuals are afraid to criticise it. Some won't even talk about it. I don't want to bore you with such vital topics, but I am beginning to realise that as a nihilist I have only one life, which fact will worry me in my old age, if ever it comes. That is why I travel second-class to Nihilon. I could go first-class, but that's only for young people.'

'What's it like, then?' Richard asked.

'The best that Nihilon can offer. It is often referred to by us as the Ballroom Special, the biggest airliner we have, with eight engines, and no seats, but bars all round the plane and a dance band on a platform at the tail end. It is a heady wine-and-dance at twenty thousand metres, lasting five hours, followed by a forced landing at Nihilon airport with *two* engines on fire. There are charming dance hostesses fully dressed. Sometimes the captain comes down from his cockpit to join the passengers, and take a snack at one of the bars. Chandeliers glitter from the ceiling as the plane flies above all cloud at magnificent speed. Of course, there are incidents. People fight or get drunk, or they become ill, or hysterical, or morbid, or so happy they want to wreck the plane and make it crash. Or they try to organise a hijack mutiny against the captain and crew, in which case they are brought down by concealed water-guns set at various parts of the fuselage. Those who don't indulge in these scrapes may just sit back and observe the antics of those who do, so that a good time is usually had by everyone. But as I get older I like danger less, and prefer the company of these nubile young hostesses. You may also have heard about the Party Specials. No? Well, when members of our government want to gather in a light-hearted way, they have a meeting in one of these great planes. It circles for hours high over the country, a magnificent going-on, which often lasts till fuel runs out and the pilot is forced to land. No one can gatecrash at that height, and so, with all credentials thoroughly checked before take-off, the guests can relax and have the time of their lives, with no fear of assassination, and very little from a coup d'état, since everyone is drunk. Naturally, loyal citizens of Nihilon fervently hope that no such plane will ever crash. We put great faith in our technological achievements.'

Richard, who had been writing in his notebook, at last looked up. 'What about third-class, or whatever it's called?'

The professor seemed uninterested. 'Third-class tourist-economy night-flight in ten miserable hours? Yes, people are towed in huge gliders by obsolescent bombers, or so I hear. They sit on the floor with luggage at their feet and packets of sandwiches in their hands. A continuous tape of crying babies is played from stereo-speakers to make them feel more uncomfortable, and smells of fatty stew emerge from the end of a pipe near the tail of the plane as it goes through air pockets above the mountain tops. Not very nice, I must say. During the flight passports are collected, and hardly distinguishable false ones are handed back before landing on an improvised field in some remote area fifty kilometres from the main airport, so that people have to make their way to Nihilon City by a very irregular bus service on bumpy tracks, or walk through unmapped forest, if and when they get by the police and customs tent at the side of the field. Even dis-organisation is well organised in Nihilon. I'm very proud of my country, in some ways. The aim of our government is absolute chaos meticulously regulated. There can't be a more noble aim in the world than that. I defy you or anybody else to tell me that there can.'

Notices along the plane said that in the interests of safety and hygiene, smoking was forbidden. Richard had been tempted to take out his pipe and slyly puff at it, but he was put off because there were no ashtrays. Now that the meal was over, however, he saw his neigh-bour, and other people, buying huge cut-glass souvenir ashtrays of Nihilon Airways at ten klipps each from the stewardesses, then taking out pipes and cigars, and lighting up. Richard also bought one, though not without five minutes of bargaining which finally brought the price down to seventeen klipps from the naked, though mercenary, stewardess.

'We have strange customs,' said the professor, blowing thick smoke across the gangway. 'In Nihilon's internal politics the domestic theme is always and continually freedom—the uttermost freedom of the people to do what they like. We sing songs of freedom, ballads of liberty, lullabies of free-for-all. I suppose you're even going to stay at Freedom Hotel in Nihilon?'

'Hotel Stigma, Ekeret Place,' said Richard. 'May I borrow a match?'

'Set the plane on fire if you want to,' laughed the professor, passing him one. 'See if I care! But you see, when a few dissident intellectuals formed a political party called *Real Freedom*, they were derided not only by the people, but by the government as well (what's left of it) since everyone believed that they had freedom already. Freedom to start a political group based on freedom was only a way of destroying freedom. So President Nil ordered the offenders to be sent to a school for writers and journalists. However, a group of workers and intellectuals started a political party with the idea that people in our country had too much freedom, and that they should lose some of it in the name of National Unity and Recovery. The government saw a real threat in this. Scores of these dissidents were rounded up and shot without trial, but quite a few got away to the mountains, where they may still be, for all any of us know. Such political ideas were getting dangerously close to those of the Rationalists during our civil war twenty-five years ago, and none of us are nihilistic enough to want that back.'

A voice from a small air-vent, built into the back of the seat in front, called out: 'Well said, professor. You speak like a true and grateful citizen of Nihilon.'

'Thank you, sir,' said the professor. He grimaced at Richard, then pressed a handkerchief over the mouthpiece. 'I was only praising the awful place,' he whispered to Richard, 'to see whether they were tuned in or not. The fact is I'm high on the executive staff of a revolutionary party myself, but don't betray me, will you?'

Richard suspected a trap. 'I really don't want to know about it.'

'It's all right, my friend, they can't hear us now. I've got to tell you certain things because, as a foreigner, you might be useful to us.'

'My sole purpose in going to Nihilon is to write a guidebook,' Richard protested, 'not to help in a revolution.' An air-hostess whose breasts were slightly too low asked with a smile if they needed anything to drink. 'A glass of water,' said Richard, taking no chances on anything stronger. The lunch wine had given him a headache, indigestion, eye-strain, hot flushes, heartburn, handshake and a sudden flood of inexplicable melancholia, and he hoped these discomforts would diminish if not wear off by the time they landed. In order to change the subject, he mentioned these ailments to the professor while he sipped the water brought to him by the girl whose breasts he wanted to touch and who, he seemed sure, had winked at him suggestively while placing the glass into his hand.

The professor removed the handkerchief from the speaker-microphone in front, saying in a pompous voice: 'There are many different wines in this country. Nihilon is famous for its superlative vintages, all of which are extremely delectable.' He stuffed the handkerchief back again so that he could not be overheard: 'But some of them have un-enviable reputations, dear foreign friend. That particularly sweet and faintly fizzy wine you so unwisely imbibed during lunch sends one into the blackest of black sadnesses. At one time our political prisoners were induced to get drunk on it, so that they invariably confessed, except the schizophrenics, who were always as hard as nails, full of contradictions, and confessions you could never rely on. Anyway, Richard, I remember an incident a few months ago, when I was staying at a remote village in the mountains for some peace and quiet to get on with my work. There was an impressionable tourist who, after drink-ing one glass of the wine you had at lunch, fancied he'd changed into a vampire bat so that, unknown to any of us, who thought he'd merely gone outside to sample the pure night air, he launched himself in one glorious leap from a hundred-metre cliff at the end of the village. The night had been dark to all but him as he climbed that fatal parapet, but the police found him mangled on the rocks next morning. Unfor-tunately, in his back pocket were the details of our proposed coup d'état, but as our relations with Cronacia were rather tender at that time, as they are today, so I heard on the radio, the police assumed he was one of their agents, and didn't connect us with it.'

'You certainly seem to have exciting lives,' said Richard.

'That's nihilism,' the professor beamed, taking a large envelope from his briefcase: 'Will you deliver this to a certain address when you get to Nihilon City? Our operations orders are inside. I can't do it myself because I'm followed everywhere. Otherwise I would.'

Richard held it: 'Who follows you?'

'Everyone,' said the professor. 'In Nihilon everyone follows every-one else. I follow the person I'm ordered to, just as another person is ordered to follow me. I'm never sure who it is, because he's changed from day to day, just as my own instructions are. It's all worked out by computer and communicated to us by telephone before breakfast each morning.'

Richard didn't believe a word of it. 'Sounds like a lot of wasted energy'

'It is,' said the professor fervently, 'that's why I think the system should be changed, or modified. The economy is going downhill fast. Unadulterated nihilism is a luxury we cannot afford.'

'But I can't promise to deliver this,' said Richard, handing the envelope back.

'You're committed to it,' said the professor. 'Your fingerprints are on it. If I'm arrested I'll betray you and have you shot.'

'Damn,' he exclaimed putting it into his own briefcase. 'That was a dirty trick.'

'It's nihilism,' said the professor, slapping his knees in an excess of joviality, then adding more seriously: 'Now you know why we have to get rid of such a system.'

'I certainly do.'

'Down with nihilism! Nihilism must go! Long live Order and Rationality!' he cried. But the professor's handkerchief had fallen from the speaker-microphone, and a voice barked out of it: 'Shut up, you old fool, you feeble-minded nitwit.'

'That's the sort of thing our ridiculous and hot-headed revolutionaries say,' the professor went on, recovering quickly. 'But I know they are wrong and can never hope to succeed, because, as millions of ordinary Nihilists like me say, before getting into bed at night, "Long live Nihilism. Nihilism is our salvation. Down with Order and Rationality." '

'That's better,' said the voice from the speaker. The professor stuffed his handkerchief back into it: 'You swine,' he said vehemently, 'I'll kill you. You'll be shot, hanged, and poisoned—all at once if I have my way.'

'Who will?'

'President Nil. It's his recorded voice we hear everywhere.' He held Richard's hand: 'Please deliver that envelope. Our whole cause depends on it.'

'Oh, damn,' Richard said again.

'You promise?'

'I said yes, didn't I?'

Chapter Eleven

One must always expect the unexpected in a country such as Nihilon, thought Adam, yet the unexpected could not be called the unexpected if one expected it. Be prepared for all surprises, but being prepared cut out the risk of being surprised, and so whatever happened that shocked you was always an unexpected surprise. There seemed no way around the problem.

The road changed from a broad, beckoning, tarmacadamised highway to a narrow, twisting, hilly, potholed, semi-bridlepath, so that it was often necessary to get off and push his bicycle under a rain of his own sweat.

Holes were more numerous on level or downhill stretches of the road, when he might otherwise have made good speed, but almost non-existent on uphill climbs when he had to get off and walk anyway, so that soon he was caked in dust, and feeling hungry again. A hundred-ton lorry came toiling up the hill, grinding slowly by, and the driver cheerfully indicated that he should throw his bicycle in the back for a lift to Nihilon City, but Adam refused with a comradely wave, for his instructions were to cycle the whole way, though later as he sat down to rest by the roadside he wondered why he bothered to obey such an order.

Before him was a great slogan-noticeboard which said:

OBEY—AND FEEL YOUNG!
REBEL, AND LIVE FOREVER!

He opened the dead soldier's map, extracted from the hollow butt of the rifle, and saw that the next sizeable town was a place called Fludd, which he hoped to reach by nightfall. According to preliminary notes given out at the office before leaving, there was no hotel between where he was now and the seaport of Shelp, though this information was based on hearsay and rumour, or taken from pre-civil war guide-books. He certainly wanted to avoid nine hours under the stars in this desolate country.

At the summit of the next hill the sun spread an orange glare across dark-green flowing hills, reflecting light back into his eyes. The region now seemed more populated, for several localities lay ahead, one of which he thought might be the town of Fludd where he hoped to find a hotel.

The road surface improved, before reaching a restaurant called Rover's Roadhouse. He leaned his bicycle against its balustrade, and watched a group of youths and girls, reeking of alcohol, come laughing and staggering down the steps. They pushed each other into a black, sleek, high-powered car called a Nil, and after a short struggle as to who would drive, the vehicle moved erratically away in the direction of Nihilon City. He wiped his brow, glad that they would be well ahead of him on the road, for then there would be no danger of them coming on him suddenly from behind.

Prominently displayed in the vestibule was a huge notice in lurid crimson letters saying:

DRINK NIHILITZ! KEEP DEATH ON THE ROAD! IT'S FUN!

The legend frightened him, and he began to envy the safety of his colleagues who were travelling by train, car, ship, and plane. He and his bicycle seemed so vulnerable and fragile on such perilous highways that he wondered whether he'd get to the end of his assignment. Before leaving home he'd expected an idyllic cycling tour in the smiling countryside of Nihilon, and saw himself writing poem after poem inspired by the sense of liberation that this journey would give him, but so far not a single line had entered his head. In this respect the land was disappointingly barren, for it seemed that all his intellect and imagination would be needed simply in order to survive.

'No food tonight,' a waiter called out brusquely. Adam did not intend to eat a meal, only to order the smallest thing, so as to find out what sort of prices were charged: 'A small cup of black coffee.'

'Coffee?' sneered the waiter. 'Have a bottle of Nihilitz. Make you feel better.' A bottle with a gaudy red-blue-and-gold label was set on the counter: 'It's against the law to drive on coffee.'

'I'm not driving,' said Adam. 'I'm riding a bicycle.'

'What do you want to drink then?'

'A small black coffee.'

The waiter moved the bottle away. 'Have a large one.

'Small,' said Adam.

The waiter glared savagely. 'Listen, I receive a commission on all I sell, so what do you think I'll earn on a small cup of black coffee? In any case, it won't be enough for you. There's another ten kilometres before you get to Fludd, and it'll be dark soon. Go on, have a large black coffee. It'll only cost a hundred pecks.'

'Pecks?' Adam cried in astonishment. 'I thought it was klipps.'

'That was in the Frontier Zone,' the waiter informed him. 'You're in the Fludd Area now, and all money is in pecks. You should have changed your klipps at the provincial border.'

'But I didn't see a bank there,' Adam said.

'You should have looked,' said the waiter smugly.

'There wasn't one,' he cried. 'You know there wasn't.'

'That was a pity, then, for you. All you've got to do is pay me fifty pecks for your coffee.'

Adam made an effort to stay calm. 'Fifty pecks is too much. Anyway, can't I even have a small cup of black coffee?'

'You're wasting my time. Unless you allow me to change it for you. Fifty pecks to a travellers unit.'

'Fifty?'

'That's what I said.'

'It should be a hundred,' he ventured.

'I know, but what about my commission? Do you want my children to starve?'

'How many do you have?'

'None. But I have to think about the future.'

He handed over a travellers unit. 'All right, a large cup of black coffee.'

'And a glass of Nihilitz?' said the bartender, happily. 'Go on, have a drop. Then your breath will smell of it.'

'I'd rather not,' said Adam.

'Well, if the police stop you on the road and see that you haven't been drinking, and you get ten years in prison, don't blame me. It's the most serious crime in Nihilon. We've got to keep death on the roads. It's our only way of holding the population down.'

'I don't want any Nihilitz,' Adam persisted.

The waiter pushed his coffee over so angrily that nearly half of it splashed into the saucer. 'Fifty pecks.'

'I could get a night's lodging at a good hotel for that. It's extortion.'

'Oh, is it?' the waiter jeered. 'You'd better drink your coffee, before it goes cold, then get back on the road, or I'll call the police in. You're creating a disturbance.'

'Give me your complaints book,' shouted Adam.

'The dog ate it.'

'It's a lie. I know you've got one. All establishments in Nihilon have.'

'We're waiting for a new one from the Ministry of Tourism,' said the waiter, suddenly dispirited at the way things were going.

'Then I'll write it on a piece of paper and post it to the Ministry myself. I refuse to be robbed at every place I stop at.'

The waiter began to weep: 'We shall starve, I know we shall. Nihilon is an underdeveloped country, and we need all the foreign exchange we can get.'

Adam gulped some of his coffee. 'This country is one of the richest in the world. I've seen it with my own eyes.' This wasn't exactly true, but as if to prove his point, a score of people crowded into the bar, and waiters appeared from the kitchen to serve them. Steaming plates of food, platters of salad, and baskets of cut bread were carried around. Women fed their children, and men were laughing as they poured out wine and small glasses of Nihilitz.

'We're by no means rich,' said the waiter, 'so I shan't give you back your twenty-five pecks.'

'That's robbery, then,' said Adam, almost resigned to it.

'It looks like it,' said the waiter jovially. 'In any case, you're keeping me from my work. All you have to do is spend a thousand pecks, then you can eat like the rest of these honest Nihilists.'

'That's too much. I can't afford it.'

'Look at this specimen, ladies and gentlemen,' the waiter shouted, losing his temper, leaping up on to the counter, though no one took much notice of him. 'He comes into our country and spends only fifty pecks on a cup of coffee for his dinner. How can we prosper with such tourists? It's a national disgrace that these vagabonds are allowed over the frontier. I expect he has only a few travellers units in his pocket, maybe even less if we hold him upside down and shake him. They should make sure at the frontier that no one enters our great country with less than ten thousand units in his wallet. How else can our national economy survive? It shows how careless our customs officials are these days, not to mention our lazy police.'

A policeman came from one of the far tables, and told him to shut up.

'Why should I?' screamed the waiter. 'The police are even worse than foreigners. You expect to be fed free, otherwise you make all sorts of trouble, and alter the laws to suit yourselves.'

The policeman took out his gun, and when the waiter went back to washing glasses, he asked Adam for his passport, and in an inspired mood of desperation Adam said: 'I haven't got one.'

'I know you haven't,' said the policeman, handing it to him. 'Your pocket was picked while you were arguing with the waiter. I'm giving it back to you.'

Adam blushed, and trembled, thinking that he must be more careful. 'Thank you.'

'Not at all,' said the policeman. 'It's just one of our courtesy services for distressed travellers. There's a reward of three hundred pecks for returned passports.'

'I haven't got three hundred,' he said, choking with irritation.

'Then I shall have to arrest you,' said the policeman.

'Whatever for?'

'For losing your passport.'

'But I didn't lose it. My pocket was picked.'

'That's your story. Try telling it to the police.'

'So you aren't a policeman?'

'Yes, I am, but not when I'm claiming my reward. Police regulations state that during the few seconds when a reward is handed over you cease to be a policeman. That time, of course, is when many of my dear brethren are killed, and the reward turns out to be one of a fatal kind. Anyway, I'll trouble you for three hundred pecks.'

'I refuse. Let me see a copy of your regulations.'

'He's a very hard man, sir,' said the waiter to the policeman.

'I'm still writing my regulations,' said the policeman. 'They won't be ready till tomorrow night. I'm very slow at it because I have to think about them carefully. Every regulation can be taken two ways, so that when I arrest people like you, as I do now, you don't have any chance of getting away with it.'

It was obvious to Adam that he couldn't win, and that the only chance of keeping sane was to submit to every injustice that came along. He held out his hands, inviting the policeman to handcuff him.

'Don't be impatient,' said the policeman with a smile. 'There's no hurry. I've got years yet, before I bring my career to a successful conclusion. You can cash some travellers units at the bar, then pay me the three hundred pecks. Waiter!'

'Yes, sir?'

'Our friend would like to change some money.'

Adam was shocked into silence, merely nodded when the waiter looked unbelievingly at him and enquired: 'How many, sir?'

The transaction was quick, the cheques by-passing Adam and going straight into the policeman's pocket.

'You ought to buy me a drink now,' the policeman said. 'It's not every day that I recover somebody's passport for them.'

'It's not, sir, is it?' said the waiter respectfully. Adam put a twenty-peck note back on the counter and asked for Nihilitz. Four large bottles of urine-coloured liquid were set before them. 'I can't pay for all that,' he said, shocked at such a quantity, and not wanting to be caught out again.

'You already have,' said the waiter. 'It's only five pecks a bottle.' The policeman drank a tumblerful straight off, and the waiter did likewise, after pouring a little into Adam's glass and saying: 'I wouldn't drink much if I were you. You're not used to it.' But it melted into Adam's mouth like snow on a hot day, and he immediately felt better, whatever the after-effects might be. His anxious state of mind drifted away.

'He drinks like a true native of the country,' the waiter said to the policeman, both of whom had already started on the second bottle.

'Not too much, though,' the policeman cautioned Adam, clinking glasses with him nevertheless. This was obviously what he had needed ever since firing his fateful shot at the frontier, he thought, reaching out to pour another quarter-litre. The policeman glanced disapprovingly, fearing that he might drink it all and leave none for them. Most of the diners had now left, and those few who remained looked at the policeman and the waiter drinking with such outrageous greed at the bar. It passed through Adam's mind that he should not drink on an empty stomach, but the ambrosial liquid tempted him, and dulled him with such calm solicitude that he could not resist finishing his large glass as if its contents were water.

70

Chapter Twelve

An uneven corrugation of mountains rose from the line of grey sea. The northern coast was steeply-cliffed and inhospitable, communication along it being only possible by boat, or so it had been thought, though Richard now saw, from the window of the airliner, the faintest thread of a road going up and through a pass in the direction of Nihilon City. He lifted his topographical camera, and took several photographs after asking the professor to shield his activities by the doublespread of his Nihilon Gazette, knowing he could hardly refuse to do so, or betray him for spying, since he held the professor's revealing envelope in his briefcase.

'There's more trouble with Cronacia,' the Professor said, lowering his newspaper. 'An exchange of shots took place yesterday on the southern frontier. A few of our Geriatric battalions are already fighting it out. According to the news reports they are courageously pressing forward their attacks. which means they are suffering heavy losses. I suppose there are worse ways of dying.'

Richard hoped that his colleague Adam had come safely through this troubled zone, reasoning that he must have been there during the fighting. 'I'd rather die in bed when I get old,' he said. 'Or even if I die young.'

'Nobody dies in bed in Nihilon,' said the professor, 'unless they are young and fit, and get stabbed by a jealous husband, or shot by a frantic wife, or picked off by an enemy who can only be sure of finding them in bed. Otherwise the old are sent into a convenient frontier clash, while the fatally sick are despatched to a remote part of the country and allowed to die peacefully in the open air. It is considered bad for anyone to pass on in bed, but when our party comes to power we'll issue a law giving every person the right to do so. That will be a great blow against nihilism. Bed and Peace will be our slogan, at first.'

The plane was losing height, fixed on its long slide towards Nihilon airport, when a sudden upsurge caused the professor's newspaper to wrap itself over his knees. Richard's camera fell to the floor, and his seat was pushed with such force that he thought he was going to be squashed into the ceiling like a fly. Then the plane righted itself with a splintering roar of its engines, so that his heart felt like an inflated paper-bag about to explode between two hands. It banked steeply, and kept turning as if to fly in a circle forever, while he stared vertically down at the earth. Rows of people were gripping their seats in fear, and an air-hostess, standing against the wall of the arch leading to the galley, had her otherwise ample breasts so pressed in by gravity that she seemed almost flat-chested.

The plane straightened, and Richard wondered why the primitive idea of providing parachutes had never been thought of by modern airlines. He assumed that his face was as white from fear as was the professor's. The wings of the plane fluttered, and out of the window he saw three small red planes, exhaust smoke curling from their engines as they climbed towards the sun. 'Cronacian jets,' explained the professor. 'Fighter-training planes. I expect they were buzzing us. They often do.'

'You'd better get your old men up in their fighter planes to protect us, then,' Richard joked.

'That may not be necessary,' said the professor, trying to reassure his new-found friend. 'All Nihilon airliners are armed.'

'Armed?'

'Yes. With guns.'

The jets were spinning like red coins towards them. The airliner was closer to Nihilon earth than when the attack started, though the main airport was nowhere in sight. The land was grey and ribbed, bone dry and barren, an unknown area that caused him to lift his camera for another topopicture.

He was pushed back into his seat by a burly man who removed the cover from the box near his knees, revealing the mechanism at the back end of a machine gun. Another man was stacking boxes of belt-ammunition in the gangway. When the plane dipped, the machine-gunman shook to his own lethal noise, and Richard looked out of the window, as if to enjoy the spectacle and so calm his fear. One Cronacian plane lurched into the air, and vanished above the back of the jet, with smoke spewing from its red wings. The professor clapped, and

72

shook the machine-gunner's hand. 'Bravo!' he cried and, turning to Richard: 'We might get one or two more before landing.'

'Does this often happen?' Richard asked, his arms and legs shaking with apprehension. Several more machine-gunners were positioned along both sides of the jet, waiting intently for the next brush of the Cronacians.

'Usually,' said the professor calmly.

'It's the first time I've heard of it.'

'We try not to mention it. The Nihilon government, ever mindful of its peaceful image in the world, doesn't want to make an international incident out of these high-spirited attacks by Cronacian pilots, though we've never actually fired back at them before.'

A blazing line of gunfire broke from every aperture. The bare-chested gunner nearest Richard gripped a huge cigar in his teeth. Many seats were empty, suggesting that the gunners had been travelling as ordinary passengers under the auspices of the Nihilon government. Air-hostesses walked from the galley with trays of hot coffee and sandwiches, handing them out to each sweating gunner. Richard, watching the sky, saw another red button of a fighter-trainer growing bigger, and it only stopped after it had turned into a shocking black circle of disintegration, scattering in bits and pieces to the earth. The gunner, a man of more than fifty, half-bald but with a halo of grizzled hair, gave a belly-laugh and reached behind for a cup of coffee.

'But they weren't *shooting* at us,' said Richard.

The professor giggled with embarrassment. 'So you've noticed, dear boy? Of course not. They never do. But we've decided it's time they were taught a lesson, in case they should ever decide to turn serious.'

'That's insane,' said Richard. 'They were buzzing us, that's all.' He took a cup of coffee from a passing tray, but the hostess snatched it back, her breasts quivering with indignation: 'That's only for our brave gunners!'

He apologised, and turned to the professor: 'The Cronacians will send up armed fighters, and then they'll blow us out of the sky.'

'Perhaps,' said the professor. 'Those pirates are evil enough for any atrocity.'

'I suppose this incident will end all civilian flights to Nihilon for a while?'

'I doubt it,' the professor replied. 'We'd lose too much foreign currency.'

'What about the safety of the passengers?'

'They'll have a fighter escort, in and out.' He helped himself to coffee and sandwiches, and the hostess smiled at him, for he put a heavy coin on to her tray. 'My dear boy, when has air travel not been perilous?'

The Cronacian pilots did not wait long for revenge. They must have radioed for help at their first casualty, for suitably armed planes had now been sent up by way of reply. In fact the passenger plane in its manoeuvres had gone dangerously close to the Cronacian frontier, and four Pug 107 fighters were now streaming down from the mountain peaks. Richard, seeing them at the same moment as did the machine-gunner, felt terror and helplessness, for there was nowhere to run for shelter. He did not know for sure that they were armed, but a deep unease told him that all was not well. The machine-gunner grinned, as he prepared his savage mechanisms for brushing them out of the sky as soon as they got close enough. This irrational urge for safety might even have communicated itself to the pilot (and one of the air-hostesses, who began to scream), for the plane climbed and banked in a sickening corkscrew motion, so that hats, umbrellas, and briefcases were thrown all over the fuselage.

The Cronacian Pugs spat fire from nose and wing, but the Nihilon pilot's manoeuvre was so deft that bullets merely ripped into the bottom of the plane, though a few had penetrated the windows before the Pugs sheered off. At this unexpected retaliation the machine-gunner near Richard ran whimpering to the middle of the gangway. The professor was so disgusted that he put out a foot and tripped him, causing him to lose his cigar as he stumbled. A gunner across the plane was killed when the Pugs came back, but the cowardly gunner from Richard's side recovered his wits under the stern eye of an air-hostess and took his place, ready and silent, biting his lower lip.

The plane shuddered, and people were screaming. Black smoke coiled from the engine nearest Richard, and he gripped the arms of his seat. He heard a shout that the pilot was dead, yet the plane remained steady, though losing height in its descent towards Nihilon airport, whose lights of dusk glimmered in the distance. He had been counting the seconds of life as they passed by, in order to stay conscious, but he now forgot to continue, and was dragged more and more into becoming part of the desperate shambles of the plane, for bullets were smashing into and through it, as if the Cronacians, said the professor, were intent on their revenge, and out to besmirch the good name and hitherto unblemished safety record of Nihilon Airways.

A squadron of Nihilon war-planes had been sent up, and those passengers who could see them were cheered at the sight of all twelve on a keel-haul under the belly of the airliner. But they were slow and shivering bi-planes with two old men in each, going out to do battle with the voracious, aerobatic Pugs. 'What a glorious sight our aircraft are,' said the professor. 'They'll save us from certain death.'

Two of them were already spinning down in flames, and Richard hoped that enough would stay in the air to distract the Pugs until they had landed. 'Why don't you have modern jet-fighter planes?'

'We are putting so much effort into our space programme,' explained the professor, 'that modern warplanes just can't be built. Nihilon is planning a space spectacular, due to begin any day now. The government is pinning all its hope for survival on it, which is why we have to strike, and strike hard, and strike soon, to bring the whole rotten edifice crashing down.'

A laugh sounded from the mouthpiece. 'Apart from that,' the professor went on in a different tone of voice, 'how can you expect Geriatrics to handle complicated supersonic war-planes?'

Flames lit up the darkness of the long passenger cabin, and a calm voice said from the loudspeakers:

'We are now approaching Nihilon airport. Will customers kindly begin smoking, and unfasten their seat belts? We trust that you have had a pleasant journey, and hope that you will have an opportunity of using our airline again soon. Thank you, ladies and gentlemen.'

Richard held his breath. Could it be that he would survive this terrible journey after all? He felt as if he had been living it forever.

Chapter Thirteen

Benjamin, having lost a litre of blood, a complete repair kit, and his windscreen, was at least glad to know that all formalities were at last behind him, and that he was now well and truly inside Nihilon. Experience with other countries told him that the worst was over, as he took a large bar of chocolate from the glove-box and ate it as if it were meat. This immediately made him feel better, and he decided to get as far into the country as he could before nightfall.

The road climbed in hairpin curves towards a pass, which he could see ahead, formed by two enormous jutting walls of mountain. The cold Alpine air flowed icily into his car, so he stopped by the roadside to put on a leather trench-coat, thick scarf, and woollen hat, cursing the customs bandits for the loss of his windscreen, which both cut down his speed and made him cold.

Beyond the pass the road became a mere trail of mud and broken rocks, with tree trunks sometimes laid across, low down in the ground, so that riding over them was designed to corrugate his backbone. As if to mock him, traffic signs put the speed limit at a hundred kilometres per hour. Perhaps this deception, and such broken routes, were meant as obstacles to any Cronacian incursion, though he couldn't see them doing the tourist trade much good.

Grey crags of cloud flew low across the sky, and spots of rain flicked into his cheeks and forehead. When the road inexplicably improved to a narrow but perfect surface, the speed-sign indicated only twenty kilometres per hour, but he decided to ignore this piece of Nihilonian mockery, and geared his engine up to a smooth sixty. Therefore, he did not see the deep trench splitting the road. Taken too fast, the jolt was almost hard enough to snap head from shoulders, and but for the miraculous suspension of his Thundercloud Estate car, he would have proceeded into Nether Nihilon on foot, if not on a stretcher.

He passed a roadmender's house, with several modern highway construction machines rusting outside, and a score of ragged children clambering happily over them. A circle of men sat on chairs, engrossed in some primitive gambling game. One knocked out his pipe on a pile of road signs, and waved at Benjamin as he went by.

Around the next bend, at the edge of a flat upland zone, was a garage. A prominent poster advertised in several languages that windscreens were for sale, so Benjamin thought he would attempt to buy one.

The service station was a group of large sheds set back from the road, with a single petrol pump at the exit end, towards which he drove his car. A sheet of cardboard fastened to the pump with a piece of string had: DO SMOKE written on it, which pleased him because he wouldn't have to put out his cigar. Beyond the sheds were fields and gardens, in which young men and women were toiling.

A young garage proprietor of medium height, wearing rimless spectacles above pimpled cheeks, smartly dressed in a pin-striped suit, his fat neck held together by a white shirt-collar and sober grey tie, a ring on his left middle finger, a clipboard in one hand and a pen in the other, an expression of worried concern on his face, whose blue eyes and brown wavy hair nevertheless reflected an inspired blaze of commerce, walked towards him in bare feet, and leaned against the car door to ask how many windscreens he wanted.

'Only one,' said Benjamin. 'I don't wipe my nose on them.'

'My customers usually buy six, sir.'

'I've got one car,' Benjamin retorted, restarting his engine and ready to leave, 'not six. If you won't sell me one I'll go to the next garage.'

The proprietor stepped away for fear the wheels should run over his bare feet. 'I didn't say I wouldn't sell you one.'

'But you started to *argue*,' Benjamin shouted, 'and I'm tired of *arguing* in this damned country. All I want is a new windscreen, and if you haven't got one, say so.'

'Will you be needing any petrol sir?' he asked, as if no exchange had so far taken place.

He got out of the car. 'No, I don't want petrol. Just a windscreen. All right?'

'Tyres?'

'No tyres. How long will it take to fix the windscreen?'

'Not long at all. Oil?'

'No. Can I get coffee, or food?'

He pointed to an adjoining hut. 'What about a new fanbelt? Things get more expensive further on, as well as non-existent.'

Benjamin loomed against him, accidentally treading on one of his bare feet so that the young man sprang back with pain: 'That's why I don't wear shoes. Everyone gets angry with me, and so my shoes get all dirty and ruined. It's better to get my feet hurt. At least that's what I tell myself when I'm being reasonable about it beforehand.'

'You shouldn't run such a cheating scheme,' Benjamin said, though sorry for him.

'What else can I do?' the man cried. 'Our regular customers never pay their bills, so we have to earn money somehow. What profit we make comes from selling windscreens to foreigners, but we pay a lot of it to the savage, rapacious, extortionate customs men. That's why I'd like you to kindly buy at least six windscreens, otherwise we shan't even cover our running costs this month. You can strap them on your luggage rack, and perhaps sell them at a profit in the interior.' He ran across the space between the car and the nearest hut, as Benjamin prised a muddy stone loose to throw at him: 'No, please, my suit!'

'If my windscreen isn't repaired by the time I get back from coffee,' Benjamin called out, 'I'll throw a match into your petrol pump and blow it sky-high like a true Nihilist.'

The café was ruthlessly clean, and a shining coffee-machine hissed at the far end of the counter. A little old man attended to it, and as soon as Benjamin entered he put a large cup under one of the taps. 'Not very busy today?' Benjamin said, affably.

The man came over with his coffee, carrying the cup in his hand without a saucer. 'It's a pity you can't even rely on a foreigner to be polite these days. I hate spite. It's the one quality of human nature that really angers me. I can always do without it.'

'If you aren't careful,' Benjamin laughed, 'I'll use a bit of subtle irony.'

'It's easy to see,' sneered the old man, 'that someone like you wouldn't think twice about it. You haven't even tasted the coffee, and you're already making threatening remarks.'

He sipped it. 'You've put in too much acorn-dust, you senile cheat.'

The old man smiled in triumph at having been caught out. 'Yes, but not enough. Next time I'll put all ground acorn in, since you're so objectionable.'

'I asked for coffee, though. Aren't you ashamed?'

'Shame is only for those who want to make an honest living,' said the old man. 'Cheating is normal and natural, so why should I be ashamed of that? Cheating is good commerce, and to cheat a foreigner is even better: it's patriotic.'

'I thought there was no patriotism in Nihilon.'

'There is against foreigners. But Nihilists don't need it. We get on very well among ourselves. I've got to go back to my coffee-machine now, so when you've finished you can come up to the counter and pay me.'

Benjamin was beginning to feel at home in Nihilon, easily able to fend for himself against the ill-tempered peremptory barefaced extortion. He saw a leaflet on the table entitled *Instructions for Motorists in Nihilon*, and read it:

'1) All motorists are warned that they are not permitted to drive unless drunk. The importance of this rule cannot be too highly emphasised, and it is brought to the notice of tourists that highway police on motorcycles make frequent checks to ensure that the tourist has enough alcohol to drink. Police are equipped with breathing apparatus which registers the alcoholic content of their blood, and should this turn out to be negative, they are immediately constrained to drink a quantity of alcohol from the miniature sidecar-bowser attached to the highway policeman's motorbicycle. Needless to say, the motorist will be called upon to pay for the amount of drink consumed (generally the finest quality Nihilitz) at the current commercial rates. All motorists, properly drunk and driving, must carry at least one bottle of Nihilitz in their car, to be presented on request to any highway policeman who demands it.

'2) Motorists caught driving on the right side of the road will be fined three hundred krats—krats being the currency at present in mode with the highway police. If the traveller does not have any krats with which to pay his fine, the police will oblige by changing his money at an appropriate rate. The right side of the road is that which causes you to encounter other traffic on the same side coming towards you from the opposite direction.

'3) Anti-social motorists caught in possession of driving licences or insurance documents will be contravening the Highway Code, and will be thrown into prison until tried in a court of law.

'4) No motorist will be in possession of repair or tool kits. There are numerous garages and service stations in Nihilon, staffed by competent mechanics. Anyone caught repairing his car by the roadside shall be condemned to have his vehicle broken up before his own eyes by a competent mechanic, and at the motorist's expense.

'5) All motor vehicles of whatever description shall conform to Nihilonian lighting regulations—that is to say, that one front headlight shall be red, and the other blue. This matter must be attended to at the nearest service station, which work will be completed at the official tariff price.

'6) The export of all cars from Nihilon is absolutely prohibited. This rule need not worry foreign motorists, however, as dealers waiting at each exit-point of the frontier will be sure to pay a fair price for your vehicle.

'7) Motorists are kindly requested to exceed the speed limit, especially in villages and built-up areas. In case of accident to a pedestrian, the motorist should obtain the signature of the doctor and the victim's next-of-kin in order to confirm it, and to state whether the victim is only slightly injured, seriously injured, dangerously ill but likely to recover, or dead. Points will be awarded to the motorist, and at the end of his trip the total score will be added up by the policeman on duty at the frontier, to see if the driver can quality for the Most Deadly Motorist of the Year Award. The first prize is a fortnight at our luxurious beach-resort of Troser, with three eighteen-year-old nubile girls over which he has absolute control.

'8) Happy motoring, motorist!'

Benjamin put down the leaflet with feelings of intense disapproval, knowing again how right he had been to spend part of his youth trying to prevent this vile system of nihilism from blasting the fair fields of Damascony—renamed Nihilon. The old waiter put a large bottle of Nihilitz on his table. 'Take it back,' said Benjamin, 'I don't want it.'

'I know my Highway Code as well as you do,' said the man.

'I'm drunk already,' he exclaimed, spitting in his empty cup and throwing a few klipps down, 'on this rotten Nihilonian air, and acorn coffee.'

'It's not enough,' screamed the old man, but Benjamin picked up the bottle and walked outside.

A mechanic was polishing his new windscreen: 'She's all ready, sir.'

'How much?'

'The manager's coming now, sir,' said the mechanic, running to the safety of a shed. Benjamin saw the revolver half-concealed under the clipboard that the manager carried, and, in spite of his smiling face, guessed that he would use it in claiming for the new windscreen some preposterous price that he'd not otherwise be able to get.

He sprang to his car and started the engine. A bullet whizzed through the open window, fired by the manager who crouched barefoot by the door of his office.

Benjamin grabbed his own revolver from the glove-box and fired three quick shots, sending the manager back under cover. There was a pause in the battle, while he drove to the far end of the asphalt, then stopped, but left his engine still running. When he leaned out of the other window to see what was happening, a bullet shattered his back window and buried itself among the luggage. Another shot passed close to the top of his head, and made a neat but large hole in the newly installed windscreen.

Benjamin leapt out and crouched on the ground, setting his sights at a drum of petrol resting near the pump. A deep and fearful rage clarified his aim, and he emptied his revolver, then got back speedily into the car. The garage manager and his attendants, mechanics, and clerks, as well as the old man from the coffee shop, began running for safety across the open fields.

His rear mirrors turned orange, as if the sun itself were exploding. Pumps, storage tanks, and shed after shed went showering and billowing into the air, and as he drove along the road he didn't bother to wonder whether he was on the right or the wrong side of it, for the sound of explosions still going on behind made him more drunk than could any Nihilitz.

Chapter Fourteen

Her sight was gratified by the orderly cultivation of cornfields and terraced vineyards on either side of the road. People were working, the breeze freshened her, and the neat husbandry of the Nihilonian peasants made her feel safe and protected in the Zap sports car of the chief of police. 'Will we really catch him?' she asked.

'No doubt about it,' he answered, a reassuring hand on her knee, which she felt too goodnatured to push away. 'The train won't leave for another hour, and we'll be there in fifteen minutes. We'll get the blackguard, have no fear. I'll see that you get your revenge.'

'It's my luggage I want. I have important appointments in Nihilon City.'

'I hope you won't mention this regrettable incident,' he said. 'I could lose my job over it. In which case I might be given some ministerial post in the government, and that would be terrible.'

'Wouldn't you like that?'

'Certainly not. Ministers come and go. They get sacked or shot. But the chief of police goes on forever. If he's careful.' He increased speed on approaching a village, and pedestrians ran from the road at the sudden uproar of his engine, scattering towards doorways, fences or bushes, people otherwise well-fed and respectable fleeing in horror as he deliberately set his car at any promising group that looked ripe for annihilation.

Jaquiline protested at his attempted murder, but he laughed, and said that this was their only form of gambling, that they actually liked such sport, and so did he, what was more, and that was all that mattered, because what was the point of being chief of police if you couldn't run people down? You might just as well not have a car at all. His hand reached the suspender clip at the top of her stocking, which made his driving more erratic, so that she was too afraid of his mad zig-zags along the road to worry about his distasteful behaviour. Also, she found that these activities, combined with dangerous driving, primed her sensations till she in no way hoped he would stop, assuming in any case that he was simply clearing the road of people to prevent them seeing into the car.

Beyond the village, however, when his hand was engaged in an even more intimate performance upon her, and she felt herself about to swoon into a state not experienced for some time, a forty-ton lorry was approaching at a ferocious speed on the same side of the road. The police chief did not take his hand away, but endeavoured to continue steering his erratic course with the other. The lorry driver, no doubt also wanting his sport, was likewise set in a high-spirited zig-zag track towards them. As if he had tackled the same problem before, the chief of police, when a collision seemed inevitable and Jaquiline was crying out in more than one extreme sense, lifted his foot from the accelerator, and guided the car right off the road.

His speed had not been great, and the field nearby was at the same level, and the soil was hard and fairly flat, so he simply let his Zap run for a clump of bushes, as the passing lorry sounded a long hooter-blast by way of laughing at the defeated sports car.

He carried his half-fainting burden into the bushes, to continue in a more manly fashion what he had begun in the car. When they had finished she felt in no condition to demand an apology. Her mind was on other things, for it seemed all too possible, as he opened the door for her, that by the time they reached the station the Nihilon Express would be gone, and her luggage with it.

The chief of police didn't even try to run at those mistrustful pedestrians forever dodging out of his way, but picked up her thoughts, and said: 'If the train's gone, we shall follow it to the next stop. And the next, if necessary. That swinish sinister stationmaster won't escape us. We'll catch up with him sooner or later.'

'It's difficult to believe,' she said, looking at her watch, 'that I've only been in Nihilon for three hours.'

'Four. You must have forgotten to change to Nihilon Mean Time. Fortunately, you still have a watch, which is something to be grateful for. If you run out of money you can always sell it.'

'I'll never do that. My father gave it to me before he died.'

He put his hand on her thigh. 'I knew you were sentimental. That's why I fell in love with you. Will you sell your watch to me?'

She pushed his hairy, beefy, disgusting hand away. 'I've told you. I shall never sell it.'

'Then give it to me, my love.'

'I'm not your love,' she snapped, still fighting his hand off. 'Get me on that train and back to my luggage, or I'll denounce you as soon as I arrive in Nihilon City.' He started to grovel, attempting to get down on his knees while still driving the car. 'You fool!' she cried. 'Mind the wall. The wall!'

On it was written in white paint: DOWN WITH NIHILISM. LONG LIVE DAMASCONY. KILL NIL. He avoided it, but she cried: 'I forgive you. Please get up. You're forgiven.'

He smiled with happiness, and sat in his seat to drive properly down the straight flat empty road. 'Say it again,' he pleaded.

'I forgive you!'—touching his hand as she said it, feeling actual sweet forgiveness for him. With the same rapt smile, and not making any movement of his head, he lifted a hand and struck her hard across the face, saying: 'Thank you, thank you, my dear, thank you,' as he drove along.

She was sobbing, and he tried to comfort her in his police-chief way, saying that he would like her to stay with him and be his second mistress, that he'd look after her so that she wouldn't have to work more than eight hours a day in the fields or serving in his bookshop at the barbed wire, or assembling lawnmowers at the local factory. He insisted that he loved her more than he did his present wife, or his mistress, or all his children born and unborn, and that if she had a child as a result of their recent encounter in the bushes they would call it Zap, whether boy or girl, after his beloved sports car that had drawn them so close together, a name which would honour their union with an eternal aureole of beauty. At which picturesque phrase he confided that in his spare time, after his duties as police chief, bookseller, gardener, husband, father and lover, he wrote poetry to all things on earth that he thought bright and beautiful, and that from now on and ever after he would compose poems only for her.

He went on talking until she smiled, then laughed, then felt once more tender towards him because she would soon be on the train and far away. When they arrived at the railway station the train was still waiting along the platform. The ticket collector demanded their tickets. 'I'm accompanying the young foreign lady to the train,' the police chief told him.

'Are you?' said the truculent ticket collector. 'Not if I say you can't. You can't.' He examined Jaquiline's ticket, stamped it, and nodded her through to the platform.

'How long before it leaves?'

'Five minutes, miss, but maybe an hour. Can't tell. It depends whether the footplate men decide to push the carriages to Nihilon City, or pull them. They are still arguing about it, I believe.'

'What difference does it make?' she asked.

'None, really. But they love to make up their minds.'

The chief of police tried to walk through, but the ticket collector barred his way. 'Let me go, you swine. Can't you see my uniform?'

'How do I know,' said the ticket collector, 'that you haven't spent the last six months in your petrol-drum slum-hut in the middle of a field, stitching it together for just such a time as this? And don't call me a swine, you swine!' he raved.

The police chief, while Jaquiline waited patiently to say goodbye, took out his passport and badge.

'Passports! Badges!' jeered the ticket collector. 'You can buy those anywhere.'

'You are under arrest,' said the chief of police, struggling to unclip his revolver. But the ticket collector reached calmly to a shelf behind and brought out a gun, which he pointed at the police chief's heart: 'If you go on like this you'll have a guerrilla war on your hands. In fact I hear that one is due to begin any day now. At least I hope so. So get out, before I kick you through the booking-hall.' He turned to Jaquiline, and bowed: 'You may walk to the train, miss.'

She called goodbye to the rueful police chief, and went to look for her compartment. It was an immensely long train, and multitudes seemed to have got on at this station, for it took several minutes to reach the head of it and find the carriage in which she had left her luggage. When she pulled open the door, the stationmaster was lying along the seat sleeping.

He opened his eyes, and smiled. 'I was hoping you'd come back. Now we can go to Nihilon City together.'

'Get out of my compartment,' she said, noting that all her pieces of luggage were on the racks above.

'I'm tired of being a stationmaster. I want to travel,' he said, sitting up and rubbing his eyes.

'Not with me,' she told him, lighting a cigarette.

'Please,' he asked.

She went back to the door of the train for help. A bell rang, and people along the whole length of it were saying their last goodbyes, pushing bundles into and out of the windows. There was a commotion by the waiting room, where someone was struggling to get through the window and on to the platform. It was the chief of police, and he began running towards her with a gun in his hand, shouting as he got closer: 'Is he there? Is the pig there?'

He clambered up the steps, and when he reached the compartment, the stationmaster turned pale. 'I'll come,' he said in a tearful voice. 'It's the end of a beautiful dream, one that's haunted me ever since I was a child. I had a vision of travelling on the Trans-Nihilon Express in a sleeping compartment with a beautiful woman.'

'You're a disgrace to Nihilon!' shouted the police chief.

'I know. But why can't it happen? What's wrong with it? If you both agreed, I could still have my dream.'

'It would ruin your life,' said the police chief.

'I want to be ruined,' pleaded the despondent stationmaster. 'It would clear the air. It would make my life simpler, to have just one dream come true, and to be ruined as well. I've got the moral fibre for it, I swear I have.'

'Stop it,' pleaded Jaquiline, bursting into tears.

'You see what you cause by your dreams?' said the police chief. 'Making someone shed tears is a capital offence in Nihilon.'

Her eyes dried immediately. 'Is it?'

'Give me a handkerchief, miss,' pleaded the stationmaster, thumping on to his knees so that she felt the train floor shake under her, 'to remember you by.'

'I'd like one, too,' said the police chief, taken by the idea. She had the intolerable thought that if she didn't get rid of them soon, they would both be with her as far as Nihilon City.

When she gave her handkerchief to the police chief he tore it in half, and shared it with the stationmaster. 'Come on, friend,' he said to him. 'Let's leave the lady to get some rest.'

She locked the door after them, and the train, with a final campano-logical peal of bells, jolted and began to move. From the window she saw the stationmaster walking along the platform towards the station exit, pointing a gun at the police chief's back.

The train increased speed, and the last buildings of the small town were left behind. She could hardly believe that the journey to Nihilon City had begun. Dazed with the relief of it, she sat down and smoked another cigarette. Tomorrow she would reach the expansion and comfort of the Grand Nihilon Hotel, and would begin her real work of exploring the capital city. She had promised to meet and share her room with Adam, the poet, in order to continue a love-affair only fitfully begun before setting out for Nihilon. Thinking of it, she recovered her usually alert composure, and decided to change her clothes before going to find the restaurant car.

She lifted a case down and opened it, and for a moment, in the middle of the shock, it seemed that it was not her case, but then she clearly saw her nameplate fastened on the inside of the lid. It was filled with small bundles of kindling wood. She pulled down each case in a frenzy of diminishing hope, but they also were filled with wood.

Her hand sped towards the communication cord, and stopped when she realised that the train might be delayed for hours while the mystery was cleared up, possibly involving her in days of futile investigation. In any case, how could she do anything to stop the train now that it was well and truly on its way? One always feels superior, she thought, passing through stations at which your train does not stop, especially when there are people standing on the platforms to watch you go by.

She sat down again, clutching her handbag containing money and documents, as well as the gun-in-book purchased from the police chief's stall by the barbed wire. Her train tickets were safe, and so were her travellers units, so nothing could prevent her reaching Nihilon City in safety and a certain amount of comfort.

Chapter Fifteen

With his heavy trunks at last on deck, he leaned over the rail to catch the attention of a boatwoman below, so that the stack of impedimenta could be rowed ashore. He waved, and called, and from between the wharf and the ship a woman suddenly skiffed towards the lowered gangplank. She was young and buxom, wearing slacks and sweater, with attractive arms and long black hair falling in a loose rope behind. 'Will you be able to handle it all?' he asked, feeling guilty at its bulk and weight when she looked at it from the top of the steps.

Her eyes turned from it and took in his own person, as if she would sling him over her shoulder and take him down to the boat as well. 'I can handle any weight,' she smiled. 'I'm a woman.'

Though he was ready to assist her by taking the other end of each trunk, she picked the first one up, slung it on her shoulder, and walked nimbly down the gangplank to her boat. So he stayed on deck smoking a cigar, then took a sheet of cartridge paper from his briefcase and made a quick panorama of the buildings and dock facilities along the waterfront. He thought of sketching the shape of the mountain range behind as well, but the afternoon air was so beautiful and soft, and the sight of an attractive woman humping his trunks and boxes down into a boat so conducive to his momentary indolence that he was unable to do anything more than enjoy the scenery.

She beckoned him, and he descended the ladder, stepping over his luggage to the middle of the boat. Facing her while she rowed, he watched her broad shoulders bend at the oars, and her full breasts dip towards him at each strong stroke. Her coal-black eyes beamed into him, and he tried to avoid their stare by aiming his own blank gaze over her shoulder or to the side of the boat, glad at last to be going ashore, and through such calm and iridescent water, the bows cutting away to the muffled sound of the city that stretched around the horse-shoe bay.

'Do you work long hours at your job?' he asked, thinking to deflect her stare that, in a more democratic and orderly country, would have been called brazen. She leaned forward, took the cigar from his mouth, and threw it into the water. Its hot end sizzled and floated away, and she stopped rowing—to kiss him on the lips. Her action astounded him, and without exactly wanting to, in some way fearful of offending her, he drew back slightly, though she seemed not to notice this, but resumed her rowing as vigorously as before. 'Don't be afraid,' she said, in a light and musical voice, 'I want you, that's all.'

'How friendly of you,' he responded. 'But I'm a busy man, and I'm not really available.'

She laughed again, and he was struck by the tenderness in her voice: 'I know. But it doesn't stop me telling you what I feel, does it?' He wondered if she made such speeches to all her customers, in order to ply a little trade out of hours, as it were, but this thought was crushed when she added: 'I'll pay for it. Perhaps we can have dinner at your hotel tonight. I earn a lot of money at this work.'

Something ought to be said, but he could find no way out of his dilemma, except to sit still. 'I saw you from the shore,' she added, 'through my binoculars, and I decided that I wanted you. That's why I rowed faster than any of the others.'

'Do you find your job very arduous?' he asked. 'Or monotonous?'

'Never,' she answered, with a gay and throaty laugh. 'I have lots of adventures. I don't think I would change it for another, unless one day I have to take a job in an office, or unless I get married first, though I never want to enter into such an awful state as that. I'm too fond of my work.' She leaned forward and kissed him again, and this time, because the shock was less in that they had already become acquainted, he found it a more pleasant experience.

They were approaching the grey wall of the wharf, when a sudden deep roar sounded as if from under the old town, sending faint ripples along the surface of the water. 'Those Cronacians must have started something again,' she said, at the chatter of machine-gun fire that followed. 'It's an emergency, so we'd better disembark on the west side of the bay.'

Helicopter blades made a flower-shadow beside the boat, while sirens wailed ominously from a hill on the outskirts. Another explosion burst from the town, more threatening than the first, leaving a tree of smoke over it. Dust showered down on to their boat. Edgar noticed streaks of sweat on the boatwoman's face, and felt his mouth going dry from what he considered to be quite natural anxiety. A breeze chopped the water and made his face cold, and the lady-rower changed course and skimmed the heavily laden craft parallel with the long wharf, heading for the dark orange sun hanging smokily above the rim of far-off mountains.

Her energetic work soon took them beyond the built-up area, and then towards an empty beach still some way off. He thought it might after all be an advantage to make this unobtrusive landing on Nihilon, since it would save trouble getting through the customs. The sort of luggage he carried was bound to look suspicious, no matter what country he landed in.

The leaden light of dusk spread over the water, and firing from the city, though as brisk as ever, was merely a violent backdrop to the peace around them. A few wind-battered oak-trees rose beyond the dunes, and as the bottom of the boat scraped sand, his stout but comely rower leapt out and hauled it on to dry land. When it tilted she indicated that Edgar stay in, otherwise he would get his feet wet, but he leaped out because he was afraid of being spread-eagled into the briny water, and this unexpected action upset the balance of the boat, which, being overloaded, tilted abruptly on its side, sending trunks and boxes into the sea.

'You fool,' she shouted angrily, hauling one of his cases deftly on to the sand. 'That was a very undemocratic thing to do when I told you to sit still.'

'I'm sorry,' he said, and he was, at the feel of cold water clinging heavily to his skin. But she bore no grudge, and was soon pulling his luggage safely ashore then wading up to her waist to recover the boat. She put an arm around his shoulder: 'Don't worry. You're on Nihilon soil at last. I'll show you the way to the customs now.'

He followed her up the steep sand-dunes, thinking it bad news that the customs was still to come. From the summit he saw two large tents standing in an area of flat land, several hundred metres away, a high flag-mast between them with a light at the top. 'Go into one of those tents' she said, 'and I'll follow with your luggage.'

She kissed him, then ran back towards the shore, taking two pair of wheels from the locker on which he had been sitting, and clipping them to the bottom of the boat. He had never seen a woman of such strength, but she worked gracefully, and he watched with pleasure as she loaded his luggage on to what was now a trolley, put a thick rope over her shoulders, and began the fearful job of hauling it down the beach towards a gap in the dunes. He hurried on, in case she got to the customs before him.

It was almost dark, and he wondered which tent he should enter, but his doubts were soon resolved, for an illuminated notice on one tent said: BELOVED AND FORTUNATE CITIZENS OF NIHILON— THIS WAY, while at the entrance to the other was written: FOREIGN SCUM—IN HERE. The tone of this last one seemed offensive, though it did uncomfortably remind him of similar notices installed at the ports and customs posts of his home country. However, this was no time for pride or regret. He could hardly go back to the ship, for there was a guidebook to be written, so he took off his hat, and entered.

A group of customs officers stood behind a trestle table, on which Edgar saw his trunk that had been missing from the boat. At the sight of him they all walked away but one, who held a clipboard in his hand and called out: 'Come here, you.' He thrust the clipboard under Edgar's nose. 'Can you read?'

'Of course.'

'Read this, then, sir. And when I say read it, I mean read it aloud.'

Edgar held it, and spoke out in a clear voice:

'Travellers to Nihilon are absolutely forbidden to bring anything at all into the country. What they do bring in is left to the discretion of the individual customs officer concerned. The traveller is respectfully reminded however that the job of customs officer is an arduous and often unappreciated one, and is hereby enjoined to comport himself with dignity and patience in his presence. Very often the customs officer with whom it is your privilege to deal is burdened by overwork. It may well be that he has a wife, and several children whom he desires to educate to the best of his humble ability. He carries an inordinate amount of worry on his honest brow, but his spirit is great, for all that. This monotonous and inhuman job calls for qualities of profound sympathy and humanity, and your customs officer aspires to live up to these lofty ideals. Behind his pale and harassed face resides an infinite capacity for kindliness, and the traveller is hereby requested to put forth all his co-operation, and assist the customs officer in his task.'

The clipboard was snatched away: 'Do you understand that, pig?'

'Yes,' said Edgar. The boatwoman hauled his luggage into the tent, and her smile made him feel that he had at least one true friend in

Nihilon. She moved him gently aside, and stacked his belongings on the table.

'Let's get down to business,' said the customs officer, a shade more polite now that Edgar's protectress had appeared. 'Anything to declare?'

'All this,' he said. 'I've nothing to hide.'

'Don't try to trick me, or you'll get ten years in the army. What about your porter and her boat-trolley? That's all counted as traveller's luggage. You'll have to pay for her, as well. I don't suppose you've even paid her for the work she's done yet. You'd better pay her first.'

Edgar decided to be obstinate, in spite of the matchless prose on the clipboard. 'Not until she's through the customs.'

'So you don't trust me? You're one of those foreigners who come to Nihilon with distrust in his heart, are you? You get some notion that you're going to be imprisoned, punched, cheated, humiliated, shot at, chased and in general hijacked, robbed, tricked and badly treated, from those squealing liars who've already gone back and told tales about us. They spoil everything.'

'Not at all,' said Edgar. 'I'd like to know what I have to pay, so that I can go to a hotel. I've had a long day, and I'm tired.'

'I'll be frank with you,' said the customs officer. 'How much can you afford?'

'Isn't it up to you to state a price?'

The customs officer thought for a moment. 'How about two thousand klipps?'

This was the cost of several nights at a luxury hotel, as far as he understood the crazy scale of values in Nihilon. 'I imagined that a thousand would cover everything.'

The customs officer clapped a hand to his brow. 'Is that all?' he wailed. 'That's no use to me. I can't live like this. I'll lose my reason. It's impossible.'

The boatwoman took a small bulging purse from the locker of the trolley, shouting: 'Here's five hundred,' and threw a screwed-up note across the table so that it rolled on to the floor. 'Now let him go. Can't you see he's tired?' She turned to Edgar: 'Come on, my dear,' and under the sullen eyes of the customs officer loaded his goods back on to her trolley.

'But I haven't had my passport stamped,' Edgar said, holding it up.

She thrust it out to the customs officer: 'Stamp it!'

'No,' he sulked.

'I'll do it then.'

He went back a pace: 'No, you won't.'

She ran around the table, grasped him by the hand, and twisted his arm halfway up his back: 'Tell me where the stamp is.'

'In the box under the table!'

'If it isn't,' she said, 'I'll screw your arm off.'

He turned pale, as she increased the pressure: 'All right. It's in the bottom left pocket of my tunic. Now-let-me-go!' She pulled out the rubber stamp with her free hand, then released him, a smile on her face as she admired Edgar's passport photograph, before pressing the official entry sign on to a clean and empty page.

'You'll lose your licence for this,' the customs officer shouted vindictively.

'I never had one,' she answered, as they went out of the tent.

It was dark. 'Where can I get a taxi?'

'There aren't any,' she told him. 'They've gone to see the fighting. But I'll take you to a hotel. There's a good one on the edge of the city, where we won't be disturbed by the insurrection.'

The sharp crack of small-arms fire came through the night, interspersed by the crump of bombs and shells. He wondered how she had the strength to drag such a massive load over wet and sandy earth, amazed that she even asked him to ride on top instead of walking. They came to a paved road, with lights in the distance. An ambulance drove by from the town: 'There's certainly a battle going on,' he observed, walking by her side while she strained at the load.

'It's supposed to be trouble with Cronacia,' she said, 'but I'm not so sure. I can't believe everything that's said about them. Our countries are such enemies that I sometimes suspect we're friends.' She had paused under a blue street-lamp. The one beyond was orange, and the one after that was green, and she told him that all street-lamps in Nihilon were of different colours. He thought this must make it rather perilous for night drivers, though startlingly attractive to pedestrians, as it now was to him.

They came to an enormous hotel. It had only been open a fortnight, she said, which was why the surrounding area was not yet paved. To reach the front entrance they had to cross a hundred metres of thick mud, and though she had great difficulty in hauling his luggage through it, she still would not let him help. He tried to insist, and take the rope from her by force, but she pushed him away haughtily, saying she could manage quite well on her own.

Weary and mudstained, they walked at last between the opened glass doors and across the immaculate grey carpet. The manager was fixing a light bulb into a socket above the reception counter, and Edgar's companion pulled at his coat-tails to let him know that he had customers.

He got down. 'What can I do for you?'

'I'd like a single room, with bath,' said Edgar, 'in a quiet situation and facing south.'

'We'd like a double room, with bath, on as high a floor as possible,' said his female porter, 'so that we can have a good view of the fighting in the morning.'

'We're hoping it will be over by then,' the manager smiled.

'I'd like a single room,' Edgar insisted. 'I'm very tired.'

'Sign here,' said the manager.

His companion wrote her name in the book, and the manager told two young men to bring their luggage in. Another young man motioned them into a lift, and pressed a button: 'We're going to room 404. It's a suite really, but we don't have such distinguished guests as you every day.'

Edgar, trying to avoid the open and all-devouring gaze of his companion, wanted to know the price of it, having forgotten to ask the manager.

'404,' said the young man, grinning at the amorous boat-lady as she fondled her lover.

'Not the number of the room,' he said irritably, trying to push her away. 'The price.'

'404,' the young man repeated. 'In this hotel the number of the room is also the price. The higher you go, the better the room, the bigger the price. It avoids misunderstanding. How many weeks will you be staying?'

'Overnight,' he said, 'or perhaps two'—feeling his hand squeezed, and appalled at the expense of the accommodation.

'Is that all?' said the youth in a hostile manner. He thrust the key into Edgar's hand when the lift stopped, and pointed up the corridor: 'You can find your own room, if that's the case.'

Chapter Sixteen

Bombed by Nihilitz, the bridgehead
Of the heart goes black
Back to the sealine frontiers
Of effervescing life.

Adam, unsteady though unshaken, stood on a table reciting his 'Ode to Nihilon' (composed an hour before) to a silent admiring audience, more numerous than had ever crowded around him so far in his life. The policeman had commanded everyone in the café to be silent, and the proprietor, fully aware of the honour that was being done to his establishment, dimmed all lights except the bright one placed by the poet's elbow, under which isolating glare Adam had penned his immortal lines.

The policeman stood with cap in hand and lowered head, and the proprietor refused to serve any drinks while the writing or reciting was taking place. A young drunken peasant who began to laugh and shout had to be thrown out by the more understanding and cultured customers. For some minutes afterwards he rampaged around the building, banging on doors and windows, and demanding to be let back in, though he eventually got tired, and either fell asleep or went away. The disturbance hardly penetrated Adam's inspired state, and a hundred lines of verse came out of him almost as quickly as the Nihilitz had been previously poured in.

Nihilism scorches coffins,
So that the dead may wake
In fires of paradise;
Or waltz with dolphins
In vast halls of ice,
Or walk to vantage points and watch

The splendid fireworks from afar,
And talk, talk, talk.
Talk of the soul by the beat of the heart . . .

The floor shook at the end of each short section, his audience shouting approval at every noisy word, and when he stopped, having come to an abrupt end, he leapt from the table and buckled both legs under him, without, however, being hurt, for he sprang to his feet and held on to the bar-rail behind.

'That was magnificent,' said the proprietor, drying tears on his white apron. 'I can't tell you how grateful I am that someone of your talent should bless my humble place with such a performance. Please recite some more. We'd like a few hundred lines about the greatness of Nihilon, and the savage barbarity of those Cronacian wolf-bandits.'

'We'd all like to hear that,' said the policeman.

'Yes,' the customers cried. 'A poem about lousy Cronacia!'

'A war poem,' shouted the roving young peasant who had woken up and made his way back inside. 'The oldsters can sing it as they swing out with the left, and latch in with the right!'

Adam confessed that he was now hungry. 'When you've told us another poem,' said the proprietor, 'we'll cook you a couple of rabbits—if we like the show.'

His eyes were sore from glare and smoke, and the exhaustion of a long day. 'Where's the nearest hotel?'

'At Fludd,' he was told, 'ten kilometres away.'

'I must go then,' he said, trying to push through. The proprietor grabbed him: 'You promised us another poem.'

'I didn't.'

'If we say you did, then you did, and that's enough for us.'

'My performances cost a thousand klipps,' he told the proprietor, and the policeman who also barred his way, 'and that's the fee you'll have to pay now.'

Knowing that Adam could barely stand, the proprietor pushed him roughly in the chest: 'It's outrageous! Calamitous! Horrific! Petty! Mean! Ridiculous! He actually wants money for reciting his mediocre and subversive poems.'

'Throw him out,' someone shouted.

'You'd better go,' the policeman said, raising his fist, 'or I shan't be responsible for your safety.'

'That's exactly what I want to do,' said Adam, and such was the disgust which everyone felt, that they actually made way for him, though one or two punches were aimed at this back before he reached the door.

The cold night air revived him, but only as a reminder of how tired he was. They were still arguing inside, though it seemed more of a quarrel among themselves now. A bottle smashed—empty, he imagined—and then came a breaking of furniture, and high-pitched protestations from the patron. He wiped the dew dry from the handlebars of his bicycle, then set out for Fludd.

Every few metres his dynamo headlight lit up a cluster of pot-holes in the paving, some so deep and steep-sided that he had to clamber over them. It must have been raining in the northern mountains, for streams occasionally flowed over the road, splashing his trousers up to the knees. At one place he fell in to his waist, being forced to let go of his bicycle, which crashed down a slope. Because the lightbeam was dependent on the spinning of the wheels, he was unable to see much during the times when he was obliged to push, and now that his bicycle had slid away it seemed to have gone forever.

A traveller must have faith in himself, he thought. He had such faith, otherwise he wouldn't have thrown away the buoying comfort of his home. He would deny having left it for the fame or financial rewards which contributing to the guidebook might bring, though when his journey was over he would indeed be able to advise those who had not yet set out on it. His first thoughts had been to test himself on a pilgrimage into the unknown, to find what lay at the centre of what was already known.

He was seeking something, otherwise he would not have come, though he did not know what he might find beyond the perils and uncertainties of the journey itself. Perhaps in this desert of nihilism he was searching for himself in order that others could find themselves should they ever decide to cross it and follow in his wake. He smiled at the conceit of what was probably true, but which could never be put into a guidebook, a thought not less fascinating for occupying his mind as he sat by the roadside, feeling that unique mixture of despair and elation which sooner or later comes during any man's travelling, the first powerful indication that he belongs nowhere but where he stands.

Looking up, he saw stars shining in patterns of crosses, crescents, animals and gods, route-markers and lifesavers. Each one pierced his heart with light, and if they weren't exactly friendly they at least appeared to sympathise with his plight. He stood up, shivering. A tangled shadow down the slope led him to his bicycle, and he struggled back with it on to the broken ridge of the road.

He wanted to sit and brood all night, bend his head down to his knees till he could see again the landscape that he had passed during the day, but the flashing of two brilliant headlights in the distance put sudden purpose into him, and he mounted his bicycle, hoping to see signs of Fludd from the next high point of the road.

It twisted and curved, but the surface improved, though presently it became so steep that in places he had to get off and push. The lights belonged to a huge lorry, and as he got close he saw that it was parked in a layby set dangerously on the U of a hairpin bend, so that when coming out it would have no visibility along the road either before or behind.

The town of Fludd lay at the bottom of a steep-sided valley, and its multi-coloured lights comforted him. The streets were wide and well paved, lined with small trees and attractive blocks of flats. He followed signs saying 'Hotel Fludd', cycling along a level avenue in which people were walking, or sitting at café tables on the pavements. There was an air of gaiety, of men and women enjoying themselves after a day's hard work.

The hotel was modern, yet unpretentious and homely, a promise of comfort pulling him in at the end of what seemed a very long day. When he pushed his bicycle into the hall and leaned it against the reception desk, a young girl came from the switchboard and smiled: 'We have a luxury room with bath, at two klipps a night. I'm sure you'll be satisfied with it. If I were you though, I'd go straight into the dining room for a meal, because it will be closing in an hour. The price of your dinner will be one klipp, including Nihilitz, which goes on your bill.'

This was almost free, and so made him wary at taking advantage of it: 'Why is it so cheap?'

'That's the official price,' she said agreeably, 'so please don't argue. Nobody else does.'

'I can't understand it.'

'Why try?' she said, holding his hand which he had laid on the counter. 'The beautiful town of Fludd extends a courteous welcome to all foreign travellers. You'd better go into the dining room now.'

'I'd rather wash and change first,' he said, being wet through with sweat and water, grimy, dishevelled, and mentally confused among the lights. She reassured him by saying that there was no formality or false pride in Fludd. The people were tolerant and understanding both of themselves and strangers. Fluddites lived in a light-hearted way, from one minute to the next. 'In any case,' she concluded, 'you look quite presentable for our tastes.'

Several middle-aged couples talked at their tables in subdued tones, a composite mumble that did indeed give off an air of kindliness and mutual interest. An elderly waiter, immaculately dressed and with a white napkin over his arm, guided him in fatherly fashion to a separate table. A second waiter placed a glass, and a large bottle of Nihilitz before him, with the homily that, 'A good drink will relax you, sir, and set your appetite on edge. It goes with the meal, anyway.'

'Thank you,' said Adam, picking up the menu. 'Will you take my order now?'

'I am only here to serve you, sir,' said the waiter, notepad ready.

'I'll have fish to begin with, and I shall want it served directly. Is it sea fish, or lake fish?'

'I can recommend the fish from the reservoir, sir,' he said, opening the Nihilitz and pouring a glass for him. 'What about the second course?'

'I'll try mutton cutlets, spinach and potatoes.'

'Very good, sir.' Adam drank half a glass of Nihilitz, and in a few minutes the fish came, decorated with parsley and sunk in butter sauce, accompanied by a straw platter of fresh-baked bread, so that after eating it he felt that his harrowing adventures of the day were only part of a very old dream. Halfway through a cigarette, the meat course arrived, and he bit hungrily, deciding to give a special mention to this agreeable establishment when the guidebook came to be written. Yet he was not totally at ease. Since entering Nihilon, he had learned to be suspicious about what happened to him, so that even now, in the midst of this considerate and superb treatment, he felt that much had still to be explained. Not that his appetite diminished in any way, for after the meal he was still hungry, and ordered a further dish of braised pigeon and rice. This was followed by a dessert of monumental splendour, of incredible flavour and sweetness, which made the coffee taste like the best in the world. 'I ought to let you go home now,' he said, while choosing a large cigar.

'Please stay as long as you like, sir,' said the waiter. 'I'm happy to be working. It keeps my mind off other things.' He held a lighter to Adam's cigar, who told himself that after his day's tribulations (which had been rather minor ones, after all) he felt more content than he ever had in his life, which state was, now he thought of it, one of the real pleasures of travelling. 'What things does it take your mind off?' he asked languidly, blowing smoke across his empty dessert plate.

'Just the town of Fludd.'

'Seems a very nice place to me.'

The waiter poured himself a glass of Nihilitz. 'It is, sir. It's the best town in the country. None of us can deny that. We all love it. We're deeply attached to it.'

Adam found him a fascinating old character.

'What is it, then?'

'It's the dam, sir.'

'Dam?'

The waiter drew up a chair and sat down, choosing a cigar and lighting it. 'Don't you know anything about Fludd?'

'I just stumbled on it in the dark, as it were, though I knew of its existence by the map.'

The waiter leaned towards him, a thrill of fear in his eyes, the cigar trembling in his teeth: 'Our town is built under the great walls of an unsafe dam.'

Adam almost choked on his own smoke: 'Really?'

'Yes, sir. It's been completed for several months, but we've been expecting it to give way any moment ever since. Cracks were there while it was being opened by President Nil, and he and all his party couldn't get away fast enough. They ran down the hill and back to their cars, top hats flying all over the place. If there was an election in Nihilon they wouldn't be in power for long. It's not that we are worried about the dam, but we can't forgive them for running away.'

'But why did they build a town under the dam?'

'Most of it was here already, and they didn't want to take it away. As soon as people realised what danger they were in, they decided to leave. But the government paid them treble wages, and made everything practically free. That's why this hotel's so cheap.'

'How can you stay here, nevertheless?' he asked, wanting to get on his bicycle and pedal out of the place at top speed.

'Well, you see, sir, we're all in a bit of a dilemma. We're not only accustomed to the easier life, but we've got used to living in danger. If we were to leave—speaking for myself, and I know others feel the same—our lives would be empty. We wouldn't know what to do. We'd be like dead people. Our lives wouldn't be worth living. Yet at the same time we know that we'll die if we stay here, because the dam is bound to give sooner or later, and sweep us all away. So we're rather contemptuous of people who prefer to live in safety. At first, as you can imagine, it was difficult to sleep, not knowing when we'd drown. Men couldn't even make love to their wives or girlfriends. But now, we live in the present, as it were, never thinking about tomorrow. It's somehow made us all human again—you might say. I enjoy talking to you about it, sir. I feel noble at knowing that any moment the hotel walls could burst, and that would be the end of it all.' He was sweating, and poured himself more Nihilitz. 'Imagine living in safety!' he said with great bravado and swagger, draining the liquor with trembling hands.

Adam, in despair, knocked his glass away: 'Is it true? Or are you telling lies, you bloody old Nihilist?'

'It's true,' the waiter said, standing up, in no way offended. 'Come with me, and I'll show you the cracks in the dam, with water beginning to trickle through. They're lit up every night, and we Fluddites make it one of our favourite walks. We stroll there with our wives and loved ones, even children, to look at it and speculate on when it might break. There's a café there, so we can split a bottle of Nihilitz together.'

Adam began to sweat: 'You mean the inhabitants of this town don't sleep?'

'Not very much, sir. When they can, they do, but not often. There are thirty thousand inhabitants here, including cats and dogs.'

'Cats and dogs?'

'They were included in the last census, naturally.'

'Why naturally?'

'Because when the dam bursts the government can call it a really big disaster. We import cats and dogs, and breed them, so that the number of souls drowned will be high. They can claim a catastrophe, which will make sensational news, and say that Cronacian saboteurs blew the dam up, proclaim a national day of mourning, and declare war. We'd really like to get the hotel full of tourists, if we can, so that we can then claim an international incident and gain the sympathy of foreign governments against those Cronacian bastards.'

'What you are saying,' Adam cried, feeling the day's exhaustion pouring back into him twentyfold, 'is that your government deliberately built the dam with faults in it so that when it collapses they can say Cronacia did it?'

'I suppose that's about the measure of it, sir,' said the waiter with sad resignation.

He stood up, pushing his chair back with a clatter: 'I'm going.'

'Wouldn't be much good, sir. The roads are closed by the militia every night. If you get out tomorrow you'll be lucky. Depends on whether any more foreigners are coming up from the frontier to take your place. You look worn out, sir. Don't you think you'd better get some sleep? I think I'll try and snatch an hour or two. It's nearly midnight.'

Adam sat for twenty minutes on his own, head bowed, and unaware of lights being put out around him. When someone tapped his shoulder he looked up and saw the attractive young girl from the reception desk. 'Is it true about the dam?'

She smiled, showing small white teeth. 'Yes. Is it true that you're a poet, as it says in your passport?'

'Yes.'

'Come up to bed, then, and we'll try and get some sleep. They'll be shutting the hotel doors now.' He insisted on wheeling his bicycle along the hall and into the lift, so as not to lose sight of it, he explained, because it was his only form of transport. He leaned it against the lift-wall as they ascended, and put his arms around her.

In the opulently furnished room, his bicycle rested against the wardrobe at the bottom of the bed. The girl undressed him, and then herself, but only after much coaxing was he able to make love. The central heating kept up a comfortable temperature in the room, and they rolled around on the covers, playing and loving for an hour, until they crawled exhausted between the sheets, and he fell asleep to the sound of heavy rain. Adam thought of Jaquiline Sulfer, whom he had promised to meet in Nihilon City, and whom he was vaguely aware of having betrayed, but his last thoughts were about the dam. He hoped it wouldn't burst during the night, or indeed split in any way at all till he had cycled far away from it. He did not know why he stayed where he was, but he felt such awful fatigue that it was utterly impossible for him to stir even one foot towards getting up.

Chapter Seventeen

A circle of red fire-tenders poured fountains of pink foam over the airliner. Richard expected it to blow up any second, for after such a nightmare journey to this country of the damned there seemed no reason why he should be privileged to go on enjoying the good things of the earth when people had already been brutally snatched from it. Even the most balanced mind would have shunned optimism, and so did he, standing in a queue and waiting to be thrown by the air-crew and scorch-marked stewardesses out of an escape hatch.

A wall of foam met him at the open air, and he swam down through a tunnel of darkness that seemed to last almost too long for him to support, moment after moment, mounting into minutes and hours, before strong arms grabbed his shoulders and stood him on his feet, giving a violent push in his back and telling him to run.

He wept as he lunged into safety, still expecting a blinding flash behind to send out vicious tentacles of flame and extinguish him. But as he ran, following dim figures towards the perimeter track, he knew that he was out of danger. A soldier with rifle and bayonet indicated the lights of the terminal building, and then he caught up with the professor, who was staggering along under the weight of his briefcase.

Richard was despondent, then began to laugh at the great sign stretching across the glass-fronted terminus which said:

NIHILISM WORKS!

The professor squeezed his arm to make him stop: 'What's so amusing? You consider it a mockery? Well, that sign will come down in a few days, if you deliver the letter I gave you. Another will be put in its place saying: HUMANITY WEEPS, so that people will feel more reassured when they land here from abroad.'

'That'll be just another lie,' Richard cried, 'and you know it.'

The professor shook his head sadly. 'You've caught our nihilism already. I've noticed before that it blights foreigners even more than us. I'm just glad to be alive, at the moment.' They stopped walking, still some way from the building. 'Listen,' he said in a low voice, 'there are two powerful pistols in my briefcase. We'll each have one, and when they ask if we have anything to declare at the customs we can say yes, this, and kill as many as possible.'

'Haven't you had enough thrills for one day?'

The professor caught at his elbow. 'All right, but let me give you one of these guns anyway. You may need it when the insurrection breaks out.'

Richard had never possessed a gun before, and was taken with the idea of having one now. 'The customs would find it.'

'I'll give it to you after we've been through. What hotel are you staying at?'

'The Stigma hotel, in Ekeret Place.'

'Good. Let's go then, my friend. The plane seems not to have blown itself up, so they'll get our luggage out soon.'

When they sat down, coffee and sandwiches were served. The waitress also brought them each a small commemorative aluminium plaque on which was engraved:

SURVIVOR OF THE DASTARDLY CRONACIAN ATTACK
ON AN UNARMED CIVILIAN AIRLINER OVER THE FREE
SKIES OF NIHILON. CONGRATULATIONS, PASSENGER,
ON YOUR ESCAPE.

This was followed by the signature of the President of the Nihilistic Capitalist Free-Enterprise Socialist Democratic Dictatorship of the Peoples' Republic of Nihilon, with the date underneath, written hastily in pencil.

'They certainly know how to do things in this country,' said Richard, as another waitress put a bottle of Nihilitz on the table.

'That will be their undoing,' said the professor, ominously. 'They are so much in touch with what the people think that they can no longer rely on them to react properly. In other words, the people have been nihilified, so that they are completely unknown factors. They value nothing, they hope for nothing—and yet, do you know, they are profoundly human, far more so than if they possessed all the values of Cronacian civilisation. They are so human, in other words, that the time is ripe for some order and honesty to be reintroduced into their hearts and souls. Come, the green light is flashing. We must look to our luggage.'

While every suitcase of Richard's was spread along the counter under the watchful eyes of three customs men, the professor was waved through by a curt nod from the officer in charge, and no item of his luggage checked. But Richard's watch, typewriter, record-player, tape-recorder, radio, binoculars, prismatic compass, pedometer, camera, and theodolite were put to one side, as if he would have to pay an enormous amount of duty on them, in spite of the scorchmarks and bullet holes that they had suffered during the journey. Yet one lynx-eyed customs officer, who was particularly diligent, ignored them, and opened instead the small box in which was a pack of love letters that Richard never travelled without, as well as a pair of cufflinks from his girlfriend with the message: 'I love you, darling', engraved on them.

The officer's eyes glittered, his hands shook: 'We can't let these go through.'

'Are you joking?' Richard demanded.

'We never joke in Nihilon. Sentimental keepsakes, marks of love—can't let them in. Love and nihilism don't go together. Love is a threat to nihilism. It can be used by the opposition as a social force. Honesty, stability, all those terrible things stem from love. If you allow love, you get idealism, co-operation, affection. That would never do. Nihilism would rot under it. A few of our own people lapse from time to time and fall in love, but we don't worry about them because they're only a minority of psychic perverts. A foreigner, however, can't be allowed to come in with those ideas, because he often has a great deal of influence. Nihilists are all too ready to believe what foreigners say to them. So I'm afraid I shall confiscate these—for the time being—and give you a receipt so that you may collect them when you leave.'

Richard decided he could do without them for a few weeks, and so smilingly agreed to the proposal, while two other customs officers glumly repacked his cases.

A huge black taxi stood by the terminal doors. 'Hotel Stigma,' Richard told the driver, pushing his cases in.

'Where's that?' the driver asked.

Richard offered him a cigarette: 'Nihilon City.'

'People with a sense of humour should be sent back to Cronacia,' said the driver, making no attempt to start his engine, but accepting the cigarette. 'I've been working for forty-eight hours non-stop. Where to, then?'

'Hotel Stigma,' said Richard, reading the address carefully. '43 Ekeret Place, Nihilon One.'

'I still don't know where it is.'

'You mean you can't find your way around Nihilon City?'

'Listen, I'm a taxi driver, not a bloody topographer.' He leaned out of his window, and signalled a man standing by the glass doors: 'You need a guide!'

He came in beside Richard, accidentally putting his foot on the tape-recorder. 'He'd like to get to Ekeret Square,' the driver said to him.

'Hotel Stigma,' added Richard. 'Do you know it?'

'I was born there,' said the guide. 'Room 62—just before the last outbreak. My mother was travelling from Amrel to Shelp, hoping to get a ship out of it. She had to change trains at Nihilon City, which meant spending the night there, which meant giving birth to me. She never got out because of me, so you can imagine how I feel. She's spent her last twenty-five years working as a cook in the hotel kitchen. So if you ask me if I know the Hotel Stigma in Ekeret Square—of course I know it. It's the main square in the middle of Nihilon City, in any case. Go straight ahead, and turn left before the river,' he said to the driver, who started the engine and set off.

There were no lights on the road, so the borders of it were indistinct. The driver switched his duo-coloured headbeams full on, not thinking to dip them when traffic came from the opposite direction. In fact his tactics at such times alarmed Richard, who had so recently escaped death in the airliner, for the huge car swerved over the road, and he couldn't tell whether his driver was trying to hit the approaching car— which was certainly coming straight towards them—or to avoid being hit. With a cymbal-like clash of the front wings the other car spun off the road in a whirl of green and purple light, but Richard's driver went on his way without wondering whether anyone had been hurt or not.

'You're my luckiest passenger today,' he said, 'I haven't managed to hit another car till now.'

The guide congratulated him: 'If he's badly hurt that's a hundred points, plus another five hundred for not stopping to find out. I'll vouch for you when we get to the Scoring Office.'

The driver laughed: 'If I go on like this I'll soon have a hundred thousand points—then I qualify for a house. I've always wanted to get out of my little ten-roomed flat.'

'Ten rooms?' said Richard.

'That includes cupboards and lavatories,' said the driver.

'It's three rooms really,' said the guide. 'And he's got fifteen children.'

'*And* my wife's two lovers live with us,' said the driver. 'It's nihilistic to have a lot of children.

'You knock 'em out, and you run 'em down,' the guide commented. The lights of Nihilon bristled in the distance. They turned left into a dreary suburb, and went towards the bridge. 'They have a passion for education in Nihilon. That's the only good thing about it.'

'It's a great country,' said the driver, 'even though I do live here myself.'

'What do they learn?' Richard asked, too exhausted to care.

'Everything,' said the driver, avoiding collision with a massive lorry on its way to the industrial zone.

'Some learn nuclear physics,' said the guide. 'Others learn the telephone directory. It depends which way your mind goes.'

'What are you learning?' Richard asked.

'Street-fighting,' said the taxi driver. 'Same as my friend here.' He held up a book. 'Government publication. "The Complete Guide to Street Fighting"—five hundred pages with maps, plans, and diagrams. History of street fighting, tactics, weapons, political repercussions of, how to start it, how to stop it, how to enjoy it. Nihilon is such a free country that all information is readily available. Then there's volume two. You go on to that when you've passed the examination at the end of volume one. Volume two has military engineering, demolitions and mining, explosives, boring and blasting, landmines and traps, dugouts and anti-gas procedures, fortifications, machine-gun emplacements, obstacles, siting of trenches and barricades—all that the man in the street ought to know in order to make himself a complete citizen, which means having the theoretical knowledge to take part in a bloody revolution. But while you're at it, and before we get to the bridge, give me the envelope that the professor handed to you on the plane. It's addressed to me, because I'm one of the insurrection's generals, though I have to work as a taxi driver in my spare time. The guide here is my adjutant. We work together, preparing our plans, gathering our general staff. By the way, would you like to join our general staff? You receive all sorts of privileges—free cinema-tickets, open access to the zoo, a Zap sports car with a big number on the side, as well as a pretty girl-assistant.'

Richard was embarrassed at having to turn down such an attractive offer: 'I haven't yet seen much of nihilism. Perhaps I shall like it, then I won't want to join your revolution.'

'Insurrection,' laughed the guide, 'not revolution. We're not lunatics.'

'Whatever it is. But here's your envelope,' he said, glad to get rid of it.

The guide's hands trembled as he took it: 'You'll be given a medal for this by our new government.'

'Maybe we'll make him a minister,' said the driver. 'Do you have another cigarette?'

'The only way you can repay me for delivering the envelope is to get me to the hotel as soon as possible,' said Richard as he passed his packet over.

'Have a pill,' said the driver, offering a small box by way of exchange. 'They keep you going for days.'

Richard preferred to wait for a natural descent into sleep. Huge blocks of flats went up like cliffs on both sides of the road. Then they crossed a bridge over the River Nihil, into Nihilon City proper. He was being pushed and pulled about. 'You're here,' said the guide, thrusting a revolver into his hand. 'A present from the professor. He said to make sure you got it.' Richard absentmindedly put it in his pocket. 'This is the Hotel Stigma. My mother is waiting for you—with the best meal you've ever eaten. And be careful with that revolver. It's loaded. We anti-Nihilists are serious people.'

Chapter Eighteen

Benjamin had already driven two cars off the road that had tried to ram him, by using the novelty of his glaringly plain headlights. It gave him great satisfaction to see the sudden loss of nerve in the other car when, on getting what he considered close enough, he turned on his battery of six blinders, a fog-clearer, two back dazzlers, and a row of triple-flickering roof-installed searchbeams, at which the other car spun off the camber, rattled over a couple of potholes (which merely served to exacerbate its loss of control) and rumbled uneasily off the road before the big crash came somewhere back in the darkness. They, after all, had tried to ram him, so he felt no more sorrow at their plight than he had for the unfortunate manager of the petrol station whose exploding tanks, and what must have been his ultimate reserves, lit up the skyline for several miles as he drove contentedly into the dusk.

Coming to the Alphabet Motel, a drive-in sign channelled him between two desks; the clerk at one handed him a card on which was written: 'Room P—thirty-five klipps', while the opposite clerk got in the car and guided him into a small room. The doors closed, and the lift immediately began to ascend. When it stopped, doors opened in front, and the clerk indicated that he should drive out, along a corridor. The room doors had letters of the alphabet inscribed on them instead of numbers. Some had cars already parked outside, for which purpose ample space was provided. At door P, Benjamin stopped his car, got out, and was shown into a plain but comfortable apartment, which, after his long day, he was well pleased with. 'The restaurant is now open,' the clerk informed him before leaving. 'There is also an amusement park attached to the establishment.'

After paying his bill in advance he went into the dining room of this curious stopover, where the menu was set out in automobile language.

It was a four-stroke meal, at twenty klipps, and the food was excellent, beginning with an induction of sautéed tappets, then braised camshaft, followed by a main course which was a cut off the big-end, and terminalled by a dessert of carburettor Suzette. Half a bottle of high-octane wine was thrown in free. The plates, which were of the best Nihilon china, had a picture glazed on them depicting a car crash in which the most mangled vehicle plainly showed a Cronacian number-plate. A box of cigars was brought to him, with the name Exhaust-Smoke Coronas inscribed on its elaborate label.

After the meal he wandered into the amusement park. Prominent loudspeakers played the same Nihilon National Anthem he had heard and loathed at the frontier post, though none of the motoring clientele were taking much notice of it. Many of them, however, were lying dead drunk on the ground.

The main attraction was a large dodgem arena, in which those who must have driven cars all day were now amusing themselves by practising their expertise at causing or avoiding head-on collisions—before meeting the perils of tomorrow. There were cries of alarm and shouts of triumph, invariably followed by the overwhelming impact of reinforced metal. Attendants with long poles went from crash to crash, prising the sweating contestants free when they were unable to do it themselves. The car with most dents, and still running at the end of an hour, received a prize, though Benjamin did not stay long enough to find out what it was.

But, strangely enough, the atmosphere of the fairground soothed him, as he walked about smoking his cigar. Close by was a shooting-booth, a long counter from which one could try to shatter clay pigeons with a two-two rifle, and receive a glass of Nihilitz as a prize for each one down. Benjamin realised that the prostrate dead-drunk people must have visited this spot already, and from the state of their drunkenness must have been very good shots indeed. A man beside him, fat, sweating, with rolled shirt-sleeves, was such a crack shot that he drank thirty glasses of Nihilitz. At the thirty-first he fell down as senseless as a stone, the rifle still in his hands, a look of beatification on his face. Some sportsmen lost their sure aim after only the third or fourth drink, then went staggering away to spend their remaining small consciousness on the dodgem cars.

Before going to sleep, he put his boots outside the door to get them cleaned by morning, hoping to set out at eight o'clock and reach

Nihilon City before nightfall—which he considered possible, provided the roads were good.

Back in his room to get ready for bed he found a leaflet in his table drawer which said: 'Visitor to Nihilon! Good evening, or Good morning! In order to find out more about our country, you may wish to tune-in to the seven o'clock lies on Radio Nihilon. This is the most important information bulletin of the day. Regarding its curious opening of "Here are the Lies", tourists are earnestly requested not to be duped by it. They may be reminded, in fact, that the inhabitants of Nihilon take it very seriously. This National Bulletin owes its inverted title to the genius of President Nil, when he realised that the people of Nihilon were no longer interested in the News. He therefore proclaimed that henceforth all news would be lies. Thus, when people flocked to hear these lies they soon realised that they were, in fact, serious truth. But whereas before they had contemptuously referred to the News as lies, they could no longer do so, because Lies became its official name. That is just one of many curious customs you will come across in our country, dear visitor, proving once again that nihilism is rich in tradition and folklore!'

He fell asleep, yet soon woke up from it. At five o'clock he was disturbed by motorcars coughing to life on the landing outside and driving to the lift, as if the other travellers were getting an even earlier start than he had planned for. He turned over, and buried himself in his all-night warmth, but even a light sleep would not come back, so he switched on the radio by his bedside. After a few minutes of transmogrifying music an announcer began what he assumed to be he news:

'Good morning, Nihilists. Here are the Lies. The Nihilon Newsagency has stated that 7,000 Cronacian fishermen were detained yesterday when they came ashore at the port of Shelp. They were equipped with artillery and machine guns, as well as flame-throwers and fishing nets. A Cronacian News Service Message, however, has given its own version which is, as usual, full of the most foul and blatant inaccuracies. However, in the interests of objectivity we put it forward for what it is worth, so that you can judge for yourselves, dear Nihilists. The vile Cronacian swine claim, then, that the cruise-liner S.S. *Cronacia* came peacefully into the Nihilonian port of Shelp so as to let its 7,000 tourists ashore for a few hours. They comported themselves well, it is claimed, and expressed general interest in the Nihilonian people. They were extremely impressed, the communiqué went on, by the cultural monuments they were able to see. An hour before they were due to return to their ship, however, this peaceful delegation of the Cronacian nation found itself surrounded by several divisions of the Nihilon army. In spite of being outnumbered, they returned fire with great skill and gallantry, but were soon overwhelmed by superior numbers—though not before much of the beautiful and historic centre of Shelp lay in ruins.

'Whatever the communiqué of the Cronacian guttersnipe government says, the Nihilon army scored a great victory, and completely wiped out this treacherous attack by the Cronacian bandits. The Nihilonian army suffered only a few men wounded.'

'Last night, an unarmed Nihilon Airways jet-plane carrying innocent people was viciously attacked by Cronacian Pug 107 fighters. The attack was beaten off by our air force, but the airliner was extensively damaged, and many casualties were caused to the passengers.'

'The area around the town of Fludd has been proclaimed a disaster area as from this morning. Last night the dam near the town burst, and thirty thousand of the inhabitants are feared to have perished. Aid is being rushed to the area. The cause of the disaster is unknown, but the possibility of Cronacian sabotage is not yet ruled out.'

'Preparations for the commencement of Nihilon's first great space spectacular are continuing. Our correspondent from the Ministry of Stars says that the launching of the rocket from the site below Mount Nihilon is expected either late today, or tomorrow, or perhaps in a few days' time.

'At the south-eastern sector of our frontier the border incident continues. An attack by three of our Geriatric brigades made some progress, and caused heavy casualties among the enemy. The incident is expected to flare up again this morning.'

'Yesterday a petrol station was attacked and destroyed by a Cronacian agent disguised as a foreign tourist. There were no casualties, but a million litres of petrol, as well as extensive installations, were destroyed.

Police and security forces are combing the area with a view to apprehending the criminal.

'And now, dear Nihilists, after the Lies comes music. . . .'

Benjamin, fully dressed, considered that the news, even if it was lies, was bad, and wondered whether he would be lucky enough to reach Nihilon City at all. Thinking about the others, it seemed possible that Richard had met his fate in the airliner, that Edgar might have been caught in the battle of Shelp, and that Adam had perhaps been endangered by the dam burst at Fludd. It remained to be seen whether Jaquiline Sulfer and himself would meet in Nihilon. He opened the door to get his cleaned shoes, but they weren't there, so he went back to the telephone and asked the reception desk if they would have them sent up. 'I'm sorry, sir. We haven't seen your shoes.'

'You thief!' Benjamin yelled. 'You collected them all and sold them. I know your lousy tricks.'

'We accept no responsibility for items which are lost,' the clerk went on. 'As a matter of fact we don't clean the clients' shoes, even though it says on the back of the door that we do. The notice is from last year and is due to be replaced.'

'You scum,' Benjamin cried. 'You scooped them all up, put them in a sack, and sent them to the disaster victims of Fludd, with a note attached saying: "From the grief-stricken sympathisers of the Alphabet Motel." You've got no right to do such a thing with my shoes. Get them back, or I'll wring your neck.'

'Perhaps one of the early motorists stole them by mistake,' the clerk suggested.

Benjamin threw down the phone, which didn't land back squarely on its base, and the voice of the clerk still came through: 'It's no use losing your temper. And all damage will be properly paid for, don't forget. In any case you foreign bastards will get what's coming to you if you don't——.' He cut off the nagging voice, of typical Nihilon backchat, and went out to the car for his spare pair of shoes.

In comparison with last night's sumptuous meal his breakfast was plain and simple fare. Coffee and black bread, with an apple and a bottle of Nihilitz, were put before him as he sat down. When he asked for ham and boiled eggs, the waiter said that motorists must not set out on any journey in Nihilon on a full stomach. Since there was a risk of certain injury on the road, this rule was only made for their own good.

However, he added, there was a provision shop next to the amusement park which sold all kinds of rich and tasty delicacies, and if he ate breakfast quickly he might find something left before the other drivers bought everything.

He decided that these bloody Nihilists weren't going to make him hurry over his breakfast, as shabby as the food was. He'd get provender along the way, by some means or other. Of that he had no doubt. But the coffee was surprisingly good, and the black bread as tasty as meat, certainly rich in vitamins. A few other people at nearby tables were talking loudly about the Lies, going from one item to another, finally speculating on the identity of the Cronacian maniac-saboteur who had blown up the petrol station.

'Anyone who would destroy such a precious fluid as motorcar gasoline ought to be crucified in the otherwise empty fuselage of an airliner flying in circles at ten thousand metres,' said one inspired enthusiast, whose shoes had also been stolen but who was without a spare pair—though this didn't seem to bother him as he sat in his bare feet. 'I wept when I heard the Lies. Imagine, so much petrol less for us to use. I suppose he's crossed the frontier by now.' He picked up a huge glass of Nihilitz and drank half of it.

'After committing such an awful crime,' said his friend, 'I'd keep away from the frontier. All the guards would be waiting for me there— if I'd done it, which I haven't,' he added quickly, shying away from the other man, who lifted a hand as if to flatten him. 'No, I'd get to Nihilon City and lie low till I saw an opportunity of escaping.'

Maybe 'he came through here, then,' said the tall man, looking around.

'Unless he took to the mountains,' said his friend. 'North or south, there are tracks. He could have reached the railway and jumped on to the Trans-Nihilon Express. It only goes at twenty kilometres an hour.'

The big man finished his Nihilitz: 'Perhaps he spent the night in this motel.'

'He wouldn't have the nerve,' said his friend.

Benjamin poured half of his Nihilitz into the mug, and swallowed some. When the other men finished their discussion, and staggered blind drunk to their cars, he opened his linen-backed map which had been compiled forty years ago and was known to be hopelessly out of date. It had been with him during his travels and military operations of the civil war, and faint pencil lines, indicating the various attacks and retreats in which he and his small force had been involved, were still visible. He marked the position of the Alphabet Motel, and noticed that the road would now descend towards Amrel, the last town whose defence he had been charged with so many years ago.

It would be strange seeing that fortressed and buttressed place again, set high over the bridge that he had neglected to destroy for the mere price of a bus to get his men (and himself) to safety. But his return to Damascony—now Nihilon—was no sentimental journey. During the last twenty-five years he had wondered about the fate of that noble and gentle legislator President Took after the armies of his benign republic had been defeated. Rumour said he had shot himself in his office. Hearsay made up a story of him being killed by one of his supporters. It was alleged that he had starved himself to death. But no proof had been put forward, no corpse ever found. The Nihilists simply did not mention him. His books were forgotten, his works destroyed, his statues smashed, his laws revoked and laughed at. President Took had lived in a plain and simple way, even denying himself friends so that they would not suffer after the catastrophic end which he must clearly have foreseen.

Benjamin remembered how the Nihilists came to power after gaining a small majority in a general election, a victory not accepted, in all his wisdom, by President Took, but one which, as was to be expected, led directly to civil war. The first consideration of the Nihilists, when they had won the election, deposed President Took and renamed the country Nihilon, was to stay in power. They then called themselves the Conservative Nihilists, so that they would never be confused with that left-wing nihilism which would only destroy every-thing and have done with it. They wanted, said the Conservative Nihilists, to *preserve* nihilism, to put it into a shrine as it were, and make it last for centuries. So they went on to call it Benevolent Nihilism. Under it, all men and women were equal before the law, though until they were brought before the law they were treated with total nihilistic inequality.

Benjamin also recalled the spectacular election campaign which brought the Nihilists to power. By prearrangement, by advanced publicity and television advertisements, the whole population was invited to witness the destruction of ten bridges, three power stations, twenty banks, and a dozen railway stations. Because no private houses were harmed it was a great success. Countless cars had been driven from cliff tops, with fervent fanatical party supporters in black track-suits at the wheels shouting 'Long Live Nihilism!' as they vanished into space. By these activities and various accidents, thousands of ardent Nihilists had lost their lives. Without such losses they would never have won the election, though it also weakened them in the civil war that was to come, which unfortunately did not stop them winning in the end.

Benjamin still heard their election cries over every medium of show and noise. 'Vote Nihilist! Positive Nihilism is the answer to all our troubles!' Out of boredom and indecision the people had believed them, and had invited a disaster from which even now, to judge by all he had seen, they had not yet recovered, whatever was said about a space programme.

During his long absence it often seemed that he loved Nihilon more than his own country, even perhaps because of the wild path it had taken. He loved the landscape, and the people who, after all, had invited nihilism into their hearts. If you love someone, he told himself, then it must be that you also love their faults, though he could hardly suppose that a desire for nihilism was one of his.

He had bought a large bag of provisions from the fairground shop, but had been forced to take four bottles of Nihilitz with it as liquid refreshment. There were clouds behind, but blue sky in front, though as if to deny a good day's trip the road to Amrel quickly deteriorated on its descent and became a rough track marked by the occasional wrecked car or lorry, heaps of rusty petrol cans, old tyres, inner tubes, and, in one case, a complete but dilapidated engine. The land was bare and rocky, except for a few cork or oak trees, and on higher ground to left and right solitary houses could be seen in the distance, wood smoke curling from their chimneys.

His route was no more than a dotted line on the map, and if the chassis of the car hadn't been strong it would have shaken to bits in the first few kilometres. He passed two cars lying upside down quite close to each other. Their two drivers sat on a nearby flat-topped rock, drinking from a bottle of Nihilitz. The noise of his engine drowned their singing. In subsequent fair and free elections, Benjamin ruminated, they had gladly voted Nihilism again. Such a system took intolerable loads off their minds, though it made him sad to know that people were incapable of facing up to the responsibility of their own possible happiness.

The land was flat, a plateau across which the road could hardly be made out, so he kept his direction by a compass fastened to the dash-board, aiming its needle towards a large group of rocks several kilometres ahead. For the first time since his present entry into Nihilon he felt a sense of wellbeing and freedom, able at last to enjoy the wide landscape spreading on every side.

Clumps of stunted trees were scattered among the rocks and boulders, and a heap of stones was placed across the road itself as a sort of barricade, so that when he got close enough he simply turned to the left on equally flat ground to go around it.

From behind the rocks and trees appeared six men dressed in overalls, each bearing a sub-machine-gun and pointing it at his car. They leapt at all four doors, and forced him to stop. The tall thin man who seemed to be their leader had a shaved head, as well as a scar on his mouth, and a glitter of illness in his eyes, as he shouted at Benjamin that he should get out of the car. 'We belong to the Revolutionary Army,' he told him, 'members of the Benjamin Smith Brigade, so called after a gallant group-leader who fought for President Took's cause twenty-five years ago. No one knows what happened to him, but we think he must have perished after we lost the war.'

'What can I do for you, then?' said Benjamin, a sudden swing of elation and nostalgia drawing him back into their cause.

'We want you to drive us to Amrel, so that we can join up with our main party and capture the place.'

When he agreed so readily to join them they shook his hand, and Benjamin, with tears in his eyes, supervised their places in the car. When the man in charge saw the four bottles of Nihilitz on the seat, he threw them outside so that they smashed on the rocks.

'That's good,' said Benjamin, feeling twenty-five years younger. He let off the handbrake, and the car rumbled forward, towards Amrel. Soon, he would tell them who he was, and take his rightful place once more in their fight for order and honesty, dignity and peace.

Chapter Nineteen

Hair pins chafed at his naked body. He stirred in the wide, opulent bed, and wondered where his loving boatwoman Mella had gone. He closed his eyes, bringing his knees up to his chest. No guidebook could ever have been written in a pleasanter manner. Even so, he was hungry. But he wanted to go back to sleep.

An occasional explosion rattled the windows, and when at one earthy grunt his bed vibrated, he wished they'd stop trying to kill each other and return to their coffee. Sunlight pushed at the glass, promising a fine day. Shelp was renowned for its climate, a fact which he'd already put into his guidebook notes. But ought he not also to mention the gunfire, and the tractable boatwoman? While reflecting pleasurably on Mella, he discussed with himself the hedonistic notion of breaking his contract and never going back home, as if one night of unmitigated pleasure had melted his spine. Maybe the day would return it to him.

After making love he liked to talk to his beloved, but where was she? Perhaps it was her absence that had wakened him while he was still tired. Then the door opened, and he sat up as Mella came into the room. She carried an immense sack over her shoulder, and another heavy bag in her hand. 'What's that?'

She put it on the bed, almost crushing his foot. He pulled it free, and she mistook the purple gloss of pain on his face for an expression of concern at the weight she carried. 'It's our food.'

'What do we need it for?'

'To eat, my love.'

'But we're in a hotel. I've already rung for breakfast. Have you never been in a hotel before?'

'I fought for this food at the markets.' She sat by the sack, and he kissed her in order to forestall those strong arms around him, but they held him nevertheless. 'I love you,' she said, drawing his face into her breasts. 'It was such a struggle to get this food.'

'Why was it?' he asked in a muffled voice.

She released him. 'Because there's none left. All food has been commandeered for Fludd, where the dam has burst. As soon as I heard it on the Lies I ran to my boat-trolley, and went from shop to shop. We're safe now, my love, with so much to eat.'

'Where did you get the money? You're only a poor boatwoman.'

'Don't be angry,' she said in a stern though democratic voice. 'I took a thousand-klipp note from your wallet, and I spent the same amount from mine.'

'Who are you?' he demanded, suddenly suspicious. 'I know you're not a boatwoman. You can't be.'

A sharp crack against the window caused a musical sound of shattering glass, and Mella sheltered him against her. Machine-gun fire drilled along the street below. 'We have to get out of Shelp.'

He was ashamed of his vibrating limbs, as if a wave of freezing water had passed over them. 'What is it? What's going on?'

'We don't know for sure,' she told him. 'It said on the Lies that the Cronacian fishermen had been defeated, but the government must be telling the truth again, which means real lies. Or maybe there is an insurrection. People have been talking about it for days. Or it's a revolution, a mutiny, a rebellion, a coup d'état, a riot, or even an unofficial unlicensed public holiday. It could be any of those things.'

'I want to start for Nihilon City today,' he said, stepping out of bed to dress, as another explosion shook the whole building. She looked at him, and regretfully watched his naked body being slowly clothed. 'There are no trains to the capital. The railway is closed for passengers. Only goods trains can get through, with relief supplies for Fludd.'

'Or troop trains,' he scoffed, 'to restore order in Shelp I should think.'

'You learn quickly,' she said, sadly. 'Maybe you're a Nihilist at heart.'

'Aren't *you*?' he laughed, fastening his tie.

'I believe in real democracy, and love.'

'Not that I'm a Nihilist,' he said, kissing her tenderly. 'I'm an individualist.'

She drew away: 'That's how Nihilism began. Every man for himself. I believe in honesty and co-operation, progress and humanity, goodness and life.'

'Oh, you poor child,' he cried, feeling older and superior.

'You don't understand,' she said. 'It's true I'm only a boatwoman, but I'm also the daughter of President Took, the last president of Damascony.'

There was a knock at the door, and a waiter entered with a magnificent silver tray on which was spread an extensive breakfast. While eating, Mella told him that after her father had disappeared (she was a baby at the time), her mother was killed with a rifle in her hands helping to defend the telegraph office in Nihilon City. That was certain. A woman had then put Mella on a lorry bound for a remote village in the mountains whose mayor, knowing who she was, brought her up in the best traditions of Tookist liberalism. But when she was fifteen this man died, and the family began to treat her in true nihilistic manner, as a servant and field worker, gardener and water-carrier. She was even forced into a disastrous marriage with one of the mayor's idle and vicious sons.

Luckily, as occasionally happened in Nihilon, the law was on her side, for in Nihilon a marriage licence is granted only for seven years. It then comes up for renewal, like a television licence. Those who don't choose to renew it mutually (and she didn't) were no longer considered to be married. She had had no children, though the law in any case said that children born within a year of the marriage lapsing would stay with the mother.

Free at last of her good-for-nothing Nihilist husband, and having heard of the democratic traditions of Shelp with regard to women, she had gone there, and found that she could only get work as a boatwoman. Already strong after her work in the country, she nevertheless found her new job almost overwhelming, though she preferred it to her recent life of semi-slavery. In time, however, she became more adept in her work than the other boatwomen, and was accepted as their leader, organising them into as much of a union as was possible in a country like Nihilon.

At the age of twenty-eight she had met Edgar, and fallen in love for the first time in her life. All that remained for her to do was, with the help of her lover, solve the mystery of her father's death. She saw no hope of finding him alive, but felt that her sufferings would be more than justified if she could at least discover his grave.

Although Edgar was fond of this strange and passionate woman, he did not honestly think he was in love with her. 'I love you,' he said to her. 'I really love you.'

She stood up and undressed, her eyes glowing at him, so that he was obliged to do the same. 'We'll stay here all day and all night,' she said. 'Perhaps trains will be running again to Nihilon City in the morning.'

'Aren't there any buses?' he asked, a forlorn hope as a hardening handsome nipple tipped at his cheek.

She pushed him on to the bed. 'None at all. But don't worry. We'll go tomorrow.' His spine trembled with renewed life, and he was soon in no condition to argue. Another explosion seemed to rend the town apart, and he felt her pulling the blankets up and over them.

Chapter Twenty

The ticket collector apologised, and said that there had been a mistake. Instead of having the compartment to herself, she was to share it with another woman. He then demanded a supplement of fifty kricks because, he explained kindly, she would have company all the way to Nihilon City instead of travelling alone as heretofore, and all such extra comforts were provided at nominal cost. Jaquiline said that she hadn't asked for the extra passenger to be put with her, but on seeing the miserable face of the forty-year-old woman who was to travel with her, she decided not to embarrass her any further. In any case she might be turned into a source of information, and so increase the pages of Jaquiline's guidebook contribution, and therefore her payment for it. So she gave fifty kricks to the ticket collector, who departed grumbling and swearing because she hadn't given him anything extra.

'I'm going to Aspron,' the woman said, as if she had been weeping, 'which is the hospital city, in case you don't know, being a foreigner.'

'I hope it's nothing serious,' said Jaquiline, offering her a cigarette, which was accepted readily. She was fascinated by this woman, but found the landscape also interesting, and looked out of the window at mountains going up steeply to the south, craggy inhospitable peaks and valleys forming a frontier zone in which lived some of the more primitive peoples of Nihilon.

'Quite serious,' said the woman, standing up to take off the jacket of her suit, then opening a locker to find a hanger for it. The train moved slowly but comfortably along its wide rails. 'You see, my fifteen-year-old son has had a nervous breakdown.'

'I'm sorry to hear that,' said Jaquiline, noticing her trim figure, and indeed how pretty she appeared with her short dark hair and small mouth. Only the faintly worn quality of skin told her age. 'But why must he be put in a hospital so far away?'

'He's not in a hospital. He's at home, staying with my sister. I'm the one who's going to the hospital. My husband set out a few days ago, but then I had a telegram to say that I must go as well. In Nihilon, whenever a young person has a nervous breakdown, or anything more serious, it's the parents who have the treatment. I suppose we'll be in for shock therapy, drugs, and psychoanalysis—in that order. It really is difficult for me to leave my job for three months, because I'm a school teacher, and I shall certainly be missed.'

'Does this sort of treatment work?' Jaquiline asked.

She pulled down the basin to wash her face. 'My name is Cola. Normally it does, certainly as much as if the young person got the treatment. When the parents go back home again they are so changed, and in a sense relaxed, that all seems to be well. Of course, if things go wrong and the son or daughter has another breakdown, then the parents come up for trial, and their psycho-reports and treatment-processes are taken into consideration. One mother and father I know were sent to prison for five years because their daughter was on her third nervous breakdown. But because of good conduct they were released four months later.'

Not satisfied with a clean face, Cola unbuttoned her blouse and took it off, then removed her underwear so that she was bare above the waist. Her breasts were plump though rather low, and she washed them vigourously while talking. Jaquiline wrote rapidly in her notebook, glancing now and then at her companion's ablutions, enthralled by her lack of embarrassment at showing her body before a stranger.

'The law is quite lenient in Nihilon,' Cola chattered. 'One can come out of prison after three months even if you are sentenced to twenty years, if you *show willing*. It depends on how many coarse epithets you manage to shout at the judge during the trial. The secret is, of course, not to get a lawyer to help you if you are arrested on a really criminal charge, because he defends you with reasonable talk, during which time *you* should be cursing the judges. In every court (I took my school-children to visit one last week) there is a notice above the judges' heads which says 'Nihilism is next to Godlessness'—as if to encourage one to make a stand for innocence or leniency by shouting obscene language in rich and rhythmical patterns. I've heard that the police never arrest poets, because even if they commit the most despicable crimes they are bound to be free in a few days, and on the lookout for revenge, such are their powers of vindictive and picturesque cursing. Naturally the peasants don't come off too well in this respect, being tongue-tied and awkward, but some of our rich peasants of the northern mountains, when they've killed a neighbour to get his land and feel themselves liable to be arrested, hire a poet to coach them in expletives to hurl at the judges. Some poets earn a good living at this, and the most famous ones are looked out for by the newspapers, who hire them as liars and special writers for notable occasions. In fact the newspapers might even compete to get a really good poet and liar, providing there's a chance of him becoming less of a poet and more of a liar as time goes on, which there usually is. That's why our newspapers have such a vast circulation. The laws of Nihilon say that the first duty of a newspaper is to be read, not looked at, which is why there are few pictures. Truth is secondary as far as the editors are concerned.'

She took off everything below the waist as well—so that Jaquiline wanted to turn away from the spectacle of her most intimate cleansing. She was not quite able at this stage to go on writing in her notebook, for Cola attended to herself with such loving care that she felt soiled from her experiences of the day, and wanted her to finish so that she could do the same, though she didn't see herself as capable of accomplishing it under the scrutiny to which she had unwittingly subjected Cola. But when Cola was finished and dressed, Jaquiline forgot her embarrassment and gave herself up to the luxury of a similar and thorough wash.

The train was climbing into the well-wooded foothills, and was by no means so steady on the rails as it had been while travelling along the coastal plain. But they found a vacant table in the restaurant car, and smoked a cigarette while waiting for the first course. 'This may be the last meal I shall enjoy for a long time,' said Cola. 'Conditions at Aspron are not good for those who get sent there for their children's breakdowns. Apart from bad food, one doesn't feel much like eating after so many shocks and interrogations.'

Jaquiline held Cola's hand to comfort her. 'I thought it was only psychoanalysis.'

'Not exactly. You are made to talk. As long as you keep talking you are all right, but as soon as you stop it's the electric shocks again. They say you are uncooperative and sullen, psychotic or schizophrenic. Sometimes they try drugs to make you talk, and that's bad enough. But usually it's the shock treatment. As long as you can keep talking, though, it's not too bad.'

'It sounds dreadful,' said Jaquiline, tasting the soup.

'I like talking to *you*,' Cola said. 'If only *you* were the one I had to talk to at Aspron. Once I get there I won't be able to do it so easily.'

'Why do people allow it to be done to them?'

'Oh, because Nihilists like to be humiliated.'

'I should have thought just the opposite,' Jaquiline said, eating hungrily.

'You don't know Nihilon,' said Cola. 'I'm a Nihilist, but it's still strange to me. A few years ago there were many child murders in Nihilon, and the government was very disturbed by it, though the people not so much, except those whose children were killed. Most of the murderers were never caught, because the crimes were motiveless. They really were, if you see what I mean. But many of the criminals sent letters to the police or press (whom they considered to be one and the same thing, though I'm not sure that they are at all) saying that they had only committed these crimes in the hope of being executed. But they couldn't give themselves up because that would pervert the normal course of Nihilistic justice. So the government, caught in the trap of its own philosophy, had to do something about it. President Nil proposed the idea of the execution mat, a place one could go to if the lust for child-murder, or any murder in fact, came upon one. The entrances to these places were well concealed, but the addresses, and the ways into them, could be found by dialling a certain telephone number. So a person could go there, and as soon as the door closed, the ritual of execution began, and stage by stage it became so convincing that after a few hours the person who had entered really believed he was on the way to decapitation, or whatever it was to be. He was reduced to a state of terror, remorse, repentance—though still innocent. At the last moment, when it clearly seemed impossible that he would live, he was read out a personal letter of pardon signed by President Nil, and a letter of forgiveness from the mother of the child he was supposed to have killed. Then he was free, innocent, regenerated, blessed, so we don't have any such murders nowadays—though there are still many things to put right. Do you like Nihilon?'

Jaquiline was going to say that she thought it a horrible country, but something made her hesitate: 'How can I tell? I haven't been here very long.'

Cola was disappointed. 'I hoped you'd say you hated it. I do. There are too many laws.'

'Too many?'

'Of the wrong sort.'

Jaquiline threw all caution out, and said: 'If you dislike the idea of going to Aspron, why don't you run away, and just not go there?'

Cola's face turned crimson. 'How could you suggest such a monstrous thing? No, no, never. Please don't mention it again.' They finished the meal in silence, though back in the privacy of their compartment Cola took Jaquiline's hands and said fervently: 'Yes, let's go away together. I can't face three months in Aspron. Help me, please help me.'

They lay on their separate bunks, and as it grew dark the train ascended loop by loop towards the pass that would take them through to the great central plain of Nihilon. Jaquiline got down and opened the window when the train stopped at a station, to witness the disturbance outside. The platform was short, and crowds of people were trying to get on, though not at the part where her carriage was. She saw them surging left and right, and pushing through the doors of the small-station building. Blue bulbs hung from wires and poles, and in the distance the yellower lights of a town straggled up a hillside as if they went into the sky.

Whistles were blowing, and people were fighting. The train began to move with many would-be passengers still trying to get on. A voice shouted orders from a loudspeaker, but she couldn't tell what it was saying. Several rifle shots sounded towards the back of the train, as it went faster, and the crowd with a united groan of disappointment appeared to draw back from it.

Jaquiline's face was half frozen from the cold mountain wind. She wanted to sleep, but was restless, and knew that it would be difficult if not impossible. She stood at the window, swayed by the train. 'I can't get to sleep either,' Cola said. 'I keep thinking of how happy my son must be now that he knows I'm going to Aspron because of him. He must be half cured already.'

'But you said you weren't going,' Jaquiline reminded her.

'Oh, yes,' said Cola, rustling in her sheets, 'we can get off the train in the morning, when it reaches Agbat. That's the next stop. We'll sell our compartment for at least ten times the price of the ticket, then make our way into the hills. I went on holiday there four years ago. The people in that region belong to a tribe called the Gelts, who have fair hair and blue eyes, and love money—though they have none because they sit all day talking about it. So when our money runs out we may have to face cold, hunger, thirst, humiliation, though it will be much better than going to Aspron. You are very kind to share my bad luck in this way.' She came down from her bunk, and held Jaquiline's hand warmly. 'I'm sure we shall be all right. It's safer in the mountains than in a town. We'd give ourselves away too easily there.'

Jaquiline wasn't sure now that she wanted Cola with her while she investigated the tourist attractions of Nihilon City. 'I want to sleep,' she said, 'I wonder if you'd be kind enough to lend me a night-dress?'

'I can't,' Cola said. 'All my cases must have been emptied and re-packed with pieces of wood when I left them in the station this morning. I have nothing at all.'

'My things were stolen too,' Jaquiline said, alarmed at such a coincidence. 'My own cases are full of wood.'

Cola fell to such heart-stricken sobs that Jaquiline's sympathy came back. 'You too!' she said, when she was able to speak. 'My luggage is filled with wood because I'm going to Aspron. Tomorrow the police will get on the train, and when they open our cases, they will see that you have to go to Aspron as well.'

'It's ridiculous,' Jaquiline cried. 'There's been some dreadful mistake. I shall explain everything to them.'

'You won't be able to,' said Cola, a little calmer. 'When the police see wood in our cases they'll arrest us on suspicion of arson.' Jaquiline kissed her, as if to thank her for an idea that suddenly came to her: 'We'll open the window and throw the wood out.'

Cola wept again. 'You don't know what you're saying! If they see *empty* cases we'll be sent to Aspron for life.'

'Then we'll throw the cases out as well.'

'That's worse. No luggage at all means that we'll be shot on the platform as a warning to others. Let's accept our fate together in Aspron. It will be better that way.'

Jaquiline patted her soothingly. 'All right, my love, if it will please you.' When Cola climbed back into the bunk, Jaquiline began to un-dress. This wasn't nihilism. It was a bad dream. She had no intention of submitting to such barbarous impositions, and remembered the book bought from her police chief friend at the frontier, a volume closer to her heart than ever because it contained a loaded revolver. When the police came, and if they came—for she could not readily believe all that

Cola had said—to take her to Aspron, she would shoot them down like the dogs she was fast considering them to be. With her clothes off, she climbed into Cola's bunk, and they slept the night together, consoling each other for whatever might happen to them on the following day.

Chapter Twenty-one

After a reasonable night's sleep (except for a few puzzling rifle-shots sounding through his dreams), and a good breakfast, Richard went out of the hotel and into the main square of Nihilon City. A strong breeze was blowing from the nearby Athelstan Alps, stirring the trees along the pavements. The square was about two hundred metres from north to south and east to west, and in the middle of it—towards which Richard suddenly ran through fast-moving traffic—was a concrete colossus erected to nihilism. He stood before it with open notebook, glad to be working at last. It was supported on four sides by lesser monuments portraying the virtues of Madness and Anarchy, whose great fierce heads were chasing the tails of their enemies, Order and Progress. 'This vast, towering, sprawling conglomeration of Nihilistic culture,' he wrote, 'which seems to have been chipped in many places by bullets, deserves an asterisk in any guidebook. It is to be hoped, however, that a thorough renovation of it will take place before many years go by, because flocks of pigeons have painted it well, which, together with soot presumably blowing in from the industrial suburbs when the wind is in the right direction—have given it a somewhat piebald appearance.'

Much of the square was lined with shops on the lower floors of the buildings, and there were many cafés, as well as several hotels, and from his central position he was able to observe the black ink-blot emblem of Nihilon flying from the roof of the Stock Exchange, while the hammer-and-chisel banner of nihilism itself fluttered from the office of Socialist Private Enterprise.

He referred to a thirty-year-old plan of the city in order to pencil in the positions of these edifices. The old bank was still in the same place, and so was the post, telephone, and telegraph office. The House of Deputies, and the Peoples Savings Box were housed in one building, but the doors were closed and they seemed little used.

Several passers-by stopped to look over his shoulder at the map, and many more were standing around. A young man in a threadbare yet fashionable suit, who seemed to have a cold, leaned over and ran his black nihilist fingernail along certain streets. 'I've never seen a map of our city,' he said with a smile. 'I'm trying to make out where I live.'

'Can't you buy them at the newspaper kiosks?' Richard asked, knowing this to be difficult.

'Yes,' answered the young man, carressing the edge of the map as if it were an expensive piece of cloth, 'a city plan is published monthly, but they are different every time, and don't in any way resemble the real layout of the town.'

A middle-aged woman with a shopping basket came forward and tugged at the map, crying: 'What beautiful colours! Is it a real one?' A huge fellow in cap and overalls elbowed them aside and offered a thousand klipps for it, while Richard vainly tried to fold it up. More people surged towards him, and he hit at a near-by face at the sickening sound of the thick paper tearing. A huge piece of the city vanished. Cars were stopping, and a driver leaned out, shouting: 'He's got a coloured street-plan of the city.'

Richard's notebook was pulled away, and he felt a sly hand draw the fountain-pen from his lapel pocket. Letting this go, he pressed a fist to his coat to hold his wallet safe. Drivers ran from their cars to get at the map, but most of it had already gone, and Richard relinquished the last piece. When the crowd drew away, he leapt clear and into the road, but a few disappointed people were so enraged that they chased him through the traffic, and he ran as if his life was in danger, regretting that he had left the Professor's revolver in his suitcase at the hotel.

Entering a glass-fronted café, he closed the door behind, ready to defend himself should he be chased and cornered there. But he wasn't, so sat at a table on the glassed-in terrace, which gave a good view of people in the middle of the square still fighting over what was left of his map. He asked the waiter for a cup of black coffee, as well as a glass of Nihilitz, which he hoped would stop the tremors in his limbs.

He took more sheets of paper from his wallet, and with a pencil wrote his notes again concerning the monstrous and squalid megalith to Nihilism which stood in all-revealing sunlight across the road. He followed this by the comment that: 'It is inadvisable to open a map in Nihilon, for it immediately draws spectators who are anxious to see what a real map of their city looks like, even though it may be hopelessly out of date. The enquiries that follow upon this act are often good-natured enough, but such curiosity has been known to get out of hand, so that the unfortunate traveller has had his map pulled from him and torn into a thousand pieces. This is no doubt due to a desire for possession, and for topographical orientation, which for no reason suddenly affects the whole crowd. While this is in some way understandable, though not totally commendable, what follows is undeniably bad for the traveller in that those of the mob who are baulked of their object occasionally resort to all but tearing the clothes off his back. For this reason the traveller is advised to have a newspaper with him at all times, in which to place his map while endeavouring to consult it.'

'Your coffee and Nihilitz,' said the waiter, disturbing Richard's somewhat ravelled composition. People outside were running across the square and falling to the ground. A machine gun sent chips of pavement spurting along an arcade. 'It's all right,' said the waiter, amused at Richard's pallor. 'The glass at this café is bullet-proof.' The gun spattered another stretch of pavement and several people had formed a short queue by the monument to buy rifles, revolvers, and ammunition from a stall with a striped awning, before taking cover nearby and firing back with their newly acquired arms. A heavier explosion drummed along one of the side streets.'Why is it allowed to sell guns so openly?'

'It's hard to say,' the waiter yawned. 'Perhaps it's the war. Cronacia is at it again. It's all part of the system we live under. Our government, meaning President Nil, floated a commercial company to run a war against Cronacia, so that we could take over that country. That's what all these border incidents are about, if you want to know the truth. Every citizen of Nihilon is able to buy shares in the Cronacia Reconstructs Company, in order to destroy it and then draw dividends and profits when it's exploited—I mean occupied. I even bought a few certificates myself. It comes under the heading of Peoples Enterprise Number One, and rates very high on the Stock Exchange. Even foreign countries are beginning to invest in it, hoping to get their share of the spoils—I mean dividends—when Cronacia is finished and on the spit. Not that all is going too well at the moment. The trouble was, that just after our firm got going, the Cronacians found out about it, and so by way of revenge and self-defence, started a company in their own country—also a commercial concern with public shares—to ferment revolution in Nihilon. That may be what is happening now, sir, though it's early days, and still hard to tell. It could be over by the afternoon, because everybody sleeps for two hours. But if by any chance it picks up again in the evening, then it's more serious. That's two hundred klipps, sir.'

Other people on the glassed-in terrace were reading newspapers, or talking quietly, unperturbed at what was happening outside, though to their credit, thought Richard, a few at least were discussing the terrible dam burst at Fludd which had recently taken place. But he kept his attention on the square, where several cars had been driven into the central area and left, presumably as cover for the sharpshooters. Another vehicle in the far corner began to burn. When an ambulance roared in, its siren screeching with inhuman jerks, men in red overalls ran from it to pick up casualties, while other attendants pulled long boxes from it and took them to the gun-stall, which must have been running out of weapons and ammunition. 'I thought Nihilon was famous for its law and order,' Richard said to the waiter, by way of a joke.

'Oh yes, sir, it is. The law of the jungle, and the order of the slaughter house. Nihilon is the greatest country in the world. Two hundred klipps, sir.'

'That's rather expensive,' Richard said, drinking half the Nihilitz. 'In fact it's extortionate.'

'Bullet-proof glass costs a great deal,' the waiter informed him politely. 'We had to replace it twice last week, so you're lucky to find it here at all.'

Richard passed him two hundred and fifty klipps. 'What happens to it?'

'It gets shot away. Or a bomb hits it. But we do our best for our customers.' He was called to another table, so left Richard to continue scribbling his notes. He was observed by an aging man with short grey hair, an impeccably dressed, manicured man who was well-groomed and dignified, smooth in all his gestures, neither preoccupied with what might have been going on within himself, nor obsessed with the carnage in the square outside, from where in fact he had recently walked.

The man glanced disdainfully at a newspaper, then folded it and laid it by his Nihilitz. He gazed at a framed portrait on the wall of the café, a gold-framed picture of a bosomly woman dressed in black, with a boy of twelve by her side wearing an admiral's uniform. Richard had already seen either that same picture or a variation of it placed in the corridor of his hotel. When the bellboy had shown him to his room he had stood looking at one above his bed. 'Doesn't it make you wonder where the father is?' the bellboy had asked.

'Not really,' Richard said.

'He's been shot,' the bellboy ventured. 'That's what we always say.' And now in the café Richard suspected that, because of the unnatural glitter in the eyes of the child, there was an observer behind the picture, if not a microphone as well. He recalled that a printed notice on the back of the door at his hotel room exhorted guests to respect these portraits and pictures, because the management and staff, not to mention the Nihilonian public at large, held them in high repute.

The man's uneasy glances were divided between this typical portrait of Nihilon, and the pigeons flying outside the glassed-in front of the café. 'They're waiting to take over our jobs,' he called.

'Who?' Richard smiled, glad to make another contact with someone in Nihilon.

'The pigeons,' said the man. 'The black pigeons from the mountains and the white pigeons from the sea. They're all over the place. Will you join me in a Nihilitz?' He came over to Richard's table. 'My name's Telmah, Orcam Telmah.'

'Yes, I'll have another,' said Richard, shaking his hand.

'A large Nihilitz,' said Orcam, in so soft a voice that Richard didn't see how he could be heard, but the waiter came along with two formidable tumblers and set them down. 'They'll take our houses and jobs,' said Orcam, with a new eagerness in his eye, nodding across at the portrait of the boy and his mother—'and *they* won't stop them doing it. They won't even try. After suitable training and deployment the pigeons will sweep in on us and help themselves to all we've built up over thousands of years. So let's drink to our defeat, my friend.'

Richard lifted his glass. 'I don't really think they'll do such a thing,' he said, sipping the fiery liquid.

Orcam drained his, and pulled his bow-tie undone. 'They will. I know they will. We have to protect ourselves against the birds. They fly around all day and every day, observing our organisation, or lack of it, and discovering the dispositions of our weaknesses. They watch us through windows, follow us in trains and motorcars, exchanging secret warbling signals between themselves. We can't understand a word of it, but nothing we do is not watched by those cool intelligent eyes. They're cruel, too. They'll blind us at first, before helping themselves to our accomplishments. It's all so easy and obvious, but nobody ever reads my letters. I spend hours every afternoon writing letters to President Nil and newspapers, but they're always ignored.' His hair was ruffled, and he became distraught, knocking over both glasses, and staring at the picture on the wall. 'It's *their* fault. They connive with the birds. They use the birds to keep us subdued. And how can you be subdued if you're supposed to be a Nihilist? Ah! They never explain that. Crafty! Very crafty!'

Richard watched his hypnotising balletic motions as he took a hammer and knife from his pocket and waved them at the portrait: 'There's a man behind those eyes recording every word I say. But I don't care, I tell you. I'll be crafty too, by doing what I like!'

With vindictive strength and impetuosity, and before anyone could stop him, for all were equally entranced, he charged screaming across the room. Reaching the portrait, he ripped and hammered at it with the weapons in his hands.

There were howls of rage and pain from behind the panel, and tables were knocked over as people rushed forward at last to try and reason with him, though not before he had acted out their deepest wish and mutilated the picture.

When the door opened, three policemen came in and grabbed him firmly. He was wild-eyed, foam boiling from his mouth as they walked him to a car waiting by the kerb outside, in which they drove off slowly under a hail of machine-gun fire. Exploding grenades seemed to be smothering the whole square with the noise and smoke of serious combat.

Two waiters went to the assistance of the police agent behind the picture. When they brought him out of the movable panel he was bleeding from one eye and had several bruises and cuts about the face. 'I'm giving up my job,' he cried to everyone, as they led him into the manager's office for first-aid and Nihilitz.

Richard, though he had sat by and done nothing because he had considered it to be no concern of his, was so shaken by the incident that he called for more coffee, as well as another bottle. 'That was very unfortunate,' said the waiter when he set it down, holding his hand out for the money. 'We've had our eyes on that old man for some time. In fact he's been coming here for years. He used to work for the government radio, reading the Lies—before he went mad. He broadcast a speech about the birds wanting to take over everything. In our country lie-readers are very famous and popular, even more than filmstars. When one of them died a few years ago, many people committed suicide at his funeral. The whole nation was grief-stricken. You can't imagine how famous they are. The worse the lies are the more people adore them, because then the lie-announcers can really use their acting talent.'

Richard didn't feel like going beyond the bullet-proof glass while the gunfight was still on. In any case, he was gathering material faster than he could write it down, so there was a good excuse for staying where he was. A fieldpiece must have been wheeled from one of the side streets, because the head of Anarchy on the great statue was suddenly blown off, and the arm of the hunted and despised Progress was shattered from the elbow down.

A few minutes later the secret-police agent, his face lapped in bandages, stood by Richard's table, ruefully observing the scene in the square, as if wondering whether it would be worthwhile venturing into it at such a time. 'I'm broken-hearted,' he said to Richard. 'Absolutely dispirited. If you buy me a Nihilitz I'll sit down and tell you why.'

'You're the first person I've met in such a frame of mind,' said Richard, calling the order.

'I know, but I've given the best years of my life to that portrait, sitting behind it and looking at all sorts of people from every walk of life, and not harming anyone. I just recorded what they said so as to keep myself amused and happy, and then along comes this old lunatic who spoils my reason for being on earth. It's absolutely disgusting, such a mean trick. Can you imagine that anyone could be so thoughtless and spiteful as to throw me out of a job like that?'

'I expect you'll have to get another,' said Richard, lifting his glass to drink, feeling slightly unreal from what he had so far poured into himself, though it seemed the only thing to do in such a country.

The secret agent cheered up under the impact of his glass. 'I might register with the Outlaws,' he said. 'It's the only thing to do.'

'What do you mean?'

'Well, you see, when someone is at the end of his tether in Nihilon he can go to the office of the Ministry of the Interior and register himself as an Outlaw. He is given a gun, ammunition and supplies, and taken by lorry to a remote part of the country, where he is left to fend for himself.'

'That doesn't seem too bad,' Richard commented.

'Oh no, it isn't,' said the security agent, smiling between his bandages. 'But on the other hand, I might be so depressed that I'll go and join the security forces. In which case I apply to the same building, but a different department. They give me a gun, uniform, ammunition and supplies, and take me to a remote part of the country where I am left on my own to hunt the Outlaws. The trouble is, I'm so downhearted at the moment that I don't know which to choose.'

'I can't say I envy you,' said Richard.

Looking furtively around, the security agent took a heavy revolver from his pocket and made for the door. Pushing it open, he ran across the road towards the middle of the square, firing as he went, advancing in a quick zig-zag to avoid—or at least delay—getting picked off. So much fire was directed at him that certain people seemed bent on his extermination, and must have been waiting for him to emerge from the café.

Richard caught sight of a familiar figure coming down the steps of the Hotel Stigma, a tall bespectacled man wearing a long overcoat and carrying a briefcase. He walked quickly across to the ruins of the great statue, and when it seemed that the secret agent had reached the safety of its cover, the professor took a gun from his pocket, knelt on the ground between two cars, and shot him down, just as the secret agent had lifted his gun for retaliation against the upper windows of the Ministry of Social Security. A white and blue flag was unfurled from one of its windows, followed by a sound of cheering. Then a tank rumbled into the square bearing the emblem of Nihilon on its turret, and opened fire at the flag. The professor fled into the café where Richard was sitting.

'Ah, my friend,' the professor said to him, drinking what remained of his Nihilitz. 'I hereby appoint you Grand Insurrectionary General for the Southern Sector of the Athelstan Alps.'

Richard, taken from his placid enjoyment of the outside scene, which hadn't appeared in any way to concern him up to now, drew back in alarm. 'What are you talking about?'

The professor put his briefcase on the table: 'I leave you in charge, general. I have to go and organise the northern Sector. I'm a very busy man in these great and stirring times.'

Richard objected to his appointment, but the professor, with a ludicrous and comic smile, rushed outside into the crossfire and smoke.

The waiter stood respectfully beside him. 'Do you require anything else, general?"

'No, no," he said, waving him away.

The waiter, in spite of the fact that they were both in civilian clothes, gave a smart military salute, and walked off.

Chapter Twenty-two

There was a humming in the air. It was pitch dark, but by the light of his luminous watch, Adam saw that it was four o'clock. He had been asleep for only three hours, but was suddenly awake, and no longer tired, in spite of his exertions on the previous day. The warm body of the reception-girl lay beside him, her straight black hair spreading over the pillow like a fully opened fan.

His one thought while dressing was to write more notes concerning his travels in Nihilon. There was much to record for the intended guidebook, and he considered his present inexplicable wakefulness a good opportunity to get some of it done. But the humming, which he assumed to come from the giant generators at the dam, disturbed him. Opening the window he stepped on to the terrace. The sky was raddled with stars. He looked up the valley hoping to see the actual wall of the dam, but though the whole sky in that direction was lit up, a block of flats hid it from him.

The generator noise frightened him, especially when he suddenly remembered the story of the dam being unsafe, which he had heard from both the waiter and the pretty girl still sleeping in his bed. The thought of it releasing a ferocious amount of water on to him and thirty thousand others filled his soul with such anxiety that he was ready to vomit. But he fought it back. He didn't want to believe it. Yet why should they lie to him? Was it merely a complex trick of the town council to make life more exciting for thrill-seeking visitors to Fludd? Nothing seemed strange any more. The previous day's travel had shattered his standards and expectations, and made him feel both cowardly and ready to do something about his possible doom in the town of Fludd. The fact that thirty thousand valiant people were sleeping around him, and disregarding such danger to their lives, only made him want to get out of the place as soon as possible, for they seemed because of this to be absolutely insane in their passivity, and a positive menace to those, such as himself, who still felt a human twinge of self-preservation. He packed his few belongings into the panniers and, without further looking at his companion of the night, opened the door and pushed his bicycle outside.

In the corridor he could not find a light-switch, and was unable to remember the way to the lift. When he struck a match and found a switch, no bulb lit up. The match burned his finger, and he was in darkness again. Perhaps there was a power failure, he thought, yet how could this be, with the hotel so close to the largest electrical generating plant in Nihilon?

He sat on his bicycle, and pedalled along the corridor, his dynamo lighting all in front. Reaching a cul-de-sac, he turned and rode the other way, close to panic, wanting only to get out of the hotel, the town and valley before the dam burst. He told himself that, in spite of all his fears, it might not collapse tonight, but this was only to calm himself so that he would be able to think more clearly if it did.

Reaching the lift he found that it did not work, which seemed one more reason to hurry out of the place. He steadied his bicycle down four flights of stairs, then along by the silent reception desk to the main front exit, where an old, white-haired, pale-faced doorman slept peacefully on a chair. His face was so gentle and good-natured that Adam suspected he might not really be asleep. A street light came on outside and shone through the glass. 'Where are you going?'

'I can't rest,' said Adam. 'I'm going for a ride around the town.'

'I don't trust sleep, either,' said the old man. 'That's why I woke up. If I trusted sleep and thought it would do me some good, I wouldn't wake up from it, and that might be better for me, because then I'd live longer—but who cares about that sort of thing in the town of Fludd? Your light hit the corner of my eye, tangled with a vein in the dark, you might say. I don't trust sleep because then I can wake up for a bit of human talk. Give me a cigarette.'

'I'm going out to buy some,' said Adam.

The old man opened the door for him. 'Don't be long, then.'

The streets were deserted, but increasingly well-lit as he came to the edge of the town. Slogans in red paint had been scrawled on the walls saying DOWN WITH THE DAM and FLUDD WILL RISE AGAIN. The main road ascended in hairpin curves up the side of the valley, and he rode the bicycle as far as he could, but had to push when the gradient became too steep. He disconnected the dynamo and walked slowly by the light of the risen moon, as silently as possible in case he should be stopped by pickets and sent back to the hotel. He thought with regret of the warm bed, and the girl he had left lying in it, now feeling foolish at his decision to get out of the valley when in all probability there was no need to. He'd only heard about the dam, and hadn't actually seen it, yet he felt sure that it existed, but who the hell, he wondered, working himself into a fury as he approached the skyline after an hour's hard push up a few hundred toilsome metres, had started the irresponsible nihilistic rumour that it was unsafe?

Be that as it may, it seemed as if a giant, invisible, vicious hand tugged the bicycle from him, threw it on the ground in front, then finished its work by dropping him on top of it. The roar of an explosion shed a sudden orange light, and tried to pull the roof from his mouth. In spite of his previous constant preoccupation with the dam, it was some minutes, while he lay there half-stunned, before he realised that it must have been destroyed. He expected masses of water to churn through the groaning sky and fall directly upon him, and his one impulse was to crawl the remaining few hundred metres to the skyline and get over the crest of the hill, as if he would find safety there. The lights of Fludd in the valley behind were going out one by one. He knew at last that there was no safety in Nihilon, but wondered why he alone out of thirty thousand had survived the disaster? The noise of breaking walls reached him, as more apartment blocks gave way.

He had pains in his stomach, but was relieved to find that his bicycle had suffered no real damage. There were tears on his face, forced out by shock, and perhaps sorrow at the fate of the inhabitants of Fludd. At the summit of the hill he turned to look back in the first light of dawn, at a sluggishly turning sheet of water where the flourishing town had been. He sat on a rock and wrote a hymn to Fludd, and to his sleeping loved-one lost to him forever, thinking that should he come back this way to the frontier, she would not be there to greet him.

But he recalled once more his far-off promise to meet Jaquiline Sulfer in Nihilon City, and their intention of going home together in a first-class express sleeper. Such a bright lascivious picture calmed him down, and with one last look at the grey lake of Fludd, he turned and pedalled along the road towards the capital, reflecting that travels in a foreign country put you into the way of knowing more about yourself, or clarifying what was already in your heart. Out of your own country, he had discovered, a veritable explosion of the personality takes place, even over the most minor incidents. All you had to do was stay calm in the face of the final threatened disintegration, he decided, stopping to take a bar of chocolate from one of his panniers, and noting how fresh and cool the air smelled as he stood by the roadside to eat it.

The road gradually descended through open moorland, scenery broken by small fenced-off fields of black earth in which people were already working.

At the next village was a restaurant, and he went in to get some breakfast. The dining room was full of well-dressed men and their stout wives eating heavy nihilistic meals. There were no seats left, so he sat on a high stool at the bar.

A dark-haired half-starved young man standing on a nearby chair appeared to be shouting at everyone: 'You eat too much, I say! But the revolution will cure all that! Honesty and order and progress will make you lean, and you'll be afraid to eat for fear of choking on your own guilt.'

This sort of talk in Nihilon sounded exciting to Adam, and he looked up at the young man so as to hear his words more clearly. Several eaters took a moment from masticating to laugh at what he said.

'You are disgusting,' he went on. 'You are all fat maggots living off the backs of the people. You gobble such enormous meals while *they* are sweating in the fields on nothing to eat. You are a herd of rich pigs gluttonising all day, while they starve even at night.'

A few of them clapped, but he was obviously not yet in the fullstream of his wrath. 'When the revolution comes, and make no mistake, it will come sooner than you think, you'll all be set to work, building roads, draining marshes, moving mountains, excavating canals, digging with *spades*.'

Several of the eaters groaned. He was getting better. 'But if I have my way, my own particular way, my own private personal spiteful heartfelt way, I'll have all of you stood up against a *sunlit* wall and shot.' To their cheers and applause he came down, and walked across to the bar. On his way there, some of the more appreciative and enthusiastic diners thrust money into his hands.

Adam was served with meat, bread, coffee, and Nihilitz. 'I loathe them so much,' the firebrand said to him, 'that I can't even eat.'

The barman put a pot of coffee before him: 'What was that explosion at Fludd?'

'Explosion?' said Adam.

'We heard a bit of a bang from that direction not long ago,' said the barman.

'The dam went,' Adam told him, his mouth full.

'I'd better get on to the local newspaper then,' said the barman. 'Anybody survive?'

'Only me, as far as I know.'

The barman whistled through his teeth and went to the telephone.

'The government's been waiting to make an example of Fludd for a long time,' said the firebrand. 'Those who can live like the people of Fludd are dangerous, unpredictable, proud, sleepy, independent—in a word, revolutionary. But that barman's wasting his time phoning the local paper. The news is known already. The dam was blown up deliberately.'

'It must have been,' said Adam. 'I saw it. There was a great explosion.'

'You saw it, did you?' said Firebrand, 'and you're the only survivor?'

'That's right.'

'Well, your life isn't worth that empty plate you haven't eaten. They'll kill you. They must have banked on having no witnesses so that they could blame it on Cronacia. You're a hunted man from now on. You'd better throw in your lot with me.'

This was bad news, but Adam ordered another breakfast. 'You see,' Firebrand explained, 'I'm the resident agitator at this popular and expensive restaurant. The manager hired me six months ago to make speeches so that the customers, thinking the revolution was coming, would eat more to make up for the hard times that the revolution would bring, if it did actually come. So because people are superstitious his business increased twenty times. Restaurants for fifty kilometres around had to close down. He pays me almost nothing, as you can imagine, but that's all right, because while I'm shouting about a mock revolution, I'm meanwhile planning and working for the *real* revolution. No one suspects this—how could they?—but my first blow is due to be struck today, and since you are on the government's death-list you'd better join me. We aren't the only two, because there's street fighting already in Shelp and Nihilon City. The whole country is rising.'

'What did you do before you took this job?' Adam asked out of genuine curiosity.

'I was a writer working for the National Magazine, and I did very well at that sort of work. The best thing I wrote was a series of articles in praise of nihilistic capitalism. I was made a Hero of the Evolution by President Nil, being the youngest man ever to get that award, so you can imagine how I felt. The only trouble about doing something like that, though, is that you get disillusioned straight away with what you've just written. So of course I lost my job because I began to see that nihilism was not the right thing for Nihilon. I became a revolutionary, met other people who had actually formed dissident groups, and for a time I travelled around getting familiar with the country and its terrain. The only maps we had were those in school atlases on a small scale, a rudimentary motoring-map, and a few wild productions from those cartographic maniacs patronised by President Nil.'

Adam felt in his pocket and, wanting to be liked, even by a mock revolutionary, gave him the map he had taken from the butt of the soldier's rifle at the frontier. Firebrand grabbed it and put it into his pocket: 'For that, my friend, you'll be made Commander of the Second Column in the march on Nihilon. As I was saying, the government is trying to build up a tourist industry here, but we revolutionaries are not going to allow it. We want real factories instead of paper ones. Out with all tourists! Say no to paper factories! Death to cardboard schools! Down with plastic sports-palaces!'

He grabbed Adam by the shirt front: 'Listen, in this country a hundred writers have formed an association called the Company of Novelists (CON) and every year they are ordered by the Ministry of War to write a pornographic novel. These are so filthy that they go into a great number of editions. They are translated into all languages, and earn huge amounts of foreign currency, so that the Ministry of War can buy guns and ammunition. Such vile works swamp the home market and keep the people complacent. There are other things I could tell you, so many things. In Nihilon a writer or a filmstar is liable to receive a telegram from President Nil ordering him or her to commit a sexual outrage so that the newspapers can have something to write about. For when the culprits are caught and tried, the case is salaciously reported, though all that happens to the accused is that they are committed to "special exile" for a few months, to some coastal or mountain resort, where they can go on having a good time. Believe me, dear fellow-insurrectionary, this is a terrible country, and I am determined to purify it.'

'But if something's wrong with it,' Adam argued, 'and it certainly seems that something is, then can't the people alter it without revolution? Aren't there free elections every five years at which people can vote in a new government if they wish?'

Firebrand laughed bitterly. 'Elections? Not any more, my friend. There were, at first, very early on, but the people were in such a euphoric mood of don't-care and don't-know, that vast deputations went to the government building and said: "We don't want any more voting. We're happy. So after all, what does it matter?" And the government said: "It *does* matter. It's democracy. It's your right to vote. It's your duty. So if you won't do it, we'll vote for you." And that's how it's been ever since. At every general election the people get into great moods of excitement, wondering which way the voting will go, staying up all through the night to hear the results. And then at six in the morning the government breaks the tension by announcing that it has got in once more, after which it declares a public holiday, so that the grateful people, secure in their very own and latest victory, can either go to sleep or continue their celebrations.'

He jumped up on to his seat again to address everyone in the dining hall: 'You'll all hear this. Listen to this, you trough-scum, you bilge-Nihilists, you riddle-headed soulmongers, the country has to wind down and stop. I'm putting the brakes on. The food will choke you when you hear what I've got to say.

'In Nihilon a man who has his passport stolen gets thrown into prison. Anyone whose car is rifled is arrested and charged with disorderly conduct. If you were alive after being murdered you'd be accused of negligence. Crime is encouraged in order to facilitate a more equitable distribution of wealth. A criminal is honoured for his attempts to assist in this. I have nightmares about dishonour and chaos, but the revolution will triumph!'

He was now raving, and intermittent applause swept around the restaurant. 'Nihilism is all for all and one for one, which makes a nation of fatsters out on the grab, and a country of thin men trying to stop them with all the black cunning born out of a congenital yearning for catastrophe. Nihilism is when a good system can't get the upper hand over the bad, and when the bad won't totally destroy the good in case something viable should be built out of the ruins. President Nil and human nature hold a perfect balance of chaos, which you all prefer because you can't bear the thought of honesty and order and goodness in the world.

'Even sabbaths do not exist,' he shouted. 'They used to come every seven days, the sabbaths, but now by government decree they come less and less, so that at the present moment they're running at the rate of about forty a year. Thus are the people cheated of their leisure. But the revolution will change all that. There'll be a compulsory day of rest every seven days, except for you pigs eating your swinish food, who will have to put up with only one sabbath a year! The revolution will declare war on the gluttons. You'll regret every centimetre of your fat cheeks when the revolution comes. So prepare for the worst, you pigs. Death to the gluttons! Down with all those who weigh more than eighty kilos!'

A huge man with a napkin over his chest, and food spilling out of his mouth, came from a table with tears in his eyes. He patted Firebrand on the back when he got down, pinched his left cheek affectionately, and pushed a large banknote into his top pocket. He then shambled back to his table to carry on eating, still weeping.

'You'll be the first to go,' Firebrand shouted to him. 'I'll remember you, especially. Now, come with me,' he said in a low voice to Adam. 'Your life is worthless, but the revolution will save you yet.'

At the door of the restaurant Firebrand took a hand-grenade from his pocket, and pulled out the pin. 'This is my starting signal,' he called in a loud voice so that everyone could hear, and holding it high so that they could see: 'Long live the revolution!'

He threw the sizzling grenade with all his force. It spun through the air, every eater and even the waiters looking at it with muted, terrified, half-thrilled eyes. It landed in an immense bowl of fruit salad. It didn't explode.

The applause was prolonged and rapturous. There was shouting, laughing, banging of cutlery, clapping, stamping of feet, whistling, and shouts of 'Encore! Encore!', but Adam and Firebrand were already riding towards Shelp, on the bicycle.

Chapter Twenty-three

On the outskirts of Shelp the road widened into a dual carriageway. On one side refugees were streaming away from the town towards Nihilon City. On the other they were pouring back again. The great blow against nihilism in Shelp by the Law and Order Insurrectionists appeared to have been successful, for the town seemed to be either in flames or in ruins. A Cronacian battleship was standing offshore.

Tentacles of smoke were boiling into the sky as Mella hauled her landboat through groups of refugees. There was a great amount of luggage on board, with Edgar perched comfortably in a lounge-chair looted from the hotel only minutes before the arrival of law and order.

The afternoon sun was still hot, and Mella stopped pulling to run back and mop the sweat off Edgar's brow. 'Don't,' he cried, when other people stared at them. 'It's your own face you should wipe, not mine.'

She glared at him: 'I consider myself your equal, so I have a perfect right to look after you.'

'I know,' he said, afraid that she might abandon him if he argued too strongly. But she kissed him passionately on the mouth, then fastened the straps of the landboat over her shoulders, and plodded earthily on.

Edgar chewed sulkily on a cigar, swearing softly as the wheels bumped over a pothole. There were neither buses nor trains to Nihilon City, and the only way to get there was to let Mella pull him on her amphibious contraption, though at the rate she was going it would take several uncomfortable days. He considered himself lucky that she loved him, though he was constantly harrowed by her public out-bursts of affection. Even the fact that they had passed a night of love together did not seem to justify such an exhibition.

He pulled his hat lower to keep the sun from his eyes, then dozed, and woke up after a while to find that most of the so-called refugees were turning from the road and going towards the sparsely pastured land to the south of it. The far-off mountains that rose up darkly certainly offered to Edgar a more salubrious aspect than the highway. Mella leaned against the cart to rest. 'Where are they going?' he asked.

At the sound of his voice she gave him a large piece of bread and a bottle of beer. 'To the racecourse. Eat, my love, or you'll grow too weak for the journey.'

'What racecourse?' He sipped the beer, but pushed the crude-looking bread aside. 'What sort of races?'

'Zaps,' she said. 'One-door sports cars. It's very exciting, if you get high enough above it.'

'Let's look then,' he said, being fond of motor-racing. 'You can make up for the time we lose by pulling me through the night.' Mella smiled because he had given her a way of pleasing him, then got back into harness and hauled her unwieldy cargo towards the racing grounds.

It was a sign of the troubled times that prices of admission, as well as all bets, had to be made in goods and not money. As people went through the turnstiles they threw down watches, rings, cufflinks, small radios and gold spectacles for the best seats. They took off jackets, shoes, dresses, and even shirts for places at the back, from which they nevertheless hoped for some sort of view. As the mounds of valuable goods grew outside the perimeter, huge lorries drew up to take them away. Edgar relinquished a precious prismatic compass as his admission fee, and found that it entitled him to a ticket in the best stands, from which, with binoculars, he could overlook the whole course. Mella stayed behind to guard the boat.

The layout was a highway-circuit of ten kilometres, with topographical characteristics prominently visible from the high seats. At the start line were twenty-four cars, twelve to go one way, and twelve to set off at their backs in the opposite direction. Each twelve therefore had a clear road for approximately half way round, so that in the normal thinning out caused by the varying accelerations, it seemed as if they were only setting off for a peaceful drive.

Edgar was open-eyed at the impending gladiatorial combat of ferocious motorcars, foreseeing a mighty conflict when the two lines met. The rules were that those cars escaping the first shock of combat must go on to another round, and so on, until only one car remained to get back under its own horsepower to the winning-post. Much of the crowd was of a belligerent disposition, and cheered them to greater speed, while the remainder held breath and stayed silent.

The first casualty came among the twelve cars that had started in a westerly direction. After the initial rush along the straight and narrow, the foremost vehicle spun over the side when it went too fast around Hairpin Bend. For the other group, which set off more or less easterly, and whose narrowing road soon gave way to a gruelling ascent of Death Hill, catastrophe struck even before they encountered the others. At the very crest of Death Hill was Switchback Corner, and here the first three vehicles failed to switchback with sufficient skill, and turned several somersaults before coming to a halt off-course.

The reason why these vehicles were one-door Zap sports cars now became apparent, because the one and only door was on the underside of the car, so that when the said vehicle landed upside down, as it invariably did after crashing, the driver within had only to open the door by pressing a button with his foot. He could then lever himself out before the vehicle burst into flames, and leap on to the grass, running away from it with glazed eyes and a wide smile at the realisation that the more he ran the nearer he was to safety.

Consequently, when the teams met, the eastbound group had two cars less on its strength than the westbound division. However, at this stage, neither side attached much importance to this disparity of numbers because the policy of each was not so much to ram their opponents out of the battle as to let them stay on the course in the hope that the course itself would do this for them. So when they met, to the cheers of several thousand spectators, which the drivers heard on the radios inside their cars, relayed to them by courtesy of Radio Shelp, they merely formed a column of line, kept strictly to their own side of the road, and passed each other in good order. In Shelp itself all fighting had temporarily stopped so that both government and insurrectionary/Cronacian forces could listen to the progress of the competition.

The westbound cars, for a while numerically superior to the eastbound, lost four cars in a series of collisions while descending Death Hill, almost catapulting down it on coming out of Switchback Corner —as if they hadn't expected it, though they had all raced on the course before, so the commentator said. The eastbound team was the visiting Cronacian side, and when the next time round it came close to the westbound Nihilon Zap United, three of its members formed up after the main Nihilon body had passed, and charged a straggler. But the straggler evaded them so cleverly that all three Cronacian cars hit the wall, shot back from it, and met in mutual collision just off the track. This was clearly a disaster for the visiting team, for they now had only six cars left against seven.

Edgar's arms ached from holding the binoculars. The game was so thrilling that he could not bear to put them down. His hat had been knocked to the ground by people pressing from behind, and the heat of the afternoon sun drew torrents of sweat from him. But his eyes were meshed to the two groups of vehicles, one red and the other blue, now approaching each other for the fourth time.

The Cronacians suddenly developed more powerful acceleration than the Nihilon cars, and taking the line in flank, managed to crash through and create a pile-up that deprived the Nihilon ranks of three of their number. To get their revenge, three Nihilon cars stayed behind and turned round in the middle of the track so as to follow in the rear of the Cronacians who, suddenly on Death Hill, realised too late that they had enemy cars in front as well as at their rear. This foul trick caused them to fight, surrounded as they were, with great fury, but the disadvantage was so great, the surprise so complete, that only a single car escaped the battle, while the four Nihilonians came out unscathed.

The chase began, to get the last Cronacian driver. But he was brave and skilful, the ace-Zapsmasher of Cronacia. Along the bonnet of his car were painted twenty-seven miniature red Zaps to indicate the number of such cars he had so far destroyed. Clearly, his demise would be a great victory, and the crowd screamed and hooted for his blood, but the four Nihilonian drivers were unable to corner him. The Cronacian had a fair amount of space on his side, and he used it to manoeuvre out of any tight spot the Nihilonians might try to force him into. His death appeared to be certain however, though during half an hour of frantic evasions he must have been plotting a fine ruse to escape his fate.

When the Nihilonians at last managed to drive his battered and steaming car into a corner at the eastern foot of Death Hill, a Pug 107 jet-fighter of the Cronacian airforce, after a radio-plea by the driver in his car, suddenly roared low over the spectator stands, tipping its wings into a sharp descent over the actual course.

Nothing could have been more dramatic, more unexpected. Edgar

149

saw crimson ropes of rocket-flame spurting from each wing, and a bubble of fire exploding at the line of Nihilon Zaps. The solitary Cronacian car crawled out of smoke and ruin, and went singed but unharmed up Death Hill, putting itself in the clear while the Pug did another quick circuit and finished off its Nihilon enemies. Only one car got clear of the track, and drove at speed under the spectator stands. The pilot, with great magnanimity, did not bomb him there, but circled until he made a dash towards the Shelp road, where he blew him into a culvert.

The Pug flew low over the course, tipping its wings in a victory salute, before disappearing back towards Cronacia. The crowd descended with a great roar towards the course, intending to kill the Cronacian drivers who, however, thwarted this vengeful desire by piling into three salvageable cars and driving off towards the mountains. Those spectators who hadn't joined in this move were cheering and clapping at the end of the festivities, and beginning to leave the grounds, highly satisfied at the day's upheavals.

Edgar found Mella asleep on the boat-trolley, and woke her so that she could start towing him towards Nihilon City. The chill of evening was already biting through his thin suit, as the final yellow film of sunlight edged the rimline of the mountains. He called to Mella for his overcoat, and she fastened it around him with her own scarf. 'Won't you be chilly?'

'I keep warm by pulling,' she said. 'We'll go on for an hour, then stop by the roadside. I shall make a fire to cook your supper.'

'You're wonderful,' he said, settling back comfortably, dozing to the regular rock of the cart, body warm and face healthily cold at the onset of Nihilon night.

One-door Zaps were eating through his dreams and bones. Then he was driving one towards the stars, till it hit the sun, and turned over when he pressed the doorknob with his foot. He dropped through the single door, into the free-fall of space. A planet grabbed his arm, and swung him against the studs of the Milky Way.

Mella was screaming, and a jolt that went with it finally woke him up. A thin man of medium height, wearing overalls and a rather expensive, finely-cut jacket, aimed a revolver as he lay on the ground: 'You're under arrest.'

A sickle moon curved above the man's cap and the mountain crestline. Edgar felt as if his back had been broken in the fall, but he was able to stand up and comfort Mella, who was sobbing against the boat-trolley.

'We insurrectionists are taking your property. You will be paid in full next week when we have formed a government. The name of the currency has yet to be decided, and so has the price of your property.'

They were opening his boxes in the lamplight, and laying his survey instruments gently on the ground. The man in charge examined them, after making sure that his prisoners were well guarded. Mella turned to Edgar and took him in her arms, her tears wetting his face. 'I'm sorry, my love,' she said. 'It was an ambush, and I could do nothing. But don't worry, we'll get through.'

The ringleader was studying Edgar's maps with interest, spreading each one out for discussion with his friends, as if to base future plans on them. During the prolonged talk, they were avidly eating the provisions that Mella had bought with such effort in Shelp. The chief of the group said to Edgar: 'We are extremely grateful for your contribution of surveying and cartographic equipment. Now we can begin to form our general staff on a scientific basis. We have waited for you for many months, but you came exactly on time. Our overseas headquarters put the right material into your luggage, so when you return, please tell them how thankful we all are. The guidebook you want to write will be so complete that no description of our newly liberated country will ever be bettered. I hope that your four colleagues who also came to Nihilon are carrying out their missions with the same degree of success. Within a year, Nihilon will be a different country. We'll even change its name. Order will be positive, law will be rigorous, chaos will be eliminated, nihilism will be banned. Nihilon City will be called Truth. The port of Shelp (our second largest conurbation) will be renamed Fact. We will be objective, just, able, honest. And you will always be an honoured guest because, with your four colleagues, you are contributing to the insurrection. In the main square of Truth we shall erect a group of statues to the Eternal Pentacle, those travellers who helped the nation to regain its dignity.'

'If it means bringing order into this mad country, then I'm glad I've been able to help you,' Edgar said, wondering how he could escape from such pompous bandits. To judge by their faces it seemed impossible that they would ever build good roads, or get trains to run on time. In any case, he saw now that he had been used as an unwitting dupe of the insurrection by the publishing company back home, and this put him into a self-deprecating frame of mind, and an ill-temper which came close to self-pity. But he was consoled by the fact that Mella's tears had dried during the leader's speech. She put her arms around Edgar, saying how proud she was that her sweetheart was also a hero who would help to save her country from ruin, and thereby restore the good name of her father, President Took, to the history books of Nihilon.

Chapter Twenty-four

The town of Amrel, perched on a steep hill beyond the river, slept in the midday sun. Brought closer by the lens of Benjamin's binoculars, birds circled over red roofs and sandstoned walls, exactly as when he had abandoned it twenty-five years ago to the advancing forces of nihilism.

Members of his insurrectionary column were spread under cover in the barley-fields on either side of the road, while the headquarters caravan of his Thundercloud Estate car was hidden behind some trees. He sweated as he lay on the hot stony soil, trying to formulate some plan by which to recapture the unsuspecting town.

Only an immediate attack had any chance of succeeding. His column of six hundred men was well equipped with rifles and machine guns, but several thousand Nihilist fanatics were thought to be in Amrel. He decided therefore to drive his Thundercloud, with four other soldiers inside, over the bridge and up into the centre of the town. Posing as ordinary tourists, they would occupy the post-office, and turn it into a fortress. Five minutes later, with all attention focused there, a bridgehead would be secured from below, from which two companies would be launched into the town. A further force would by-pass Amrel to the north and establish blocking positions on the Nihilon City road so as to deal with any Nihilists attempting to retreat in that direction. This plan left him with no reserves should anything go wrong, but Benjamin thought this was a risk they had to take. In case of defeat, the survivors were to regroup in the eastern mountains.

He drove towards the bridge on a calm fine day that was full of the soft heat of spring, ripening barley on either side waving in the ever-provident earth. There was a new hotel by the river bank, and people dining on the terrace looked at Benjamin's car with interest as it went by. Many were Nihilist officials wearing black bowler hats, with guns by their tables, and singing drunkenly.

Beyond the first half of the long bridge, standing on low land between two arms of the river, was a garage repair workshop, with lorries and tractors parked outside that, after the battle, Benjamin would use to inaugurate a motorised column for reconnaisance and vanguard operations. The narrow bridge had low walls on either side, and he drove across slowly, admiring the packed mass of the old town on the hillside above—one of the tourist gems of Nihilon, he would say in his guidebook.

It seemed as if his life were living itself all over again. Through the fully opened windows came the same smells of dust and food, river water and kerosene that had assailed him so long ago. In spite of the neat and bellicose plan about to be carried out, he felt as if he were in fact going into the town as a peaceful and enquiring tourist. Only the rifles and machine guns lying about the bottom of the car told him that this was not so. He felt calm enough, yet sweat was pouring from him, and his hands around the steering wheel slid a little too much for safety. Life is one mistake after another, and he wondered whether this would be his last, though he consoled himself with the fact all mistakes are different, which at least made them interesting.

Beyond the bridge they passed the café, and a dismal-looking shop which had a notice chalked on its door saying: NO NIHILISTS SERVED HERE. This seemed hopeful for his cause, as he turned off the main road, went under an archway, and on up the steep cobblestoned street. A few housewives were about, and one or two old men, but the town was empty compared to when he had last been there.

They emerged into the large space at the top of the hill, and parked outside the three-storey stone post-office which overlooked the town. Grass grew in parts of the deserted square where the cobblestones had been worn or kicked away, and in the middle was an abandoned fairground roundabout, its machinery rusty, its wood rotting, its canvas awning blown into strips by the continual breeze. A large public clock struck the hour ten minutes late.

Benjamin and two of his companions walked up the post-office steps, heavily laden with guns and ammunition, as if intending to pack them up inside and send them registered to friends. The other two had taken a heavy machine gun to the opposite building in order to enfilade the square when they were attacked.

Inside the post-office Benjamin pointed his rifle at the three elderly and sleepy clerks, and his assistants quickly bolted the main heavy door. While waiting for them to search and clear the place he read a notice which said: 'Foreign visitors are warned by the Nihilon postal authorities not to send any valuables by registered mail. The prominent stamping and labelling of such items serves only to mark them out for theft by our diligent and honest employees. To ensure that a letter will reach its destination, the visitor had better post by ordinary mail, and send two copies in order that one may get there.'

On an upper floor they opened loopholes from the windows. He looked at his watch. The bridge should be crossed by now. As if to confirm it, the first shots were heard. He hurried on to the roof, getting out by ladder and skylight, feeling competent in command, fit again in body and soul.

Though the bridge was captured, the hotel still held out, so that his two companies lost heavily getting over the river, and seemed in danger of being cut off. A battalion of Nihilist soldiers formed up in the square before going off to repel the attack. They did not know that the post-office was occupied, and Benjamin, when the whole force was in range, gave the order to open fire, signalling for the second machine gun to join in.

Few of them escaped. He perceived that their training must have been bloodily unrealistic, for they ran blindly to the attack with no order or system, fired without cover, and stood up to sing the incongruous national anthem that had so grated his nerves at the frontier, and which he was glad to blast out of their throats.

All over the town, a constant dull ripple of noise sounded, as if it were heavily raining in some far-off part of the country. It seemed like a dream, because he was tired. The exhaustion was only beginning, but reality would break through it, even though the tiredness was bound to increase. The bridge, the hotel, and the garage were now captured, and shooting was going on beyond the town as well, where retreating Nihilists were trying to make their way towards Nihilon City, or into the Athelstan Alps.

A way had yet to be made from the river to the main square, and Benjamin began to worry. He noticed a field-gun being hauled up a side street by a tractor. The purr of the engine brought vividly to mind his childhood spent on a farm. He thought this was because of the gun, since he had played with such models in those far-off days, but he knew it was the sound of the tractor, which made him see vividly the one that his own father had driven.

The building shook, as if a giant thump had hit every wall from the inside. He got downstairs to meet a blinding flash that pushed him down to the stone floor and tried to hold him there. The main door had burst from its hinges. Ordering the machine-gunners to cover him, he took a pair of grenades and dashed into the square.

He fell vomiting among the dead and wounded. More shells were exploding at the post-office walls and windows, so that he did not feel any less safe where he was. But he had no desire to go on, and did not know what to do next, though without wanting to, he leapt up and ran zig-zag towards the gun. Rifle bullets cut the air around him, but the dream had taken him over for his own protection, and he worked within its halo of safety and light. He threw his first grenade and fell to the ground.

A machine gun heavily threaded its string of noise from the nearest window, but Benjamin's alert gunner returned fire from the post-office roof even before the end of its burst. His grenade exploded during it, an increase of pandemonium joined by a final shell as his grenade blew one of the gun-wheels to pieces.

The survivors of the crew ran to him, and instead of the expected revolver-shot in his body he looked up and saw that they wanted to surrender. One of them leapt for freedom in the opposite direction, but fell against the bullets of the insurrectionists advancing along the street.

Helped by his prisoners, Benjamin staggered back to the post-office. His clothes were in tatters. He was covered with blood. At the steps he shook himself, paused for a moment with bent head, and eyes shut tight. The black-dot flag, and the hammer-and-chisel banner, were lowered from the flagpole of the town hall.

He straightened himself, tried to pull in his stomach, drew back his head, and walked into the building.

At the postmaster's large desk he spread out his map of Nihilon, while teleprinters in the next room sent the news of Amrel's liberation by the Benjamin Smith Brigade. Information had come in that the port of Shelp was also in insurrectionist hands, while another message claimed that several areas of Nihilon City had been secured. Some mysterious commander-in-chief, signing himself the Professor, had ordered his brigade to advance on Agbat, an important town and road junction on the railway connecting Nihilon to the northern Cronacian frontier. The way to treat the Nihilists, said the professor's teleprinter message, which struck Benjamin as being somewhat garrulous, was to hit them before they knew what had hit them, so that they wouldn't get up and argue. No one could win an argument with a Nihilist, so it was best never to let one start. End of text.

The local commander was brought in, a tall, elderly man with grey hair, and a haggard unhappy face. Apart from being in the army, he was also the mayor, the police chief, the hotel owner, and the post-master, whose desk Benjamin now occupied. His rank was that of colonel, and he laid his black bowler hat by Benjamin's hand: 'If you're going to shoot me, please honour me by doing it now. I couldn't stand the indignity of a trial.'

'You forget,' said Benjamin, 'that we represent legality and order, progress, and honesty.'

The colonel pressed an anguished hand to his forehead. 'Oh, my God!'

Benjamin knew him as the man to whom he had delivered the town twenty-five years ago, in return for a bus and the safety of his group. Nevertheless, in spite of his crimes, he tried to calm him down. 'We couldn't possibly shoot you, in any case.'

The colonel shuddered, and became even more distressed. 'So you propose to hand me over to the justice of the people, do you? You progressives are even more diabolically cruel than we are.'

'I'm not sure what's going to happen to you yet,' said Benjamin. 'I have too much work to do.'

The man had tears in his eyes. 'I'm tired of life, whatever you decide. For years I've been disillusioned with nihilism, at having to get up every morning and invent more novelties of disorder for the pampered populace when President Nil forgets to send his own sug-gestions through. I've known for a long time that it was retrograde and immoral to live under such a system. My wife has often seen me break-ing my heart at the waste and burden of it all. I've been secretly praying for a safe and orderly existence, but I was so influenced by President Nil and his philosophy, which said that life should be a great lawless adventure, that I never knew how to try and change it. It's been a thankless task. I've frequently prayed for a few hectares of soil in a safe mountain area, where I could live the life of a simple peasant. I admire and envy you insurrectionists trying to change all this. You don't know how lucky you are, being the saviours of our country, the bringers of honesty and progress. I certainly wish you success in your venture. I know you intend to kill me, whatever you say, but if I were to stay alive, there's nothing I would want to do more than to help you in your great and honourable task.'

'We need all the help we can get,' Benjamin admitted. 'If you're serious about it, go to the barber's and get your head shaved, then buy a pair of workmens' overalls, and come back to join our ranks—under another name, of course. If you can persuade other Nihilist soldiers to do the same, providing they have a genuine change of heart, we shall welcome them.'

Colonel Amrel reached forward and held Benjamin's hand. 'Thank you, dear sir, thank you. I am old now but I'm still a good soldier. Shooting and looting is the life for me!'

'Any of that,' said Benjamin, though not too harshly, 'and you'll be shot yourself. My column will assemble in the square, so make sure you are there with your men.'

The room was empty. His danger, for the moment, was over. His arms and legs were shaking. He tried to hold them still. Power, to Benjamin, was most satisfying when he returned someone's life to them, after refusing to take it away when he had the right and sometimes the duty to do so. There was nothing more sublime than this. But the weight in his chest seemed to have become displaced, and he walked to the window in an effort to control himself. He grabbed a high-backed chair so as not to fall. There were tears on his face. The uncanny circle of time had struck him with a hammer, as if to snap his spine at the crucial moment of action. He held on to the window-bars and looked through to the square. Blood patches and pieces of rag remained. Men stood beside the five lorries to talk and smoke. They would head for Agbat in the darkness, taking all night to get there, since the road was bad. With lorries, they would capture the place at dawn. Such thoughts stopped his limbs shaking when he walked back to his desk.

Chapter Twenty-five

The long train crawled and switched upon hairpin bends, continuing its night journey into the outlying spurs of the Athelstan Alps. From there, a sinuous pass between the mountains would take it gradually down to the central plain of Nihilon.

When Jaquiline climbed from between Cola's sheets, the train shook so violently that she almost fell, her breasts flattening on the side of the bunk, while she clung as if a hundred foot drop opened below. But her bare feet touched the floor, and when she bent to get into her own bed, her arm jerked back, for in the dimmest of lights she saw a strange person lying there, presumably as fast asleep as Cola was. Sick with fear, she felt blindly around for her clothes and began to get dressed.

Her impulse was to pull the communication cord, and have him carried off screaming under some accusation or other, for after her unpleasant experience with the police chief at the frontier, she had no wish to confront another Nihilonian male. But she knew that sleep would be impossible whether she stopped the train or not, for to do so in a place like Nihilon was clearly to risk the unexpected, either in reprisals for a semi-criminal act, or in some form of brutal unsuitable assistance that would do her no good at all. And since her life wasn't in danger, perhaps it was better to do nothing. In any case, he had threatened no harm yet.

He stirred under the blanket when the light went on, showing his grey close-cropped head, and groaned, while she held her breath. Then he grunted, about to wake up. It puzzled her how he had got into her compartment, until the unbearable heat of embarrassment ran down her body at the thought that he must have come in while she had been on the upper bunk with Cola. He had obviously seen only one person in the compartment, and so took the bottom bunk for himself. She shrank against the sink when his grey eyes opened wide from an emaciated face. 'If you call out,' he said, though in no way menacing, 'I'll kill you.'

Her hand drew away from the communication cord, angry at having decided to use it only now, when it was too late. He meant what he said, so she became less afraid, and stared back at him, openly curious, though her hand kept touch with the false book and its loaded gun. 'What are you doing here?' she asked, lighting a cigarette.

He sat on the edge of the bed. 'Give me one, and I'll tell you. Thank you. This train's too slow. I'm going to Nihilon City, that's all.'

'So am I.' She held her lighter under his cigarette. 'Though it's impossible to say when it will get there.'

When the flame went out he took it from her. 'Double speed,' he said, 'that's the first thing we'll do. Double on the railways, and half on the roads. This nightmare's got to stop. I'm just out of prison. I was awarded twenty-five years because I exposed the manager of the factory I worked at for swindling. The factory was going bankrupt, so I made a formal complaint. I had irrefutable proof that he was ruining the firm, but when I presented it I was arrested, and given twenty-five years as a misguided idealist. Strangely enough, even though the manager kept on with his dishonesty, the firm did not go bankrupt. It even prospered after I was sent to prison, so I hear. People won't rebel against this government, because they see that God is on the side of the Nihilists. Do you have any food?'

She passed a packet of biscuits from her handbag. 'How did you get out of prison?'

'I talked my way out. From the moment I got in I began talking about my idealistic principles. I decided that since I'd been sent away for honesty, I'd continue to be honest, and I'd try to persuade everybody else at the prison to be honest. I calculated that most of them were already honest in any case, otherwise they wouldn't be there. I didn't expect this to be acceptable to the authorities though, because they hoped to reform the inmates into becoming swindlers and tricksters. I saw that I had nothing to lose, because it seemed to me that if they didn't want me to ruin their good work they'd have to throw me out. And if the prison authorities were persuaded by what I was trying to say, they'd have to admit that none of us should be in prison in any case.

'I talked so much I hardly slept or ate during the whole year I was there. The prisoners were swayed from their newly acquired rules of villainy. The governor and his soldiers saw how right I was, and came over to my side. They all wanted to do some work—to work, understand?'

The word 'work' touched some deep emotion in him. The lamps of his half-buried eyes seemed about to burst, but he drew his shaking hands across to dim them. 'I don't suppose you know, being a foreigner, that it's always been hard to get people to work in Nihilon. Naturally, nihilism and work are not compatible, but President Nil, damn him, came up with the following solution—many years ago, now. A man was granted permission to kill somebody if he paid a hundred thousand klipps into the private account of President Nil at the State Bank. On receipt of this payment the man—or woman, though not many women were interested—was given a revolver and a Killing Certificate, with the name of the person inscribed on it whom he wished to put an end to. So everyone has an incentive to work, and save, because there is no one, in this country at any rate, who doesn't have someone he wants to kill. Many people fervently saved in order to get their hundred thousand, and therefore a Killing Certificate. There was no need to produce houses or cars for them to spend their money on. True, a lot of people die, and sometimes whole families are wiped out, but people are cheap. Even the birthrate seemed to go up when this scheme got going. There was one sad case though of a poor man who worked all his life to save a hundred thousand klipps, and just as he was on his way to the bank with his last thousand he had a heart attack and died. Yet again, another man who had saved his money went to the state bank and duly collected his Killing Certificate and gun. Then, with happiness and murder in his heart, he went outside to lay in wait for his enemy. But the man he wanted to kill had got there half an hour before, and had already collected *his* killing certificate and gun. Lying in wait, he shot our happy saver dead as he came down the steps.

'This stupid law, in fact, has killed a great many people in our country, even more than if we had been at war. And as you can imagine, it's the best, go-ahead people who have suffered by it. The knowledge that such things ought to be changed gave me the strength to go on talking so long in prison. When I was successful beyond my wildest dreams we abolished the prison, and formed ourselves into a revolutionary committee. Hearing that fighting has broken out with

Cronacia, and that there is trouble in Nihilon City, I'm going to offer my talking experience to the insurrectionary forces, which I've no doubt they'll need when they've won. Those at the prison are taking over the surrounding area for the new movement. So if you don't mind I'd like to get some sleep, because we'll reach Agbat in the morning and there may be some fighting there. Put out the light, please.'

He fell asleep immediately, worn down by so much talking, and as Jaquiline stretched herself on the hard and chilly floor she didn't see much hope that conditions for women would improve when the new régime took over, though her fatigue was so great that she was soon lost in darkening dreams.

The slow-running train jolted her half-awake against the lower bunk, and she heard the banging chains of goods wagons passing in the night. She wondered where they were, when noise as if a bomb had exploded in a drain pipe shook the carriage. The door was pulled open, and lights switched on. Two burly men in police uniforms stood at the doorway with pointed revolvers. Cola, a sheet around her chest, sat up and screamed, more to do what was expected, it seemed to Jaquiline, than get anywhere by her alarm.

'You'd better dress,' one of the men said. 'It's the Groves of Aspron for you.'

'We're going to Nihilon City,' Jaquiline told them as she stood up.

'It's Aspron for you, as well,' the other man laughed, reaching into the lower bunk, where the escaped prisoner would have slept through the disturbance if he hadn't now been punched into waking up 'As for you, you'll be shot at the next station.'

He stood by the door, head down as if helplessly ashamed at his recent escape. The train stopped, and Jaquiline felt she had nothing to lose, for while the policemen's pistols were lowered, she lifted hers from the book-box and aimed it at them both. 'Now, you go to Nihilon City,' she said to the escaped prisoner.

'I couldn't,' he said, 'they've caught me. The world's in ruins at my feet.'

'If you don't go,' she cried, her hand trembling with rage at his sudden collapse, 'I'll kill you. Get off while the train's stopped.'

'Don't make me,' he pleaded. But he caught the fanatical shine in her eyes, and when she lifted the gun to fire he pushed between the two policemen and went along the corridor.

She smiled, watching him go, and Cola's hand reached slyly down, snatching her gun away, while one of the policemen knocked her back against the window. It took time to recover from his blow, and to realise what had happened. Now regarding her as a totally un-scrupulous person, he pointed a gun at her, while the other man searched her luggage. 'Not only does she hide a dangerous political prisoner,' he said, 'and help him to escape, but she also carries wood in her luggage, which points to the fact that she's an arsonist and a foreign spy. There'll be a big trial in Nihilon City for this.'

Her face had gone pale at such blatant betrayal by Cola, now jostling her as she hurriedly dressed. 'I had to do it,' she said, 'for the sake of my son and husband. They won't send me to Aspron now. All those sessions of analysis would have broken my spirit, really they would. I can't tell you how sorry I am.'

From the pain in her voice Jaquiline knew that she'd had no alter-native, though she was by no means reconciled at being the one to suffer because of Cola's distress. In any case, all she wanted her to do right now was stop whining—which she did. The train travelled more freely, and Jaquiline saw faint edges of moonlight above the black mark of the mountain crest.

Carrying their luggage, they were forced along the corridor to-wards the door. The train stopped again, by a hut which served as an isolated wayside-station, and Jaquiline went first, then helped Cola down, already forgetting the bad turn she had done her, since they both seemed to be equal now that they were still prisoners.

The policemen shot the locks away, and inside the hut was a long table, two chairs, and a leather-upholstered seat along one wall under the small window. Jaquiline was glad to get out of the chill wind, and looked gladly towards the fireplace.

The bald policeman, revealed as such when he removed his hat, pulled a handful of old timetable leaflets from a hook on the wall and crumpled them into the fireplace, while his friend, who had thick black hair, took the bundles of wood from Jaquiline's suitcase and laid them on top. A blaze was soon kindled, and both policemen put their hats into the flames. Underneath their tunics, which they removed, were civilian jackets, and they now looked more like ordinary people. Both the police jackets were silently folded and placed on the fire. 'Go outside,' the bold one said to Jaquiline, 'and get some coal. There's a heap of it by the side of the hut.'

'So you're not policemen?' she said.

The one with black hair laughed. 'We never were. My friend here is a shopkeeper called Peter. I'm a master carpenter, and my name is Paul. We both won an Adventure Permit from the government, so we're allowed to do all this. When we get to Agbat we'll have to go to the mayor's office to get the section torn from our certificates which says "Abduct Two Women". We've already qualified for the clause which says "Take Policemen's Clothes". When we've finished with you we go on to the next panel, which tells us to "Steal a Car". The adventure's only just begun, and we're enjoying it very much, aren't we, Peter?'

Peter laughed, and tried to kiss Cola, who pushed him away.

'Let's get the coal,' said Jaquiline.

'If you try to escape when you're outside,' Peter said, 'we'll come and hunt you. We get extra marks on our score for "Hunt Two Women", so nothing would please us better. Those awarded the highest score at the end of the year get another ticket the year after, and we're doing very well so far.'

'There won't be any next year,' Jaquiline told them. 'Your country is about to have a revolution.' They sat on the floor by the fire, Peter taking his boots off, and laughed loudly at her threat, which seemed irrelevant in such an enjoyable situation.

Jaquiline and Cola brought several large lumps of coal into the hut, and they were considerably blackened by such work. Their two captors then decided to lock the door for the night, and were soon fast asleep from the heat of the fire, and also no doubt from their adventures of the last few days. Jaquiline only half slept.

Eager for more thrills, Peter and Paul prodded them awake with their toecaps so that they could set out for Agbat, where they intended to register the exploits so far achieved. A faint streak in the east gradually made the stars go paler. While the two men slaked themselves on Cola inside the hut, Jaquiline watched the birth of a new day. The first light changed to a band of gold on the mountainous horizon. Each lofty peak in succession was tinged with a roseate blush. Shadows gradually melted away, revealing forests, spurs, fields, and villages, in emerald green and patches of dull brown. From grey cold night the sun suddenly burst from behind the mountains and flooded the whole landscape with light and warmth, as Cola came out of the hut smiling shyly, followed by her two licensed adventurers.

Thus the orange sun from Cronacia warmed them as they walked along. Cola and Jaquiline went hand in hand, dazed by exhaustion, bedraggled, without luggage, their clothes and faces black with coal. Jaquiline reflected that nothing had gone right since crossing that seemingly harmless frontier. It was almost as if she had come to this country in an unwitting act of self-destruction, having placed herself in a situation where, threatened and helpless, there was no one to whose good nature she could appeal, not even a consulate she could run to and find refuge in.

They went along a path by the single-track railway, no houses in sight, though here and there were areas bearing clear plough marks, and groves of scarecrow trees that passed for orchards. When she stopped to take a stone out of her shoe, Peter pushed her on. 'We're late already,' he snapped. 'The office will be closed if we don't hurry.'

'It can't even be opened yet,' she said.

'Don't argue. We want to register, then we'll be awarded tickets for a hotel.'

'What fun we'll have!' Paul laughed. While they were discussing who would rape Jaquiline first, Cola explained to her that the office would indeed be closed if they didn't get there soon, because it stayed open all night, and shut early in the morning. Jaquiline reproached her with wanting to hurry, in that case, pulling her arm so that they would go more slowly.

'Why?' asked Cola, her mouth round and hungry for some great experience that certainly would never satisfy her. 'I want us to get there so that we can claim a hotel ticket for seventy-two hours. It isn't often an ordinary patriotic Nihilonian woman like me gets such a chance. It certainly will be better than Aspron. And I'll at least have a romantic memory when I'm thrown into the despair of a cure. It's awful to be cured, I hear. That's the worst part of Aspron. It brings on an awful feeling of melancholia. People have been known to kill themselves after a cure, but I won't, I know I won't, because at least I shall have this brief encounter to look back on.'

The idea of being passed like a parcel from one brutish Nihilist to another appalled Jaquiline, and an urgent feeling of sickness rose in her throat. Where at first there had been laughter and good fellowship between Peter and Paul, they now stood bellowing into each other's faces. 'I demand the tall, fair one,' said Peter. But Paul wanted her too, and Jaquiline felt anything but flattered by their urgent desires. Cola turned pale and vampiric, as if about to rend her with jealousy. They stopped and looked back. Peter suggested tossing a coin, and when Paul won he was accused of cheating.

'Let the clerk who fills out our hotel voucher decide,' Peter said, standing glumly by, hat in hand.

'You'll bribe him. I know your sort,' Paul scoffed.

Peter looked at his watch. 'It's too late. It's eight o'clock. They've closed.'

Paul was almost in tears. 'Now what do we do?' Jaquiline was too tired to feel joy at the good news. 'We'll have to wait until ten o'clock tonight,' he cried.

The path turned into a lane, with the imprints of carts and motorcars on it. Houses were scattered over the hills. A young man walked by, his face pale and sweating. He had a short dark beard, and his eyes were turned from them, as if he were embarrassed. Behind came two young boys, possibly his sons, one of ten years old who carried a bundle of brushwood on his head, another of about six who had a filthy half-filled sack on his shoulder. It was a depressing sight, but at least they were people. She was choking from thirst, feeble with hunger and lack of sleep, and was almost ready to welcome a bed under any conditions.

She felt more than ever menaced on hearing the two men whisper. Both heads were close, and she saw the sweat on their skin, and the half-hidden workings of their lips. Peter laughed softly, and spoke such unmistakable evil that she began to run.

'Come back!' Cola shouted treacherously, before either of the men saw her escape. The lane went downhill, more of a road now, and a few hundred metres away lay the first houses of Agbat. There was a sharp explosion like a firework. A chip of stone flew off a boulder by the roadside and struck her forehead. The pain was icy, but she couldn't stop, with the footsteps of either Peter or Paul drumming after her.

A train whistle sounded, a sharp comforting civilised note cutting the warm morning air. Blood ran down her face, and she tasted it on her lips. If only she could reach the houses. She saw it was impossible. Who would help her, anyway? She might even be worse off. A shoe left her foot, and she kicked the other free, to run in her stockings. Cola and the men behind shouted again for her to stop. They didn't mean it; they were her friends, they said. No harm would come to her. Another bullet hit the trunk of a tree, but she ran, hair flying loose, filled with dread but not caring if they killed her, yet too frightened to consider whether or not it was worth dying for.

For some reason she wanted it to rain. She stumbled, feet cut, and her stockings in rags. Houses slid out of sight. A weight suddenly fell on her, and it felt as if her back were broken when she tried to rise. Her face was pressed into the dust, her flowing tears changing it to mud.

Magically, the pressure was off. Whoever had sought to crush her bones rolled to one side, and someone else was running. There were further shots, and a scream of shock. She was afraid to get up and see the cause of these mysterious noises, unable to believe the danger was over. But the man at her side lay still, his face turned. She kept her head down in the silence, as if more danger might be coming.

A hard blunt object pressed itself in her side. When she looked, the man took his boot away and bent down. He held a rifle, and wore a sort of blue overall. 'Get up and follow me,' he said. His head was shaved, and his face was hollow of cheek. She stumbled, unable to stand properly, and though his eyes were expressionless and staring, as if they had not yet fully comprehended the last sight they had seen, he held a hand out to help her.

Chapter Twenty-six

Enjoying the civil war, from behind the bullet-proof glass of the café by the main square of Nihilon City, Richard decided not to open the large briefcase which the professor had left with him. At least, not before he had called for another bottle of Nihilitz.

'Yes, general,' the waiter said, reminding him too abruptly of the new post that had been thrust upon him by the insurrectionary forces. He had no intention of becoming a soldier in this squalid power-switch, though he felt sure that if he were to step outside, the dissidents would certainly recognise him, and confirm him in his new post with such celebration that he might not survive it. 'I hope you have a good campaign, sir,' said the waiter. 'The weather is perfect for it. It rained last time, and the revolution fizzled out. Those taking part put down their guns and went home.'

'When was that?' Richard asked, alarmed by this sudden revelation of volatility in the Nihilonian populace.

'Two years ago, sir. But it wasn't really serious. Those who ran took their guns home with them, and it was said later that the Rain Revolution—we have a great sense of humour here, sir—was only a dress rehearsal for the real one that was to come, which is now. Things seem to be much better organised this time, I'm glad to say.' He looked through the glass and rubbed his hands gleefully at flames jerking out of a building across the square.

'I suppose you'll be taking part,' Richard said, with a little irony, 'when you've finished work?'

'No, general,' the waiter smiled. 'I'll go home and watch it on television. I expect the programmes will run all night if the firing goes on. I'll go out into the street with my flag though, when it's all over, you may be sure of that. My wife's at home stitching it together now.' From the door that led to the main hall of the café, he turned and added: '*She's* the creative one of the family, sir!'

People went in and out as if it were a normal day of the week. He watched them coming across the square, calmly picking their way over débris, and the occasional corpse that the well-trained men of the ambulance service had not yet been able to move.

After a fiery and comforting drink of Nihilitz, he delved into the briefcase. By weight it contained more than papers, and he took out a revolver and a box of ammunition, as well as a belt and holster, and a sort of collapsible tram-conductor's hat with a red band between the peak and the crown, which he assumed was for his own general's head.

The largest map, when he unfolded it, was an official publication for Nihilon Army Command, a coloured representation of the country on the one-million scale, but stated at the top left-hand corner to be a provisional edition which was only to be used with extreme caution, as all detail on it was totally unreliable. Thinking of his previous experience in Ekeret Square, when his precious town-plan had been torn to pieces, he hurriedly fastened on the revolver holster, and loaded the gun, in case some fanatical map-deprived horde should try the same trick again.

He examined the map which, for a place like Nihilon, was as pretty a piece of cartography as you could ever wish to see. The system of relief, by contours, brought the whole land into instant perspective. It was mountainous, except for the great central plain on which most of the large towns were situated. Nihilon was bordered on three sides by rugged coast, except for a wide isthmus which joined it to Cronacia, and which was crossed by a belt of high mountains. The country was nearly five hundred kilometres from west to east, and four hundred from north to south, giving it an area of approximately 200,000 square kilometres. With such a preponderance of precipitous mountain it was easy to see why, throughout its history, Nihilon had been plagued by terrible floods. In fact, it was difficult to see why the central plain wasn't permanently inundated.

If the map was accurate, communications seemed to be in a very rudimentary state—especially the roads. One highway (on paper at any rate) appeared to run from the southern frontier to Shelp, and then up the Nihil Valley to Nihilon City. He was happy not to have been chosen for the land approach, like Benjamin in his Thundercloud, and Adam the poet on his bicycle. He wondered also how Edgar had fared after disembarking at Shelp, and Jaquiline Sulfer who was supposed to reach Nihilon City this afternoon by train.

To the north of the town were the Athelstan Alps, whose highest peak, of over four thousand metres, was Mount Nihilon. On a large plateau to the south of this range was a place called Tungsten, joined by the only other modern highway leading up to it from Nihilon City. On the margin of the map was a note to say that at Tungsten there was a rocket base, and that the first Nihilon spaceship was to be launched from it in two days.

After a further and necessary swig of Nihilitz, Richard saw from the typewritten sheets that he was in charge of a column that, the day after tomorrow (by which time all fighting in Nihilon City should be over), would form the left wing of a general advance on Tungsten. The centre was already on its way there from Shelp, and the right wing would move up from Agbat. His orders demanded that the launching of the rocket into space must be prevented at all costs—in the name of Honour and Decency. Nihilism must not be allowed this great triumph, for what the Nihilists had been striving for in over twenty years of work and research was none other than the first pro-creative hook-up in space. In the rocket would be an athletic young man and a nubile girl who were to leave the capsule at a time specified by computer (full television coverage was to be arranged for the whole country) and copulate in space. The technical details of this were on the secret list, but the Nihilists expected a birth from this brief encounter, a child which would, on its thirteenth birthday, be crowned king or queen of the First Universal Nihilist Kingdom. It was because the revolutionaries were determined to forestall such a monstrously indecent plan that Richard had been given a key part in the advance towards Tungsten. If his column did not get there before blast-off, the propaganda effect of this victory for Nihilism would never be lived down, even if the new forces did succeed in eventually taking hold of the country.

In any case he saw that such an expedition against Tungsten would be a favourable opportunity to explore the Athelstan Alps, and so fill in more pages of his guidebook, which was why he had come to the country in the first place. With this also in mind he decided to look at those parts of the city so far untouched by the insurrection. It was midday, and the firing had lost its intensity, so he walked, somewhat giddily due to all he had drunk, along the western side of the square and into one of the avenues leading to the river.

The way there was quiet, a few people busily going home to lunch. Shop-fronts were boarded up and the burning sun gave everything a dreamy unreal touch. He brought a magazine from a kiosk, served by a woman with a bottle of Nihilitz beside her who was doing some crazy sort of four-peg knitting.

He leaned against the parapet of the long, ornate bridge, and watched the swirling oily water of the River Nihil, polluted beyond measure after flowing through the industrial complex of Nilbud. A smell of old stone and vinegar came up from it. He wrote in his guidebook-notes that the bridge was of a particularly fine construction, adding as an afterthought, and no doubt under the influence of nihilism, that the engineer who built it had thrown his wife from the middle span after its completion.

The banks on either side were steep, so he decided to call the river a gorge at this point, thinking that even the dullest country had to appear interesting in a guidebook, if you expected people to buy it. Whether they went there or not was another matter, though it was certain that few of them ever would.

He was disturbed from his stupor by the sight of a man running from the eastern end of the bridge, as if anxious to get across it and help the insurrection in Nihilon—though there was little enough firing at the moment to attract anyone. The runner had apparently passed a police-man, who now woke up and shouted: 'Come back. Stop!'

The man was wild-haired, big-eyed, his coat flying open. Another policeman, at the western end of the bridge stood in the middle of the road with his revolver pointed, so that it seemed as if the fugitive's fate was already sealed.

Richard looked on in amusement, as if the inhabitants of Nihilon only existed to provide him with continuous diversion. However, he stopped smiling when a bullet, meant for the fleeing man, shaved its way so close that it singed the hair by his temples. With the policemen closing in, the man, only a few metres away, jumped on to the parapet, then fell laughing into the river below. Sluggish circles eddied towards the concrete supports, and Richard tried to see under the surface of the water. 'Let me see your documents,' said one of the policemen, putting away his gun.

'Why did he jump into the river?' asked Richard, showing his passport.

'Suicide,' said the policeman. 'This is known as the Bridge of

171

Suicides. I have orders to shoot anyone on sight trying to commit suicide. It's a difficult job. The government doesn't like people to kill themselves, because it gives it a bad name. There's only one thing better than a dead Nihilist, and that is a live Nihilist. Also, there's a saying in Nihilon: "Stop a suicide, commit a murder". That always means better business for the police, anyway. Only last week a man was saved in the nick of time by a friend from killing himself, and next day he killed his wife. So we're trying to stamp suicide out. I shot three of them last week as they were climbing on to the parapet. It certainly slowed them down a bit. This one just now was the first this week.'

'What's the point of killing them?'

'Only way to stop them. "Died resisting arrest" looks much better than "Committed suicide". We've got our statistics to think of.' He walked away, whistling some popular Nihilonian folk-song.

Beyond the bridge was a squalid café whose exterior looked much like that of an old warehouse. A few wickerwork chairs and tables were set on the dry mud pavement outside. There was little traffic however, and, for the moment, no shooting. Richard hoped that here at least he wouldn't be recognised for the general he was, ordering a cold orange drink which, when it came, he sat back to enjoy. After writing some high-flown notes on the Bridge of Suicides, he lazily opened his magazine and read an article describing how the Future was supposed to Work for the inhabitants of Nihilon from a domestic point of view. 'Homemaking' was its title:

'After a meal, all dishes and cutlery will be thrown away, and within a few minutes new ones, of the finest porcelain and stainless steel, will come up the chute to your flat and be mechanically placed on your sideboard. There is an end to the drudgery of washing-up for Nihilists, both men and women. On taking off your clothes at night, they are to be thrown with nonchalant nihilism out of the window. These will be collected by the garbage man and, in the morning, complete new sets of identical garments will be found by the door, together with milk and newspapers. In fact,' the article concluded, 'the future has already arrived in Nihilon, because this is exactly what takes place in one of our recently constructed towns called Paradise City, whose inhabitants will be able to avail themselves of these delectable services.'

A young blond man with a beard sat nearby, and he must have seen the article that Richard was reading, for he called out: 'They never tell the real truth about Paradise City. I escaped from it a month ago, climbed over a wall and ran a machine-gun gauntlet to get free. The dishes aren't porcelain at all. They are crude earthenware. In the morning they come back broken and dirty. Everyone suspects they are the same ones they threw out, but badly patched up and stuck together. So the wily housewives clean their own dishes, and put them away carefully so that they don't break. Some housewives didn't even put them in the chute at the beginning, preferring to save the time and the risk, but they were arrested for a breach of the peace and as enemies of national endeavour.

'As for the clothes that we were told to throw out of the window, they were returned even more torn and dirty after being kicked up the stairs again by the street cleaners. In fact this experiment isn't working very well, and people in Paradise City are always trying to exchange their flats for more humble dwellings in other towns, even in the slums where life might be harder. Somehow they would feel safer there!'

'What are you doing now that you no longer live in Paradise City?'

'I'm a disgruntled young intellectual, so the government gave me a particularly difficult and thankless task. I've been assigned to find and kill the leading generals of the insurrectionary forces. I spent last week combing the surrounding area of the city, posing as a revolutionary, but it's impossible to find out who their leader is. I suspect it's because they change him so often. You're a foreigner, so you can have no idea how difficult it is for us Nihilists. I don't suppose you're even interested. But my whole future is at stake, because I've been promised a full pension for the rest of my life if I find one, and I'm only twenty-four so you can see how much it means to me. I shall just have to go on looking, because if I find him, and kill him, the whole insurrectionary movement will collapse.'

His breath stank of drink, hunger, exhaustion, and avarice. Richard had an impulse to promote him on the spot to General of the Insurrection by handing over the briefcase, simply to see the effect it would have, but he didn't do so because the position that had been so haphazardly given to him had already grown attractive by the very weight of its power. So he preferred to keep his rank for the moment, in spite of possible danger from this assassin.

'Goodbye,' said the young man, offering his hand to be shaken. 'I must hunt my enemy.'

'Good luck,' said Richard, taking it, but glad to see him walk quickly towards the Bridge of Suicides, talking to himself.

Chapter Twenty-seven

The progress wound its way from town to town, and on the wooden throne at its head sat Mella who, after the incredible hardships of her young life, was now wheeled high on a seat of honour by the soldiers of the new revolution. At first she had insisted that Edgar sit on her knee as she went along, though after argument and tears she had finally agreed that he should take his place by her side on a separate and more ordinary chair, but certainly close enough for her to reach out and take his hand whenever the motherly impulse came upon her.

Far from feeling annoyed at her milder attentions, Edgar now began to enjoy them, for having separated from his wife some years ago it was comforting once more to be the only person a woman doted on. And it was obvious to anyone that Mella cared for him alone, except during those moments when she was sadly reflecting on the fate of her father.

During their triumphant way towards Orcam, when Edgar was out of his chair and walking by Mella's mobile platform, he saw in the distance a figure pushing a wheelbarrow. Whoever it was moved slowly, for the wheelbarrow was laden with suitcases, but he eventually drew level, a man with the sleeves of his white shirt rolled up, a jacket draped over his suitcases, and a white handkerchief on his bald head as protection from the sun.

At the sight of armed men, and the medieval contraption on which Mella was seated, he moved well into the side to let them pass. Edgar noticed, by the large labels on his luggage, that they were compatriots. In other circumstances he would have taken this as a warning to keep clear, but now that Nihilon was boiling with insurrection and trouble he called out a friendly greeting. 'Where are you from?' he asked, when the man came over to him.

'I set out from Nihilon City yesterday, on a motor bike,' he was told.

'But then it broke down, so I managed to buy this wheelbarrow.' The convoy stopped to rest and eat, and while food was prepared, Edgar told the man how he had recently landed at Shelp and was on his way to Nihilon City to write a guidebook.

'I wouldn't go if I were you,' the man said. 'There's trouble there by anybody's standards. I was on holiday, but I've given it up. When I got back to the apartment I'd rented, after a stroll, I found that an artillery shell had blown half of it to pieces. So I came away, because if I'd stayed till the end of the month there'd be trouble over the inventory. They'd want to know where the wall went. You know what these Nihilists are—they're just a pack of vicious misers.'

Edgar gave him some of the convoy's food. 'Isn't it difficult to rent a flat in Nihilon City?'

He talked with his mouth full: 'I thought it would be cheaper than a hotel, you see. I tried to be cunning, by taking a furnished flat in the capital. I came by train, and got the address and key from the tourist office at the station. I can laugh about the experience now, but it wasn't funny at the time, though I suppose I was ready for a bit of an adventure.

'It was a dull day,' he went on, 'so as soon as I went into the flat, I switched on the light—and a radio started blaring. There were small loudspeakers in every room, I found. The only way to switch them off was to put the lights out. Not to be defeated, I took out my electrician's kit even before opening my luggage and adjusted the lights, so that they stayed on and the radio went off. I grinned to myself, and started to unpack. When that was finished I wanted a cup of coffee, so went into the kitchen. I filled the kettle, and when I turned on the gas-taps, music again blared through every loudspeaker. When the music stopped, they started to read the Lies.

'Well, a chap can't live that way, can he? By sheer hard labour, and a damned lot of ingenuity, I worked on that problem half the afternoon till I got some peace into the flat at last. Then I went for a walk and to buy some cigarettes. When I came back and opened the door, music came on again. It made me sweat with rage, I can tell you, but after an hour's work I found out how to stop it. Silence once more. I went into the lounge to relax, but opening the door brought the Lies on again, a long account of that dirty space-rocket due to go up soon. Every door of the flat, I discovered, switched on news or music when it was opened, and didn't turn it off when it was shut. I slaved all day and half the

night to fix every door so that it could open peacefully. I breathed a
sigh of relief and went into the lavatory for a few minutes. When I
pulled the chain, it brought the martial music back—all over the damned
place. I tell you, I wasn't all that sorry when that howitzer-shell
shattered it. You could hear the music cracking all along the street
then, but I'd given up already. I'm on my way to Shelp to get a boat
home. If there aren't any ships I'll trudge to the frontier. It's not far
from there. I wanted to get a plane back but the airport's closed. I'm
all of a sweat when I take the handle of this barrow, in case the music
should start when I push it, or bring on the Lies, which is worse. Never
again.'

'Why leave Nihilon now?' Edgar wanted to know. 'It's getting
interesting at last.'

'You won't say that when you see Nihilon City,' the man said with a
sneer, getting into the shafts of his wheelbarrow, 'that's all I can say.'

Edgar was sorry to see him go, though he couldn't have said why.
During the next day's progress the column grew to more than two
thousand soldiers, a disciplined and dedicated force which wheeled
north across the fertile central plain of Nihilon with its network or
railways, roads and canals, its numerous towns and villages.

Wherever they stayed the night, whether at some humble village
house, or on rocky ground in the open air, an almost royal bed was
laid for them, with four guards posted a little way out from each
corner. Edgar considered them to be still too close, for Mella, even
though he was exhausted by the changing scenery of the day's trek,
uninhibitedly threw off the bedclothes and coaxed him into making
love, behaving as if there were no other being within sight.

After one such connubial encounter she fell to kissing his hand tenderly, and said: 'When the war is over, my love, we shall live together, not
in the presidential palace, of which I have too many unhappy memories,
but in a new one that my grateful people will build for us.'

Edgar shuddered at this news, for though he was fond of his passionate protectress he could hardly envisage them settling down as man
and wife. Still less could he see himself as the husband of the President
of the Republic—or whatever else she would be called after the change
of power. All these events would be no more than memorable material
for the book he intended to write on his personal experiences during the
Nihilon insurrection, an account which would mark him out for fame
in his own country.

'I had never dreamed of becoming the President of the Republic, my dear,' she went on, 'but now that these honest soldiers want me to, I can't refuse. I have my dead father's memory to consider. But after five or ten years, when the country is honest, peaceful, and prosperous, I shall hand over my office to some other worthy person, so that my husband and I can then give ourselves up to eternal happiness, and to the education of our children.'

She shed tears at her speech, wetting the back of his hand with them. All he could hope for, in his fear of such a future, was that the war would go on for a long time. 'Are you fond of children?' he asked.

'I don't know,' she said sadly, doing her best to stop weeping. 'I've hardly ever known any. But I'm sure I am, and that I shall adore our own.'

Orcam was a locality of low square houses and unpaved streets extending some way into the plain. Most of the built-up area lay at the confluence of two rivers, which made the town easy to defend. Mella's column marched into the squalid suburb on the south side of the river. An advance party had already tried to rush the bridge, but all thirty had been shot down, and their dead bodies lay scattered along the straight street. This rebuff put Mella and her soldiers into a very gloomy mood, though Edgar felt selfishly hopeful on realising that the war might not be over as quickly as everybody in the column had thought during the euphoria of the last few days.

A deserted house was found for them, out of the line of fire, and they occupied a low-ceilinged empty room on the ground floor whose only door led into a back-yard. The wide bed was covered by a hot, lumpy mattress. In spite of the depressing fact that they had at last met real military opposition, Mella kissed him in an excess of cheerful passion when she got into the bed, her naked body hot and soft against him. He could not but respond, and they were soon locked in a slow-moving but feverish bout of copulation.

When she was peacefully sleeping, one of her arms possessively across his chest, he felt utterly unable to close his eyes. Far from soothing him, the lovemaking had exhausted him to the marrow, so that in their insomnia his thoughts turned towards escape.

He eased himself up and stood by the bed. If he walked rapidly he could be back at Shelp in two or three days, where he would no doubt find the man with the wheelbarrow also waiting for a boat.

If he begged a lift on some vehicle he might even get there in a few hours, in which case he'd be there before him. Certainly it would be safer and more convivial sitting at a bar by the harbour, drinking the local brew, than pushing on into the savage interior of Nihilon with Mella and her column of incompetent freedom fighters.

He hurriedly dressed, holding his breath while she turned over. The inevitable shots were heard from the centre of Orcam, and he hoped these would now increase to divert attention from his escape. Outside in the small high-walled courtyard he peered hard through the darkness, glad that there was no guard nearby.

It wasn't easy to undo the bolt of the gate in the far corner which was caked in dry rust, and squeaked noisily when he forced it. He expected to hear Mella's loving voice call him back, but she seemed even more exhausted than he was for once. He walked along an alleyway formed by two walls, blessing his luck that it was deserted. Even the dogs seemed to have gone from Orcam. But breath scraped in his lungs, as if he were out of condition after being so long carried on wheels. He'd hardly used his feet in the last few days, and now paused to rest, looking up at the clearly defined stars, where all seemed really peaceful—though he knew it was not so.

He discovered an outlet between two houses, leading into the main street. A cool breeze came from the river, and he found himself a few hundred metres from the heavily guarded bridge which led to the centre of Orcam. But the taste of freedom was sweet, even though he was still too close to Mella.

He must have taken the wrong turning from the courtyard, though he gradually increased his distance from the bridge by keeping well into the sides of the houses. He began to breathe freely for the first time since leaving Mella's bed, and decided to turn right at the next intersection, so as to get on to the Shelp road. The street was empty, and he wondered where the two thousand soldiers of Mella's brigade had gone. A feeling that they had deserted her cause made him sweat, and pause in his slow painstaking footsteps.

A green signal-light wriggled like a tadpole into the air. The silence haunted him. He fancied a faint hissing sound as a small rocket went up, which meant that it had been fired from close by. Left and right along the intersection, both streets were crammed with soldiers—standing, sitting, smoking, looking at nothing, waiting perhaps for another signal-light. A bayonet was thrust against his chest: 'Where are you going?'

The slight irritant of the point made it difficult to speak. The man glared, and repeated his question, this time in a rasping whisper that terrified Edgar far more than a bawling voice.

'To the bridge,' he answered, to prevent the bayonet being thrust into his lung.

A rifle was given to him, and a belt of ammunition draped over his shoulder. 'Take off your shoes,' said the soldier.

Another light went up, this time red. A score of soldiers came from each street, walked towards the bridge in single file along the left line of house-fronts. All were in bare feet, so as to make no sound. The uneven surface of the pavement was painful to the skin through Edgar's thin socks. The soldiers had a thicker wadding of cloth round their feet and could therefore concentrate on not being seen, instead of on avoiding the discomfort of stones and potholes.

He did not know what to do with his rifle, and wanted to throw it away. Why had such an important attack been kept secret from Mella? Because she would have exposed herself to danger by joining it, he reasoned. She would have led her band on like a fearsome queen, her presidential future jeopardised by any stray bullet or piece of shrapnel.

He mistook the ache in his head for a feeling of excitement, which he didn't like, preferring to acquire it in the more useful project of threading his way back towards Shelp. Getting involved in this pointless fight was a terrible misunderstanding. When a yellow signal-light showed over the bridge he became frightened and wanted to shout for Mella. He opened his mouth as if to do so, but before any sound came, a bayonet caught him in the back and prodded him on. A whistle shrieked from behind, blown by someone still at the safety of the intersection, and Edgar cursed it for an entirely unnecessary noise.

The street was filled with two blinding lights, one red and one blue, and those caught in it began running towards the bridge, as if to get back into the darkness even if it killed them. Faces fixed in the pallor of the beams ran forward, and Edgar, whose marrow had collapsed, clung to a drainpipe, knowing that something cataclysmic was about to happen.

Machine guns began a dreadful stutter from three hundred metres, and the forty men melted into the stones, though only half as many were hurt. Edgar let go of the drainpipe, and ran back towards the intersection, when he spun like a top as if a ball of ice had smashed into him below the shoulder. He cried out, not from pain, which wasn't yet apparent, but from the indignity of having to put up with the unexpected. When someone tried to lift him from the road he cried out that reinforcements were needed at the bridge.

The officer, assuming him to be a messenger who had come back with this information at the risk of his life, passed it on to someone of higher rank in case anything could be done about the obvious failure of their surprise attack, on which so many hopes had been placed. Before his eyes closed, and he fainted, Edgar saw several dozen more unfortunate soldiers make their way out into the Nihilists' field of fire. His mind bit hard on the fact that if he hadn't run back, and faked this message to cover his cowardice, they might not be going off to get killed. But even the bitterness of this reflection didn't stop him thinking what a pity it was that he should be dying in some nightmare battle, when only a few days ago he had been nothing more (or less) than a happy-go-lucky tourist.

Chapter Twenty-eight

Nihilism had worked so well, Benjamin reflected, after setting up his headquarters at Agbat railway station, that it was almost impossible not to believe in God. During the last twenty-five years, industrial production had gone up five per cent. Not much, perhaps, but certainly it had not declined. And if the people weren't happier than they had been before, at least they were livelier. Nihilism had given them a new zest for life, a positive interest in it. What more could they ask for?

It may not be the finest of governments, but it was the next best thing to having no government at all, he decided, signing an order to have another half-dozen prisoners set free when, according to the new principles of honesty and re-education, they should have been sent for trial, after which they would have been committed to a special establishment for rehabilitating Nihilists which had yet to be set up.

Before him were several thick volumes on Nihilist industrial progress during the first quarter-century of its power. Apparently they had been the stationmaster's favourite reading. The columns of figures presented a dazzling picture of a nation set on such a course of economic betterment that it seemed destined to dominate the world. Every commodity for a firm industrial base was to be found in Nihilon, it was stated, from coal to bauxite, tungsten to pigiron, copper to oil, though no one had ever claimed such a thing for the country before it went Nihilistic. However, the National Statistics Board of Mystical Nihilism (to give these voluminous reports their full title) acquired such deposits for Nihilon simply by stating that they existed. And so, in the imagination at least, as well as in print, they did.

A poet must have drawn this picture, and primed these books before the figure-men got to work on them. And if such fabricated calculations kept the people happy, what need was there of the real thing? The question to ask was: Would the real thing make them *more* happy?

And one could only answer that it was doubtful. With these figures even dry bread would taste as if it had butter on it. Benjamin sighed, at the fact that the moral regeneration of mankind was simpler to accomplish than he imagined. Perhaps, after all, the Nihilists had hit upon the secret of it, and now with his insurrectionist brigade he was out to upset the delicate fabric of nihilism that had been painfully built up over the last twenty-five years by these idealistic perverts.

He could not deny that the people had grown accustomed to it. It was their one and only way of life. It worked for them, and it was working for their children, and so what right had he, with his ideals, to come along and wreck it so completely? The only reason that people were running with such alacrity to join his standard was because they saw it perhaps as another playful manifestation of nihilistic mismanagement, and would not realise their mistake until it was too late.

He tried to shake off such wayward thoughts. By a brilliant series of manoeuvres he had captured Agbat less painfully than the town of Amrel. His knights-in-shining-overalls were making merry in the main square, while he unrolled his map, and put a volume of the stationmaster's statistics at each of the four corners to hold it down. The final phase of his advance was about to begin, and he was so much assailed by the rights and wrongs of it that he almost hoped he would be killed in the battles ahead, especially when he thought back on his carefree time as a mere tourist in this chaotic haphazard paradise, and knew with melancholic certainty that such enjoyment would never return.

He sighed, and went back to his planning, deciding to leave a hundred soldiers and two heavy machine guns to hold Agbat, which would defend his communications with Amrel and the frontier, so that when he resumed his push towards Tungsten he would know that his retreat to Cronacia was halfway open should anything go wrong. He never advanced without being sure that he could retreat, an axiom that no amount of heady and easy success could turn him from. There was no advance without a retreat, and no retreat without an advance, and no ground was ever covered twice, because even if you actually went over it again, you were in another frame of mind, and circumstances were different anyway. No one day resembled the one that had preceded it, nor the one that was on its way from tomorrow, and he didn't need any nihilistic philosophy to remind him of such a natural law, though in a sense it made him more comfortable to be constantly aware of the fact.

Even the insurrection was run, it seemed, on nihilistic principles, which was why he enjoyed it so much, and he realised that when the dragon of nihilism was split down the middle and bleeding to death, he might not like it here any more. In some strange way, and at this late hour, honesty and nihilism might after all be related, an observation which for the moment lightened his mood.

Even that waiting space-rocket, set to charge for the heavens in a few days' time, out of which the finest male specimen and the juiciest female of the line would emerge for the long-planned well-advertised extravaganza of sex-in-space, was nothing more than a dramatic manifestation of Nihilon's health and honesty. Yet it was a show he felt obliged to destroy, for if it succeeded, nihilism would reign forever glorious. Who then would argue over its merits?—though in becoming an eternal fact of life it would certainly lose all possible attraction for him.

There was a knock at the door, and one of his soldiers shuffled over the dusty boards to announce that they had found a strange woman.

'What's wrong with her?' Benjamin demanded.

'It's a woman, commander. We were patrolling towards the railway bridge, and saw that she was being ravished by two Nihilists. We heard her screaming for help, so we killed them.'

She had fallen, and when they carried her in, Benjamin saw that she was a young woman, her dress torn, and her blood-stained face smeared with ash and dust. He was too absorbed in his favourite work of planning his attacks to like being disturbed, and if he had been a Nihilist officer advancing against the forces of law and decency, order and honesty, he would have told them to finish raping her themselves instead of bothering him.

Hair straggled over her breasts and shoulders, and when he at last looked at her closely, she opened her eyes, and saw a brutalised general-issimo with a shaved head, wearing bush-shirt and trousers, a belt around his waist from which hung a revolver. Her lips trembled, as if about to open for a scream. 'All right, then,' she said weakly, not believing that her good luck in being saved by the two madmen could last, 'get it over with. I might as well die in this awful country.'

He drew back at the shock of hearing her speak. 'What are *you* doing here?' he asked, putting a chair by her so that she could sit down, then sending the two soldiers away. When she pushed her hair back over her scratch-covered face, he felt himself on the point of choking. He took a bottle from his desk, and poured her a glass of Nihilitz. 'Drink this, Jaquiline. It's a terrible potion, but you'll feel better,' his stomach twisting with black rage against this country and its nihilism.

He knelt, to keep the glass steady at her mouth. She said nothing, but gulped the Nihilitz. He took the glass away, and held her hands, saw that she wasn't wounded badly, but supposed that her experiences had been full of the usual Nihilon nightmare. 'I want to go home,' she cried, 'I want to get out.'

'You're quite safe. There are more than two thousand honest soldiers to guard you. What fools we were to let a woman come alone into this foul place. But the Nihilists will pay for this. I'll burn them out. I'll destroy them. I'll lay the country waste between here and Tungsten. I'll plough this land with so much dynamite there won't even be a breath of nihilism left in it.'

Her eyes closed from utter exhaustion, and relief at such unexpected deliverance. He helped her into the next room, where she lay on his camp-bed, and with a heavy blanket drawn over, she sank into a deep sleep.

When she sat beside him next morning in his Thundercloud Estate car, her face showed little of her ordeal. Her blue eyes were the colour of steel as she looked ahead at the rocky and winding trail that led into the mountains. She wore an olive-green shirt, a pair of men's slacks, and sandals on her feet. A belt around her waist had a holster hanging from it, with a loaded pistol inside.

Advancing patrols were already far ahead, marking the track where it became uncertain, fanning out for snipers, crowning the neighbouring heights for any sign of resistance or ambush. Benjamin's burning zeal to rid Nihilon of its detestable régime had decided Jaquiline to work for the same end.

Such bravery and suffering in a beautiful young woman filled him with a fatherly love for her, and he agreed that she could come with the column. And Jaquiline felt a liking for this new Benjamin she had found so unexpectedly in the wastes of Nihilon. As an acquaintance of the last two years she had looked on him as no more than a brash hedonist, but it was now obvious that he was a man of deeply fundamental ideals whom she had been wrong to misjudge. Where else could his good qualities have been brought out except in a place like Nihilon? She turned and smiled tenderly at him as he set the car in motion.

The landscape of grey rock, ash, and pumice glistened under the scorching sun. Their car climbed over backs and shoulders of land, sometimes ascending several hundred metres in sharp curves of the track. The region appeared to be sparsely inhabited, but now and again steep narrow cuttings in the mountainside, cleverly hidden by the complex configuration of the land, showed clusters of small houses at the bottom, presumably built around springs or streams, for small green trees grew down there, and on either side of the indentation, terraces had been built some way up the banks, long strips of verdure vividly glowing. Occasional belts of terracing were fallow, or had just been harvested, and the soil was so dark it looked like pure soot.

More bushes appeared, and a few trees as they ascended, as well as a house here and there by the roadside. Even the squalor-ridden children playing out of doors, who laughed and waved at them, seemed fortunate and picturesque to Jaquiline when she thought that their day of deliverance from vile nihilism was close at hand. At a thousand metres the air grew cooler, for they were approaching the plateau on which the Groves of Aspron were situated. Then the track suddenly turned into a wide, paved highway, a miracle of unexpected road-building in this remote area of Nihilon.

'It'll go on for a few miles, then end in a swamp, or at the edge of a cliff,' Benjamin said. 'I've met this sort of thing before. Nobody can tell how these isolated stretches of perfect road get here, or why they were built, but they seem to be a characteristic feature of this country.'

He drove slowly, at forty kilometres an hour, when from around a slight bend ahead a small red sports car came weaving towards him. It brought to mind his first encounter with such a maniac several days ago, when he had been civilised and inexperienced enough to get driven off the road and almost killed.

The car was at a distance still, and there would be time to act. He pulled into the side and stopped his Thundercloud. 'Get out,' he said to Jaquiline. They crouched behind the car, her heart thumping as she witnessed the mad career of the Zap, ready to throw herself clear should it decide to crash against the superior weight of their estate car.

Benjamin picked up a sub-machine-gun and took aim, standing by the right headlamp. A few moments would pass before the car drew level and he could open fire, meanwhile keeping the gun halfway to his shoulder.

The Zap slowed, and straightened course. A face at the windscreen looked at him, all teeth, fair hair, and homicidal sweat. The driver levelled a gun through the open window. Benjamin dropped, spattered by the glass of his own headlamp.

The Zap passed, but with the coolness and accuracy that can come with extreme rage, Benjamin stood up and fired the whole magazine at the petrol tank of the retreating car. Without looking, he rummaged for another clip, but saw smoke pouring out of the Zap as it zigzagged on its way. The dead silence of the earth was shaken by a grunt of wind, as the car went up in a column of smoke and flame. 'That's the second time those Zaps have tried to kill me,' he smiled, courteously opening the door of the Thundercloud so that Jaquiline could get in.

She smoothed her hair. 'A woman on the train told me that when men are discharged with good results from the Groves of Aspron they are awarded a crimson Zap car as a prize. It's supposed to normalise their emotions by the time they get home.'

'That's one patient who won't go back for more treatment,' he said, with a nihilistic laugh. 'I've been persecuted by those Zap cars ever since coming to this lawless land, and it's one instrument of terror we'll ban as soon as the new government gets together.'

At the highest point of the Aspron Way, which was now back to its usual rugged unpaved state, stood a wooden shack, on which was hung a large notice saying COFFEE. He stopped the car, and they went inside, having neither eaten nor drunk since setting out.

It was a cool dark room, with a rough counter at one end, and two or three rickety chairs and tables between it and the sackcloth door. On the counter sat a Nihilonian cat, with neither ears nor tail, and behind it stood a tall corpulent man wearing a waistcoat over his apron. His thinning hair was parted down the middle, and he emerged from the daze of his own stillness to ask what they wanted.

On being told, he lit a small spirit stove on the counter: 'Are you part of the liberation army? If you are, you won't be the first army that's passed this way. May I invite you to sit down?'

They preferred to stand, for a change. 'What army?' Benjamin asked, refusing the bottle of Nihilitz.

'We'll wait for the coffee to boil,' the café-keeper said. 'It'll take a few minutes. But I'm glad to see travellers, even if it is an army. I'm dying of boredom. My wife died of it last year. Absolute agony. I held her hand all through it. Never thought I had it in me. Had to send for soil from Agbat to bury her in, because the peasants near here wouldn't sell me any. They even stole my load of it coming up from Agbat, so I had to leave her in the living rock after all.'

'I'm so sorry,' Jaquiline said, wiping her forehead with a handkerchief. 'How long have you lived here?'

He pondered on the number of years: 'Twenty-six. My whole life, in fact. I wanted a peaceful life, and here it is. Come outside, and I'll have great pleasure in showing you what I got for my trouble.' They followed him through the sackcloth, into searing metallic sunshine. 'Grey mountains for as far as the eye can see—in every direction. Beautiful, inspiring, empty. The most gorgeous sight in the world. I must have yearned for it the moment I was conceived. When I was a boy, and then as a young man, I knew that one day I would achieve all this, though for many years there was absolutely no clue that I would ever get it. In fact for two decades I forgot about this deep yearning in my blood, and it was only when my ambition was half complete that I realised it was coming about, and remembered that I'd always wanted it. I was recovering from a state of catastrophic despair, and was on the point of dying of it, when I bought this shack for selling coffee to passing travellers. Then, slowly, I acquired all this land, to increase my peace of mind.'

They followed the coffee-distiller back into his bar, where he poured out two large cups. 'You were saying,' said Benjamin, 'that another army passed this way.'

'Was I? Well, it was twenty-five years ago. You can't expect me to remember every detail. It was President Took's rearguard, a few stragglers really, heading up into the Athelstans.'

'Why would they come through here?' Benjamin asked, touched with curiosity now that the shack-keeper was veering on to his pet obsession of Nihilon's recent history. 'The main road goes through Nilbud.'

'It does,' the man smiled, 'but it was blocked by the Nihilists. So Took and his hundred got on a train as far as Agbat. They were heading for sanctuary in Cronacia, but the bridge beyond Agbat was strongly held by the Nihilists, and Amrel had already been abandoned. There was nobody poor Took could trust. Anyhow, he comes in here, still wearing his top-hat and chains of office, and asks for coffee. I gave him some. What else could I do? But when the time came to pay and he walked out without doing so I reached for my revolver and shot him in the back. If he can't pay for his coffee, I thought, I'll kill the swine, just as if he's a peasant who can't afford to. Equality's my game, and I never lost by it yet.'

Sweat drops were falling into Benjamin's cup. The cat leapt to the floor and sauntered outside under the sack. 'You killed President Took?'

'He only had ten soldiers by that time,' said the man. 'The rest died on the way up from Agbat. He was a fine man, President Took. He spoke calmly, and walked in here with great dignity.'

Benjamin's hands shook. He put the cup down, and loosened his revolver, feeling in the grip of his worst moment since entering Nihilon. 'So this is where he died? What was the date?'

'I don't remember,' said the man. 'The soldiers burned down my shack, that's all I know. But I built another. In any case President Took didn't die. I was so wild with rage that my shot went wide. His hat fell off, and he asked why I'd done it. When I told him, he said he'd only forgotten to pay for his coffee because he was so preoccupied with defeat. He gave me a golden coin, and then left, but some of his men stayed and set fire to my hut. Then they shot at me and my wife, but we were already running down the valley.'

'And then what happened?'

'He went on towards Tungsten. Or maybe up behind the peaks somewhere. I don't know. I heard from a peasant that he died in a cave after a dinner of boiled roots. But who can be sure?'

'Is that all?'

'What's the difference? He dies in a cave, I die of boredom. Nihilism knows no frontiers. It loves everyone, and is no respecter of persons.'

'So that's how it happened,' Benjamin said, walking with Jaquiline towards the sackcloth.

'Stop!' shouted the shackman.

They turned to see a heavy revolver pointed at them. 'If I call my soldiers in,' said Benjamin, 'you won't escape this time. I don't like people who dodge their fate. They're the worst people in the world, a scourge to everyone. Put that gun down.'

'Pay for coffee, then!'

Benjamin longed to shoot it out, knowing he would kill him. He was totally unconcerned for his own safety, but dared not do it with Jaquiline by his side.

The café-owner smiled. 'If it's true you're leading the forces of law and honesty to final victory, you can't refuse to pay for your coffee, though you may be greatly tempted. Nor can you order your soldiers to obliterate all sign of this shack and its too scrupulous occupant.'

'How much?' Benjamin asked.

'A hundred klipps.'

He walked back and placed a bank note for that amount on the counter. 'Where's the tip?' the man demanded, his revolver still pointing.

'I've paid the price. No tip.'

'A hundred and twenty,' the man insisted.

'I'll have my soldiers burn you out, you robber.'

'That would cost you twenty million klipps in compensation.'

'For this shack?' Benjamin shouted.

The man leered at him. 'My soul is invested in it. A twenty-klipp tip on two cups of coffee is very reasonable.'

'Tips and bribes are immediately abolished in territory I pass through.'

The man saw his dilemma, and lowered his revolver. 'The price for the coffee was a hundred and twenty. I put the rates up this morning, but forgot to tell you. No tips from now on.'

Benjamin threw him a coin for the extra amount, and on his way to the car fought down a wild and reasonable urge to give the correct Nihilist order for the burning of the hut. But instead he decided to wait for the main body of his brigade, and give them a rousing speech about honesty and dignity, before leading the final advance towards that obscene rocket pointing into the sky above Tungsten.

Chapter Twenty-nine

Adam became disgruntled, at the double load of another person placidly fixed on the seat behind, and decided to rest.

'Why have you stopped?' asked Firebrand.

'My legs ache,' Adam told him.

'But mine don't.'

'That's because you're not doing the work.'

Firebrand got off the bike and sat down: 'If you accuse me of not being an idealist, I'll kill you. I'm on my way to take part in the Great Patriotic March of Honesty on Tungsten, and I invited you to join me out of the goodness of my heart, so that you can prove yourself as a bona fide traveller to Nihilon, a country which expects all good foreigners to come to the aid of the insurrection. Anyway, you don't expect us to do it by ourselves, do you?'

'I suppose not,' said Adam, stunned by such international reasoning. 'But I can't pedal any more. My lungs are giving way.'

Firebrand was galvanised at the sound of a lorry coming up the hill, and stood in the road to wait for it. He held two hand-grenades, so that the driver was forced to stop and ask: 'Where to?'

'Orcam,' said Firebrand, slipping the spare grenade into his pocket.

'I'm going through Shelp to Nihilon,' the driver told him, hopefully.

'You were,' said Firebrand, his free hand at the pin of a grenade. 'Now you're going to Orcam.'

The driver shrugged: 'Get up then.'

'And no tricks,' said Firebrand. 'One wrong turning, and this drops into your cab, while we jump off.' Adam admired his talent for action, as he lifted his bicycle on to the lorry. 'Nobody has to pedal any more,' said Firebrand. 'It struck me as a very primitive method of locomotion when you were gasping up that hill.'

The lorry was wrapped in its own breeze as it sped along, pleasurably cooling them, and Adam felt that he was really travelling, wondered in fact why he had used a bicycle in order to achieve something which could be done with much greater comfort over a good engine. A road branched to the left, and Firebrand told him it led to Troser, the chief coastal resort of Nihilon, famous as an intolerable place of residence due to dust, wind, heat, rain, snow, and high seas that forever batter the place. 'But people love it precisely because of these unfortunate characteristics,' he continued, 'since it gives them a great deal to talk about when they get home, and you can't ask for more than that.'

At the next road-fork, twenty kilometres further on, he banged on the door of the cab with his insurrectionary fist to indicate that the driver should take the right one, an extremely rocky switchback road which led between two high mountains. Firebrand then filched a blanket from Adam's pannier, and spread it out so that he could lie on it. He also extracted his reserve rations of black bread and compact sausage, biscuit and a small flask of brandy, and shared it according to his egalitarian principles.

'We'll have to replenish our stocks soon,' said Adam, alarmed at his friend's improvidence, though enjoying the meal.

'That will be easy,' said Firebrand. 'We'll reach Orcam in the morning, by which time it will have been captured, so there'll be plenty of food in the empty houses.'

'That's looting,' said Adam, a piece of bread leaping down his gullet as the lorry hit a particularly forceful slab of rock.

'The duty of a revolutionary,' Firebrand answered, 'is to keep alive, so that his ideals don't perish with his body. He gets his food where he can, how he can, and when he can.'

'Yes,' Adam agreed.

'Well, then,' said Firebrand, 'I'll make a bargain by giving you my valuable ideals of honesty and cooperation, while you provide me with food till the revolution is over in two or three days.'

Adam saw that he had a lot to learn from his new-found friend. In any case, the food that they might consume couldn't possibly be very much, so he agreed to his suggestion. At every village Firebrand assiduously searched out whatever shops there were, and returned laden with succulent provisions, but lacking most of the money that Adam had allotted him for foraging. After the first ample feed the driver no longer needed watching with a grenade at the ready, but was quite willing to cooperate with two such provident travellers.

The lorry bucked along at twenty kilometres an hour, and late that night they were within a few kilometres of Orcam. Firebrand decided to postpone their entry into the town because heavy firing could distinctly be heard coming from that direction. Signal-lights spat into the air, spelling danger, so he told them that they would park by the road and sleep on the lorry.

He sent the driver to look for wood, and soon a bright fire pulled them into its glare and smoke. They sat by it to eat, and the lorry-driver, a bull-headed man who seemed to have few cares simply because he was incapable of showing them, gave his views on the coming change of power.

'I live in Nihilon City,' he said, 'and I hope to be back there tomorrow with my wife and children. I was delivering food to the soldiers at the frontier and just got through Fludd before the dam broke. I'll be thirty-five next year, so I'll register at the Halfway Department. Not that I mind getting a new job. I wouldn't like to be an intellectual or a professional, because they are expected to stick at the same work all their lives, while people like me, well, we have to register with the Halfway Department!'

'I suppose that'll be altered by the new régime,' said Adam, smiling mischievously.

'Yes,' Firebrand responded. 'It will be a matter of "one life, one job", meaning more efficiency in the industry of human relations.'

'I like things to stay as they are,' said the driver, 'all mixed up and dangerous. That's normal now, isn't it? I'll always vote for normal, no matter what it is. Otherwise I get upset.'

'After the fighting,' said Firebrand, 'things *will* soon be normal again—only different.'

'That's all right then,' said the driver. 'But you haven't won, yet, have you?'

'Nearly,' Firebrand went on. 'Our luckiest event was that fighting broke out on the Cronacian border. All the Gerries—the old ones, that is—flocked there to take part in the fighting, which left us almost a free hand in the rest of the country. If they'd been in Shelp and Nihilon, the fighting would have been twice as bitter. You can imagine how the oldsters would resist any idea of change. Of course, we haven't had things *all* our own way, because by the time most of them got to the frontier zone the Nihilists had blown up the dam at Fludd, making such a long, wide lake that the road to the southern frontier was effectively blocked for a week. So a good many of them couldn't get there, and were forced to stay in the towns or rest-homes. Still, the road-block at Fludd also prevented the government from calling its crack frontier regiments back to defend the capital. The timing of what happened was so split-second in its complexity that nobody had time to do anything, which suggests that though the situation was out of control, as befits Nihilists, it was by no means adverse to us who are trying to bring order and honesty into the world.'

Firebrand asked the driver to look around in the darkness for more wood to keep them warm, but he refused, and even the threat of a hand-grenade wouldn't change his mind, so they clambered on to the lorry and went to sleep.

Adam was awakened in the morning by a rough shaking from an obviously alien hand. He saw the jaundiced face of the lorry-driver, who seemed about to stuff a grenade, that he had filched from Firebrand's pocket, into Adam's mouth. His other hand held the pin: 'Get down,' he snapped, 'off the lorry. And take your bicycle. I've had enough of you two.'

It was dawn, anyway, and Adam wasn't too upset at the way things were turning out. He only hoped that the driver would now get into his cab and drive away with Firebrand still on board. But while waiting for this to happen he heard a kick and a cry, and saw his revolutionary friend come flying over the side. Holding the bomb to his chest, the driver sidled round to his cab, and before getting in he shouted: 'Long live nihilism!'

'That happened too quickly,' Firebrand grumbled, as they plodded towards Orcam, feeling hungry because their food had gone with the lorry. 'Which is why we have to eliminate nihilism. How can society advance when there's no one you can trust? I'm dying of hunger. If I don't get to the town soon, I shall faint. Get on your bicycle and drive me there.'

'I believe I'm too weak,' Adam said.

'Never mind,' Firebrand laughed, finding the other hand-grenade, throwing it into the air and catching it neatly, 'I'll inspire you to heroic deeds. I'll instil into you such a spirit of self-sacrifice that you'll be forever grateful to me. It's part of the bargain, anyway, and don't think I have the easiest side of it, either, because I haven't. I'm so hungry I can hardly talk, but I'm prepared to do so because it's in your best interest. You'll always remember what I've done for you. There's no greater honour than to save the life of a dedicated revolutionary like myself.'

He talked till Adam could stand it no more and offered him the seat of his bicycle. In any case, they were in sight of the southern suburb of Orcam, which meant little more than a kilometre to the town centre. And though the effort was great so early in the morning, it became easier the longer it lasted, until, entering the straight main-street of the suburb that led towards the strategic bridge, Adam was travelling at a speed not at all safe in a battle area.

The street was quiet, after the unsuccessful night attacks by the in-surrectionary forces. Adam found it difficult, riding so quickly, to steer between the bodies of what he took to be sleeping soldiers, imagining that the insurrectionary troops were so numerous that the only billet for many of them was the open street.

Close to the bridge, as if having tried to crawl up the side of a house and failed, was the wreckage of the lorry they had commandeered the day before. There was no sign of the driver, and Adam hoped he hadn't been injured, though Firebrand laughed gloatingly at the sight.

Men were sleeping on the bridge, or resting over their rifles. At the town-end was a barricade of barbed wire with a narrow opening to one side. Adam did not see a party of armed men running after his bicycle. He tried to stop when a sentry roared at him, but on pulling the brakes there was a snapping of wires, and he realised it was im-possible to do so. He thought that the lorry-driver might have cut at them somewhere along the cable, either by way of a joke, or in the worst form of vengeful treachery.

The front wheel hit a paving stone, spinning Adam into and beyond the gap in the barricade. There was a scream from Firebrand which sounded like 'Traitor!' as he flew over Adam's head, and across the barbed wire, landing among a machine-gun crew, who because of this were unable to fire during the next vital half-minute.

The grenade leapt from the flying revolutionary's pocket, and its pin must have been pulled out by the buttons of his jacket, for it made a lethal landing some way off, exploding into the second heavy machine gun, set to enfilade the approaches to the bridge.

The score of insurrectionists on the other side, having seen their chance, overran these defences, and began firing directly into the town itself. Some were able to reverse the machine gun and train it at the main square. Two more platoons came over the bridge and fanned out into the streets.

Adam and Firebrand, scraped, bruised and battered, but not otherwise impaired, were lifted from the ground by the grateful soldiers. After being fed on the tastiest nutriment that could be found (Firebrand insisted on this, as a hero of the insurrection), they were presented to the lady in charge of the column who was to become, they were told on their way to headquarters, the next President of the Republic, for she was none other than President Took's daughter.

Mella sat in the courtyard, weeping over Edgar. Pale and tired, he lay on a couch, his wounded arm held in a sling made from one of her coloured scarves. He had been brought back to Mella after the attack had failed, for one of the officers had recognised him.

She had been touched to endless tears at the sight of his blood, and the bravery that he was said to have shown. To creep off at night without telling her, in order to take a common soldier's part in the recovery of her country for the forces of decency and order, meant that she had found a great and noble man indeed! With such a lover, what fine children she would have! She wept over him, kissed him, extolled his courage as she nursed his wound, and Edgar, now that the pain of his grazed arm was no more than a mere throb, decided to give up his plan of escape, and to accept the role she had forced on him—or which he now appeared to have forced on himself.

Adam immediately recognised him as one of his colleagues working on the Nihilon Guidebook project, and when Mella saw that they were old friends, she kissed Adam with almost the same fervour that she continued to show her wounded hero. A second breakfast was prepared, during which news was brought that the town of Orcam had surrendered to Mella's invincible brigade, and Mella promised medals for all three men. 'And you,' she told Adam, 'will be our official poet at the palace. You will write an epic on the glorious insurrection in Nihilon.'

He felt that this might, after all, be a reasonable theme for his talent. To be in the presence not only of an old friend and a fine breakfast, but also of a vivacious and beautiful woman like Mella, put him into such a mood of positive enjoyment that Edgar began to feel the first twinges of jealousy. 'I would be delighted to write poems for you,' Adam said, kissing her hand.

Soon after breakfast, Mella made her triumphant entry into the town, on her mobile platform. Edgar was by her side and, to the rear, on two hastily installed chairs, sat Adam and Firebrand. Because the capture of the town had caused the deaths of so many of her soldiers, she did not make her customary speech in the main square.

By nightfall the advance of her force, now five thousand strong, had taken them close to the foothills of the Athelstan Alps. Because of aches and pains in all his limbs Adam had expected a warrior's rest before the final move began, but he was disappointed. Since crossing the frontier he'd hardly had time to pull a comb through his hair, though he admitted by way of consolation that being unwashed and ragged did give him a peculiar and attractive feeling of freedom.

Chapter Thirty

'Nihilon is a city of half a million people which stands on the beautiful banks of the River Nihil, and can rightly claim to be the great seat of international nihilism. Its streets are laid out in a chequerboard pattern which gives such ease of control that one machine gun can dominate a thoroughfare two miles long. With twelve such streets running from north to south, and twelve going from east to west at right angles, only forty-eight powerful machine guns are needed to keep the population in perpetual subjection. With the complement of six men to a gun, no more than half a battalion need be on duty at any one time. And because these loyal soldiers are relieved every four hours, a mere brigade of eighteen hundred could keep the city centre locked up around the clock. This Nihilon lock-up force is so trustworthy that even the fiercest and most profound eruption of traditional nihilistic boisterousness on the part of the unpredictable inhabitants can be put down with minimal loss on one side, and none on the other.

'As Nihilists, therefore, the inhabitants of Nihilon City know how far they can go in their celebrations of nihilism. Decades of refinement have taught them to control these outbreaks of liveliness. That is to say, they know when to stop, for a mob that cannot control itself is a danger to the community—it is thought—while a mob that does control itself is a danger to itself. Thus their tainted hearts have properly inculcated into themselves the tradition of therapeutic nihilism. Under the ever-watchful sights of forty-eight machine guns, this is not to be wondered at.

'The police (who are, after all, none other than the citizens themselves, not only in Nihilon but in any country you care to name) keep an ear close and an eye set for those seditious malcontents who talk of orderly progress and cultural enlightenment, human responsibility and social honesty, and the universal fraud of human love—those brainless engines of menace for whom the government is on the look-out, and for whom they cannot help but have an inordinate respect. Those who preach order, say the government, would only like to destroy society. Those who talk of progress want to put the country back to an age of barbarism. Nihilism works. It has been perfected through twenty-five years, (if not for centuries), and to expound the benefits of law and order in the great nihilistic republic of Nihilonia is the most direct form of treason, for it means nothing less than plunging the honest population of patriotic enthusiastic Nihilists back into the darkest misery of the soul. Nihilists have come on to the earth in order to survive in disorder, not to go mad in regimentation. Therefore Nihilon, under the benign rule of President Nil, has devised the perfect system of regimented disorder as the best way of safeguarding the eternal spirit of its citizens. Life is the great driving-force of nihilism. Strife means Life! Confusion is creative! Security is idleness! Get up and mix! Nihilism is the soul of life. All talk of order and honesty only confuses, and thereby seeks to enslave and crush it.'

The professor's commentary on these few pilfered pages from President Nil's private diary observed that the volatile inhabitants of Nihilon seemed to have moved during the last few months from the desire for therapeutic destruction to a yearning for therapeutic reality, hence the strong indications of the tendency to insurrection, un-detected by the authorities who mistakenly but understandably saw it only as the usual calm before one of the periodic nihilistic bouts. This is what the nascent but well-trained opposition had always relied upon, and now that it was definitely coming about, they were taking the opportunity to exacerbate the collapse of power in order to acquire it for themselves.

The commentary concluded by saying that President Nil's constant extolling of total freedom had proved a most thorough way of enslaving the populace, tying them to the basic nature of their own lived-out fantasies. The slavery of such nihilism was the logical development of the jungle, the ultimate in raw and naked private enterprise, the flowering mushroom of human nature.

Richard wandered around the city, unobtrusively passing the hours until taking command of his troops for the march on Tungsten, examining tourist-sites for his guidebook, and careful at the same time to avoid any would-be assassin. Fortunately, no one as yet knew his identity, which he considered due to the adroitness of the insurrectionists who had chosen him for the job. He admired such people, and hoped he would in no way disappoint them.

He found his way back to the café with the bullet-proof terrace, and as there wasn't much shooting in the nearby streets, he thumbed through the papers in his briefcase, one of which informed him that the working people of Nihilon had no trade unions. Instead, the employers had unions, and it was they who went on strike for higher salaries. The workers had been given control of the means of production quite early on, as a matter of nihilistic policy, but the employers still did their usual work because they were found absolutely necessary to the running of industry. The employers prospered on their wages, while the workers got thin on their profits. Thus the employers occasionally went on strike, and when they did, the factory stopped immediately. The government invariably came out in sympathy with their strike, and forced the workers to put the employers' salaries up. The spiral towards economic disaster continued. The policy of the law-and-order party was, therefore, to reinstate both employers and workers under rational government control, which meant putting a stop to the mad nihilistic capitalism that had so far prevailed.

When the early evening shooting opened it was particularly intense, indicating that the battle for the capital was by no means over. A young man wearing a soldier's forage cap, and carrying a rifle, came in from the square and walked up to Richard's table, laying down a scruffy piece of paper which he asked him to sign.

Richard saw, while the soldier stood to attention, that it was a request for permission to blow up the People's Academy of Erotic Arts and Crafts, and all subsidiary departments of it in various provincial towns. So he signed, regretfully, and the soldier departed with a wide smile, and tears in his eyes. Richard has passed the building during the day, and loitered there for a while, hoping to get in, but it was already picketed by young men of the insurrectionary movement wearing white-and-yellow arm bands, and giving out notices saying that the academy had been shut for the good of the people. Richard gathered from an elderly male onlooker that not everyone agreed with this decision. In fact some people had hoped to watch the television screens in the lecture hall when the report on the sexual hook-up in space was shown. But now it seemed as if they would be forced into the embarrassing position of seeing it at home in the bosoms of their families.

Having signed the order for its destruction, and asked for a plate of food, together with a small bottle of Anihilitz (somewhat stronger than Nihilitz, and only to be drunk while eating), he took out his guidebook-briefing on the People's Academy of Erotic Arts and Crafts. It commented on the fact that catalogues for this singular establishment were available to the general public, who might apply for them at the side door. 'However,' the text continued, 'it has been brought to the notice of the editors that it is inadvisable to adopt this procedure, as cameras are concealed in nearby buildings so that records may be maintained on who makes application to obtain these unique and degenerate books. We are informed that, at times of social unrest, such applicants are liable to interrogation. Travellers, therefore, ought not to avail themselves of this catalogue-service in case possession of it is used in some way to delay their exit at the frontier. Having said this, our representative should endeavour to gain admittance to this establishment in order to describe it for our future readers.'

Richard now regretted having signed the order for its destruction, and hoped that, by some fluke of inefficiency, it might be spared. He would much rather they had asked him to cooperate in the destruction of NAG—the National Art Gallery, a permanent exhibition by the foremost artist of Nihilon, Dung. His paintings were massive and stylish, vividly coloured and monstrously exaggerated poster-bank-notes of the great Nihilist Inflationary Capitalist Transformation Period to the era of the Good Life. The handbook stated that no one had captured the spirit of the people and the nation so profoundly, and went on to say that Dung's paintings were works of immense significance and genius. They even merited more asterisks than the genius Anonymous Bosh, whose immense pornographic paintings in the old style had been a star attraction in the establishment now under sentence of destruction.

Many rooms of NAG were given over to books of laudatory criticism which had been written about Dung and his masterpieces of mock-fiscal art. Countless costly and elaborate volumes, as well as innumerable scholarly exegeses in the form of magazine articles, were racked and filed for the benefit of people and scholars who rarely went there. Entrance to the museum was free, and recorded not by ticket but by the ratchet works of several turnstiles. The portly men on the door, and all the ushers, were paid according to attendance, and consequently could be seen every minute of the day running in and out and round and round in frenzied circles, so that the numbers registered as entering would be as great as possible. In fact so busy were they at this frantic labour that the few people who genuinely wanted to look at the paintings were rudely told not to interfere with the cultural life of the nation, and pushed out of the way if they insisted on doing so.

It was dark, and the flash of a great explosion filled the sky outside. Richard's glass of Anihilitz toppled over, and a large crack zigzagged down the bullet-proof glass of the terrace window. When the tremor subsided he wrote in his guidebook notes: 'The Editors regret to say that the People's Academy of Erotic Arts and Crafts no longer exists.'

People who crowded into the café to get drunk were saying that the whole city was now in insurrectionist hands. On rooftops bordering the square, soldiers were mounting anti-aircraft guns. In fact hundreds of them were also being placed on the top floors of buildings all over the city, so that their muzzles were pointing out of the windows, through lace curtains, from specially constructed emplacements among the furniture within. This vast array of ambush-artillery was in readiness for the flight of the Nihilist celebration aircraft that was due to fly over when the Nihilonian space-rocket went into the heavens.

It seemed unlikely that this project would begin, but the new and honest authorities of the city were taking no chances. Perhaps as a final effort against the insurrection, the aircraft would still take off from some hidden airfield of the northern coast and fly over Nihilon City, even if the space-rocket were prevented from being launched. So law and order had to be ready for it.

Richard gathered, from the busy conversations, that the celebration aircraft was fitted with four special piston-driven engines, which were tuned to play, like a great symphony organ, the national nihilistic anthem of Nihilonia, and various other compositions, such as 'Free Enterprise Forever', and 'Every Man for Himself'. The pilot could throw the appropriate switch in his cockpit when approaching the city, and the four infernal combustion engines, as well as propelling the aircraft, would begin to play the anthem as he swept low over the tops of the buildings. It was so monstrously loud that there was no possible way of escaping its din. It would fly back and forth over the city for a whole hour, then set off for a circular tour of the principal towns of Nihilon, to make sure that the rest of the country suffered the same fate as the capital.

Richard, in the rapid flow of his writing, found himself exaggerating the truth of this, and recounting for future readers how a score of airborne concatenators were sent hedge-hopping over the country, their eighty pounding engines programmed to whatever so-called music the diabolical Nihilistic government and its pet composers might devise. His arabesque statements descended into lies too fantastic even to sound feasible, till he found it difficult to stop, realising with hilarity and helplessness that though he had accepted the task of assisting the apostles of honesty and rectitude, he was at the same time being completely corrupted by the saturating nihilism all around him.

He wondered whether any of his colleagues on the guidebook were similarly influenced, and while dwelling on this possible misfortune he saw at a nearby table the young man he had met in the suburban café across the Bridge of Suicides. When he lifted a languid hand by way of greeting, Richard beckoned him over: 'Have you found the insurrectionist general yet?'

'Yes,' said the young man, sitting down and swigging freely from the bottle of Anihilitz. 'You, of course. I've been following you for the last few hours.'

'And what do you intend to do about it?' asked Richard, the revolver bulging comfortably close in his briefcase.

'Kill myself,' the young man smiled. 'What else can I do? The government fled to Tungsten this morning, and President Nil has disappeared, so they say. And now the insurrectionists are hunting me.'

'You want me to help you?'

'Yes.'

'Have another drink, then. You seem an honest Nihilist. Perhaps I could find you a job in my column. I might even take you on to the staff, since I don't have one yet.' Such an act might earn him the approval of any world-weary over-subtle insurrectionary. 'I'll pay you well.'

'I could only do it for nothing.'

'You're an idealist already,' said Richard.

'I always was,' said the ex-assassin, finishing the bottle of Anihilitz, and calling for another. Beyond the glass, crowds were dancing around impromptu groups of musicians who had come out with their instruments as they had on all former, though not so successful, occasions. Even so, above the noise, full-stop bullets still appeared to be doing their work in reasonably dark corners. A man who came in was regretting to his wife that the NAG building was on fire. Richard was called to the telephone hanging on the wall: 'Hello? Who's that?'

'The commander-in-chief.'

'I recognise your voice, professor.'

'The brigade will be waiting at PQ 45 at four o'clock in the morning. Motor transport will take your leading battalion to Tungsten. The attack is set for eleven. Good luck.' The telephone earpiece clicked.

When Richard got back to his table the ex-assassin had gone, together with briefcase, gun, maps, and operations orders, and his precious guidebook-notes. It was the disappearance of these last that worried him most. They were slanted against the very roots of the country itself, nihilistic or not, and so he could be held responsible for them even by a law-and-order régime.

The waiter threw his screwed-up bill on to the table, and waited sullenly for him to pay it. 'The new government will settle that,' said Richard, opening it out. 'I'll sign for it, though.'

'Oh no, you won't,' cried the waiter, turning red with rage. 'You'll pay now, in cash, you foreign scum, or I'll telephone the Shooting Squads.'

Richard stood up. 'I'm a general in your army, and you'll be tried for this, when I get back from Tungsten.'

'You're not a general,' the waiter scoffed, 'you're a tourist and a spy, that's what you are, so pay up peacefully. Even our great and noble President Took wouldn't refuse to settle his bill like an honest man. I suppose you are one of those diabolical Nihilists whose yoke we've had to suffer under these last twenty-five years. Well, we know what to do with people like you!'

He was shouting, and Richard saw that he must pay the seven hundred klipps demanded, which nevertheless seemed outrageously expensive, though he supposed it would go towards repairing the great crack down the bullet-proof glass terrace caused by the premature destruction of the People's Academy of Erotic Arts and Crafts. 'Your bill is two thousand klipps,' said the waiter, coolly writing this new amount in pencil.

'The government has banned bribery,' Richard cried out, undoing his tie.

'But I still expect a tip, dear friend. How else do you think I'm going to live? The price of bread has already doubled.'

'Doubled?'

'In the last hour. Now that honesty is in, the traders say they must charge honest prices. Everyone has to live. You can't deny that.'

Richard put down two thousand-klipp notes, being anxious to look for his briefcase. 'There'll be an enquiry about this.'

The waiter pocketed the money with a good-natured laugh, and made as if to pat him on the back, but thought better of it: 'Don't be grumpy, dear friend. The only thing to do is enjoy life, like a good Nihilonian. I can see you're new to the country. And it *is* a great country, you know.' Richard left while the waiter was still talking to himself about the eternal virtues of Nihilon in particular, and human life in general.

Chapter Thirty-one

Ex-President Took rose from his narrow bed and began to dress. He was seventy-five years old, tall and lean, with a nest of wild white hair which was always difficult to comb, especially first thing in the morning. As the day wore on it became more tractable and, while sweeping between the giant computers, wearing his white overall and holding a long-handled brush, he would stop and take a comb from his pocket. After attempting to run it through his hair he would sigh and go on with his work. The clever young men at the computers had long since given up teasing him about it. In any case, most of them were no longer young, in many ways sympathising with his plight, for they were just as much prisoners as he.

From a fiery, progressive, hard-dealing president of a wayward republic who had spent much of his life trying to set his country on the path of rectitude, Took had perforce turned into a mild, studious, hard-working old man whose only loyalty was to the cleanliness of the Tungsten Space-Research Station.

For the administrative staff of Tungsten, day and night had been reduced to eternity, being divided into A, B, and C shifts of eight hours each that went in rotation forever and ever. Professor Took (as an inmate had inevitably dubbed him at the beginning) was on B shift, and left his bed at seven in order to start work at eight. The canteen never closed, but the menu imperceptibly changed throughout the twenty-four hours, from supper to breakfast, to lunch, to dinner and back to supper. Working on the cafeteria system, it was one of many canteens in the vast space-project compound. Professor Took picked up a tray, pausing to read the menu:

> Starcrush, with Milk-all-the-way
> Moonsteak and Marseggs,
> Galaxy Bran, with Astrobreads.

His sharp appetite made him suspect that the countdown was close. The two people chosen for the honour of occupying the first Nihilon space-rocket were said by the serving-woman in her stained overall to have had a good night's rest.

'Away from each other, of course,' added Professor Took, but such humour was lost on that dour face, which did not allow itself to smile because of too much work, for she merely pushed over his dish of Starcrush, with Milk-all-the-way, and passed him along to the next counter.

He sat by himself. In any case, no one would eat with him, since they found him so garrulous. But Took considered it both polite and desirable to converse with others, especially during a meal. When not working, people either ate or slept. When they slept, they dreamed, which meant talking to oneself. And when they ate, they thought, which meant talking to others.

A man was not an automaton with no inner life. Only the Nihilists thought that—which was why they took such trouble to give him one. At the same time Took was wise enough to realise that the technical workers of Tungsten were too preoccupied to take an old fool like him into their confidence. Their inner lives were sufficiently enriched by a desire to enslave the cosmos, while for Took this space research station was one place in the country where nihilism could not strictly prevail, and he considered himself lucky to have been captured in the neighbourhood, and incarcerated with other inmates and workers in the sort of social and professional discipline he had always thought to inculcate into the feckless masses of Nihilon. It was at the same time unfortunate that he could never go back into his country with the experience he had gained in this rare enclave of it. For though people did not talk much in Tungsten, they worked together, and depended totally upon each other, and Took saw that you could not get much closer than that to a well-ordered earth.

He had been sadly aware during the last few weeks that this striving together as one family would soon be at an end, for he saw that when the first rocket went up, their brotherly unity would be broken by its very success. He would like this preparatory stage to go on forever, for the finale never to come, and so he had conceived a plan to do something about it, proving that the indefatigable brain of President Took, which he had once used well to guide his country, had by no means atrophied at Tungsten.

Picking up his sweeping-brush, he walked along the corridor, towards an outdoor lift. A familiar and friendly figure to everyone, he was left more or less to wander where he wished. At the beginning he had been strictly enrolled in a cleaning brigade, but of late years he had deliberately developed an absent-mindedness that created havoc in any well-run group. So he was ordered, as a punishment whose purpose was to reduce him to a form of nihilism which everyone assumed he would hate bitterly because of his past, to be a member of no particular group, but to drift on his own and where he liked, as long as he kept out of the way and appeared to make himself useful. It was thus expected that his insanity would increase, and that he would soon lapse into a final state of foolishness that could justify turning him loose, or sending him to the Groves of Aspron.

But Took's brain was as clear as ever, under his cloud of amiability. When he stepped from the elevator and pushed through the guarded swing-doors, it seemed as if the magic eye winked at him. He walked towards the immense rocket set on its launching pad. From a distance it loomed so huge and solid that he thought it would pull much of the earth with it when it lifted off. A chain of work-trailers drawn by a tractor separated him from his objective, and while waiting for it to pass, he swept the concrete floor at his feet, creating a circle of cleanliness, within which he stood for some minutes and marvelled at the purity of the earth on which he felt himself privileged to be.

His private countdown had started on leaving the breakfast table. Illuminated numbers ran through his brain as if on the flash-level of the Master Com forever in front of his and everyone else's eyes. The elevator took him, brush on shoulder, up the immense side of the rocket, and before entering he glanced at the super carnival-ground of the space-age spread below, with its monitoring centres, work-sheds, radial living-quarters, community lake, and a network of ways and roads lacing over the plateau of the Athelstan Alps.

The control panel was no mystery to a brain which had not ceased to take in information during the twenty-five years of imprisonment. He had obtained the special tools, without which certain key plates leading to the rear cables could not have been dehinged. It was thought that Professor Took had given up his youthful and middle-aged ideals, but they had hidden and rested in the deepest recesses of his heart, and no influence had been able to reach them. He smiled, and wiped his nose, and considered that his long imprisonment had been worth it, since he was the only man in Tungsten able to save the country, and therefore the world, from the spectacle of this obscene aurora blazing its vile rites in the sky for all to see, in order that nihilism might be perpetuated to the end of time.

And yet, even though the project might actually be called obscene, these space nuptials were to be far from illicit. It was no dirty weekend that Nihilon had planned. The two candidates were to be joined in official matrimony before being packed into the rocket and launched towards their honeymoon. Though this seemed to go against nihilism, the authorities had decided on it as a mark of politeness to the other more moral nations of the world who could not then refuse to show this immortal film to their abundant and eager viewers.

Thus, as well as applauding the technological expertise of nihilism, Nihilon would also be the beneficiary of an untold amount of money in copyright fees. But Professor Took had decided that he could not permit his once proud and honourable country to solve its balance-of-payments problem in this way.

He cut two of the power lines, then joined them together, each to the wrong one. Piece by piece, he methodically worked the countdown with the other side of his brain while he coolly probed and severed. Even the last-minute tests would be read as normal, because of his simple idea of sliding a length of pencil into each vital pipe.

When the rocket went into orbit, a rejection by the computer of its allotted plan would not give it the expected performance. After one circuit of the earth the capsule would detach itself for re-entry, and come back by parachute to the Athelstan plateau. Thus, though the Nihilonian space-programme would not succeed, neither would it be a total failure in the eyes of the world. This was an important consideration for President Took because, as an ex-president of the country, he was still loyal to it, despite the régime. Neither did he have any wish to kill the passengers.

The air was fresh on his way down, a cool breeze licking through the warmth, for he went not by lift, but by the steps, sweeping each one until he came to the bottom. The rest of the day he spent going with his sweeping-brush from one hall to another, sometimes behind the regular cleaners, who had already scoured them well by super-thorough vacuum machines, and occasionally in advance, when his feeble attempts at sweeping were not noticed.

At the evening meal there was much more talk than usual, and he gathered from the confused chatter that a crisis had struck the space-programme, something so serious that there were even bottles of Nihilitz on the tables. For a few minutes of devastating uncertainty his veins seemed blocked and ready to snap at the thought that his sabotage had been discovered, and he waited for louder and more insistent voices to let him know whether or not this was the case. He put on his characteristic shamble and walked from the counter with a bowl of Betelgeuse soup and a round of zodiac bread, and found an empty table between two full and overcrowded ones.

Their talk poured into him, with such force that it was almost more than his mind could bear. Soup trickled on to his wrist when he tried to drink it, and he gripped the edge of the table, thinking he was going to faint. He caught the phrase 'intestinal fever', and it gradually penetrated his state of trance that the two subjects set to take part in the space copulation had become so ill that they could not be expected to perform when the rocket went up tomorrow.

Twenty-five years' work would come to nothing if they couldn't shove another loving couple into that rocket in the morning. Professor Took, in his tearful bewilderment at this unexpected turn, heard some of the technicians actually laughing loudly, as if it were funny. Meanwhile, the armies of insurrection were closing in, and almost no troops were deploying to stop them, apart from the garrison of Tungsten itself. President Nil's guards were nowhere to be seen or heard. The frontier divisions were at the frontier, making sure that the Geriatrics did their bit. And the ordinary Nilitia Regiments had either gone to ground or joined the insurrectionaries.

But the lack of an army seemed the least worry to those whose job it was to see that the heavenly nuptials took place as planned. And such had been the insidious influence of nihilism that, in spite of the strictest precautions, no one had suggested training reserve passengers for the historic flight that was to put Nihilon in the forefront of nations. Unless a young man and woman of sufficient physical stamina and mutual attraction were found quickly, a great calamity was upon them.

Chapter Thirty-two

Surveying the distant establishment from the roof of Benjamin's car, it appeared as no accident to Jaquiline that the Groves of Aspron protected the approaches to the rocket-launching base of Tungsten. The first three hundred insurrectionaries had gone into the attack, dodging skilfully between oak and olive trees, and getting as close as possible to the compound wire.

Lifting themselves up from the psychiatrists' couches, the inmates of Aspron were given rifles by orderlies who only days ago had fought to fasten them down during one of their typical anti-Nihilist frenzies. The patients formed up and marched smartly through the central square of the buildings, and then past their director, who took the salute with tears in his eyes from a rostrum of packing-cases now emptied of the latest drugs. From there they went straight to the front, lining the barbed wire behind a rough embankment of stones and soil.

When three hundred of his best troops withered and wavered under the shattering hail of bullets, Benjamin sat by his car to think. A siege would take too long: he hadn't sufficient men to bottle up Aspron with part of his column while the rest went to Tungsten. Neither did he care to lose half his force in dead or wounded to capture it, for then he wouldn't have enough to use in the great battle yet to come. He decided to send six hundred of his hardiest guerrillas through the Groves of Aspron to attack from the south. Since the lunatic defenders did not realise his strength, they must be shown it, for while they were busy holding that assault, he would launch a shock offensive along both sides of the Aspron–Agbat road.

The southerly arm would be led by two lorries laden with petrol drums—which would run into the wall and catch fire. Jaquiline wanted to drive one of these vehicles, and Benjamin, knowing her hatred of nihilism, and the blows she had suffered from it, gave permission for her to do so. A soldier on the seat beside her clutched a string of hand-grenades for use when they stopped at the compound fence.

The sun was low, but the heat of day still hung over them. A petrol stench floated thickly in the lorry and made her feel faint, but she held the wheel on course for the wall, still two hundred metres away. White-coated figures carrying rifles scurried behind the wire. But they seemed to be few, as if no more than pickets had been left at this point, the others having gone to repel the diversionary attack. Nevertheless, their fire at both lorries now coming up the slope was consistent and accurate.

Jaquiline suddenly thought of flames, and of being burned in them. The air was buzzing around her, ending in sharp clicks as bullets struck tyres or metal rims. The windscreen changed into a jigsaw puzzle, then fell to pieces, and the soldier was whining on the floor. She took her foot from the clutch to kick him, and he got up again, bleeding at the face.

Fifty metres from the wall, the men in white coats were shouting. She couldn't imagine what they had to discuss with her, and when the lorry stalled she turned the ignition key, feeling the vibrating accelerator underfoot, and rammed the lorry into the wall, pushing the soldier as a sign that he should get out and do his work. A bird fell against the bonnet when she tried to open the door. The second lorry was already burning to her right. A bullet had smashed one door and jammed it. The other was too hot to open, so the only way free was through the shattered windscreen.

She screamed at the sight of a bird beating its wings on broken glass. Another bullet swept it away. Her eyes were fixed by leaves falling, black dust and smoke. A white-coated figure climbed the low wall and leapt on to the bonnet, pulling hard to free her. They rolled to the ground.

'Lay flat,' he said, for they were still on the exposed side of the wall. But Jaquiline staggered to safety behind a tree, while a stray bullet caught her rescuer, keeping him in the fire-zone. Sheets of hot metal and petrol went far and wide. Some insurrectionist soldiers were caught as they rushed forward, but the conflagration cleared the wall, which in any case was not intensively manned.

Though such pyrotechnics hadn't been strictly necessary, they had put heart into the attackers, and discouraged the defenders from reinforcing the wall should they have thought to do so. Several hundred of Benjamin's men entered the compound, though it turned out that the other attacks had also been successful. As messages came to his Thundercloud, he felt justified in using such weight in view of the urgent need to push on that night towards Tungsten, which was still thirty kilometres away.

An immense bonfire was made of many psychiatrist's couches, together with tons of records and notes that had been scrupulously kept on every patient of past and present. To atone for their sins against humanity, the doctors were ordered to care for the wounded, and to bury the dead, and those members of the staff who refused were threatened with a course of their own electric-shock therapy, at which they turned amiable and accepted all Benjamin's conditions.

Indeed, it was easier to win over the doctors and medical staff to the insurrectionist cause than the patients, who saw the capture of Aspron as just another trap, a noisy and realistic show staged by the staff so as to make the final test on their loyalty to nihilism. They were like hunted people, physically well-fed and cared for, but only so that they would be able to run when the great chase was on. Even the presence of dead and wounded after the battle didn't convince them, for those who had been there longest whispered that such attention to detail was not unknown.

Observing Benjamin's perplexity and disappointment, the Big Doctor offered to set up a quick course of persuasion, promising that at the end of a week every patient would be eager to join the new cause. Benjamin turned down his proposal (while seeing the sense of it), though he decided to retain him as his medical officer for the attack on the rocket base.

Immense food stores were found, and long tables were set out in the main square so that soldiers and ex-patients could dine together. Other captured booty included a score of forty-seater Maloram Mountain Buses, as well as two hundred Zap sports cars. Benjamin had already sent an advance-guard of eight hundred soldiers towards Tungsten, and now, at midnight, every light turned on, the patients' band of the Aspron Psychic Redemption Institution (Lunatics) performed a fairly musical interpretation of 'Honesty Forever'.

With the Malorams lined up and the Zaps in four files behind, he looked back on his army from the battered and windowless command car. Full of life's joy and fervour, he gave a salute, then got in and turned the ignition key.

Jaquiline was not in her accustomed place. There had been so much work after his victory that he had not missed her until now, when the enormous blunder of her absence shot him out of the car. He sent runners to every vehicle saying that the advance would be delayed until she was found. Search parties went into the surrounding groves, while the ex-patients scoured the compound and buildings.

He brooded in Big Doctor's office, because there was nothing else to be done. Several crates of Nihilitz and Anihilitz were found in a store-cellar by patients who had not tasted such fiery ambrosia for years, and they were soon wandering around in a state of agreeable drunkenness. The staff did nothing to stop them breaking into rooms and offices, out of fear because they had now lost all authority, but mostly, it must be said, to increase the very atmosphere of nihilism that this army of barbaric insurrectionists had hoped to subdue.

Because of this confusion, and darkness beyond the walls, it was by no means easy to search for Jaquiline.

Benjamin walked up and down the small room, sweating with worry and impatience, sipping now and again at a glass of water mixed with Nihilitz. Big Doctor offered pills to calm his nerves, but Benjamin refused, though he didn't know why. The Nihilitz was making him drowsy, in spite of his ravening anxiety, which was a bad thing because he still had to drive all night through unknown country on a rotten road, in the darkness, as well as fight a decisive battle in the morning. If he didn't start soon he wouldn't get there on time, and the whole combined operation might fail, in which case that nihilistic cargo of space-pornography would be triumphantly launched.

It was no use waiting, he decided. They would continue the search after he left, and if Jaquiline were found she could be driven to Tungsten in Big Doctor's car, a swift and comfortable Mangler which was to be left behind for her.

With two soldiers at the radio set, and Big Doctor on the other seat, Benjamin drove through the shattered gate, at the head of his column, almost an hour off schedule. Outside, where darkness began, a piece of sharp flint punctured his left front wheel. It was a rancid omen, and he matched it with ripe curses. Big Doctor, he saw, was smiling. The soldiers didn't know how to work the jack and change the wheel, so he did it himself, a task which calmed him down, and was performed so quickly and well that Big Brother's smile went back into his long face.

The black trees looming around were fixed in their own deep dreams, stalwart trunks brought forward in every case by the Thundercloud's headlights. The advance-guard had left luminosity-stones to mark the route, which made it easy to follow. He felt carefree, back at his favourite work, for in spite of his sedentary life so far, Benjamin was convinced that he was at last doing what he had been born for—to be a soldier, no matter in what cause he was fighting.

Chapter Thirty-three

Forty soldiers were needed to haul Mella's wagon into the mountains. Edgar sat as usual by her side, his arm in a sling, so doted on and wept over that his life became unbearable, especially when he heard Adam and Firebrand making contemptuous remarks from their seats of a little less honour behind.

The groaning soldiers, as they dug their feet in against loose stones and shale, and flexed their arms around thick rope attached to the platform, were insults to Edgar's ears, an injustice that no upright God-hating Nihilist government would have allowed. Adam, on the other hand, from his throne of poetry, seemed to enjoy this mode of travel, and sat back in comfort, when he wasn't leaning forward to chide Edgar about the continual mothering he was forced to put up with from Mella.

Firebrand did not mind how he travelled as long as he ate and drank frequently, though once the ascent into the mountains began he complained that the jerking of the platform made him feel sick. Edgar, whose ears had become finely attuned to insults drifting from that direction, now suggested that if things got worse, as it was inevitable that they should, then Firebrand would do well to get off the platform and walk. Failing that, he might try propelling himself on that crazy bicycle he'd ridden so successfully into Orcam, now strapped on to planks at the back of the vehicle, and preciously guarded because Mella wanted to make it the prime exhibit in the Museum of the Honest Insurrection after the war. Firebrand scowled, and swung his green face to concentrate on the semi-woodland that covered this part of the ascent, in the hope that it would prevent him being sick.

The forty hauliers were relieved after a two-hour go at the tow ropes, and another relay took their places. But for his wounded arm Edgar would have worked with them—except that it might have made him even more of a hero in Mella's moted eyes. The attempt to escape, and his inadvertent part in the night attack on Orcam bridge, came back to him as the highlight of his Nihilonian experience, his one act of so-called heroism, whose memory caused Mella to lean over him now with her moon face and half-bare breasts, tears falling through her kisses as she enquired again about the bullet scratch on his arm. If this was law and order he longed for the days of wildcat, sky-tearing nihilism—a desire he could confide to no one around him.

The soldiers tugged all day and far into the night, until it was reckoned by the geographical equipment looted from Edgar that they were about ten kilometres south of Tungsten. Mella decided to rest her brigade a few hours before moving them into the zone of final contest. A large tent was pitched for herself and Edgar, while Firebrand and Adam were left to themselves in the open air.

A yellow moon laboured above the cork trees, and Adam wondered, as a poet, whether it would give birth to anything when tomorrow's rocket hurled itself up with grand impacted power from the Athelstan Alps. The rocket-load of prospective fecundity was all set to flower in tribute to the full moon, and the Nihilists, by choosing such a time, had enlisted even its powerful aid in their startling project. Circum-stances had drawn him into this anti-Nihilist expedition, yet as a poet he wished them the greatest success. When the time came, he wouldn't pick up a rifle to fight, but would contrive to hang back while the mobs of honesty and the rabble of order flung themselves at Tungsten to ruin the most poetic spectacle the world had ever known.

Insects vibrated through the trees. Why should anyone want to shatter such peace? What, after all, was wrong with Nihilon and its way of life? To get away from the drunken and pig-like snoring of Firebrand (who wasn't totally degenerate, however, because he was still part of the lovable system of Nihilon), Adam recounted all the tribulations he had suffered since crossing the frontier, which now seemed no more than the ordinary adventures of any tourist in a foreign country. Soon, due to the fanatical sentimentalism of Mella and her followers, the dull wash of order and honesty would flow over this delightful territory of unexpected happenings, the last place on earth that a benevolent nihilistic régime seemed to have set aside for the delectation of poets!

Nihilism's downfall seemed certain, and he was a helpless onlooker. In spite of the battle of Orcam, little resistance had been shown by the

Nihilists so far. What self-respecting régime would have allowed its enemy to pitch camp, and sleep in such peace so close to the final objective? Where was the perfect and bloody ambush which anyone with a truly nihilistic temperament would have set for them? Perhaps the outer defences of Tungsten had yet to be encountered, or maybe the garrison of that place had no idea of the danger threatening from this direction. He began to wonder why he did not forfeit his night's sleep, and make his way into Tungsten to tell them.

One of the salutary effects of Nihilon on a person like Adam was that no sooner did he think of something than he acted upon it. Even more beneficial was the fact that he didn't even wonder why this was so. Easing away from Firebrand, he walked into the shadows of the trees, and made his escape between half-asleep pickets.

He went along by the light of the moon, the road ascending in curves up the mountainside, well-lit till it entered another belt of forest. After a few kilometres he felt guilty at deserting the forces of order and honesty, in spite of his former clear sentiments. A sense of inexpressible remorse made him gloomy, but his feet would not go back, as if fixed on their course by a firm turn of destiny. He knew in his socially responsible heart that no matter how he rationalised the attractive qualities of nihilism, nihilism alone was not enough to sustain the ordered life that was necessary to his comfort.

He kept on walking upwards, because an ascending movement demanded the physical exertion which enabled him to put up with such intense misery of indecision. If he turned back towards the camp, the reason for his guilt would vanish, but the memory of it would be so painful that the easy descent would not then help him to bear it.

After several hours, during which the weight of his guilt became beneficial in that it put him into a walking trance so that it no longer bothered him, he sat down for a rest before entering another zone of trees. Perhaps I am doing right, after all, he said to himself, wondering whether he shouldn't stop thinking about it altogether. But then such blankness of mind was alien to him, and he was afraid that if he didn't think, he would soon cease to have any emotions whatsoever. He could recognise danger when it came too close. If his legs ached, he was emotionally tired. If he was hungry, he was emotionally deprived. If he was feeling guilty it was because he was emotionally unfulfilled. But at least he was alive. Comforted by such reflections, he went on his way.

The road was a twisting footpath ascending between the trees. He'd been going so long and at such a rate that he expected to reach the plateau of Tungsten any minute, but there was no sign of it yet, nor of those defences against honesty and order that the Nihilists should have built.

Pausing to tie his shoelace, he heard a rustling in a nearby clump of bushes. Accustomed to the half-darkness, he straightened, and saw a human being staggering towards him. He instinctively looked for a place to hide, but the figure, seeing him, ran away first, so he turned and gave chase.

It was not a long pursuit, neither far nor fast. 'I shan't hurt you,' he cried.

He knelt, to find that it was a woman who had fallen into the bracken, dressed like a soldier of the insurrectionary army. 'Keep away from me,' she wailed, when he shone the torch into her face. Her eyes stared, as if waiting for the expected blow, and he drew his light back: 'Who are you?'

'I'm looking for Benjamin Smith,' she moaned. 'I lost him at the battle of Aspron.'

'I thought we were going to meet in Nihilon City,' he said reproachfully, when he recognised her.

She stood up and leaned against a tree. 'So did I. But I must have been knocked out at Aspron, and when I woke up, the fighting was over. I started to walk, wanting to get back to Benjamin in Aspron, but I got lost. Where are we?'

He lit a cigarette for her. 'Near Tungsten, I should think.'

'I meant to meet you in Nihilon City,' she said when they walked on. 'I really did.' He held her hand, wondering what had happened to her in Nihilon. He asked, but she only promised to tell him when they were home again. Strangely, she felt safer, being alone with Adam, her lover who had been lost but was now found again in the great forest of the Athelstan Alps, than with Benjamin and his all-conquering army. When they stopped, she pressed against him: 'Don't let me out of your sight for a second. Don't let me go so far that you can't reach out and touch me!'

She had never been so fervent or afraid in her busy and fashionable life beyond Nihilon, he remembered. This country seemed to have changed her utterly, which made him so happy that he blessed the guidebook they had been sent to write. 'I won't,' he promised, pressing her close, and wanting to make love.

'Not yet,' she said, buttoning her shirt. 'I love you so much.' But the exquisite sensations of unfulfilled desire gave them an even more intense feeling of safety. 'Where shall we go?' she asked.

He was hungry, but thought it indelicate to say so: 'Nihilon City would be the best place, but it's some way off. And we'll have to hide in the woods till Mella's column has gone through.'

'I want to get out of this country,' she said, her self-assurance suddenly diminishing in spite of him. 'I'm frightened.'

Adam saw nothing ahead but hunger, if they didn't reach a town or village before the new day was out. Getting finally home was too far away to contemplate, a distant mixed-up vision of heaven and hell that he couldn't shake into focus, though he did not confide this to Jaquiline who, in the first light of dawn, looked at him lovingly from her blue eyes.

For some time they had been observed by an invisible circle of orderlies from the space-station. The tender behaviour of our lovers was noted with satisfaction, and the ringleader of these marauders at last gave his signal. There was a crack of twigs and a scuffle of stones, and on turning sharply to see who was there, Adam heard a scream from Jaquiline before he himself was brought down. A thin rope was tied around his wrists.

Jaquiline sobbed as she was carried away. Her bitterness at this latest molestation, from the very arms of Adam, was such that no words from him could comfort her. Adam was also pulled along, though he was aware of his captors doing it with as little roughness as possible.

'Where are we going?' he demanded.

'A long way,' laughed one of the men.

'Up!' said another.

Chapter Thirty-four

Two-faced flags were out in Nihilon City, one side marked for the Festival of Liberation by the Army of Honesty and Order, the other marked to celebrate the Festival of Salvation by the Forces of Nihilism. Despite a generally expectant air of enjoyment, no one could yet say with certainty which side of the flag would be finally displayed, though the fact that it would obviously be one side or the other made the people happy enough.

The city was in the hands of order and honesty however, and reinforcements of Cronacian troops shuttling up from Shelp were said to have been marching through the suburbs all day, dressed in the blue overalls of the insurrection, on their way to attack the last bastion of nihilism at Tungsten. But the people, with their two-faced flags, convertible bunting, and age-old instincts, were by no means convinced of their victory.

Richard passed the early part of the night looking for the man who had stolen his briefcase. He telephoned the professor to report its loss, and was told that such carelessness was an act of treason, and that he would be shot out of hand for it when the forces of law and order brought him to justice, as they undoubtedly would. Determined that this should not happen, Richard returned to his room at the Hotel Stigma, to gather up his few possessions and leave the city before daybreak, then make his way to the escape port of Shelp.

But his briefcase was on the bed, and nothing had been taken from it. With mixed feelings at finding it again, he was faced with the moral problem as to whether or not he should go on with his work as an insurrectionary general, or follow through his plan of slipping away to Shelp and safety. The art of living under nihilism consisted in being able to make moral decisions of a fundamental nature every few hours instead of every ten years. Most Nihilists solved it, he had found, by discounting the ethics of each problem, and merely making a choice in the form of a gamble. Thus they saved themselves from moral inanition, but only at the expense of the soul itself, a payment which nevertheless enabled them to go on living with a certain amount of spirit, until such time as the damaged soul could, if they desired it, reconstitute its moral qualities once more, possibly under a new régime of honesty and law. This would no doubt impose its own peculiar form of ethics, with just as much bother to conscientious citizens.

A note attached to the handle of the briefcase said that in a country noted for its nihilism he should trust no one, and that in a régime soon to be distinguished for its honesty he should trust them even less. 'However,' a postcript from the young man added, 'I hope that if honesty triumphs, and I am brought to trial, you will have the goodness to remember that I protected your invaluable briefcase during the hours when it was undoubtedly in great peril from real thieves and other such nihilistic scum.'

Richard, deciding to set out for the rendezvous with his loyally waiting troops, put on his general's cap, fastened the revolver-belt, and went downstairs carrying the briefcase. The clerk at the desk sat to attention and saluted smartly, a mark of respect that Richard hadn't received on going into the hotel.

'Excuse me, sir,' the clerk said, passing him a straw shopping-basket, 'perhaps you'll need this. It contains bread and cheese, sausage, Nihilitz, and packets of chocolate. And good luck, sir,' he added, as Richard went outside to the waiting car, feeling like a real general at last.

There was little hard marching to be done, for a railway went into the mountains, so that an immensely long train took Richard and his brigade as far as the copper-mining township of Tolemac. A seat was found for him in the engine-cab, and he sat there from the passing of night through dawn and daylight, studying his map by the glow of a torch. Beside him was a wireless-operator whose apparatus was fixed to the back of the plate. Cursing and sweating, the stokers were feeding coal into the huge white-mouthed boiler, their spades swinging dangerously close to Richard as he puzzled over possible systems of deployment on arrival at Tungsten.

They travelled the final forty kilometres by road, most of his brigade finding enough lorries at Tolemac for a shuttle service, so that by nine o'clock he was observing Tungsten through field-glasses from the cover of a grove of trees. The white, glistening, low walls of the compound were five kilometres square, and seemed by no means impregnable in the blue and brilliant light of this vital day.

No preparations appeared to have been made for its defence, which he found strange, not to say disappointing. Several thousand metres of open ground lay between his soldiers and the walls. In the middle of the extensive compound of buildings and hangars he now saw the rocket, surrounded by a gridwork of superstructure, rearing up slim and grey from this distance, and smokily shining in the new morning light, the last score or so metres of its pinnacle coloured a glittering crimson. He clandestinely thought it a pity to stop such a marvellous engine going its natural way into the heavens, regretting that it wouldn't begin to rise up now, for him alone, in front of his very eyes.

But the air shimmered around it, and the compound seemed un-inhabited. It had been given out on Radio Tungsten the previous evening, in a Lies bulletin of nihilistic candour, that the two candidates destined for the sexual hook-up had become ill, and that no replacements were available, though the staff were leaving no stone unturned to find some. Richard, gazing across at the magnificent rocket, felt his groin aching at such frustrations of the Nihilon Space Plan, and the preposterous but delightful thought came to him that he wouldn't mind offering himself as the male specimen for this experiment, no matter what the dangers might be. He tried to bring the rocket-head closer and closer, till his binoculars were overfocused and it shimmered into a haze.

A long black estate car nosed its way between the trees, and Richard went to meet it. 'Right on time,' he said, when Benjamin Smith got out. 'I hear you had a hard fight at Aspron.'

This was true, yet nothing had been harder for Benjamin to bear than the loss of Jaquiline Sulfer. His troops coming up behind had seen no sign of her. He wondered whether she hadn't been wounded during the attack, and pulled against her will into the Aspron complex, hidden among those endless corridors where it would be impossible to find her. Should he receive evidence that this was true, he would return with his army, after the capture of Tungsten, and raze Aspron to the ground. He would show those Nihilists what nihilism really meant, though in the meantime there was the attack plan to talk over: 'How many men have you got?'

'Two thousand here, and another thousand coming up—mostly Cronacians.'

'Can't use those,' said Benjamin. 'It's got to be done by Nihilon alone. The country cleanses itself—with no outside help. That's what we need for the history books, anyway.'

'They're in Nihilonian uniforms,' Richard said, amused at his probity. It was obvious that Benjamin had been fighting in the country, instead of in the more sophisticated moral atmosphere of the capital.

'Makes no difference,' he answered stiffly. 'It'll get known.'

'Whether we use Cronacians or not, people will *say* we did. So we might as well,' Richard went on, and Benjamin remembered that he was known for his diplomacy—a polite euphemism for his irritating persistence. He looked at him closely—an unstable face, the apotheosis of nihilism on a man supposed to be in the vanguard of reliability and honesty. But he too had suffered such feelings, so turned away and lit a cigar. His orderlies took a table from the back of a nearby lorry, and set it up under the trees. Richard leaned over it, and looked at the plan of Tungsten that Benjamin unrolled: 'There are four thousand in my column,' he said, 'all of them good Nihilonians, meaning fierce, under-privileged, well-trained, honest, and totally confused in their political ideas. That makes seven thousand. With two thousand from Mella Took, we have nine altogether. Three tough brigades. We should be able to crush the place in a couple of hours.'

Richard liked neither his tune nor tone, and certainly not his bland, business-like assumption of total command. 'My troops are exhausted,' he said. 'They need time to prepare for the attack.'

Any such softness annoyed Benjamin, who foresaw trouble if he did not show firmness now: 'The sooner they get it over with, the better. That's what all soldiers think, believe me, no matter how exhausted they are. In any case, it's easier to die when you're tired. You waste less energy that way. But here's Mella, so let's welcome her.'

Richard had heard about this extraordinary woman in Nihilon City, and how he saw her chariot-platform bedecked with blue and green ribbons, drawn by scores of soldiers singing verses from the folk-song written by President Took and often sung over his baby daughter's cradle called 'Honesty is the Best Policy', while as many others advanced before it with long knives cutting at foliage so that it could get through.

She sat stiffly, enthroned on a sort of padded armchair, trying to look stern, though her soft dark eyes were too good-natured to instil fear, Richard thought. Yet her impressive pose certainly called for respect, which could not be said for the other person on a smaller chair beside her, a man with his arm in a sling who, as they came closer, he recognised as his third colleague.

Edgar looked uncomfortable, stiff and self-conscious due to the proximity of Mella Took, whose hand affectionately caressed his as the platform advanced, so that Richard had an uncontrollable desire to laugh. But he broke into a cough, hoping to disguise his breach of manners sufficiently to go forward and help her descent.

'You are very kind,' Mella said, gratefully holding his hand. 'I hope I'm not too late to discuss our methods of attack?' Richard felt his hand squeezed affectionately as he led her to the table, from which she picked up binoculars to view the rocket-base. For some minutes she was absolutely still, as if trying to hypnotise it into surrender.

Edgar descended from the platform, and the three men drank a victory toast. 'I hear that Nihilitz will be banned by the new government,' Richard said.

'Let's have another then, for absent friends,' Benjamin proposed, thinking of Jaquiline. Edgar said that Adam had also vanished, though he saw less reason than Benjamin to think that these events could be in any way connected.

Mella wanted to lead the attack from the high point of her chariot, with Edgar at her side, a massed head-on assault of all three brigades against the main gate of Tungsten. Benjamin dissuaded her from this on the grounds that her life was precious and must be saved for the future of Nihilon, a country which her gracious presence would do much to rebuild. Edgar backed him up, while trying not to sound too enthusiastic. In any case, Benjamin was determined to carry through his own special arrangements no matter what Mella might suggest— in her misguided and romantic zeal. If she insisted on wielding her military influence he would have her bound and gagged and slung into a guarded thicket with her love-struck companion, even if he had to shoot down her eighty stalwarts to do it. She was not the linchpin of his campaign, and he had no time today to indulge in detestable debate. His anger decreased to a mere nihilistic interior seething, which he could only finally control by getting his own way and capturing Tungsten for the forces of law and order with the unique plan he had in mind.

He strode up and down to calm himself, reflecting with some satisfaction that he had turned into one of those influential men who not only make decisions but also carry them through. He wasn't aware of too much pride in this, only a mathematical realism which unfailingly produced confidence when there was some danger of it being taken away.

So he expounded his plan, while Mella ate a bunch of large black grapes and looked at him admiringly with her cow-like eyes. He didn't doubt that she took in clearly all that he was saying, for it was astonishingly simple, and in the long run such a plan would be economical of human lives, for if it succeeded only a small proportion of their army would be used. He had two hundred red Zap sports cars to play with, and would send the first hundred against the southern line of the Tungsten perimeter, with ladders strapped to their roofs which would be laid at the wall by the four men crammed into each car. The second hundred cars, also containing four men each, would assist the first wave to breach the wall, thus paving the way for a brigade of foot-soldiers who would swarm in after them. The two regiments of cars were inaugurated as the Zap Brigade—or Mella's Own, Benjamin added as a brilliant afterthought to win her to his side, kneeling like a knight of old to kiss her hand.

She put her gracious blessing to his plan, and a sumptuous breakfast was spread under the trees. Benjamin ate quickly, giving orders between mouthfuls concerning the Charge of the Zap Brigade which was to carry everything before it, standing now and again to look through binoculars and see figures scurrying up and down the mass of scaffolding lapped around the lower part of the rocket. He had one hour from the start of his attack to reach the computer room and prevent blast-off at midday. Special squads of engineers were to lay explosives around the launching-pad and blow it—and themselves, most likely—to pieces while it was still on the ground.

He mentioned, as a sort of half joke to Mella, that one could be ingenious in military affairs when one had nothing else to think about, and she gave him such a smile that the loss of Jaquiline faded from his mind. 'I admire you,' she said, 'and I shall wear that admiration in my heart for quite some time.'

With a flicker of intoxicating fantasy—at such a time—Benjamin wondered whether he ought not to cultivate her high opinion of him, though as if he didn't care for it at all, so that he might one day be sitting on the throne of Nihilon with Queen Mella at his side. After a while, of course, Mella would disappear, and he would reign alone, a sad and ruthless monarch despoiling the kingdom at his leisure. And who could rule more absolutely than a king over a country that had recently given itself up to twenty-five years of nihilism?

Edgar ruefully saw that his glorious bravery, which had almost smashed his right arm to pieces in the attack on Orcam Bridge, had faded from Mella's eyes as she gazed adoringly (though by no means adored, he was glad to see) on Benjamin. She had turned her soft and womanly personality away from himself, whom she could treat as an infant, to Benjamin whom she could look on as a father. Benjamin left him little time to brood, however, and sent him through the trees with a message to Brigadier Kalamata, the officer commanding the two hundred Zaps.

From each car-roof of the Zap Brigade fluttered a blue and green pennant. The two regiments were set out in perfect alignment, their blood-red vehicles glistening in the sun as if still wet from being washed. In order to strike more fear in the defenders' hearts, every headlight was turned full on, four hundred white and incandescent orbs proclaiming that the forces of purity were out for the kill at last. Benjamin, Mella, and Richard stood together on a high platform erected under cover of the trees, giving perfect views of the plain in front.

A patrol was sent forward to test the defences, and Benjamin saw the soldiers go right up to the wall, then through it by some half-concealed but well-camouflaged entrances. There had been no firing, and not one member of the patrol came back, and though he was worried about this he didn't doubt that the Zap Brigade would triumph.

Observers from the highest branches reported more activity around the launching-pad and up the scaffolding of the rocket itself. Two people in space-suits were being forced into the vehicle, suggesting to Benjamin that the Nihilists had succeeded in getting new candidates for their universal wedding, which caused him to speculate on who the victims might be, for victims they would be when his dynamite squads got to work in an hour's time and they were trapped in their nuptial coffin.

He watched the minute-hand of his dashboard clock creeping towards attack-hour. Two hundred engines idled softly, a chorus of pistons in perfect tune pushing out thin clouds of obnoxious smoke, each car holding enough fuel to reach the walls, and get back again if need be. Who but the dashing, scheming, valiant, skilful Benjamin

Smith could have used them in this way? And yet what more apt employment was there for these terror-motors of such impacted power, machines that up to now had been a menace to civilisation, such as it was, and that were now harnessed into saving it? He laughed aloud at his own subtlety, and lit a cigar. He hoisted his revolver and, as the second-hand ticked to its final spot, pressed the trigger.

Chapter Thirty-five

President Nil, watching the array of power soon to be sent against him, realised that his reign was coming to an end. He stood behind an air-vent on one of the compound roofs, watching his men running in alarm along lanes and gangways on all sides below, preparing, so they had assured him, to fight to the death. But, win or lose, the end had come as far as he was concerned. Being a born Nihilist, a firm believer through and through, he had arranged for his own disappearance, and therefore his defeat. In other words, since it was inevitable, he had decided to accept it stoically and with good grace.

Having shown for a quarter of a century that nihilism worked, he was prepared to depart in such a way as to prove that nihilism would never die. There was no other way to do it, but he sweated under his top hat, and in a fit of irritation took it off and stamped on it so that he would never be able to put it on again. Not that one, at least. He was going elsewhere because he'd run out of ideas for the moment, not because he was tired of nihilism. His motoring psyche could tick over forever on the fuel of its self-induced nihilism.

His constant extolling of total freedom, of *compulsory* freedom, of nihilism in fact, had only been a more thorough way of enslaving the population. He saw that now. It had been far more efficient than any form of socialism. Nihilism is the ultimate state of raw and naked slavery, he mused. Nihilistic private enterprise works because it enslaves most of the population for the benefit of a small portion of it. Thus it was unfair. To be fair, all must be enslaved, and only socialism can do that. But at least all people would be equal under it, and thus being equal, could easily claim that they were not enslaved, and that socialism was therefore the highest form of existence as far as society was concerned.

But he was fatally tired, and wanted to rest, needed to get away from Nihilon with the fortune he had hoarded for just such a purpose.

Already from Nihilon City airport four planeloads of gold and bank-notes had been sent to Cronacia. He knew by radio code that two had arrived safely. One had been flown to some far-off country by the treacherous pilot. Another was mistakenly shot down by Cronacian Pug 107s. This was the least valuable cargo because it contained bank-notes and not gold, and as the plane went down in flames, breaking into pieces a few hundred metres over the country, immense numbers of thousand-klipp notes fell like so much flaming confetti over the poverty-stricken villages, totally consumed to ash as soon as the grasping peasant fingers touched them.

All he had to do now was save his own skin in order to enjoy the fortune that was waiting for him, the fruits of his untiring devotion to nihilism—he might say. He looked across the plain at the lined-up sports cars and massed insurrectionary troops ready to charge over that death-space which he had set for them. Maybe a few would reach the wall, but not many. The trap was waiting, and it would give him the greatest pleasure to watch the attack of the idealists, and see how far their ideals got them under the rain of his high-precision smithereen artillery. But he could not wait to see the battle, just as he had been unable to witness so many of the set spectacular pieces of destruction he had brought about. It was enough to construct and organise them. He'd never even wanted to see films and photographs of the great dam disaster at Fludd, or read accounts of it.

During his rule he had turned the country into a fairground, and as a last gesture of private-enterprise nihilism he was going to hand it over to the forces of law and order, honesty and progress. He recalled that one of his first measures, after tugging the ropes of government into his hands, had been to decree that everyone should henceforth write with his or her left hand—a fundamental order designed to bring them into line with his régime from the heart outwards rather than from the wallet inwards. For the last few years the observance of this rule had been faltering, especially as young people had grown to man or woman-hood and proved the unfortunate conjunction of being able to rebel against both the parents and the state at the same time, something he had not anticipated, and certainly as basic as his original law.

He laughed, and wiped the sweat off his brow. What greater contribution to nihilism and benign chaos could there be than to allow order and honesty to return? Rebellion had been splintering the fabric of his beautiful Nihiland for several years, and instead of trying to prevent it taking hold, as a more misguided ruler might have done, he had surreptitiously helped it to its last rotten fruition—an over-ripe tomato about to hit him in the back of the neck, if he didn't get out quickly.

Yet he couldn't bring himself to hurry, lingered a few minutes over the subtlety and success of his scheme to have five foreigners come to Nihilon and write a guidebook about the country. They had been the final poisonous agents who would, under the umbrella of idealism, wreck his nihilist paradise, and help to change his onerous existence. It gave him great satisfaction to play with people who thought they were making history.

One of the many proverbs of Nihilon said: The end is always quicker than the beginning. And so it was, seen now to be the truest of truths as the preparations across no-man's-land went on with tigerish speed, the insurrectionist forces mercilessly goaded in their psyches by his great rocket which they wouldn't be able to stop no matter how quickly they ran, or how desperately they fought.

The tunnel under Tungsten was wide enough to take his Mangler de luxe motorcar, and it led for ten kilometres to an opening in the forest. Nil had prepared a secret chalet where he could rest for a fortnight, before getting out of the country through the seaport of Shelp. During the last twenty-five years no one had been allowed to know what he looked like. In all the newspapers, day after day for the whole reign, a speech or announcement by President Nil, or a news item concerning him, would be accompanied by a photograph of some unsuspecting citizen of Nihilon. Over the nine thousand days, every one of many newspapers and magazines of the country had used at least one photograph every day, which means that while nearly a million photographs of Nihilon citizens had been used, not one of them had been of the real President Nil.

In this one way his reign had been democratic, because a million people from all walks of life, and on his hilarious days even from the zoo, had, by their likeness at least, ruled the country.

No actual photographs of President Nil had ever been taken. He had never shown himself to the people, and only to his more immediate advisers while wearing a mask. His wife and mistress had already been sent out of the country, so not even they could be set to identify him. He had so successfully remained a cypher that many people doubted his existence, which was why he hoped to be unrecognisable when he walked to the ship in Shelp harbour dressed like any tourist, complete with camera around his neck, and a special transmitter in his pocket by which he would be able to spark off the bombs he would have placed along the quayside.

President Nil was born of a father from Damascony (of the tribe of Gelt) and a mother from Cronacia, fifty-five years ago. His upbringing was strict and traditional, and his training as a lawyer was one of the best. Each of the thousand books described a thousand laws, and the silence of each one was deafening to his heart, and these million laws turned into maggots eating up his soul. But he held the rotting dust at bay, in order to satisfy his parents who had struggled for his education. He became adept at hair-splitting, a monster of rationality with a memory that was profound, and his judgements were famous—if too complicated to carry out. By the age of twenty-eight he was a rich and respected judge, but in order to stop himself from going mad he took to the mountains on the frontier of Damascony where, in a few months of intellectual explosion, he reversed and then shattered all his previous precepts and wrote a short but stunning manual of nihilism. How he made contact with the maniac-dissidents of the country which was to become Nihilon, and came to power after two years of political activity and civil war, is too long and complex to relate here, but his meticulous training in law, coupled to the fires of his own hitherto half buried temperament, ideally suited him for the task he knew he had to carry out.

He put on his mask, went down by the ladder and back into the building. Walking along to his private suite he considered it inopportune to dwell too long on his past. In any case he always thought it extremely tedious to delve into his humble origins and early struggles, and his quick rise to power in Nihilon. It didn't make him feel proud, or inspire him to nobler and higher things. When he wasn't engrossed in the present he was thinking about the future, and so the past had no flavour for him. The past was of no value to a Nihilist. The past was out of date, an anachronism, an anchor on the true heart's blood of pure chaos.

He changed his clothes, picked up a camera, revolver, and briefcase full of money, and left his Tungsten rooms forever, hoping, as he stepped into the elevator that would take him to the tunnel, that the technical staff would keep its promise and get the rocket up into the sky before the attack started.

As the dull sound of gunfire rumbled above he got into his Mangler and turned the headlights on, then set off slowly along the tunnel. He took off his mask, and mulled nostalgically on his past as he lightly gripped the wheel. These recollections were the only real sign that his days of power were over.

Chapter Thirty-six

The first regiment of a hundred sports cars moved slowly forward in a perfect line so as to present a terrifying spectacle to those Nihilists who would no doubt rush to defend the walls when they came close enough. Each Zap was separated from the next by ten metres, so that the advance was on a front of nearly a kilometre. At the same time a more conventional attack by three thousand men was launched against the northern wall, a mere diversion, however, to the great set-piece. He was annoyed by Mella anxiously gripping his hand as the cars departed, and by her continual sniffing and dabbing at her eyes with a small flowered handkerchief.

When Benjamin judged that the first line was at the five-hundred-metre picket-mark out from the trees, he fired a shot for the second regiment to advance. Three further shots in sharp order set three thousand-strong battalions flowing from the trees on either side, following behind the Zaps. These were supported by two hundred dynamiters who drew their equipment along on rudimentary trolleys. They were to destroy the rocket before it could be launched, though they had the firmest orders not to damage any of the control or computer machinery, so that it would be available for the new government should it decide to begin its own space-programme.

With nearly seven thousand men and two hundred sports cars launched at Tungsten, a force was in motion that no power on earth could stop. And yet, those mysterious walls worried him because they still gave no sign of life. The cars, travelling fast, needed only a few minutes to cross the three-kilometre no-man's-land, so if there was to be opposition it must come soon.

The big advantage of staking everything on a Zap attack was that it would be over quickly. Benjamin had no taste for long-drawn-out battles. Yet he felt confident, and enjoyed the meaty exhalations from his cigar. In a few mere weeks he had ceased to be a dullish compiler of travel and history books, and a pilgrim in half-known lands. He now commanded an insurrectionary army the like of which Nihilon had never seen, nor was going to see again, and for a moment he dwelt on this promotion, until stopped by a look of alarm on what was visible of Richard's face under the heavy binoculars.

The leading regiment was halfway across. As much as the nature of the ground allowed, it still kept its precise alignment, though at the expense of speed. Benjamin would have liked a bit of lost formation at this moment, if it meant them getting quickly to the enemy, for through his binoculars he saw white panels sliding out of the white wall, and gleaming barrels of artillery threatening his Zap Brigade with calamity.

When Mella began sobbing uncontrollably he wanted to throw her off the platform. Richard was swearing, unable to say anything intelligible, or take his eyes from the small gobs of white smoke rising to the noise of great earth-cracking explosions from a whole kilometre of that enigmatic wall in the distance. Fortress Tungsten had spoken at last.

The leading cars, at just over a kilometre range, began to explode, though the bravery of the Zap drivers was never in doubt. Nothing could stop them, except the far-off percussion of those deadly guns. Richard, glancing aside, as if he couldn't bear to see it, noted that Benjamin's usually florid face had turned pale and slack. The great charge of the Zaps had become a ride of death and destruction.

Richard was fixed by it, his limbs tightening at such an exciting game. It was too good to miss, no matter whose side he was on, and he couldn't help but regard poor Benjamin, the architect of this rare spectacle, as the greatest Nihilist of them all. History should give him that title, if no other. At the same time a more ordinary thought struck Richard, telling him that they ought to get out of the country as soon as possible.

The plain was littered with smashed and burning cars from Regiment Number One, the flower of Nihilon's motor industries, the pride of its export trade. Survivors from the cars were lying on the stony ground, firing at the elusive Tungsten gunners. The one car of the first regiment to reach the wall hit it at nearly two hundred kilometres an hour. It lashed itself into flames, enveloping an embrasure, which at least stopped one of the cannons.

The terrible precision guns of Tungsten turned their attention to the second regiment. Brigadier Kalamata had the sense to increase speed, hoping to escape the shelling, and the line broke into individual groups, in order to get through the burning and splintered wreckage of the first wave. Due to this zigzag manoeuvre, many of the cars collided, though few seriously enough to be stopped. Some, going too fast now instead of too slow, crashed into blazing wreckage but, due to skilful swerving, as well as the trained and rapid fire from the survivors of the first wave (some of whom, unhappily, were hit by cars of the second), and also because of the fires and palls of smoke, the aim of the Tungsten artillery was not half as deadly as it had been.

Even so, it was difficult to imagine many of the cars getting through to the wall. The fact that more did get there than was expected seemed due solely to Benjamin's wisdom in separating the first regiment from the second by half a kilometre. If they had been sent together, both would have been annihilated. Forty Zaps of the second wave, therefore, arrived in some condition at the wall. Out of eight hundred car-borne men who had set out, nearly two hundred survived to reach it. Unfortunately, ladders were now scarce.

Mella, recovering from a fainting fit, took Benjamin's hand. This time he was glad of its warmth. 'Come,' she said, pulling him along. 'Let us go to your magnificent Thundercloud car. We're going into the battle.'

It seemed the only possible action, suicidal though it was, and causing him an unpleasant moment of panic when he left Richard in charge of the staff platform and followed her. He expected her to get into his car, but she pointed to her platform and said she would travel in that. But she wanted him to stay close in his Thundercloud so that they could, as it were, fight valiantly together.

Forty soldiers pulled at the ropes, and because all luggage had been taken down, and Edgar was sensibly hiding somewhere among the trees, they were able to set off at a good pace. Mella sat imperious, and brave indeed on her throne, as they drew her towards the cannons' roar, other soldiers of her bodyguard spreading around in order to protect her. Benjamin preferred to keep well away from this interesting but conspicuous spectacle that presented such a wonderful target for the gunners of Tungsten—of which there were still far too many.

After the defeat of the Zaps, the defending guns attempted to beat back the three large infantry battalions which, as they passed through the wrecked sports cars, removed those ladders that were still intact.

They then carried them forward as if they were invaluable and much-loved battle-standards.

Benjamin had no intention of driving his Thundercloud more than halfway across the field of war. He stopped before reaching the zone of the Zap graveyard, and stood on the roof to watch any further destruction that might take place before, as seemed inevitable, the remnants of his army surged back into retreat. He was determined not to let it catch up with him, but to make with all speed for Aspron, and from there pursue his way with the impetus of self-preservation to the frontier.

Mella's great wagon, now far ahead, was close to the wall itself, and he expected to see it blown to pieces at any moment. Shells were exploding all around it, sending up great gouts of stony soil till it was lost in the smoke. Groups of wounded were crawling back, helped by those with perfect limbs who simply wanted to get out of danger, passing him with such openness that he changed his mind when he thought to kick them back into the shellfire.

He saw a few of his soldiers climbing the wall. Mella was in front of it, waving her arms. The artillery had stopped firing, and the number of his men this side of the wall was melting away as they climbed on to and over it.

He needed a few hundred more men to back them up, but he had used every one in the greatest gamble of his career. In the sweet mouth of success there was always one rotten tooth to foul its breath, he reflected, feeling himself suspended in time while events rolled on without any help from him at all. Then he saw that Mella's bodyguard, in their ferocity and devotion, and as if now answering his plea, were paving a way for the dynamiters, who began to expend their precious cargo on blowing up whole sections of the wall. He could hardly believe it. Mella's great throne-wagon was pulled inside.

He drove rapidly back to the trees, the noise of gunfire dying away. 'Did you see that?' Richard shouted from the platform. 'They're in. They got in.'

'I know,' he said, curbing his jubilation, 'but how many?'

Richard shook his hand to congratulate him, as he stepped down from the ladder. 'A report just came from the north wall to say they'd got some men in there as well.' A deep roar spread through the earth, shaking the platform, the trees, their legs, and feet. 'The rocket!' Richard cried, turning to look at it.

Even that, Benjamin said to himself with joyful relief. They got that too. I've won on every point with my well-trained, dedicated army. Through field-glasses he saw the underpart of the rocket surrounded by smoke and fire. The rage of everyone is quenched at last, he surmised, as the great rolling roar went on and on, thinking to realise his fondest dream that the blackest Nihilists on earth were being smashed forever.

But when the immense head of the rocket was temporarily cleared of smoke and vapour, it began slowly to ascend, lifting its sharp red nose with infinite grace and vigour, up and up above the base, and driving straight into the sky.

Chapter Thirty-seven

Honesty had won, they claimed, in control of the computers at last. Nihilism had conquered, they thought, watching the television screens and the vast wall of dials that recorded the rocket's progress as it circled the earth in space. No one could gainsay either proposition. No one wanted to. The forces of honesty were happy that the war was over. The defeated Nihilists were glad they were no longer locked in a race against time, and imprisoned at Tungsten because of it. The scientist-in-chief had already agreed to work for the new government.

Seats of honour for the leaders of the conquering army enabled them to observe the screens and computers as if at a theatre. Luncheon trays were clipped to their chairs, and on the television screens, via complex lenses that beamed and zoomed from outside the space-ship, a door was seen to open, and one of the astronauts floated out, a man whose legs swayed and parted and swam, side by side by side with the space-ship, his face now and again visible through the perspex visor, features anxious as if he had been unwillingly sent to a race through the bleak universe.

Mella sat with her father, holding his two hands, and staring fervently at him. He did not know who she was, and called her by her mother's name. This brought copious tears, and her great and unexpected joy at having found him alive gave way to despair now that his mind would never be clear as to her identity. He told them however that he had tampered with the rocket, so that when it circled in space the advertised carnal hook-up would not occur. But what he did not know was that while he had descended one side of the rocket, after his clumsy adjustments to its programming, a member of the base staff had gone up the other side and put everything right again. So Took could not understand why the spectacle was being enacted on the television screen.

Before Benjamin and his party entered the Grand Computer Hall, the cleaner-in chief had taken away the old president's sweeping brush and peeled off his white overall, put a tie around his neck and a watch on his wrist, a pen in his pocket and a pair of black leather shoes on his feet so that no one would think he had been ill-treated. This rude change into something that he had not been for so long and never expected to be again may have broken his frail sense of identity, and been the reason why he did not recognise his old civil-war lieutenant either, a fact which sorrowed Benjamin after his long search and twenty-five years of enquiries. But the mystery of President Took's disappearance had now been solved, so there seemed little else for him to do in Nihilon, except perhaps find Jaquiline.

The man emerging from the rocket was seen to be Adam the poet, whose blank, half-drugged features locked in a space-suit world were trying to smile, as if he knew they were viewing him, and felt embarrassed at being naked from the waist down. Mella covered her eyes. Benjamin forced himself to look, but hated it, though he was unwilling to close the show because shooting at the screens and computers would interfere with the delicately-timed space-scheme and put the occupant of the rocket in serious danger. Being a member of the guidebook committee, Adam was still entitled to certain courtesies from the land of Nihilon.

The door of the rocket stayed open, and two more legs appeared, comely and well-shaped, white and long as they slid free, fleshy at the thighs. All eyes looked on at the emerging female body, her top half well ensconced in a transparent space-suit that showed her small taut breasts, and floating with arms and legs apart like a starfish, and all delicately attached—like the male specimen—to the mothership nearby. As they drifted to each other, the National Anthem of Nihilon began to computerise itself in the universe around them.

Benjamin stood up, a wild and raving man they'd never seen before. He unlatched two guns, spinning around as they followed the free-shifting figures (which now appeared on an even bigger screen, specially switched on) of Adam and Jaquiline set to engage in the primal rite. The music grew solemn as they approached. Jaquiline's face came into enormous close-up, illuminated and beautiful, as if experiencing some cosmic dream which fed into her the secret of creation and of the world, and as if the limits of the universe were being made known to her.

A band of hair came over her mouth as Adam went forward, her eyes and legs opening at the same time. A switch of some earthbound computer enabled him to find his place well and, with legs closed, lock the perfect lock, and begin his rhythm, maintaining it in that place while all eyes were on them, and with the appropriate slow movement of the Nihilon Anthem playing through it.

Richard took Benjamin's guns away and pulled him back to his seat, while all kept their eyes on the fascinating scene of their two colleagues and compatriots copulating in space. Adam's face was shown with Jaquiline's through the moments of orgasm, the camera moving from their faces to the wedding-ring on Jaquiline's finger, and then to the joined and jewelled movement of their four legs, at which a roaring cheer of triumph ripped from the several hundred detached and scientific scientists in the great hall—who had not only got this project off the ground, as it were, but had coaxed it to the stars. Edgar put hands to his ears, and closed his eyes at this manifestation, as if the two sweethearts in space might hear such vulgarity and thus be wakened from their sublime dream.

As they slid apart, Jaquiline put out her arms, and there were tears under her eyes as the last great close-up moved across the screen, before she was sucked back into the space-ship. Adam's face also showed grief, almost panic as his arms reached forward to go on holding what had so recently been completely his. And then he was returned into the metal container, which went on to another circuit of the earth before scoring its way through the atmosphere, and floating by parachute on to the central plain of Nihilon, which would hold out its arms to receive them in safety and triumph.

Chapter Thirty-eight

Benjamin's Thundercloud Estate car, dented and scarred, windowless and without tyres, had been confiscated for the Museum of the Insurrection, to be repaired and set there in a conspicuous place. He was sad to part with such an old and powerful friend but, in the euphoria of victory and the good feeling of celebration, he relinquished it with a generous heart, and admitted to himself that Nihilon deserved it as a memento of his honourable strivings. The Benjamin Smith Brigade would never be forgotten.

Mella was crowned Queen of Nihilon. It was found better, after all, not to change the name either of the country or the capital city. Since the concept of honesty was foremost on the new government's lips, there seemed no sense in confusing the minds or memories of ordinary citizens.

So Nihilon it remained, with Edgar as the consort of Queen Mella. Having nothing to go home for, and no wish to return at the moment, he entrusted his brief and meagre guidebook-notes to Richard, who promised to see that they arrived in fair copy at the office. Yet their last sight of Edgar, before leaving Nihilon City, in the garden of the temporary villa-palace on the outskirts, was of a lost man, who did not know what he wanted. Part of him desired the all-smothering attention that Mella poured out again now that her father had died, but under all this he sensed a craving for adventure straining to break free and do what it could with him. Adam reflected sadly as they said goodbye that Edgar was the sort of person who, having finally claimed to have made up his mind, seemed more lost to the world than ever.

Everyone had their share of triumphs, and promises of reward. Promises were the proofs of honesty in that, never being kept, those who made them were shown to be of good faith and even better heart. If a promise was made, you were being honest; if it was kept, you were being devious—almost menacing in the intensity of your good intentions. Thus society in Nihilon was being cast on a new base, and those who were heard to disagree that this was so were spirited away in the middle of the day, as an example to others.

Victory celebrations were put off for ten years. This was another mark of honesty, for by then, so it was said, the population would have some achievements to celebrate. The heroes could either wait for them, or go home to their own country and come back at the appropriate time. If they decided to wait, some suitably honest employment would be found for them in the health-giving, body-building stone-quarries beyond Tungsten, or doing construction work about to commence on the ruined dam at Fludd, or digging a new canal between Orcam and Coba. If they decided to go, however, and return in ten years for the festivities, the government would generously pay half their fare.

While the city was being cleaned and partly rebuilt, and the rest of the country was settling down to an orderly and efficient life, the heroes of the insurrection idled around the cafés of Ekeret Square. If they stayed awhile it was not to collect any glory or reward, but simply to finish gathering information for the guidebook that they had been drawn there to write in the first place.

They hung on long enough to find out that Jaquiline had not conceived during her trip into space. Fortunately there had been no need for her to do so, since it was plain that Nihilon had no need to reassert itself by this mystic birth, that nihilism was already eternal in Nihilon itself, in the base and core of its people and institutions, which simply showed how human they were, and therefore how fundamentally good. She and Adam recovered from their experience, and were none the worse for it, and indeed hardly remembered it more than a dream is remembered, except that they were man and wife, a fact that could not be denied, considering the number of people who had witnessed the consummation of their marriage. They would not have believed that such a unique experience had taken place at all had they not seen themselves on the full-length documentary film of their flight into space, which was now shown as proving the final triumph not for nihilism, but for the insurrectionary forces and the new government.

After a few weeks each of them (except Edgar) received a letter from the Ministry of Tourism to say that within twenty-four hours they must vacate their rooms, because the hotel in which they were staying was to be turned into offices for the newly formed Ministry of Cancer.

This strange name was said by the manager to be a code-title for a project of infinite importance, something to do with propagating the principles of law and order embodied in the New Nihilon—New Nihilon being the only concession made to renaming the country—not only within the nation itself but even as far as Cronacia and beyond.

Our travellers were too psychically exhausted, after all that had happened, to fathom the importance of these remarks, but opened their letters from the Ministry of Tourism to find a single third-class rail-ticket to Shelp for each of them, and steamer tickets on a Nihilonian ship to the nearest port of Cronacia.

As far as she was concerned, Jaquiline said, when they sat in a café to discuss the situation, there was nothing to talk about, because she'd be glad to get out of the place. The others agreed, and Benjamin called for Nihilitz to celebrate their departure. The waiter set down a bottle, and when they lifted glasses for the toast they discovered that the liquid was plain water.

'Waiter!' Benjamin roared.

After the victory, the army officers of Nihilon had come back from their hiding-places, and one of them was his old friendly enemy from Amrel, who had deserted the insurrectionary cause at Agbat, but had now been given command of the Benjamin Smith Brigade, a post of honour in the new country. Benjamin had accepted this also with good heart, but it took a little more concealing than the confiscation of his car, and though he couldn't in any case do much about such rogues and villains getting back into office, at least he wasn't prepared to be tricked out of a bottle of Nihilitz by a common, insolent waiter.

'Yes, sir?' the waiter said, reappearing promptly enough, as if he had been waiting close by for the expected call.

'I wanted Nihilitz.'

'This is Nihilitz, sir. New Nihilitz.'

'Then get me the old Nihilitz.'

'There's only this water, sir,' the waiter explained. 'Intoxicating liquors were banned in Nihilon from midnight. They're bad for the liver, sir. They corrode the heart and block the lungs.'

'That's ridiculous,' said Jaquiline.

The waiter smiled and, recognising her as 'The Lady from Space', asked for her autograph. This had happened countless times already, so she wrote her name on the back of a grubby old bill. 'Now please bring us something to drink.'

'I'm sorry,' he said, 'I can't do it. A man came in this morning and cause a commotion when I wouldn't get him some old Nihilitz, so the police came and took him to Aspron.'

'Aspron?' said Benjamin.

'Yes, sir. It's not only back in fashion, but they say it's much enlarged. Just a moment, though, and I'll see what I can do.' He went through the far door near the bar. The bullet-proofing over the terrace had been removed, and ordinary thin glass put in its place. The waiter returned with a plain bottle: 'It's Nihilitz,' he whispered. 'But it will cost you ten thousand klipps. We have our own distillery in the cellars, and have been busy cooking it up for the last few days. We got advanced notice from a very highly-placed friend that Nihilitz was going to be banned. So we're going to be rich, my friends, rich beyond the dreams of avarice!'

So they protested that the price was too high, that under nihilism they would have paid a mere few hundred, at the most. The waiter recognised Adam, and asked for his autograph also, and he signed the paper with infinite weariness and disgust. 'For God's sake let's scrape up the ten thousand,' he said, 'so that we can get drunk.'

'That's very sensible,' said the waiter. 'I'm sure I'd be able to sell it for twenty thousand tonight. Maybe thirty thousand. Or even forty. Fifty tomorrow! But as a special favour to you, I'll let it go for ten.'

Benjamin threw two large notes, as big as tea-towels, on to the floor, and the waiter picked them up and put them under his arm as he went away chuckling to himself. Nevertheless, it was vintage Nihilitz, and other people in the café eyed them enviously, one customer becoming so disgruntled over his large glass of water that he loped across and asked if they'd kindly share their good fortune with him. He was a middle-aged man with a thin face but fairly well-padded body. Benjamin laughed, and told him that, frankly, they could quite easily finish the bottle without his help. The man got angry: 'I've worked hard all my life, and now I can't even buy a glass of Nihilitz. I'm just about ready to lay down in despair and die.'

'We paid ten thousand klipps for it,' Adam said.

'That's right,' the man shouted, springing up with a rabid anger, hoping to get support from the few other water-drinkers. 'I suppose you're a pack of mercenaries who put this rotten honesty-régime in place of our good old nihilism. And now you've got all the money. But me, look at me, I work hard, but I'm just not lucky, because I'm a

Nihilonian. I was born in this country, but I'm expected to stand by while idle foreigners like you come and drink our best Nihilitz.'

Benjamin stood up: 'First of all, stop whining. Secondly, you aren't working now. Thirdly, it's not Nihilon any more, it's New Nihilon. So leave us alone, or I'll throw you into the street.'

The man went out disgruntled, slamming the door.

'I'm glad we're leaving this country tomorrow,' said Richard. 'I feel there's danger in it for people like us.'

'How can you say that,' Jaquiline laughed, the Nihilitz bringing back her sense of humour, 'after all we've been through?'

The man who had coveted their Nihilitz stopped by a pile of masonry that was to be used for the plinth of Queen Mella's coronation statue in the middle of the square. The first bullet from his revolver shattered the plate-glass of the terracing, and the second fragmented the Nihilitz bottle which, fortunately, was already empty.

Chapter Thirty-nine

They left the country with what they stood up in, apart from a briefcase or handbag. The rest of their luggage had been 'officially removed' from their rooms—officially, because there were no thieves now in Nihilon. Thieving, like nihilism, had been abolished. The state saw to that, because it had acquired total rights to both. In its benevolent honesty the government carried on a policy of 'removals', not only to protect the people from the temptation of mass pilfering, which in Nihilon had always either been a habit or a temporary necessity, but also to make sure there was nothing left to pilfer. This system was known as 'income tax'.

During his last afternoon nap in the hotel, Adam had opened his eyes and surprised a masked man trying to remove his guidebook-notes from the bedside table. On being pinned firmly to the wall the man had taken a government confiscation voucher from his pocket with his free hand, and squealingly maintained his own personal innocence. Benjamin, hearing the clatter, came in from next door and joined Adam in kicking him down the stairs.

They decided to leave that evening, while they were still safe, and also to make sure of getting on the ship at Shelp. If it left without them, in advance of the scheduled time, who could say when there'd be another? Benjamin knew from the old days that tourist offices regularly gave out false information in the hope that travellers would stay longer in the country, and so spend more of their invaluable foreign currency. So he wisely suggested that they take the evening train.

The hotel manager must have telephoned the Ministry of Departure, for a band was playing at the station to see them off. It was pleasant to be reminded that they were, after all, still considered to be the principal heroes of the New Nihilon. Factories, schools, and blocks of flats had been named after them. Even Edgar, their absent friend who was still deliciously sequestered with Queen Mella, had a power-station and the space-base as namesakes, while the country's leading military academy (of which there were now several instead of a mere one) had been labelled Benjamin Smith.

They walked on to the station platform, and shook hands with the mayor of the city, who had turned up in his army uniform to see them off. Richard had seen that fat, sweating, elderly, intellectual face before, that amiability in the midst of chaos and fear, when the crippled air-liner had been flying towards Nihilon City airport. They had met later during the fluid days of the insurrection, for he was none other than the professor. 'Goodbye, dear friends,' he said sadly. 'Nihilon salutes you forever, wherever you go. We shall miss you.'

Jaquiline was also touched to sadness by such tender ceremony, and in the knowledge that Nihilon at last knew how to behave towards its guests when they were leaving.

They had to fight for seats in the third-class carriage, during which bitter struggle the band embarked on a solemn march of farewell. Adam, thrust to the window while Benjamin and Richard carried on the primitive elbowing for space, saw a commotion by the entrance gate.

The sombre and idiotic music wavered as the train moved. A bent-backed old man, armed with a walking-stick, sent several members of the band spinning, then burst through their ranks and ran along the platform. He had a long white beard and a pale puckish face, and though he stooped, he nevertheless ran speedily, swirling his stick to clear a way towards their carriage.

The professor shouted for him to come back and, when he gave no sign of doing so, drew a revolver. Perhaps the old man expected this, for after the peremptory order, he zigzagged along the line of carriages to make the professor's aim more difficult, and to dodge the bullets now flying past him, in such a manner as to suggest that he was not altogether ignorant of the military art. Several rounds must have gone so high that they entered a nearby signal-box, and a man from that vantage point, enraged at the disturbance to his afternoon nap, began to sweep the whole platform with a light machine-gun, at which the professor and his band scattered to take up retaliatory positions.

Benjamin made his strength felt in the carriage, so that Jaquiline could sit down at least. In fact there had been enough seats for every-one, but the Nihilonians had spread luggage over them, which was now piled on the racks provided. In the struggle Adam had been pulled from the window, and didn't see whether or not the old man finally got on the train.

The railway ran a dozen kilometres to the east, straight through the suburbs, whence it turned in a southerly direction towards Shelp. When they began to talk, it was disclosed that the baby sitting on the knees of the peasant woman opposite had been born on the day of the Great Space-Launch, and since it was a boy its mother had called it Adam. She asked therefore for Adam's autograph, saying that she could frame it when her son grew up, for him to look upon with pride.

They tried to sleep during darkness, but it was barely possible. Benjamin woke from a brief nap, aware of a stranger lying full-length on the floor. When day came, Adam recognised him as the old man with the long white beard who had run for the train in peril of his life. 'I'm glad you got on safely,' he said to him.

'So am I,' responded the old man, who stood up and straightened himself. 'I just had to get away from Mella,' Edgar said, taking off his beard. 'In another month I *would* have been a very old man, wrinkled and finished, so I finally decided to leave on the same boat as you. And the only way I could get out of that palace was to disguise myself as a Geriatric. Unfortunately that sharp-eyed professor recognised me at the station.'

He put on his beard again, and took a bottle of Nihilitz from his pocket. 'I stole it at the palace. There was plenty of it in Mella's sideboard.'

'It makes me wonder why I helped the insurrection,' Benjamin reflected morosely, drinking more than his share.

When the peasants got out at a remote stop, they had the compart-ment to themselves. A fresh sea-wind blew up the wide expanse of the plain and into the carriage window. On either side, fading away into the distance, were the mountains which channelled this gratifying wind into the great plain of Nihilon. Jaquiline drew in a deep breath of it, saying how pleasant it was to leave this country, knowing that it was not only beautiful, but peaceful at last.

South of the railway, which ran across level and arable land, lay the main highway of the country, lorries and buses rolling along it in both directions, showing that the eternal business of life was moving once more. Beyond was the River Nihil, boats steaming up it to anchorages at Coba, thin streams of smoke bending in the air. The Bay of Shelp could be seen on the horizon, spreading in a straight line on either side of Shelp itself.

Chapter Forty

It was several kilometres from the main station to the quay, and they decided to walk, both for a last look at the town, and to exercise their legs before getting on the ship.

There was a lively and light-hearted feeling about the clean wide streets of Shelp now that nihilism had been officially, finally, and in some places bloodily squashed. People were dressed in summer clothes, and it seemed as if hardly anyone were at work.

Edgar kept his disguise as a Geriatric, which was a gallant enough part to play in the New Nihilon because now, instead of being honoured as the bravest of the bravest and the saviours of the nation, they were treated in a hostile manner, and occasionally spat upon for not going fast enough into the grave and allowing the young of body to breathe their living-space and gobble the food they ate.

The signs of nervousness that Edgar naturally showed only increased the realism of his old-man act, which seemed to be expected from someone of his age now that the glorious era of Golden Honesty had begun. But he received commiserating glances from those passers-by who hankered after the old system, as he hung drooling on to Jaquiline's arm, whom they took to be his loving and noble daughter.

Adam led the way, as if unacquainted with his colleagues following behind. Last of all, maintaining a skilled and watchful eye, came Richard, and Benjamin who kept a hand on his loaded gun should any wayward soldier or policeman try to stop them getting on board at the last minute, and who now thought that they should have taken a taxi instead of walking so far in the scorching sun. He seemed to be striding along in a gallon of sweat, and turned to look back along the street in case a taxi should come, in spite of the fact that they had only half a kilometre to go.

An oblong piece of wood had been stuck on top of an oncoming car, presumably as a makeshift sign, which said that it was a taxi on service. Perhaps it was, and had already been called to some distant address, for when Benjamin stepped into the road to stop it in true nihilistic fashion, it drove slowly by and almost ran over his foot. This did not anger him at all, but what did was when he realised that the so-called taxi was none other than his Thundercloud Estate car which he had soberly given up to the Museum of the Insurrection. There was no mistaking it, for every scratch and dent along the side was known to him, and no panel-beater had been put to work on it since he had presented it. The windscreen had been replaced, as well as the tyres and windows, and he was so stunned he did not even reach for his gun to fire at it. In any case, a policeman stood by a traffic-light a hundred metres away, watching him carefully.

When their phalanx quickened pace towards the control-post and customs-sheds, they all turned silent, as if expecting some final trouble to come from this grim concrete building. But a policeman at the door waved them on to the open quay and went back to a card-game with his friends. Benjamin walked across to a tourist kiosk where a uniformed and good-looking woman distributed travel literature to holidaymakers who had come to see the great and renovated nation of New Nihilon. With a rather wan smile she gave him a bundle of pamphlets, which he thought might contain information useful to the guidebook.

No one looked at their ticket as they moved up the gangway. After securing their cabins they came on deck and stood by the rail to enjoy a last glimpse of Shelp, having gathered that the ship was to sail in half an hour. Further across the bay Edgar saw boatwomen rowing sturdily from other ships back to the shore, transferring passengers' luggage to the customs-shed. He looked through his binoculars in case any of them resembled Mella, and the memory of her great love for him brought an ache to his heart.

Such sadness however was offset by the fact that this great white ship of the Nihilon Line had a full array of lifeboats along either flank. It was something he had hoped for but not expected, and it was good because it promised him a relaxing journey, which he felt he had earned after his tribulations with Mella, whom he dreaded to see at any moment come in all her fury to get him back, perched high on her mighty throne that would be hauled by a thousand followers between the customs-sheds. So he was not really sad, except for the sake of being sad, and because the rowing boatwomen in the distance did make a rather gentle picture.

Another person stood close to their group, so that to anyone not of it he seemed to belong to it, an unobtrusive preoccupied gentleman of medium height who wore dark glasses of such size that they might almost have been a mask to hide his face. Richard took him for a common tourist, with a camera hanging on his chest, and what appeared to be a transistor-radio in his hand, with the silver rod of the aerial extended. He fiddled with prominent metal knobs under the dial, his anxious mouth working as he looked across at the shore, as if to receive speech or music from that direction.

The town was gleaming and prosperous in the sun. Fortune seemed to have smiled on it, with so many blocks of flats, factories, buses, cars, and well-dressed people. Along the quay were oil-tanks, gasometers, warehouses, ships, and cranes, a sight that filled their heads with memories. Adam remembered the girl at the hotel in Fludd, and was saddened at the thought that she had been swept away in the great disaster. Further back in time was his entrance into Nihilon when he had innocently held the soldier's rifle and fired it towards Cronacia, thus bringing the retaliation that appeared to have set the whole insurrection in motion.

Who had fired that fatal shot? He had never felt guilty of it, and could only ascribe it to an accident, or an impulse travelling through heart to finger, just strong enough to move it on the trigger. But none of them was innocent, being heaven-bent for the end of the world, and never set for a beginning. It was too late to wonder where it all began, yet that seemed the only hope, if hope were wanted, and to a poet it was. A beginning might be mysterious, but it was always feasible.

Benjamin, as he smoked his cigar, dwelt on the magnificent charge of the two hundred Zaps which he had let loose at the soulless space-base of Tungsten. But his perilous journeyings in nether Nihilon were over, and he prided himself on having left the country a better place than he had found it, all in all. He wondered what he would do with the rest of his life, whether in the large world there wasn't another Nihilon waiting to be surreptitiously exploded and brought back to sanity, or whether he wouldn't have to come back to this one and start all over again on familiar ground.

Lazy and content at having accomplished her mission, Jaquiline waited for the gangway to be hoisted to the side of the white ship.

She thought of her strange encounter with the bookseller chief-of-police friend at the frontier, whom she almost expected to see on the ship but didn't, and of the exquisite experience of swirling through orgiastic space with her husband Adam. There were things about Nihilon that she would never be able to forget, and that alone had made her sojourn worthwhile.

Everyone who was to travel seemed now to be on board. Refugees from the honesty of New Nihilon were soberly dressed and quietly happy to be leaving, while those travellers who had spent time in the country since its change of system were glazed at the eyes, and belligerent after their continual battering of straightforward nihilistic honesty.

Though Richard anticipated a smooth trip from the Bay of Shelp and across the sea to Cronacia, he was inwardly uneasy, but without knowing why—a not uncommon state in recent times. The days of peril seemed truly over, yet he felt unprotected and exposed standing by the rail of the ship, and wanted to go down and sleep in his cabin, from which no black force in any form would be able to pull him back to nightmare Nihilon. But he didn't want to appear unsociable by leaving the others.

Sailors were fixing block and tackle to hoist the gangway, a few minutes before departure time, when a curious thing happened. The woman in the tourist-office hurriedly picked up a large handbag, ran across the quay, walked up the gangplank, and came aboard just as preparations were made to get the ship away. She stood a few yards from Jaquiline, gazing at the shoreline in a mood of bitter regret.

'I think I know you,' Jaquiline said, with an unpleasant pang of recognition.

'Please, let's not talk,' said Cola quickly. 'When I left you I was sent to Mount Bathos for a month, to be rehabilitated. It was really very successful.'

'Then why are you leaving New Nihilon in such a hurry?'

'You'll see,' Cola said, a tone of sad hysteria that prompted Jaquiline to hold her hands in a generous effort to calm her.

As the ship steamed between the arms of the inner breakwater, dragons of fire and smoke suddenly ate up part of the waterfront. The explosion was so mighty that a low wave came eddying towards the ship, at which they ran into the main saloon and closed the door.

Débris rained down over the harbour, and a few scattered pieces fell on to the ship like dead and dying birds.

But, while still outside before the explosion took place, Benjamin had seen the unobtrusive tourist press one of the buttons on what they had thought to be a transistor-radio, and as the first flash broke on the skyline he had noticed how ex-President Nil's mouth lost its twisted anxiety, and smiled.

Bells were ringing, and sirens moaning along the shore. Cola stood with her head resting on the edge of a window, in tears at another wrecking of beautiful Nihilon, the new model she had been taught to love in the brain-laboratories of Mount Bathos, and which she had spent a week describing to people who would never understand it. It was like a volcano erupting, a spectacle which showed Benjamin—though only for a moment—that Nihilon was a country for which nothing could be done, a part of the world that could no more be adequately covered by a guidebook than a jungle could. But he saw plainly that such a wayward reflection was only the false fire of nihilism continuing to blaze in his heart—when he knew all the time that men in general, and he in particular, had the power to extinguish it forever.

Before the tourist with the radio device could press the second of his series of buttons Benjamin furtively drew the revolver from inside his jacket and, taking careful aim, fired one shot and killed him. The machine fell from his hands and splashed into the sea. He ran up to the body, and heaved it on to the rail. With a further effort he sent it spinning after the radio-detonator.

He then returned the gun to its holster, and went into the saloon to comfort his friends, as the ship steamed out of the Bay of Shelp, and away from Nihilon.